TASK FORCE ONE

BOOK II OF THE ALISTAIR SAGA

J.M. KÆ

TASK FORCE ONE

By J.M. KÆ
© Copyright Information
Year of Publication 2023
United States of America
First Edition
All Rights Reserved
Paperback ISBN: 979-8375451619
Hardcover ISBN: 979-8375457970

No part of this book may be reproduced or transmitted in any form or by any means, graphic, electronic, or in print, including copyright, audio recording, or by any information storage system without the written permission of the author.

Disclaimer: Persons, places, incidents, and actions written in this book and the Alistair Saga story are a work of fiction. Any resemblance to real persons, places, incidents, or actions written for the purpose of the story is coincidental.

All comments or questions can be addressed to:
www.joannakurczakwriting.com

TASK FORCE ONE

*It Matters Not How Much A Heart Shatters.
The Destined One's Love Holds The Power
To Heal And Restore All The Heart's Broken Pieces*

≈ Chapter 1 ≈

Chicago. The Windy City. The city of lights and the city of... crime. Although it may not seem as such to some, it was the very reason why Rigel Alistair chose to settle down in the Jewel of the Midwest. This was the city where its heartbeat pounded day and night. Rain or shine. Regardless of the season of the year. But perhaps the main reason why Rigel's gut feeling led him to Chicago was the fact that someone like him could blend in without being noticed. Not because he was a criminal, but because he was a vigilante with a conscience of a good cop and a hidden gift of figuring out who stood on the right side of the law.

As one of seven siblings, Rigel stood out as the one who always walked on solid ground. He knew who he was, and he accepted it. All of it. While his siblings took time figuring out who they wanted to be in life or how they wanted to cope with their parents' untimely deaths, Rigel did not waste one second on pondering, wondering, or deciding what to do. He chose to fight for righteousness. Even if it meant doing so on his own terms. Or under the name concealing his identity. Not just for his sake, but for the sake of his siblings.

To the outside world, he wasn't Rigel Alistair. He was Rigel Brzozakiewiczowicz, a Detective with the Special Task Force of the Chicago Police Department. His unit dealt with cases and criminals who breached the rules of the law not only by breaking it, but by manipulating it to fit their corrupt views of the world. Murders? He'd seen those. Revenge? His best friend would attest it was Rigel's daily bread. Corruption? Fighting corruption in the City of Broad Shoulders was as obvious and evident as the city's well-known association with Al Capone.

To those who dealt with him daily, Rigel was Detective Brzozakiewiczowicz. He was a loner. A maverick. An introvert with the peculiar ability to somehow figure out who the bad guys were. If there was an unsolved case, Rigel knew how to close the case in less than a blink of an eye. Cold case? Even better. And no one around him suspected Rigel knew how to read minds with one look into someone's eyes, but more importantly that he knew how to read hearts with one shake of someone's hand...

"Look who finally decided to return my call?" The voice on the other end of the phone line sounded more amused than annoyed. Though Rigel made the call while driving along the Magnificent Mile through downtown Chicago on a late Friday night, the man on the phone knew Rigel called when he could, not when he decided to do so.

"I was busy... Those lines at the donut shops seem to go on for miles, especially in November," Rigel chuckled and knew his best friend appreciated a good bout of sarcasm instead of an apology for calling back two days late.

"Did they run out of onion bagels?" Sebastian Lipa, Rigel's best friend, the only person in the city aware of his identity, grinned at his own comeback. "You should watch Your figure with those bagels. Those buns of steel will turn toward the south someday."

"Don't worry about my bagel intake. It will be a sad day for Chicago if I find out the city ran out of onion bagels."

"You and Your onions, man," Sebastian chuckled. "How on earth will You ever find a woman willing to put up with You and Your love of onions?"

"That would be her problem. I don't have a problem with it."

"Of course, You don't," Sebastian laughed and shook his head. "So, what are You up to? It's a Friday night. It's cold and rainy. It's after 9:00 p.m. Your shift ended a while ago."

"It never ends in this city," Rigel sighed and turned the volume up to hear his best friend better through the car's speakers. "Crime doesn't go away when the summer ends. Especially for me. Sometimes I wonder how I sleep at night."

"Alone. You sleep alone, my friend. Those onion bagels do You more harm than good."

"Sometimes I wonder what Your wife sees in You, dreamboat," Rigel laughed and felt better because conversations with his best friend were usually the only thing that helped him unwind after hard days at work.

"She sees my buns of steel. Which, by the way, are still in the same shape after all these years," Sebastian teased Rigel.

"No problem there, they barely existed before. They barely exist now, too," Rigel bellowed out a laugh.

"Happyski, maybe You should exercise those buns of steel instead of Your tongue. We both know You're not getting any younger," Sebastian chuckled at his own brilliance, only to receive a jab in the ribs from his wife accompanied by a rather warning stare.

"That was a weak comeback," Rigel grinned, suspecting the reason for his best friend's less-than-insulting response.

"Oh, I have better ones, but Kasia's glare stare forces me to play nice," Sebastian replied and blew a kiss across the kitchen to his beloved wife.

"Give my best to Your wife," Rigel bellowed out a laugh.

"She's seen Your best, and feels sorry for You," Sebastian laughed as well, pleased with himself, until he saw the way his wife looked at him. "And she said to apologize. So, I apologize - for You not getting any younger."

"Sebastian Lipa, You play with fire," Rigel laughed even louder. "I almost feel sorry for You, man. Almost."

"Funny, she just said the same thing," Sebastian smiled but straightened up the moment Kasia took a few steps his way.

"Then again, I do feel sorry for You," Rigel clicked his tongue and smiled, when an incoming call came through. "I have to go, dreamboat, duty calls."

"At this hour? They don't pay You enough," Sebastian shook his head.

"It's not about the pay. And they wouldn't call if it wasn't important."

"You say that every time."

"Because it's true," Rigel grinned. "Kiss Your wife from me."

"You wish," Sebastian winked at his wife and ended the call.

"Happyski, what took You so long?" A woman's scratchy voice rang in Rigel's ear as he picked up the second line.

"My face was stuffed with a bagel," Rigel smiled.

"Onion bagels are not good for You," Nicholetta Stormstrong scolded the best Detective on her Special Task Force.

"That's not a problem for me, Chief," Rigel replied, recalling his conversation with Sebastian from a moment ago.

"Not yet, it's not. But someday it will. Anyway, that's not why I called."

"No? And I thought my bagel intake was at the top of priorities in the department."

"It will make it to the top if You don't watch Your wisecrack responses," Nicholetta warned him but smiled, nonetheless.

"Sorry, Chief," Rigel straightened up in his seat. "What's up?"

"Someone called in a murder," Nicholetta said in a reserved tone of voice.

"That's nothing new," Rigel rolled his eyes.

"That may be so. But someone called in a murder at the Mayor's Office. From the Mayor's Office."

"That's new," Rigel raised his eyebrows and rubbed his five o'clock shadow beard.

"Tell me about it."

"Any idea who the victim is?" Rigel already began thinking of the fastest route to the Mayor's Office, anticipating the Chief's coming request.

"Not as of yet."

"Any idea about the motive?" Rigel asked and turned to the nearest street.

"Not as of yet."

"Was the press notified?" Rigel continued with his usual questions.

"Not... as of yet."

"I wonder why?" Rigel clicked his tongue and reached for the control button to turn on the Police Department emergency signal in his undercover Dodge Challenger Hellcat SRT.

"No one is to find out about this," she warned him. "At least not yet. This means no radio contact through the usual channels, and definitely no signal."

"Got it," Rigel retrieved his hand.

"Call me when You get there."

"Already on the way, Chief."

"Oh, one thing You should know. Maybe two," Nicholetta added before ending the call.

"I'm listening," he turned the car toward one of the downtown alleys for a shortcut.

"The Mayor is out of town, so whoever did this not only has access to the Mayor's Office but knows how to get in and out undetected," Nicholetta advised him as she pulled up a list of all employees at the Mayor's Office on her laptop.

"What's the second thing?" Rigel slowed down as he pulled up to the main street only to speed through it to enter another alley.

"The person who found the body is the Mayor's new intern. New and pretty shaken up as it is. Watch Your step - and Your mouth - so we don't get called into the principal's office for bad behavior again."

"Me? Get called into the Mayor's Office for bad behavior?" Rigel grinned with mischief. "There is no way that will happen twice in one month."

"Then I wonder why he requested for You to take the lead on this one?" Nicholetta replied in a tone of voice that told Rigel she was not joking. "Personally."

"Same here..." Rigel narrowed his eyes. The Mayor hated him. And the feeling was mutual. So, a personal request like this was not only out of the ordinary, but it was also suspicious. To say the least.

Rigel's suspicion only grew as he arrived at the Mayor's Office. The place was deserted, aside from two obviously distraught security guards, and one very frightened intern…

≈ Chapter 2 ≈

Visiting the Mayor's Office may be considered as a sign of distinction or recognition. But not to Rigel. To him, it was a reminder of how much he disliked the guy. The dislike was more than skin deep. Much more. And it had nothing to do with the fact Rigel used to consider the Mayor's sister to be his significant other. Or that the Mayor blamed him for his sister's untimely death in a plane crash immediately following their breakup...

How was Rigel supposed to know his relationship with Camilla Lucchese would end in such a way? Or that it would end at all? Some say that it takes a lot for a woman to fall for a man. That may be true. However, it takes just as much for a man to fall for a woman. Even more so for a man like Rigel. Not because he was a maverick who swore off all women. It was because he was the son of his parents, two undercover agents who exposed an international ring of double agents, and he swore to protect his family's identity. He finally thought he met someone he could trust with his identity and his heart. He was proven wrong in a way that broke his heart. A heart he decided to close for the rest of his life.

Even if he disliked the man, Rigel had to admit Mayor Vincent Lucchese was the leader of the city. If nothing else, the chair he filled demanded diplomatic sort of respect. Why? Because the moment Rigel learned of the crime he had come to inspect, he became intrigued. And he never left the sight of a case that intrigued him. Never.

"Evening, gentlemen," Rigel sent a casual salute gesture toward two guards waiting for him near the door to the Mayor's Office on the 5th Floor of the Chicago City Hall and ran his hand through the soaking wet hair.

"Evening, Detective B.," said one of the guards. Just because he knew Rigel, it did not make pronouncing his last name any easier.

"Hey, Owens," Rigel nodded. He decided to forego the temptation of asking the guard to state his full name. This was not an occasion for witty nuances. "Hey, Slingman."

"Hey, Rigel," the other guard waved at him.

"I've been told You have something for me tonight?" Rigel allowed the men to lead the way into the Mayor's Office. He unzipped his brown weathered leather jacket and ensured his gun holster was secured in its rightful place.

"We're fresh out of onion bagels," Owens chimed in, hoping to sound witty. It resulted in narrowed eyes on Rigel's part, and a warning gaze from his guard partner.

"Duly noted, Owens." Rigel directed his ice-cold stare from Owens toward Slingman. "Can You point me toward the location where the victim was found?"

"Sure thing. This way," Slingman inclined his head and directed his steps toward the room where the Mayor's desk was located.

"Who was the last person to leave the office tonight?" Rigel asked the guard as they walked to the room where the body was found.

"Well, the last to leave was the cleaning crew, about an hour and a half ago. They all left together," Slingman advised him.

"It's a bit early for the cleaning crew to sweep through here, isn't it?" Rigel raised his eyebrow.

"You sure know the schedule around here," Owens chimed in, again receiving an ice-cold glance from Rigel.

"It's my job to know these things." Rigel fired back stoically and decided his energy would be better spent on other aspects of the evening rather than wasting it on a conversation with Owens. He did not need to announce to the guards he was aware of the Office's schedule because he visited the office when Vincent was first elected, during the time when he and Camilla were still together. Nor that he knew the cleaning crew by name. Nor that he knew about the Office's bi-weekly winter half-day policies, which suspiciously coincided with the gruesome discovery.

Rigel realized how accurate his decision proved to be the moment Slingman opened the door to the office where the body had been found. Not because Rigel saw the body, but because he saw a frail petite young woman sitting on the couch facing the Mayor's desk.

"Who is she?" Rigel asked without looking at the victim's body. Something about the young woman got to him. She was frightened. She was shaken. She was scared. Yet, that wasn't it. He couldn't pinpoint what it was about her that struck at his gut.

And then, he realized what it was. Her mind was void of any thoughts. Any at all. And that bothered him. How was he supposed to read her thoughts if she didn't have any?

"We didn't touch it," said Slingman after a moment of prolonged silence.

"What?" Rigel blinked his way back to reality, intrigued by the simple fact someone with no thoughts at all caused him to lose his concentration.

"We did not touch the body," Owens repeated, and this time earned a nod from Rigel.

"Who found the body?" Rigel asked Owens, aware of the answer.

"She did," Owens pointed to the young woman sitting on the couch.

"Who is she?" Rigel asked, recalling his superior's words.

"She's the Mayor's new intern," Owens advised him in short.

"How long has she worked here?" Rigel began with a series of his usual questions. He did not bother to write down the answers. He never did. His memory was as good as his talent for reading people's minds.

"About two months. She's a linguist," Slingman noted.

"She's a linguist working at the Mayor's Office?" Rigel narrowed his eyes on her. So, she spoke different languages? So, she could think in many different languages, but now chose not to think at all? Not even a single thought? That detail added another layer to his slowly growing suspicion.

"Yes. She's excellent with people. She pretty much handled all the calls requiring a translator all by herself since she started working here," Slingman added.

"You said the cleaning crew was the last to leave. If that's the case, what about her?" Rigel looked at Slingman.

"You asked who left. You did not ask who stayed," Owens chimed in again, and again his timing and misplaced sense of humor were off its intended mark.

"I will be sure to modify the questions going forward, just so You can answer them accordingly," Rigel said dryly as he looked at Owens and waited until the man felt the cold sweat roll down his back, then turned to Slingman since the man was more mindful of the severity of the situation. "Why did You allow her to remain with the victim's body?"

"She wouldn't move. She called us up here after she discovered the body, and we found her just sitting there. She would not talk. She would not look at me. She wouldn't even accept a bottle of water I offered to her," Slingman scratched the back of his head as Rigel crouched down to examine the body.

"Did You call the coroner's office?" Rigel asked without looking up at Slingman. He swallowed hard at the sight of the victim's appearance, though not because of how the victim looked. He did so because of what he saw. And because he saw it before at other crime scenes. The victim laid on his side, with an obvious gunshot to the head and clear additional shots to the chest. Just how many shots were fired at the chest would need to be determined upon the coroner's arrival, but if Rigel had to guess, he would bet his paycheck the coroner would find three bullets. Hollow-point bullets.

"We did not call the coroner. The Mayor said he spoke with Your boss, and she was arranging it so it does not get out into the press yet," Owens chimed in. "The Mayor is trying to avoid a scandal since he is out of town."

"He is?" Rigel looked up at Owens. "And where is he?"

"Visiting his family out of town," Owens replied dryly.

"And where is that exactly?" Rigel held his stare on Owens before looking at Slingman.

"Sorry, Detective. We're guards, not office employees. We would not know that. But she would," Slingman pointed at the frightened young woman sitting silently on the couch.

"Alright," Rigel nodded, rose, and walked over to the couch.

"Good luck with getting through to her," Owen muttered, much to Rigel's growing annoyance with the man.

"Slingman?" Rigel turned toward the man.

"Yes?" The guard replied.

"Take him out of here, or I will." Rigel narrowed his eyes on Owens and waited until both men left the room before addressing the woman. "My name is Detective Brzozakiewiczowicz. Would You mind if I asked You a few questions before the coroner arrives?"

The woman neither replied nor moved. So, he crouched down and looked into her eyes. And his own reflection in her golden honey-brown eyes caused him to hold his breath - even if she did not pick up on it. He swallowed hard and tried a different approach.

"I am going to have to ask You to come with me to the conference room. The coroner will be arriving shortly, and we must clear the area before he comes," Rigel spoke calmly and extended his hand toward her.

The young woman looked at him with a distant gaze, then down at his extended hand, then back at him, and nodded.

"Good," Rigel offered her a faint smile. "What's Your name?"

Though he asked the question, he did not hear her answer. And not because she whispered. She didn't. She answered in her usual delicate tone of voice. It was because the moment the skin of their hands touched, the moment their fingers grazed against each other and her hand fit perfectly in his, Rigel's brain shot a bolt of hot lightning through his body. Was it a gut feeling related to the case? Was it his inborn talent for reading people's minds? Was it his ability to read people's hearts? Whatever it was, it shook him from head to toe because of the single thought stuck in his mind.

'She's the one...'

He blinked. Twice. And rose to his feet all the while pulling the young woman up from the couch. But if he thought the whisper he heard rushing through his mind was enough to shake him to the core, he was mistaken. It was what the young woman said that twisted knots in his stomach. And it wasn't something complex. She simply revealed her name.

"My name is Jade Alistair."

Those few simple words caused his stomach to twist and his heart to stop. Not just stop. It caused it to skip a not-so-silent beat…

≈ Chapter 3 ≈

For a man who read minds, Rigel was at a loss for words. In a way he could not explain. He had come to the Mayor of Chicago's Office to inspect a crime. That was his job. His daily bread. What he trained for and what he expected out of his occupation. But he never expected to be shocked by what he would find at the crime scene. And this time, the shock he received was so bewildering he... fell speechless.

Rigel tried to process what happened. He read people's minds. No one aside from his family and his best friend were aware of it, but he could read thoughts as easily as drinking his morning coffee. Yet he couldn't, for the life of him, read the mind of the frail young woman who stood before him, still holding his hand. Why? Because her mind was void of any thoughts - at least until she took his hand and looked into his eyes.

But that wasn't the only reason he fell speechless. The moment the young woman's delicate hand touched his, a single thought rushed through his mind. A thought both intriguing and bothersome at the same time.

'She's the one...'

Rigel was accustomed to hearing others' thoughts rush through his mind. Quite frankly, he was used to them, though not those exact words. It was the way his talent for reading people's thoughts and hearts came through - it was the way he could figure out if the suspect was guilty or not, good or bad, lying or not. And yet, he was stumped. Though he heard those words the moment their hands touched, there wasn't a bad bone in the young woman's body. Not one bad cell. She wasn't an innocent creature - no human ever was, but the woman who held her hand in his had a good nature. She had a good heart. She had a gentle and light soul. So, reading her heart perplexed Rigel to say the least.

And then, there was the matter of her name.

Jade Alistair...

How was it possible the woman who stood before him shared his mother's name? At first, Rigel thought the woman was trying to prank him. But he brushed the thought aside - she neither knew who he was nor was she aware of his identity. Only Sebastian was aware of it aside from his family. And Rigel was sure his best friend would never reveal the information. So, without any other logical choice, Rigel accepted her words as true. Even if it was the only information she wanted to reveal to him. Although...

'His eyes...'

That thought flashed through Rigel's mind so unexpectedly it caused a smile to appear on his face. So, the young woman did think after all? So, she wasn't totally out of touch with reality? So, she... noticed his eyes?

"I understand this may be a difficult moment for You. I will try not to make it any more difficult than it has to," Rigel advised the young woman as he slowly led her out of the room, somehow still holding onto her hand.

'His voice...'

"Jade, can You tell me how You came across the victim's body?" Rigel asked, trying to keep his composure as best as he could. The young woman was either taken by his appearance or hoping for much more than he was willing to offer at the moment. Besides, if he questioned her about her thoughts, then he would come across as being the one interested in her since she was not aware of his ability to read her thoughts.

"How do You know my name?" The young woman asked with suspicion and narrowed her eyes on him, which was quite a challenge since he towered over her by a good 10 inches.

"You... told me Your name a moment ago, remember?" Rigel looked down on her, raising his eyebrow.

"Did I?"

"Yup," he nodded and led her toward one of the chairs in the conference room.

"Oh," she looked down and sighed. As she began to sit down, she inadvertently kicked the chair's wheel with her heel while turning to sit down, and it began to roll away. She did not see it, but Rigel did. Quick on his feet, he pulled her toward him instead of allowing her to fall.

"What are You doing?" She asked, shaken, pressed against his chest. When she looked up at him, there was more fear in her eyes than before, but still no thoughts he could read. It unsettled him in more ways than he was willing to admit.

" You kicked the chair with Your heel, and it began to roll away. I had two options - to let You fall to the floor or pull You toward me. I chose the latter," he replied in his usual tone of voice, but nothing about what he felt was usual. Nothing.

"Thank You for the save," she mumbled and reached for the chair.

'Those broad shoulders...'

"So, can You tell me what happened tonight?" Rigel asked, not quite sure if he was referring to her discovery of the victim's body or to what happened from the moment they met. One thing was certain, though. Her thoughts were beginning to interest him to the point where he contemplated going out of his way to see if he could bring those thoughts out of her.

"Well, I stayed at the office to put in a few extra hours. I worked at my desk, but I heard something, so I went to check what could have made the sound," the young woman said slowly.

"You heard a sound?" Rigel watched her for any kinds of signs she could be lying. It was his routine. A part of his job, but to be honest it was a part of who he was. He liked analyzing people. He did not judge liars, nor did he praise those who were honest with him. People were who they were, and a lie did not change that - it just made trusting them impossible.

"Yes."

"What kind of sound?"

"The kind that made me notice it?"

"Jade..." he leaned forward as he sat in the chair facing her, placing his elbows on his knees while linking the fingers of his hands together. "May I call You Jade?"

"No."

"Why not?" He responded, surprised.

"You don't have my telephone number," she said bluntly.

"What?" Rigel tipped his head back at her response.

"You asked if You could call me. I said no, because You don't have my telephone number. You are a Detective, but are You always this forgetful with what people tell You?"

"No, I..." He was stumped. He never thought someone could play on his words so easily. "I did not ask if I could call You. I only asked if I could call You Jade."

"What's Your name?"

"Rigel," he said, unsure why he revealed it to her, but if it resulted in the young woman continuing to speak with him, he figured it wouldn't hurt. Then again...

"Well, You may not call me, Rigel," she stated bluntly, causing minimal eye twitch in the corner of his eye.

"Are You always this difficult?" Rigel sat back in his chair and tried his best to remain calm.

"Are You always this direct with women? Or just the ones You interrogate?"

"I am not direct with women," he said through his teeth.

"Oh, so You are just this direct with me?" She stood up and wondered why the man sitting in the chair across from her was sent to the Mayor's Office instead of any other Detective in all of Chicagoland.

"I am not direct with You!" Rigel raised his voice, which rarely happened, but he could not help it having heard her thoughts. He rose from the chair, and inadvertently closed the distance between them. "You are not my type!"

"Well, it makes two of us, then." She looked up at him with bolts of amber lightning in her eyes. "Do You need me tonight?"

"What?!?" He tipped his head back, not only because of her odd question but because of his own reflection in her eyes, for the second time that evening.

"I do not feel comfortable speaking with You now. If You don't mind, I will go home and come to Your Police Station."

"Alright." Rigel nodded and figured it was best they parted ways before he lost control of his temper completely. He took out his wallet and pulled out a card from one of its compartments. "This is my contact information. Please call me if You remember any details that might come to You. No detail is too small."

"Alright, Detective." She looked at it. "I may just call You Rigel."

"Fine, Jade." He shook his head and did not bother to hide his grin at her odd ability to play on words as she walked away.

Nor did he bother to hide his puzzled look the moment he heard a knock on the door to his house and opened it to reveal Jade standing there, with the season's first snowflakes falling gently behind her back...

≈ **Chapter 4** ≈

He never got caught off guard. Never. At least that's what he thought until recently. But Rigel was surprised to find the petite young woman standing on the other side of his screen door. Not only did she find the location of his house, but she also did so in record time.

What bothered him most about his current predicament was the fact he did not tell her where he lived. Nor did he intend to do so. But there she was. Jade Alistair. Standing at his doorstep. Looking at him without so much as a blink of an eye - with the same absent stare he saw in her eyes earlier in the evening. Since the notion of being pranked by anyone on the force or his best friend was out of the question, he had no choice but to open the door, albeit reluctantly.

What bothered Jade, aside from suddenly feeling foolish for going out on a whim and deciding to visit the close-minded Detective because she remembered a detail from the crime scene, was the fact she was looking straight at him. And not necessarily into his eyes. Why? Because the man standing before her opened the door shirtless. Dripping water from his just-showered hair, down his bare back and perfectly sculpted chest. Wearing dark-washed jeans, zipped but unbuttoned. With a towel in his hand.

'Holy pecs...'

Jade's not-so-indirect thoughts struck Rigel as both amusing and bothersome.

"Hi, Jade," he greeted his unexpected guest through the screen door.

"Detective."

"I'd say You were the Detective."

"No, I am the intern."

"I know – " Rigel paused and debated whether he should explain the rhetoric of his statement.

"Then why did You say I was the Detective?" Jade crossed her arms at her chest.

"You are standing at my doorstep."

"Correct."

"You are speaking with me," he said in the same half-annoyed tone of voice.

"Correct."

"Considering I didn't tell You where I live, I'd say You must be one damn good Detective," Rigel noted with sarcasm and rubbed the towel on his wet and now cold hair.

"Of course, I am not. You told me where You live."

"When did I do that?" He narrowed his eyes on her and tried to recall their prior conversation.

"When You took out Your wallet and pulled out Your card," she replied in a way that made him feel almost insulted. "I notice details."

"You do?" He didn't know whether to be impressed with her or mad at himself for letting his guard down enough for someone to see where he lived.

"Yes. That's why I'm here," she nodded. "I remembered something about the victim. But I noticed something else, too."

"And what might that be?" He asked, intrigued by the reason why she decided to come by his house instead of simply calling him about it.

"It's cold outside, I walked here for a good hour, and You still did not open the door so I could come in."

"You... walked here? In this weather?"

"Yes."

"Why?" He asked, impressed more than he would have preferred.

"My mom took the car to visit my aunt, and I am not a fan of public transportation."

"Why?"

"Personal choice. May I come in?"

"Right. Sorry," He shook his head and opened the screen door, letting her inside. The cold November night breeze caressed his bare back in a way he did not care for one bit. He was used to rough nights while on duty, but not on his personal time.

"Did You just move in?" Jade stood near the door and took in the view of his living area. It was almost bare to the bones, with a long dark blue rug the length of the living room and dining room, three tall plants by the window, two barstools by the kitchen island, a kitchen without any personal items or equipment beside a cordless kettle and a toaster. It looked almost uninhabited.

"Nope. I've called this place home for the last 5 years," he replied without giving it a single thought. And again, wondered why he told the information so easily to her. "Why?"

"It looks... lonely.".

"It looks like my house.".

"Is the upstairs just as lonely?" Jade asked before she could stop herself.

"Nope," he crossed his arms at his chest, flexing his muscles.

"Oh," was what she said, but Rigel heard much more.

Those muscles... Don't look there, look into his eyes...

"My bedroom's upstairs," he noted with a smirk to see her reaction since her thoughts offered him a sense of amusement he had not felt in a while.

"I don't need to know that." She blinked and looked into his eyes. "Why did You tell me that?"

"You asked if it's just as lonely upstairs. I simply answered Your question," he flashed a wide grin.

"Are You always this direct with women? Or just me?"

"Do You always knock on men's doors shortly before midnight? Or just mine?" His grin widened because he knew he scored a point in his favor. Then again...

"I have been raised better than to go for a quick-mouth show off. I have come here because of the crime that was committed, not because of Your looks!"

"I'll keep that in mind." Rigel washed the grin off his face, but flexed his pecs again to prove a point. Just as he thought. She simply could not NOT look there.

"Keep those pectoral muscles to Yourself. Better yet, put on a shirt. You'll catch a cold in this weather," she scolded him, but it only amused him even more.

Pectoral muscles. Nice one, Jade! You really had to call them that?!?'

"Fine. I'll cover my pectoral muscles if they bother You so much," Rigel remarked, flexed them once again, and walked into the laundry room next to the kitchen to retrieve a sweater.

"Your muscles don't bother me!"

'Yes, they do!'

"Yes, they do." Rigel repeated the words he heard in her thoughts, grinning to himself as he pulled a white turtleneck sweater over his head.

"I did not come here to speak about Your muscles!"

"And yet, here we are." Rigel walked back into the kitchen, noticing his guest did not move from where she stood. "Would You like some coffee?"

"It's too late for coffee."

"But not too late for an hour's walk?" He asked and poured water into the kettle.

"You play on words, Detective."

"You seem to be good at that Yourself." He set the kettle and leaned on the kitchen island counter, gesturing for her to sit on one of the barstools. "Please, come in. You've come to talk, so let's talk."

"Alright." She removed her winter coat and boots and walked toward the kitchen island. It was then that Rigel noted just how petite and fragile her body looked. She was no taller than 5'2", 5'3". Her raven black hair reached way past her tiny waist, which complimented her South American complexion, and accentuated her natural glow.

"Tea?" He gestured at her with cups retrieved from one of the cupboards.

"I would appreciate it," she smiled but the smile disappeared. "I apologize for coming over this late tonight. I tend to act on a whim if something is important to me."

"Do not apologize for it," he shook his head. He disliked being caught off guard but disliked when people did something intentionally then asked for forgiveness. "Now, what did You remember?"

"It may sound strange, but when I found the man lying there near the Mayor's desk, I came around him to see if he was alive. He had passed on, unfortunately, but I noticed a single green thread in the palm of his hand."

"Which hand?" Rigel asked and passed the cup of hot and pungent tea to her.

"Right hand. The hand that laid on the carpet."

"Are You sure?" He asked to be certain.

"Yes, he laid on his right side, and his left hand laid across his chest."

"Alright," Rigel recalled the crime scene in his mind, and recalled seeing the green thread himself. "I will be sure to examine the thread. It sure did not fit the crime scene."

"You might say that."

"Why do You think so?"

"Well, when I first saw the man lying there, the thread was in his right hand. But when I went back to the room to retrieve my laptop before leaving, the thread was down on the carpet, beside the body," she paused, a bit unsettled.

"But I did not touch the body. Neither did You, right?" He asked, narrowing his eyebrows. He recalled the green thread in the man's right hand but could not recall if he noticed that the thread had been moved.

"I would never touch someone's body after they passed on."

"Alright. Did You notice anything else?"

"Not that night, but I do remember seeing the man who had been shot twice before at the Mayor's Office. Both times that man appeared to have been in a bad mood," she looked into her tea and twirled the cup in her hands. "But there was one more thing I remember about him."

"And what is that?" Rigel paused as he was about to bring his cup to his lips.

"When someone comes to visit the Mayor's Office, they usually are announced and wait to be called into his office. Whoever this man was, he must have been acquainted with the Mayor because he walked right in."

"Acquainted or threatened," Rigel said before he could stop himself.

'Exactly...'

That thought of hers surprised him. Could she know something she did not want to reveal? Could she tell him more if he pushed it now? Probably not. He also knew better than to question a witness on something so important in the vicinity of his own four walls.

"I think we should speak about it tomorrow. Can You come by the precinct tomorrow?" He turned and set his cup down in the sink. When he turned back around, she was right in front of him, startling him. So much so he took a step back.

"I don't bite," Jade narrowed her eyes.

"I didn't say You did," Rigel raised his eyebrow.

"You jumped. I wonder why I scare You so much?" She kept her eyes narrowed on him.

"You don't scare me," he shook his head, wondering why someone as delicate as she could make him... jump. To prove to himself he was NOT scared of being near her, he decided to offer her a ride. "It's late. Let me drive You home."

"What if I won't let You?" She took a step back and crossed her arms at her chest.

"I... I didn't mean anything bad by it. I have no ulterior motives, Ms. Alistair," he raised his hands to prove it.

"Alright.".

"Alright."

"But I must tell You that You've come undone," she leaned forward and set her cup down, almost forcing him to take another step back. If he wasn't raised to be the man he was, he would have cussed out loud at his own foolishness.

"I most certainly did not."

"Sure, You did."

"And why do You say that?"

"Your button is undone." Saying so, Jade turned and walked to retrieve her winter coat.

"Which button would that be?"

"Your jeans button," she added with a smirk, leaving him stunned, dumbfounded, and at a loss for words...

≈ **Chapter 5** ≈

Filling out crime scene reports was the best part of the job - said no Police Officer or Detective. Ever. Though it was a part of Rigel's daily routine, it did not mean he would ever get used to it. Or that he would like it. Or that he would one day fall immune to the crimes one human being committed against another. That was something he would never get used to. Never.

Maybe it was part of his blood, or a part of his conscience? Or perhaps because of the way he was raised? At some point in life Rigel decided if bad people were to be punished for their wrongdoing, good people had to exist to make sure justice prevailed. Whether lawyers played devil's advocate, so the bad guy walked. That was not up to him. He realized that first year on the job. No, it wasn't up to him to judge people. It was up to him to catch the bad guys and put the fear of karma in their hearts.

Rigel felt that exact way as he looked over the crime scene report pertaining to the victim found by the woman who played on his words the night before, and one who kept popping back into his mind ever since they met. The moment his thoughts traveled her way yet again that morning, Rigel leaned back in his chair at the precinct and sighed while rubbing his eyes.

"If I didn't know any better, I'd say You might be bothered by the fact the Mayor called in a personal favor by asking for You to take the lead on this one," Rigel's Task Force partner,

Detective Alex Stepka grinned from ear to ear as he walked toward their dual sided desk with two cups of coffee.

"You don't know better," Rigel replied with a sour face, already sensing the crude taste of the way Alex brewed coffee.

"Really?" Alex chuckled.

"First of all, it did not bother me I got called in for this case," Rigel stretched his arms up and then crossed them, linking his fingers behind his head. "Second of all, I doubt anyone would look at it as calling in a favor."

"I would," Alex grinned. He passed the cup filled with a liquid of questionable color of creamy mud to Rigel and sat down on the edge of the desk.

"You would also assume You make better coffee than Your wife," Rigel accepted the beverage and took a sip, grimaced, but smiled, nonetheless. "You don't, sunshine."

"That's not what she says."

"She loves You, she has no choice," Rigel chuckled, realizing how much he needed a momentary mental break.

"Of course, she loves me." Alex puffed out his chest. "I'm the best catch in the city!"

"That's not what she said, sunshine." Rigel laughed wholeheartedly now.

"Hey, insult me and I might tell Maria to stop making those onion bagels You love so much," Alex pointed at his partner.

"You wouldn't dare," Rigel said grimly.

"Maybe," Alex flashed his pearly whites. "Anyway, what do we have?"

"Well, we have one victim, one possible witness, four bullet holes, no suspect, and no weapon found at the scene," Rigel sighed, bothered by all the items he counted and at seeing an eerie similarity between this case and others he was working on in secret from everyone.

"Why do You say we have one possible witness?" Alex narrowed his eyes on Rigel.

"Because Ms. Alistair found the body but did not witness the crime," Rigel said in plain words.

"How hard could it be to find the bad guy if the crime took place at the Mayor's Office?" Alex moved his shoulders up and down. "We'll make sure the witness talks, and then it's smooth sailing for us."

"It's the talking to the witness that will bend those sails of Yours, sunshine." Rigel smirked and took another sip of the coffee, grimacing at its taste again as Alex pointed toward the door.

"Who's that?" Alex stood up and flexed his muscles at the young woman walking toward them.

"That would be the possible witness." Rigel set the coffee down on the desk but did not rise from his chair.

"Did I tell You how much I love getting partnered with You?" Alex muttered, running a hand through his hair.

"Happyski! There's someone here to see You!" The Officer who manned the front desk walked toward both men with Jade walking shyly beside her.

"Oh, I am not here to see Detective Happyski. I am here to see Detective Brzozakiewiczowicz," Jade asked, confused.

"They are one and the same, Miss Alistair," the Officer smiled at her. "It's just easier to refer to Rigel by his happy nature than by his name."

"He has a happy nature?" Jade raised her eyebrows, causing the Officer to bellow out a laugh.

"Only when Detective Stepka makes coffee for everyone else but him." The Officer patted Jade on her shoulder as they stopped by Rigel's desk. "She's all Yours, Happyski."

"No, I am not!" Jade protested and sent Rigel a thunderous look.

"No, I did not mean..." The Officer began to explain herself with a baffled look when Rigel waived his hand.

"That's all right, Barb. She won't get it anyway," Rigel sent the Officer a half smile. "I'll take it from here."

"Good luck," the Officer offered him an all-telling smirk and walked away.

"I most certainly am not all Yours." Jade looked down at Rigel, who still sat in his chair.

"I never said You were." Rigel looked at Alex, then back at Jade. He wondered whether to read her thoughts intentionally, or whether to wait for them to scream at him as they did the night before. Since he was in a better mood than moments ago, Rigel decided to add a little pep to his morning. He rose from the chair, and stopped no more than an inch from Jade, forcing her to look up. The look they shared could have been an innocent one if it didn't last as long as it did.

'Oh, wow... Jade, control Yourself!'

"Thank You for coming by to give Your statement, Miss Alistair." Alex chimed in, aware of the way his partner seemed lost in the young woman's eyes and caused both Jade and Rigel to turn their heads his way in unison.

"Thank You, Detective..." Jade all but curtsied when asking for his name.

"Detective Alex Stepka." Alex inclined his head, flexed his muscles, and smiled from ear to ear.

"Nice to meet You, Detective Stepka. I can't say I felt the same way about meeting Your partner," Jade returned his smile without looking back at Rigel.

"Don't I get any points for driving You home?" Rigel asked, which resulted in a raised eyebrow from Alex and a glare of a fiery temper from Jade.

"I did not pull Your arm to drive me home," she said bluntly.

"Leg," he grinned.

"What leg?" She asked, confused.

"My leg," he smirked.

"What about Your leg?" Jade narrowed her eyebrows.

"Nothing. You said You did not pull my arm. I think You meant to say that You did not pull my leg," he sent her a full-blown smile, when he saw Alex looking at him. "Am I right, Alex?"

"I guess," Alex scratched his head, but found it puzzling how Rigel was able to figure out Jade's train of thought.

"She's a linguist," Rigel explained, seeing his partner's confusion.

"That... explains it," Alex said more to himself, still as puzzled as before. "But I thought she was an intern?"

"Yes, I am an intern." Jade explained with confidence, looking at Rigel "And I most certainly am not a Detective, nor am I Yours."

"Most certainly not." Rigel flashed his cocky smile and made sure to do so with his dimples showing.

'Those dimples! How rude!'

"Ready for that statement, Miss Alistair?" Alex chimed in again, feeling ousted from the conversation.

"Yes. The sooner I provide the statement, the sooner I can leave."

"Alright," Alex nodded. "Would You like some coffee?"

"Say no!" Exclaimed the men and women standing near them.

"That hurt!" Alex exclaimed back.

"Not as much as drinking Your coffee," Rigel laughed, shaking his head back.

"I can see why they call You Happyski," Jade noted and sat in the chair beside his desk.

"Oh, it has nothing to do with his happy laugh," Alex announced and sat in the chair behind his desk adjacent to Rigel's.

"Then why?" Jade raised her eyebrow.

"Have You ever tried pronouncing Rigel full name?" Alex grinned with sarcasm.

"Rigel Brzozakiewiczowicz," she said without the slightest pause or mispronunciation, causing Alex's grin to disappear.

"Like I said, she's a linguist." Rigel moved his shoulders up and down, sending Jade the kind of a look that brought a smile to her lips. But it was her thoughts that brought a smile to his…

≈ **Chapter 6** ≈

Sitting in a chair as stiff and as uncomfortable as physically possible, Jade felt more insignificant than she ever felt in her life. She disliked Police precincts on principle. Her past did not make dealing with law enforcement any easier. Especially in a foreign country. Especially when the person interrogating her raised her blood pressure - more than the proverbial notch.

Even if the headstrong Detective Brzozakiewiczowicz did not look at her, she could not help but feel his gaze pierce through her. Right through her. And even if she did not look at him, Jade was... secretly analyzing the way he looked, the way he spoke, the way he seemed grander than life as he sat in the chair behind his desk in a crisp white shirt creased only by the leather holster strapped across his shoulders and his wide muscular back.

Though Jade reminded herself time and again she was not the suspect, nor was she guilty of anything aside from coming across a crime that did not make sense to her, she still felt uneasy about it. Even more so, the more answers she provided, the more questions Rigel and Alex had in mind.

"You indicated You were alone in the Mayor's Office. How did You know You were alone?" Rigel repeated that question twice in the span of an hour. He wasn't looking to discredit Jade's story. He was looking to strengthen it.

"Everyone left early. I passed the cleaning crew on my way into the Office. We spoke briefly, and they informed me there was no one left in the Office," Jade repeated the same words, as if on autopilot.

"In other words, the cleaning crew indicated to You that You would be alone. Is that correct?" Alex asked as he jotted notes of his own since Rigel held the file in his hands.

"Yes," Jade nodded.

"So, technically, You did not check each of the Offices to see if anyone was still at the Office?" Rigel continued Alex's train of thought, nodding to his partner in agreement.

"No, I did not." Jade shook her head. "Why would I doubt the cleaning crew's words?"

"I didn't mean to imply You should or should not have doubted their word," Rigel twisted a pen in his hand. He did not take notes, so holding the pen was a form of staying focused.

"You just did," Jade puffed out air, adjusting her position.

"I did not. I just want to make sure we rule out any colleagues of Yours that could have committed this crime," Rigel clarified and paused twisting the pen. "I also want to figure out how the cleaning crew could have cleaned the Mayor's Office but left without discovering the body."

"I wondered about that as well," Jade sighed and looked at Alex. "How could they have cleaned and not seen that poor man?"

"What makes You so sure they cleaned the Mayor's Office at all that day?" Alex leaned forward in his chair.

"Because they clean it every time they come?" Jade answered his question with hers.

"When did the Mayor leave to visit his family?" Rigel decided to try a different approach. Maybe instead of asking Jade what she saw, asking what she did not see could offer additional information that may seem insignificant to her but not to him.

"He left shortly after 5:00 p.m.," Jade answered matter-of-factly.

"Yesterday?" Rigel tipped his head back and narrowed his eyes on her. "Didn't the Office have shorter hours yesterday?"

"Yes," Jade nodded.

"If the Mayor left at 5:00 p.m., how come the security guards said the cleaning crew was the last to leave the Office?" Rigel sighed, confused.

"Because the Mayor left on Thursday," Jade replied with sarcastic undertones. "Isn't it obvious?"

"Now it is." Rigel grit his teeth, unable to stop himself, and looked at Alex. "What did I tell You about bending those sails?"

"It's definitely obvious now." Alex shook his head, sensing a growing headache. He rose from the chair. "I need coffee. Anyone want one?"

"No!" A chorus of those around them exclaimed in unison, causing Jade to let out a delicate laugh that released the tension in her stomach, and oddly enough - in Rigel's as well.

"How about we take a little break from the questions?" Rigel asked her when Alex walked away in the direction of the kitchen area.

"I would appreciate it, Detective. I don't like answering all these questions," she said quietly.

"Trust me, it hurts much less answering them as a witness than it does as a suspect," Rigel offered her a faint smile.

'Trust You? I would rather drink Alex's coffee instead!'

"Alex! One coffee!" Rigel laughed sincerely at her thought. And then... realized immediately that he heard Jade's thoughts and not her spoken words. Which only meant one thing. He was now stuck with another cup of his partner's preposterously tasting beverage. Begrudging Jade instantly for something she didn't even know she had done, he narrowed his eyes on her.

"What?" She tipped her head to the side.

"Nothing," he muttered the response.

"That was NOT nothing. The way You looked at me was not nothing." Jade replied and leaned in closer to examine him.

"I said it was nothing," Rigel leaned back, feeling suddenly uncomfortable in his own chair.

"I say it was something. Did You..." Jade raised her eyebrows, then opened her eyes wider. "Did You just read my mind?"

"Of course, not." Of all the human beings on the surface of the earth, of all the times he read minds, of all the moments in his life where he chose to use his talent... this was the one time he did so unconsciously and NOW he was discovered? NOW?!? And by HER?!?

"Prove it," Jade challenged him, and felt immensely better to turn tables on him.

"What?" Rigel puffed out air but leaned in closer to ensure that whatever she said next would not be said louder than it had to. As a matter of fact, he decided to lean in so close that it would ruffle her feathers. He failed... miserably. It ruffled feathers, but not hers.

"Prove You did not read my mind," Jade whispered, propped her chin on her hand as if for unnecessary support, and leaned in even closer, almost closing the distance between them.

"And how do You suppose I do that?" He whispered as his mouth ran dry. Unable to stop himself, he held her gaze until his mind filled with words that weren't his.

'Take a sip of the coffee that Your partner Alex brings, and I will find a way to kiss You...'

There. She thought it. She really did. She was sure her thoughts fell deaf of their intended mark. But she was wrong. Oh, so very wrong. He heard her, and for a man who chose to spend the rest of his life without a hand that held his, Jade's thoughts intrigued him. Not only that. They made him wonder for a split second of time. A split second of time he realized instantly he wouldn't be able to take back.

He looked down...

Down to her lips...

Ever so slowly...

And traced the contour of her lips with his eyes...

Whether she was willing to believe or deny it...

"What did I tell You? I knew my exceptional coffee making skills are going to grow on You one day," Alex walked up to the dual desk with two cups of coffee in his hands.

"Thanks." Rigel grit his teeth, not entirely because of the coffee he would soon be forced to taste.

"Are You sure You don't want it?" Alex asked Jade, but he had no idea her thoughts did not move past Rigel's lips she was now looking at.

"I would rather not answer that question."

"Suit Yourself, but the offer stands if You need it," Alex advised her and received a thunderous look from his partner.

"I think we are done here for now." Rigel straightened in his chair. "We will call You if we have any more questions."

"Was it something I said?" Alex wondered out loud.

"No," both Jade and Rigel answered in unison.

"I see." Alex nodded to himself and took a sip of his coffee so no one would see his growing smile. It appeared his headstrong partner met his match in a tiny-framed and just as headstrong Miss Jade Alistair.

"Alright," Rigel rose to his feet. "Like I said, I will call You if I need You."

"Interesting." Alex said to himself in a not-so-quiet way.

"WE will call You," Rigel corrected himself by almost hissing the words at his partner.

"You won't." Jade countered his suggestion and rose from her chair.

"Are You sure about that?" Rigel almost snapped his neck as he looked down at her.

"Of course," she smirked.

"And why is that?" He asked and did not know why his temper kicked up a few notches.

"You gave me Your telephone number, but I did not give You mine," she said with confidence, earning another smile from Alex.

"Very interesting," Alex repeated his observation.

"Your way of brewing coffee is interesting," Rigel fired back at his partner.

"Not as interesting as THIS," Alex offered him a wicked grin and made a circling gesture pointing to Rigel and Jade.

"Your partner has a poor sense of humor," Jade advised Rigel as she narrowed her eyes on Alex.

"Just be glad You didn't get to taste his coffee," Rigel shrugged.

"I will remember that." She nodded, then paused. "Did You figure out what that green thread could be from?"

"No, not yet." Rigel felt a sudden tug at his gut. It wasn't because Jade offered him a faint smile that reached somewhere deep. It was because there was no mention of a green thread in the list of evidence. And he checked that list twice.

"Alright," Jade sighed. She leaned in over Rigel's desk. She wrote down her telephone number after all on a blue post-it note and handed it to Rigel. "This is my telephone number. You know where to find me."

"Thank You, Miss Alistair," Alex bid her goodbye since Rigel kept silent.

"It was nice to meet You, Detective Stepka," Jade inclined her head and walked toward the door after she waited for Rigel's goodbye which never came.

She was almost at the door when she decided to look back. What would it hurt? It wouldn't, since she was convinced Rigel wouldn't even notice her among the sea of Police Officers and Detectives. She realized just how wrong she was when she looked back and saw him looking straight at her all the while he downed the entire cup of coffee Alex offered to him - in one single gulp...

≈ Chapter 7 ≈

A week had gone by from the day the crime had been committed at the Mayor of Chicago's Office. Short seven days yet one long week at the same time. A lot had happened since then, yet little changed in Rigel's eyes. And all of it had unnerved him.

The crime had been committed - some may say it was nothing new in the land of Chicago. Even if that crime was committed in the Office of Chicago's landlord, so to speak.

The Mayor had been questioned from the vicinity of his private home in the Bahamas at first and not at the Police precinct - again, nothing new. There were politicians who knew how to work the system, and Mayor Vincent Lucchese was an example of just that. He did, eventually make his way to the precinct to provide Rigel with his statement, but he did so four days after the crime was committed. This did not bother Rigel as much as the fact that Vincent Lucchese decided not to cut his family's lavish vacation short after finding out that a crime was committed at his Office, right in front of his desk.

The man who fell victim to four bullets fired at him was a Police Officer - that may not seem shocking to some, but it did to Rigel. That would have been enough to motivate Rigel to put the killer behind bars. However, there was more. Why? Because he had seen the same exact fatal injuries before. His former partner, Sebastian's brother, was killed in the same manner. Same exact manner. That was why the crime he was called upon to investigate took on a personal meaning the moment he saw the three bullets fired at the victim's chest and one at the man's head.

Tried as they might, none of the evidence Rigel and Alex had gone over directed them toward any leads which could result in catching the killer. Just as it didn't in the other nine cases over the past years. All those cases were deemed robbery related. Closed as resolved. No correlation between them. But Rigel knew better. The Alistair blood flowing through his veins knew better.

And then, there was the issue of the evidence itself. Or rather, lack thereof. Case in point? The single green thread Rigel saw at the crime scene. Correction, the single green thread that both he and Jade had seen. Even if he could somehow talk himself out of seeing that thread, he could not dismiss the fact Jade saw it as well.

Nor could he dismiss the nagging feeling that he... somehow missed her. And Alex's constant reminders of her existence did NOT help Rigel one bit.

That was why Rigel praised the heavens above that Saturday morning came when it did. It was his day off. A day he could spend far from his job, far from his duties, and far from his persistent partner. A day he would finally visit his best friend Sebastian for a much needed and well overdue evening where he wouldn't have to think about things that troubled him daily.

With that thought in mind, Rigel decided to take an early morning drive down the Lake Shore Drive. He liked Downtown Chicago. Its mix of cultures. Its strips of greenery and nature in an otherwise industrialized jungle. Its contrast between the tall glass buildings and the water edge horizon of Lake Michigan. The Clarence F. Buckingham Fountain. The Navy Pier. The Bowman and The Spearman monuments known as The Equestrian Indians. The Millennium Park with the famed Cloud Gate - The Chicago Bean as it has been dubbed by those who ever heard of it.

It was a cool November morning. It was cloudless. It was sunny. It offered a light breeze silently announcing a change of the weather. It was a perfect time for him... to call the woman he could not get out of his mind or from under his skin. And he told himself there was nothing ambiguous about it. After all, he was a lead Detective on the case assigned to him. She was a witness in the case. He was going to call her to see if she remembered anything new about that day which could help in the case, and maybe he would ask how she was doing. Maybe. That was all. And it would have been all, if only Jade had picked up the call.

She did not...

So, he called again...

Again, the call went unanswered...

Mad at himself now more than at Jade, Rigel dropped the phone on the passenger seat, and decided to go to the one place in all of Chicago that offered him a sense of peace. He directed his car off the Lake Shore Drive and drove around the Soldier Field Stadium. He paused briefly as he passed the Chicago Police Officers Memorial, thinking of his late partner and dear friend Eryk Lipa. Eryk was the reason why he joined the Task Force. He was the reason why Rigel believed he could make a difference. He was the reason why Rigel became suspicious of a string of fatalities plaguing the Chicago P.D. ranks.

But that laid in the past. Regardless of the possibility that the past murders he was secretly investigating could have been related to the most recent one, Rigel knew he had to shake the gut feeling twisting his stomach into knots. He needed to clear his head so he could go back to work and catch the person who dared to pull the trigger on a man in uniform.

After parking his car by the Adler Planetarium beside the Burnham Harbor Marina, Rigel puffed out a resigned gulp of air and sighed. He leaned over the steering wheel, crossing his arms over it, and rubbed his eyes. All he wanted was a moment of silence. A moment of peace. A moment to feel like an Alistair again, capable of handling whatever it was that troubled him. And just at that moment his telephone rang. Swearing to himself, he looked over to the passenger seat, picked up the phone, and chuckled.

"Jade Alistair." Rigel answered the call, grinning instead of being mad at her for not picking up in the first place.

"You called me, Detective Happyski?" A gentle voice greeted him, muffled a bit by what Rigel assumed was a windy breeze.

"I did." He replied, suddenly feeling awkward about it. Why? He didn't know. And that turned his grin into a frown.

"You did," Jade repeated and decided to wait for his explanation for the call. What she received instead was a prolonged moment of silence. "Are You here?"

"Am I here?" Rigel shook his head at the odd way she formed the sentence.

"Yes, are You here in the conversation?"

"Oh, You meant are You there." Rigel grinned again while knots began to loosen in his gut.

"There where?" Jade replied, confused.

"Nowhere," he chuckled. Goodness, did that little confusing exchange of words help him, even more than he was willing to admit.

"Oh," she sighed. "Did You need me for something?"

"I..." How on earth was he supposed to answer THAT one? He swore to himself because of the blunt directness of her question and cleared his throat. "I called to see if You remembered anything related to the murder case that could help us with the investigation?"

"I did not, and You can read my mind if You do not believe me," she smiled to herself.

"I do not read minds." Rigel grit his teeth. He decided then and there that calling her was a bad idea after all. Even if she did not believe him now, Rigel was certain that she would find a way to mock him for it in the future. And then, he blinked. What future? Why would that even come to his mind?

"Don't You?"

"No, I don't."

"Could have fooled me by the way You drank Detective Strepka's coffee all in one gulp."

"I did gulp that cup," Rigel narrowed his eyebrows, aware of what she meant, but decided to flip the conversation on her. "I drink coffee all the time. I also gulp it up from time to time. Especially when it comes to Alex's muddy coffee. Why would drinking coffee mean anything other than what it was?"

"No reason," she cut her reply short, feeling conscious of her foolish thoughts the last time she saw him, when she shrugged because of the breeze. She immediately scolded the brisk wind for sweeping her hair up as she sat on the lawn behind the Adler Planetarium, unaware that he heard her thoughts.

"Where are You?" He asked, stunned at the serendipity of it, and turned off the car's engine without waiting for her response.

"Here," Jade responded at the ridiculousness of his question.

"Alright. Let me ask You again before I lose my sanity," Rigel puffed out air and exited the car, slamming the door in a not-so-gentle manner and began walking toward Lake Michigan's waterfront behind the Planetarium. "Where are You right now?"

"Here, by the Adler Planetarium," she replied with sarcasm and rolled her eyes because she didn't think her current location was any of his concern. "And where, Detective, are You right now?"

"Here..." he whispered, ending the call the moment she turned, and their eyes met...

≈ Chapter 8 ≈

What could scare a man built strong enough to fight criminals, both local and international? Realizing his peace was stirred by internal factors and not external ones. Especially when he was unable to bring himself to stop thinking about the woman who sent ripples through his mind by simply being herself.

Jade Alistair. Rigel could have sworn she was not his type. Not that he had one. He decided long ago trusting someone with his feelings was not for him. It sucked, it hurt, and he knew it. But deciding not to get hurt again sounded far better than trying to patch up a heart that had been shattered into pieces.

And yet, this was different. Why? He had no clue. Maybe because of the woman Jade was? Though she seemed attracted to him, even if she denied it, she did not pursue him. He heard her thoughts, but those were intimate glimpses into who she was on the inside. Inside, she was a delicate and gentle soul. Rigel could feel it and sense it without the necessity of touching her hand. Outside, though, it was a whole other matter...

"Detective Happyski." Jade greeted him calmly as she sat on a blanket spread on a patch of dried-up grass near the water edge of Lake Michigan behind the Adler Planetarium, though her heart paced in her chest at a speed she was not confident enough to reveal. "I find it odd that You came to my secret place."

"Let's call it even since You came to my house," Rigel walked up to her.

"You told me where You lived," Jade narrowed her eyes on him.

"Like I said, let's call it even," he grinned. "Mind if I join You?"

"It is a free land, Detective. I doubt You need my permission to do anything," she replied shyly, taken with the way he looked against the bright blue sky in a washed out leather jacket.

"It isn't a NO, then?" He asked and inclined his head.

"No," she smiled shyly.

"So, it is a no?"

"No," she denied it, narrowing her eyes on him. "Yes. I mean no, it is not a NO. You confuse me."

"That makes two of us," he smiled and sat down beside her, making sure to keep at least an arm's length distance between them.

"Is there any progress in the case?" Jade asked on purpose, trying her best not to concentrate on the way his presence made her feel. Or the way the scent of his cologne perfume hit her senses as the breeze carried it her way. Or the way his eyes pierced right through her.

"None." He exhaled heavily and picked up a dried-up strand of grass. It wasn't out of boredom or consternation. It was to keep his hands from accidentally reaching out for her. "That's why I called You."

"I apologize but I haven't remembered anything new from that day or about that poor man," she replied with undeniable undertones of sadness.

"I figured, but thought I would try anyway," he offered her a faint smile.

"Well, I am glad that You did," she said before she could stop herself. "It has been a bad past week. Seeing You kind of made me feel better."

"Why do You say that?" If the question did not make him feel dumb, the way she looked at him did.

"First of all, I found a dead man in my employer's office. And second of all, everyone at the office stopped talking to me now, even the Mayor."

"Why?" Rigel asked, surprised by her words. "You are not the suspect?"

"I am not, but everyone is suspicious of me. They think I will go to the Police if I overhear them saying anything about the case, the man who died, or the Mayor."

"Why the Mayor?" Rigel asked, puzzled. "The man is a donkey's arse, but he is not the suspect either?"

"It sounds like You know the Mayor personally?" Jade raised her eyebrow.

"I do," he nodded, then immediately corrected his statement. "I did."

"Oh," she tipped her head. "Care to share Your point of view of the Mayor?"

"No," he replied in short. He did not mean to put an invisible distance between them, but he did. And she could not get past that.

'I am sorry I asked...'

"I understand," she said shyly, and brought her knees closer to her chest, wrapping her arms around them. "Well, maybe that is also a part of the reason why no one at the office wants to speak with me."

"How so?" Rigel turned to her more now, unconsciously, and unintentionally.

"My colleagues say You are not to be messed with. You have a reputation of being stern and hard like steel. Since You were chosen by the Mayor to take the lead on this case, and they know I have spoken with You, they think I would run to You to cause trouble," she explained and moved her shoulders up and down.

"Would You?" He asked before he could stop himself.

"Would I what?"

"Would You run to me?"

"Would You want me to?"

'It would depend on the reason...'

"It would depend, I guess," he paused and looked deeper into her eyes. He told himself it wasn't to read her mind. Not at all. At all.

"On what?" She narrowed her eyebrows, contemplating whether he really did read minds.

"On whether You would have a choice to do so or not." He decided to word his response in a way that would mislead her. And hoped it worked.

"I am afraid I do not understand. What does choice have to do with it?" She turned slightly toward him.

"You see, running to someone when there is no other choice is easy. It is in our human nature. An instinct. But running to someone at a moment when life presents many other options takes guts."

"You have an old soul, Detective," she inclined her head toward him. "You guard it well, but it speaks through Your words."

"That... is a keen observation coming from someone who met me a week ago." He did not mean to offend her and was glad to see she did not feel that way. Instead, she smiled from her heart, sincerely, and deeply, perhaps for the first time since they met.

"My father taught me to look at people through the prism of their soul, not through the reputation of others," she turned toward the Lake's waterfront again.

"He is a wise man," Rigel nodded.

"He was. I miss him dearly." Saying so, Jade sighed heavily, and Rigel did not need to read her mind to realize her father had passed on.

"How old were You when he passed away?" He asked, hoping for an answer.

"Too young for it not to bother me," she said with tears in her eyes, recalling the day her family found her father's body. She hugged her knees tighter because of it, unaware Rigel read her thoughts and tried his best not to reach out to comfort her.

"I miss my parents as well." The moment he said it, Rigel realized Jade was the first woman he ever mentioned it to. It was also the first time in his life where he let his guard down without it bothering him.

"Did they pass away long ago?" Jade turned back to him.

"Yes. It sucked. It still does," he replied quietly and looked down on his hands instead of looking into her eyes.

"You must have taken it hard. Something like that changes a person," she leaned in toward him in a gesture of sincerity, sympathy, and understanding.

"I did, but my older brother took it much harder." He did not know why he said it. He just did. It was neither a revelation nor admission of who he was, but it had a profound effect on the moment they just shared. "May I ask You something?"

"Yes, Detective."

"You call this spot Your secret place. Why?"

"Because it is."

"Care to share why?" He inclined his head a bit.

"No," she smiled when she saw his facial expression. "I come here because it reminds me of home."

"And where is home for You?"

"São Paulo," she sighed and closed her eyes.

"It is a beautiful city," he smiled, having visited that city on more than a few occasions in the past.

"It is," she agreed but felt a sliver of fear run through her.

'It has its secrets, too...'

"I am sure You would rather visit São Paulo than feel this cold Chicago breeze on Your cheeks," Rigel tried to get her to talk about herself a bit more.

"No," she replied with sadness in her eyes.

'I can't...'

"Do You want to know how I found You here?"

"How?"

"Would You believe this is my secret place as well?" He grinned and watched as his admission cheered her up.

"I don't think so."

"And why not?"

"I have been coming here for the last two years, and I have never run into You."

"You haven't?"

"No. I would have remembered You."

"Would You?"

"I don't know what Detective Alex may have told You, but You are pretty hard to miss in a crowd," Jade grinned, and noticed the more she spoke with him, the calmer she felt.

"Oh, so You admit I am pretty?" He teased her.

"No, I..." she rolled her eyes. "That is not what I meant."

"So, I am not pretty?" He asked and flashed his pearly whites in a purely cocky way when she shook her head in disbelief.

"I doubt You need anyone to approve or disapprove of Your looks, Detective," she chuckled, fully aware her cheeks burned ruby red - and not because of the weather.

"Agreed," he nodded. "Are You hungry?"

"You are certainly a man. If it's not Your looks You think of, then it's food," she noted with amusement.

"You are wrong on both accounts. But I am hungry. Care to join me?" He stretched out his legs before standing up.

"I must say that question was much nicer than the ones You asked me at the precinct," she advised him.

"Like they said, I am a stern Detective. Hard like steel. But I also have a softer side in private," he clicked his tongue and twisted a few knots in her stomach with that simple gesture.

"I will keep that in mind. What sort of breakfast would You have in mind?" Saying so, Jade decided to take him up on the offer of a shared meal. After all, it was a late morning, she was hungry, and it was an innocent invitation.

"Ever had bagels for breakfast?" Rigel rose to his feet and extended his hand to help her rise from the blanket.

"As long as wherever You decide to take me has onion bagels, I am in," Jade replied, unaware she took his breath away not only by mentioning his favorite choice of bagels, but also because he heard the same whisper of thoughts the moment her hand touched his when she accepted his hand.

'She's the one...'

≈ **Chapter 9** ≈

Sitting back on a comfortable couch at Sebastian's home in the Roselle suburb of Chicago, a week after enjoying breakfast with Jade over onion bagels, with a glass of his favorite brand of golden, smooth, and perfectly chilled whiskey, Rigel smiled as he twirled the glass in his hand. The sound of the whiskey stones complimented the bellowing sound of laughter that filled the living room.

To some, Saturday evenings were meant for family gatherings. To Rigel, they were about family, yes, but the one he chose. Far from his real family, from his six siblings. And maybe he preferred it that way to some extent? Life was what it was, and those who sugar coated it often ended the day on a sour note.

The group of friends who became Rigel's family were a close-knit circle of individuals he knew he could trust. Though, only Sebastian, his Polish highlander best friend, was aware of his identity. An identity Rigel could not risk exposing. Not after Sebastian's brother died, and after Rigel's heart was left void because he once thought he was strong enough to let love into his life. It surprised Rigel to find out years ago Sebastian and Alex were close friends. Now, he felt grateful they were.

"Look at Happyski. It took him less than a month to melt faster than ice cubes in whiskey," Alex pointed to his partner with his own whiskey glass as he leaned back against the kitchen counter.

"That's why he can't take ice cubes," Sebastian chuckled while his magician of a cook wife brought out a plate of her famous homemade cheesecake.

"Real men prefer whiskey for its own taste, and don't bother to sissy it down with melting ice," Rigel smirked.

"Too bad I don't see one here." Maria's twin brother and Alex's brother-in-law Marek offered Rigel a cocky smirk as he sat on the couch across from Rigel.

"At least there are men here who can take whiskey instead of ice cubes," Rigel flashed his pearly whites at Marek.

"Hey, I am on a diet." Marek muttered back as his cocky smirk disappeared.

"I see." Rigel raised his glass in honor of Marek's plate topped with grilled Polish sausage, sauteed onions, and perfectly seared steak.

"What I see is a man who can't hide that puppy-eyed gleam in his eyes whenever I mention the name Jade Alistair," Alex decided to defend his brother-in-law. "And I thought falling for a witness was not his thing."

"Seriously?" Sebastian narrowed his eyes on his best friend.

"You should see him at work," Alex nodded, unaware Sebastian and Rigel shared a silent look because Sebastian just learned of Jade's full name. "He even tried to cover those puppy-eyes moments by gulping up repeated cups of my coffee."

"I don't know what You are talking about?" Rigel stopped twirling the glass in his hand.

"Sure, You don't." Alex chuckled, oblivious to Rigel's thunderous gaze. "Two weeks passed since the two of You met and You can't stop thinking about her. And You're going to tell me You had no idea she would drop by the precinct yesterday with a box of Your favorite onion bagels, right?"

"Favorite onion bagels?" Marek wiggled his eyebrows. "Did You tell her about them? Or does she like them as well?"

"Both." Alex cackled.

"He's a goner," Marek bellowed out a laugh "Might as well bring her along on our camping trip next week."

"Leave him be," Alex's wife Maria scolded them. "It could be just a coincidence that this... Jade likes onion bagels."

"No, it's not," both Alex and Marek shook their heads.

"I need some air." Rigel rose to his feet. He was not amused when the conversation turned toward Jade's subject. Nor by the accuracy of Alex's words. He crossed over to the patio door and stepped out into the cold late evening air, foregoing the necessity of his jacket. He needed the brisk November air to cool down his simmering temper.

"Are You alright?" Sebastian joined Rigel on the patio, closing the door behind him so they could talk in private.

"Yes," Rigel all but clenched his jaw.

"No, You're not." Sebastian walked to where Rigel leaned over the patio terrace's railing and leaned his back against it.

"No, I'm not," Rigel said quietly.

"I can see that. Mind telling me why this Jade Alistair bothers You so much?"

"Beats me," Rigel moved his shoulders up and down.

"She beats You?" Sebastian cocked his eyebrow.

"No!" Rigel straightened up. "She talks just like that."

"Who?" Sebastian asked, amused.

"Jade Alistair."

"Does her name bother You? Or the woman herself?"

"Both." Rigel rubbed at his eyes. "My mind went blank when she told me her name. Damn it. I froze for a moment, and that never happened before."

"So, the fact You found a dead body at the Mayor's Office had no effect on You, but she did?" Sebastian wondered and turned to lean over the railing.

"Pretty much."

"I'm sure her name is a coincidence," Sebastian advised Rigel without looking at him. "There's no need to lose Your cool over it, no matter what Alex says."

"There's more," Rigel looked up at the moon.

"How much more could there be? You met her two weeks ago. Even if she got under Your skin, she'll disappear from Your life when this case is over."

"I heard her thoughts."

"And that's new?" Sebastian sent him a sarcastic grin. "News flash, Happyski, You've done that before."

"We'll it's not the fact I heard her thoughts that bothers me. It's what I heard that does," Rigel grit his teeth.

"And what did the thoughts reveal that's got Your sissy briefs in a twist?"

"That she's the one..." Rigel whispered, refusing to admit he was afraid to say those words any louder.

"Seriously?" Sebastian raised both eyebrows now and patted Rigel's back in a brotherly way. "Hate to tell You, but that's exactly what I heard when I met Kasia. And my heart knew I was done for."

"Shut up," Rigel hissed out.

"Can't deny true love, man. You just can't." Saying so, Sebastian clicked his tongue and decided to walk back inside so Rigel could process his own thoughts. He was about to open the patio door when Rigel's phone rang. Sebastian paused and watched as his best friend lit up like the moon itself when he saw the name on the telephone's screen.

"Jade Alistair." Rigel smiled as he answered the call. And then, the smile disappeared in an instant because he heard Jade's thoughts. "What's wrong?"

"Good evening, Detective. Sorry for calling at this hour, but..." Jade paused as he cut her words short.

"Where are You?"

"I dropped my mother at my aunt's house, and I am on my way home, but I cannot get past this feeling someone keeps following me," Jade tried to speak calmly but Rigel did not fall for it. "It may sound foolish, but I hoped to speak with You, or someone, until I got home safe. I hope You don't mind."

"Nonsense," Rigel replied in a tone of voice that revealed to Sebastian how much his best friend cared about the woman he tried to deny having feelings for. "How far are You from home?"

"About twenty minutes, depending on the traffic closer to Downtown," Jade replied while looking in the rear-view mirror.

"Take the longer route to see if whoever is following You gives up. I'm on my way," Rigel clenched his fist in a bout of a temper he did not bother to hide from Sebastian. "I will call You in a moment when I'll get in the car, alright?"

"Yes, Detective," Jade agreed, grateful. "I'm sorry for calling but I didn't know who else to call without worrying my mother."

"Don't apologize," Rigel looked at Sebastian. "I'll call You right back."

"Duty calls," Sebastian nodded at Rigel. "Or rather, the call of the heart does."

"Shut up," Rigel narrowed his eyes on his best friend.

"So, I shouldn't comment on the fact You seem to know where she lives already?" Sebastian wanted to lighten up his mood but knew Rigel's mind was already miles away.

"I'd punch You if I didn't feel bad about it afterwards," Rigel frowned at Sebastian and went inside to retrieve his jacket. He rushed to his car not because of Jade's words, but because of her thoughts and the ill feeling he wasn't able to shake off that something bad was about to happen...

≈ Chapter 10 ≈

It took Rigel 20 minutes to travel the distance from Chicago's suburb of Roselle to Downtown, where Jade lived. The worst part about getting to her house as fast as possible wasn't the distance, though. It was the little One-Way streets once he exited the I-290 E. The streets he knew like the back of his hand, which never bothered him before, now seemed too narrow and too long for their own good.

The fact the engine of his Dodge Challenger Hellcat SRT worked at max speed as he cut through the traffic with his Police Department signal activated did not bother Rigel. The fact Sebastian bluntly pointed out his knowledge of Jade's address did not bother him, either. The fact he not only heard Jade's thoughts of worry but felt her fear in his gut did. And the Alistair gut was the one thing that detected danger better than his gift of reading people's minds.

If Sebastian questioned him about it afterwards, Rigel would admit with his hand on his Staccato P gun - which he already sensed he was going to have to use that night, that he read people's minds so he could predict which way they would pull to the side when they saw flashing lights in their rear-view mirror.

What kept him sane was Jade's voice flowing through the car's speakers as he rushed to her house. If she kept talking, it meant she was safe. Still safe, Rigel corrected himself at some point. She did not know about his gift, so she could not have foreseen that even though she reassured him she was calm, he disregarded those words because her fearful thoughts whispered at him with full force of her true emotions. And it only got worse when she arrived home. Then, those thoughts shouted at him louder than even he could have understood why...

"How far are You from home now?" Rigel asked because of the urgency feeling in his gut he could not overlook.

"I am parking in front of the house," Jade advised him, glad to have arrived home despite her worry. She tried her best to downplay her growing fear, but she could not fool Rigel. "The car that followed me drove past my car and turned toward the main road. I think I am safe now."

"No, You are not." Rigel's ice-cold tone of voice sounded even more ominous in his own ears.

"But the car left." Jade sulked. "I know how to be cautious. I called You to feel safer, didn't I?"

"But You are not out of harm's way yet," Rigel shook his head and pressed the gas pedal, only to be cut off by a red light and a CTA bus. He slammed on the breaks at the last moment and turned to the alley right before the intersection. "Stay in the car."

"But I am right in front of my house?" Jade countered his words. "There are no other cars driving by."

"That's even worse." The seasoned Detective's blood in him knew better than to allow Jade to drop her guard. "Whoever followed You would wait for the moment You wouldn't have witnesses near You."

"You seem too paranoid, even for Chicago standards," Jade tried to lighten up, but did a poor job of hiding her trembling voice.

"Says the woman who felt it necessary to call me on her way home on Saturday night," Rigel puffed out air to release the tension. And then swore to high heavens as Jade hung up because of his poorly worded comeback.

"That boor!" Jade grit her teeth as she exited her car.

Though she was still scared, her anger at Rigel momentarily overshadowed her sense of logic. So much so, that she remembered leaving her purse on the front seat of the car as she stood at the gate of the fence surrounding the front of her row house. She stumped the ground, rolled her eyes at her own carelessness, and turned around to go back to the car. The man she saw standing between her and the car caused her throat to lock up, making it impossible to scream for help even if she needed to do so.

"A bit late of an hour to be strolling around, wouldn't You say?" The tall and stick-thin man spoke casually as if instilling fear of life in others was his daily bread.

"I doubt it," Jade planted her feet firmly on the ground and breathed as calmly as possible. Fear was one thing. Bluff was another. At least she hoped so.

"I would assume a pretty little something like You carried half her life in a purse to make Yourself look tough, but I see You left the house without one," the man smirked wickedly as he puffed out the last bits of smoke from his burning out cigarette.

"Some women don't need a purse to feel tough," Jade replied and crossed her arms at her chest. She seemed confident, but she made the mistake of looking around for any sign of Rigel. The man noticed it in an instant.

"Robbery sometimes backfires if a woman is dumb enough not to carry one around." Saying so, the man dropped the cigarette and stepped over it with his shoe, putting it out as sparks of wicked excitement appeared in his eyes.

"I..." Jade hesitated, damning herself for not waiting for Rigel like he asked. "I actually left my purse on the front seat of my car. You can have it, just please don't hurt me."

"The purse was an excuse, although..." the man chuckled, looking in the direction of Jade's car. He regretted it immediately. The moment he took his eyes off Jade, his body got slammed against the passenger door of her car so hard he didn't even get to hiss out from pain.

"You got some nerve attacking defenseless women!" Rigel grit his teeth in anger and held the man without giving him a chance to turn his head.

"I am not defenseless!" Jade fisted her hands in anger, but that anger mellowed down when Rigel glared at her.

"Which part of 'STAY IN THE CAR' sounded like a suggestion rather than a request?" Rigel asked her as the man he held down tried to wiggle out of his hold.

"Well, the part where You made me end the call," she moved her shoulders up and down.

"I made You end the call?!?"

"Yes!" Jade shouted at him.

"We will talk about it later." Rigel inclined his head in her direction and decided to turn the would-be thief around. He grabbed the man's arm, twisted it, grabbed the man's shoulder, and turned him around. "I'll be damned..."

"Detective B., what a small world!" The man choked up out of fear. The light from the light post was enough to reveal how the man's face paled in a matter of seconds.

"Lucky Knuckles." Rigel narrowed his eyes on the man all the while tightening his grip on him. "It is a small world, indeed."

"You know each other?" Jade raised her eyebrows, surprised to say the least.

"Definitely." Rigel replied slowly, emphasizing every syllable.

"Unfortunately." The man whispered, fearing for his well-being, which was something he didn't take lightly.

"Definitely unfortunate for You." Rigel grabbed the man by the jacket and raised him off the ground with such ease it caused Jade to cover her mouth with her hands. "What are You doing here, Lucky?"

"I felt like taking a walk," the man replied, then grunted as Rigel thrust him against the passenger door.

"Wrong answer." Rigel hissed out. He didn't have to read Lucky's thoughts to figure out the man was lying.

"Fine," the man raised his arms in defeat. "I saw her walking and figured she would make an easy target if I grabbed her purse."

"Wrong again." Rigel clenched his jaw and set the man down while still holding onto his jacket. "Who paid You to follow her?"

"Nobody," the man shook his head in denial.

"You were paid to follow me?" Jade asked, confused, and surprised. "Why would anyone think I am worth following?"

"Someone obviously would," Rigel looked at her, losing his concentration because of her thoughts.

'That's impossible. No one knows I live here...'

The moment Lucky figured something happened to Rigel's train of thought, he thrust all his strength at Rigel, pushing him toward Jade. Rigel released his grip on the man, turning to shield Jade from anything Lucky would have tried. But the would-be robber disappeared between the parked cars.

"Are You alright?" Rigel cupped Jade's face and caressed her hair, making sure she was unharmed.

"Yes. Thank You," she nodded and debated whether to accept his concern or not.

"Grab Your purse and let's get inside before Lucky decides to change his mind and comes back," Rigel grabbed the keys to the front gate of her row house.

"Yes, Detective," she nodded and did as he asked.

"I still cannot believe You just hung up on me and put Yourself in danger," Rigel rushed her inside the house, making sure to lock the front gate and the door to her house.

"And I cannot believe You just invited Yourself into my house," she replied stoically.

"You must be joking," Rigel sized her up and down. "I saved You out there and You question my motive behind it?"

"That is one way of looking at it," she crossed her arms at her chest.

"You called me asking for help. I drove here like a madman. I nearly knocked out that idiot of a robber and You wonder why I came into the house with You?" Rigel placed hands at his hips as his temper stirred.

"Aren't You hot under the sweater, Detective?" Jade sized him up and down with a cold stare in her eyes.

"What?" He blinked, stupefied by her statement.

"Aren't You hot under the sweater," she repeated with undertones of annoyance mixed with a bit of temper. "You know, angry?"

"If You're going to quote an idiom, do it correctly. It's: aren't I hot under the collar," he looked at her and wasn't sure if he should laugh or grind his teeth at her.

"That's what I said."

"Sure, you did." He decided it was best for him to leave before he got angrier at her more than he already had, or before the evening would turn into something Sebastian would have summed up as an 'I told You so'. "I'm leaving. Call me if Lucky bothers You again."

"Fine," she rolled her eyes. "Thank You for Your help."

"Don't mention it," Rigel nodded and turned for the door.

As he did, Jade followed him with her gaze. Her sadness at seeing him leave turned into fear for his life as she saw a red dot at his back. She knew what it was. She recognized it in an instant. She shouted his name in her thoughts because her throat locked up in fear for his life. She leaped toward him pushing him down to the floor as hard as she could, landing atop him as a slew of bullets pierced the windows, ending up in zig zags all over the walls of her kitchen and living room...

≈ Chapter 11 ≈

His mind went blank. His heart skipped a beat. And it had nothing to do with bullets flying all around them. Rigel couldn't care less about the sounds, the shrapnel, nor the danger the bullets posed to them as he and Jade laid on the floor of her dining room. What he cared about was the echoing sound of his name ringing in his head.

He was the Detective. He was the one who served and protected those around him. He was the one who looked danger straight in the eyes and faced it with his head held high. But this time... This time it was he who was saved. He was certain of it. More certain he ever was in his life. Because Jade saved him. Because she pushed him out of harm's way. Because she wasn't afraid to stand between him and the flying bullets.

When the bullets ceased to cut through the air, the silence raised Rigel's level of awareness of everything around them. But, above all, it raised his awareness of Jade's small-framed body lying on top of his - shielding him from danger.

"Are You alright?" Jade embraced his neck while her braided hair, now disheveled, laid across his cheek.

"I should ask You the same thing," Rigel whispered into her ear and tightened his arms around her. He held onto her and tried to process what just happened. He assessed the situation with whatever brain cells were working, still taken aback by the fact that she saved him, not the other way around.

The only thing he was able to recall clearly was the sound of Jade's voice. He heard her calling after him, though in his mind and not in his ears. He felt the thrust of strength she had to use to push him. He turned around right before his back hit the floor with a resounding thud, right before the bullets began to fly...

"Are You hurt?" She asked in a trembling voice but kept embracing his neck, still too scared to raise her head, or to even open her eyes.

"Again, I think that is a question I should have posed to You first," he breathed heavily and tried to read her thoughts. He sighed an enormous sigh of relief as he did not sense any thoughts of pain in her mind.

"I am sorry I pushed You..." Jade muttered. "I did not mean to push You so hard. I just wanted to push You out of the way."

"I doubt this sort of... effort warrants an apology," he eased his embrace and caressed the back of her head.

"You didn't tell me if You are hurt?" Jade opened her eyes now, feeling calmer because of the way he held her.

"I didn't," he replied, more steadily. He switched his arms so the hand caressing her hair embraced her waist, while the other hand brushed away her braid from his cheek. And then, he kept the hand there, on her cheek.

"Well, can You tell me if You are?" She raised her head slowly to look at him.

"I am," he whispered because he saw his reflection in her eyes, and it... scared him.

"You are hurt?" She tried to rise to her elbows so as not to cause him any more pain, but he tightened his grip around her waist.

"I didn't get hurt."

"Are You certain?"

"Positive," he smiled and caressed her cheek. "But we seem to have two problems on our hands - aside from the obvious damage done to Your house."

"Oh?" Jade opened her eyes wider. "And those are?"

"You will need another place to stay." Saying so, he allowed his eyes to travel from her eyes to her lips.

"I can stay with my aunt. My mom and I can stay with her for a while."

"That's right. Your mom lives here as well," he recalled, scanning the room for the damage all around them. "It was very fortunate she wasn't here to witness this."

"Goodness. I could not forgive myself if something happened to her."

"Neither could I. Whoever did this will pay for putting Your life in danger. I promise."

"I don't think I was the target," she shook her head.

"Why do You say that?"

"Do You want to know why I pushed You before the bullets broke the windows?" She asked and, as shy as she felt, allowed her eyes to journey from his eyes up to his hairline, then back to his eyes again.

"Why?"

"When You turned around to leave, I saw a red laser dot on Your back, near Your neck," she shook her head to rid her mind of that memory, but not before he heard her thoughts of fear for his life. "Rigel, whoever did this knew to point the gun at You. Not at me. I am nowhere near Your height."

"You may be shy, but You are a keen observer," he smiled at her. "You are also hard as nails."

"No, You are."

"That's the gun," he smirked.

"What gun?" She tipped her head back a bit, oblivious to his pun.

"Never mind," he chuckled, feeling relieved that she was unharmed.

"What's the second problem?"

"What second problem?" He asked, wondering whether her way of thinking rubbed off on him.

"You said we have two problems. What is the second one?"

"This..." He did not bother to offer her a verbal explanation. It wasn't necessary. It wasn't needed. All he needed to convey was poured into the kiss that rocked them both. He brought her lips down to his, while his hand cupped her cheek. He raised his head to meet her halfway and had to admit finding her hands wrapped around his neck for support... filled him with even more excitement for the kiss.

Maybe he did not mean for the kiss to feel so urgent.

Maybe he did not mean for it to feel so profound.

Or so fulfilling.

But it did...

"Wow..." Jade whispered breathlessly once the kiss ended, much too soon for her liking, which Rigel figured out instantly because of the piercing gaze she offered him. He saw her passion in it. He saw her desire. He saw his own in it as well.

"Wow is right."

"Actually, You're wrong," she whispered in a trembling voice.

"Why?"

"Because we now have three problems."

"What's the third one?" He replied and didn't have time to read her thoughts.

"This..." she whispered against his lips, causing them both to forget they laid on a floor covered with debris and broken glass. The hands that caressed her cheeks now held onto her waist. No, they held onto her. Rigel all but lost his mind because he chose to let go of the restraint that usually kept his emotions at bay. He let go. And held on.

"Wicked woman," he breathed heavily as they heard Police and Fire Department sirens coming in the distance.

"Is that a good thing?" She raised herself up on her elbows, worried.

"Definitely. But this has to stay off the record."

"This mess?" Jade pointed toward the debris all around them.

"No, this mess." Saying so, he looked deep into her eyes. "I have to stay on this case to catch whoever did this. If my boss finds out we're... involved, she will take me off the case faster than You can say Brzozakiewiczowicz."

"Brzozakiewiczowicz," Jade smirked with mischief.

"Wicked woman," he kissed her again.

"But what will You tell Your boss? How will You explain being here if she asks?"

"The truth. Even about Lucky," he cleared his throat as they sat up on the floor.

"Do You think he could have done this?" She wondered and accepted his hand when he helped her up.

"I don't know. He doesn't have the guts to hold a gun. Let alone fire one at a cop," Rigel replied, though not completely sure of it.

"Should I stay away from You for a while?" Jade asked, worried, when Rigel turned to look around the room. She did not want to put his life in danger any more than it already was.

"What?" He turned to her.

"I do not want You to get in trouble. I also do not want You to get hurt," she linked her hands. "Maybe I should stay away from You?"

"I never want to hear You say those words again," he reached for her, wrapping his arms around her. "We will solve this, and You will not have to look over Your shoulder to see if anyone out there is trying to hurt You."

"If only it were true," she embraced him, not entirely referring to what just happened...

≈ **Chapter 12** ≈

Rigel grit his teeth as he filled out the report for what happened at Jade's house. His first-hand account. On an early Sunday morning. Since crime did not seem to take a day off, neither did he. And, apparently, neither did Nicholetta Stormstrong. The woman who considered him to be her best Detective on the Task Force. She now sat in her office and tried her best to reassure the Mayor that the crime committed against his new intern was in no way, shape, or form related to the murder discovered in his own Office.

As for Rigel, considering all the danger they were subjected to, he had to admit that more good came out of it than bad. Except for his beloved Dodge Challenger Hellcat SRT. Whoever shot at them felt compelled to empty a round of bullets at his car, and another at Jade's car. But Rigel was willing to overlook that detail. Why? Because the little outburst of perpetrator's anger worked in Rigel's favor.

Case in point? The bullets that pierced his car, Jade's car, as well as the windows of Jade's living room.

Those bullets and their signatures rubbed at Rigel's gut instinct. The Alistair hunch he was born with screamed loud and clear in his mind that the bullets fired at them would match... the bullets that were fired at the Police Officer who was found at the Mayor's Office. Namely, at the man's head. And his hunch did not stop there. It forced him to review the information and crime scene photographs pertaining to the murders of Police Officers he was investigating in secret.

He had done a lot of digging through endless reports and evidence gathered at those crime scenes. Although the bullets found at the crime scenes were labeled as having been fired from the Police Officers' own guns, Rigel knew better. Moreover, only shell casings from the bullets shot at the Police Officers' heads were described in detail in the reports. But not the ones fired at their chests. In all the cases. All of them. The shell casings from the bullets shot at the victims' chests were not noted anywhere in the reports. None of them. Even when the photographs from the crime scenes left no doubt in Rigel's mind the bullets were fired from two different guns and were of a totally different caliber.

That part of all the investigations bothered Rigel. Why two different guns? Why two different bullet signatures. Why two different shooting styles? But, above all, why only one type of the bullet was listed in the reports?

And, now, he knew why. The two different guns, bullet signatures, and shooting styles did not match because of the individuals who pulled the triggers. Could the half-wit Lucky Knuckles stand behind all those murders? It could not have been that simple. Rigel knew perfectly well the man who attacked Jade possessed neither the brains nor the guts to do so. Lucky may have played a part in the murders, but he was not the mastermind behind them.

But there was more. The bullets fired at the victims' heads did not match the ones fired at their chests not only because they were fired by two different individuals. They did not match because they were fired for two very distinct and vividly clear reasons. The bullets fired at the victims' chests were meant to kill them. The bullets fired at their heads were meant to serve as one last effort to ensure the victims would be silenced once and for all just in case the men somehow survived the first three shots. And that boiled Rigel's blood - the way only Nicholetta understood.

He was also now convinced he would need to reveal his findings to his superior...

"Overthinking has a potential of frying one's brain," Nicholetta directed her words at Rigel as she stood in the doorway of her office, leaning against its threshold.

"If only I had one," Rigel offered her a faint smile. He sat back in his chair and continued to click the pen in his hand.

"I would reconsider that statement if You don't want those imbeciles out there on the streets to laugh at You," Nicholetta chuckled.

"They do it anyway." Rigel sighed, frowning in a way Nicholetta recognized as a sign something troubled him.

"What's wrong, Happyski?"

"Besides the usual?" He mouthed. "Let's see... My car's been shot at. I was shot at. My witness was shot at."

"Like You said. The usual." she moved her shoulders. "I need a break. Bring all those reports You've got hiding under that pile of rubble on Your desk to my office. And fetch us some good coffee before Alex gets here. I can't stomach the taste of his coffee on a Sunday."

"Got it, Chief," Rigel replied with a nod. He wondered how she was able to figure out he wasn't just working on the report pertaining to the shots fired at him and Jade the night before.

"Thanks." Nicholetta accepted a cup of black and pungent coffee from Rigel once he made his way to her office. "Do me a favor and close the door. I don't want Alex to hear me praising Your coffee. If he does, he'll spend the next two years forcing me to try different ways he'd brew it until my stomach gives out."

"Sure thing, Chief," Rigel chucked and closed the door behind him with one swift move of his foot.

"Now, tell me what's really bothering You," Nicholetta set the coffee cup down and got right to business.

"Always keen on details, right Chief?" Rigel smirked in his cocky way.

"At my age, I have to," she chuckled. "What have You got there, and why haven't I found out about it sooner?"

"How mad would You get at Your favorite and most handsome Detective if I told You I've been working on something without Your knowledge?" Rigel passed the slim stack of files to her.

"I'd point out to You are not that handsome, and then I'd advise You that little happens in this office without my knowledge," she smiled with the biggest fake smile she ever offered to him.

"Ouch." Rigel chuckled and sat in the chair on the other side of her desk.

"You deserved it," Nicholetta advised him without taking her eyes off the first folder she opened.

"Ouch again," he laughed, noticing she did not.

"Where did You get this?" Nicholetta skimmed over the first file. She closed it, dropped it on her desk, and opened the next file only to review it in the same manner.

"Closed cases aren't that uncommon. I... borrowed the files for a day or so..."

"Some of these are a couple of years old," she looked at him in a stern boss-like manner.

"I did say I borrowed them for a day or so."

"Understood," Nicholetta concurred. "Now, why do You have these files?"

"I like to read up on old cases."

"If You like to read, I have dozens of unsolved cases." She set the unread files in her hand down on the desk. "Why do You have these files, Rigel?"

"Because, Chief, these aren't solved cases. At least not to me," he said so boldly she had no choice but to believe him.

"I... agree."

"What?" Rigel raised his eyebrows, surprised.

"I agree." She rose from the chair. "It's a sad day covered with dark clouds when we have to bury our own. Even darker if it gets labeled as simple robbery."

"Chief..."

"I know. Believe me, Rigel. I know." She sighed heavily and leaned back on the cabinet behind her desk. "Signing off on a report when the evidence points to a robbery does not mean I believe it - or that I agree with it."

"Then why sign off on it if the gut tells You otherwise?" He crossed his arms at his chest to cover up his anger.

"Politics." She sighed, rubbing her eyes.

"Bullshit." He fired bluntly and did not bother to apologize.

"Got that right." Nicholetta clicked her tongue. " I am glad someone finally had the brains to give the files a second look."

"So... I am not in trouble?"

"Not unless You stop looking into these cases."

"All right. But I have to ask You for something." Rigel rose to his feet and walked over closer to her so no one could hear his request.

"Is it important?" Nicholetta asked, already aware it was, otherwise he would not ask about it.

"Jade Alistair." He said stoically but Nicholetta sensed there was something in the way he said that name.

"You want to be taken off the case?"

"No such thing. I want to make sure she has protection going forward," he said and meant it. "I would like to ask for permission to keep watch over her. Effective immediately."

"Effective immediately? You want to keep watch over a witness on Thanksgiving? " Nicholetta tipped her head to the side. "But it's Your time off. I approved it months ago?"

"Agreed. But this is important, Chief."

"That's asking a bit much. Even for a witness in a murder case, don't You think?"

"No." Rigel shook his head. "And it is strictly work-related."

"Strictly, huh?"

"I have a feeling whoever shot at her is linked to all these murder cases. If I am right about this, the bullet signatures from last night will match the ones fired at those murdered cops."

"You have a feeling, huh?" Nicholetta raised her eyebrow not only at the fact her best Detective felt compelled to protect Ms. Alistair personally even before she asked him to do so because the Mayor called her earlier that morning, but also because it appeared Rigel seemed to put a rush on the lab with regards to the bullet signatures. He had a gut hunch, and that gut of his was usually right. "Permission granted. But be forewarned if anything happens between now and the President's visit to Chicago two weeks from now, You will have more than a couple of reports to read over at Your desk."

"Desk duty?" Rigel grimaced.

"Yes. Consider Yourself warned."

"Yes, Sir. I mean ma'am. I mean Chief," Rigel saluted her with a faint smile, aware he could not have smiled wider in front of his boss…

≈ Chapter 13 ≈

Thanksgiving weekend. The long weekend. It was Rigel's favorite time of the year. Hands down. Why? Because it was the only time during the year when he was able to leave Chicago for a few days without the necessity, nor the desire, to look back at the life he led. He loved Chicago. He appreciated it for what it offered. But there were times, too many to count, when he felt alone. Not because he did not have a significant other but because he did not have his siblings beside him.

If one was to ever survey the seven Alistair siblings, Rigel was the most practical one. He viewed life for what it was. Expectations did not work because people usually dropped the curtain hiding their true face after a certain period. As such, he never judged people. He watched people and their actions, but he did not judge. And he valued authenticity above all other virtues. Especially in the group of friends he came to call his family away from family. And because he did, the Thanksgiving weekend offered him four days to breathe the air as a man not burdened by the weight of his bloodline...

Standing at the doorstep of Jade's aunt's house in Chicago's suburb of Elmwood Park, Rigel frowned. But not at the weather's cool breeze caressing the back of his neck in a not-so-pleasant way on the morning of Thanksgiving Thursday. He frowned because of the knots twisting in his stomach. It was foolish. He knew it was. But somehow the idea of meeting Jade's mother and aunt made him... jittery. And he could not figure out why. Those jitters only worsened when the front door creaked open to reveal a petite woman with silver streaks in her raven-black hair and eyes just like Jade's, and an older German Shepherd of enormous proportions.

"Can I help You?" The woman sized Rigel up and down through the closed glass screen door.

"Good morning, ma'am," Rigel all but curtsied, feeling dumb instantly. "I hope You can. I am looking for Jade Alistair. Is she available?"

"No." The woman replied in a noticeable South American accent and shook her head with confidence.

"Oh?" Rigel raised his eyebrows. "She told me she was staying here."

"She is." The woman said in an ice-cold tone, crossing her arms at her chest.

"Oh," Rigel whispered, feeling out of place. "In that case, could she come out to see me?"

"No." The woman repeated flatly and narrowed her eyes as the German Shepherd began to growl. "Heel, Alsatian."

"That is one mighty dog," Rigel smiled cautiously - feeling timid probably for the first time in his life.

"He knows that."

"Right," Rigel cleared his throat. "Well, could You at least let her know that I am here?"

"No."

"Why?" There, he said it. Bluntly and firmly. Rigel wasn't sure if the woman standing before him was going to open the door and release the dog to chase him away, but at least now he would know why.

"Because You didn't say PLEASE."

"Right," he offered her a fearful look.

"Who is it, Aunt Aline?" Jade's gentle voice soothed Rigel's nerves so much he released a noticeable sigh, and by doing so received a narrowed-eyed glance from Jade's Aunt.

"Good morning," Rigel smiled at Jade and bit his lip to hide the smirk that came to his lips when Aunt Aline sized her own niece the same way she sized him up and down a moment ago.

"Good morning," Jade beamed at him.

"You did not tell me You were going out of town with a man?" Aunt Aline all but growled at her niece.

"I did not tell You I wasn't," Jade hugged her aunt and opened the glass screen door for Rigel. "Come in, they don't bite."

"I wouldn't be so sure," Rigel straightened as he walked in.

"I will be ready in 5 minutes," Jade kept smiling as she pointed him to a couch, although he decided that standing would give him a head start if he needed to run for any reason.

"Take Your time. The others left already, so we don't need to hurry," Rigel replied and noticed Aunt Aline and her trusted dog stood by the door in the same spot, watching him with suspicion.

"Who are the others?" Aunt Aline narrowed her eyes on him.

"My family."

"Parents?" Aunt Aline narrowed her eyes on him even more, if such a thing was even possible.

"My parents passed away." Rigel said with honesty. He was not sure why he said it.

"Sorry to hear that," Aunt Aline said in a much softer tone of voice. The noticeable difference in her voice made Rigel wonder why she did it, but he chose not to read her thoughts.

"Mom, can You come down and meet Rigel?" Jade called out to her mother as she walked into a bedroom she called her own for the time being. "We will be leaving soon."

"Alright, dear," Jade's mother responded from the second floor of the house.

Rigel heard the footsteps as Jade's mother made her way down the stairs to meet him. He heard the pleasant tone of her voice. And he heard... her mother's silent gasp as she made it to the foot of her stairs and looked at him.

'His eyes...'

Rigel watched the woman who looked at him all but freeze where she stood.

"Good morning Mrs. Alistair," Rigel greeted her. "My name is Rigel Brzozakiewiczowicz."

"Now I know why Jade said they call You Happyski," Aunt Aline cackled. Even the dog appeared to match the change in her stance as it began to wag its tail. "Happyski sounds better."

"Yes, ma'am," Rigel chuckled as well, but cut it short when he heard Jade's mother's thoughts again.

'His voice...'

"Did You pack anything to eat? I did, in case You did not," Jade came out of the bedroom with two backpacks.

"I did. Fresh onion bagels," Rigel replied to her but kept his eyes on Jade's mother.

"You too?" Aunt Aline rolled her eyes. "I thought Jade was the only one who ate that treacherously tasting monstrosity."

"They are delicious." He smirked with mischief, and decided that Aunt Aline was a good-natured woman after all since she laughed at him instead of releasing her guardian dog on him.

"It is very nice to meet You, Detective," Jade's mother offered him a kind smile. She also extended her hand. He accepted it without hesitation. "My name is Eliana Alistair."

"Pleased to meet You, Mrs. Alistair," Rigel inclined his head in a sign of respect and accepted her hand. What hit him first was the warmth of her gesture. Then the honesty in her eyes. Then the trust, even though he sensed without a shred of doubt that she hid an indescribable amount of sorrow. "I hope You don't mind me taking Jade away for a few days."

"I don't mind," Eliana nodded with a sincere smile.

"I do." Aunt Aline chimed in, and again her guardian dog matched her stance by growling at Rigel.

"Don't mind Aline. She is somewhat partial to Law Enforcement," Eliana explained calmly.

"We don't bite." Rigel offered Aunt Aline a smile.

"You may not, but it may be a different story where we come from," Eliana said quietly, and immediately cleared her throat, afraid she said too much because of the look Aline sent her. A look Rigel picked up on without trouble.

"How long will You be gone?" Aunt Aline asked suddenly.

"Four days."

"Time away from this place will help take her mind off what happened in the last few weeks," Eliana noted.

"Where are You going?" Aunt Aline demanded to know.

"Tennessee."

"A change of scenery will be good for her," Eliana said softly.

"If Your parents are not going, then who is?" Aunt Aline crossed her arms at her chest. Suddenly Rigel imagined her as one of the guards at the holding cell at his precinct.

"Jade told me Rigel's friends will join them," Eliana advised her sister-in-law before Rigel was able to open his mouth, saving him from Aunt Aline's piercing gaze.

"But You said Your family was going. Why did You lie, then?" Aunt Aline asked bluntly.

"My friends are my family," Rigel replied politely. "They became my family after my parents passed away."

"Alright, Aunt Aline. That's enough." Jade scolded her aunt. She grabbed a thermos with hot tea and the backpacks, one with food and one with clothes and went to embrace her mother. "I love You. I will call You once we arrive in Tennessee. Let's go Rigel, before they ask You questions You may not feel comfortable answering."

"It was nice to meet You Ladies. Alsatian," Rigel bid them goodbye but chose not to pet the dog out of fear of getting bitten - not necessarily by the dog...

≈ Chapter 14 ≈

The drive from Chicago to Rigel's favorite part of Tennessee usually made him feel as if it went on for endless hours. Chattanooga was a beautiful place, but 9 hours of driving could tire even the most experienced and seasoned driver. And yet, this time around it passed as if in a blink of an eye for Rigel, all because of the woman who sat beside him in the passenger seat and watched with awe in her eyes as the scenery changed on the other side of the window.

It surprised Rigel to hear Jade hadn't left Chicago since the day she arrived in the city a little over two years before they met. It also surprised him how interesting it became for him to hear about her Aunt Aline and Jade's mother Eliana. But, above all, it surprised him how little she spoke about her family back in São Paulo where she was from.

He did not push her for answers. He knew well enough it was neither the time nor place, and not the level of comfort Jade would have needed to feel free to speak about something she obviously kept secret for a reason. He felt the same way about his past, his family, and especially his gift of reading people's minds and hearts. Though, he hoped Jade would someday reveal her past to him. Even if he chose to keep that hope to himself.

"I hope You don't mind how long it's taking us to get to Chattanooga," Rigel inclined his head and advised Jade. "We should arrive at our destination in less than an hour."

"Oh, I don't mind." Jade offered him a sincere smile. "I often wondered how the rest of the country looked. I used to look at photographs of different states online, but photographs fail to bring out the feelings one gets when they see this country's beauty in person."

"That's a bit poetic, isn't it?"

"No. Just honest," she replied without looking at him. She was too captivated with the view of the hills of the Cumberland Plateau and Chattanooga's scenery bathed in the hues of the setting sun.

"If You like it now, You should see it in summertime."

"I am sure it is beautiful any time of the year," Jade smiled at him and looked back at the view in front of her, missing the gleam in his eyes.

"I am sure it is," he whispered, not referring to the scenery.

"Do You come here often?"

"Twice a year, three times if I'm lucky," he lowered the volume of the music, seeing Jade began to open.

"How about Your friends?"

"They try to come once a month, though they stay longer in the summer."

"And You really think they will be okay with me coming along with You?"

"They will be more than okay. Alex will be there, too, so You can feel safer."

"Will he make coffee for us?" Jade wondered, raising her eyebrows because Rigel bellowed out a hearty laugh.

"Not if I can help it!" He continued to laugh at Jade's perfectly timed question.

"Is it really that bad?"

"Worse!" He laughed again. "But thankfully his wife's cooking makes up for it."

"Is she a great cook?"

"Maria? She rules the kitchen, especially with her onion bagels," Rigel smiled from ear to ear.

"She... makes them herself?" Jade opened her eyes wider.

"Yup. As they say, the way to a man's heart is through his taste buds," Rigel winked at her.

"Don't You mean through his stomach?" She smirked.

"Now who's correcting who?" Rigel raised his eyebrow, impressed.

"Oh, I did not mean to do that. Sorry," Jade lowered her eyes and linked her hands together.

"Don't apologize. We are friends, right?" He smiled. "And, yes, the way to a man's heart is through his stomach."

"So, all a woman needs to do is learn how to make onion bagels and get through to Your stomach?" Jade tried to make a joke to lighten up the conversation, and it backfired in the most unexpected way.

"No."

"Oh?"

"She would need to get through to my heart," he said quietly, but the tone of his voice sent a shiver down her spine.

"Oh," Jade replied and swallowed hard, unaware that it wasn't her verbal reply that caused a thunderous gaze in his eyes, it was what she thought that did.

'Be careful, Jade. You are not his type...'

"We're here." Rigel announced suddenly and directed his pickup truck down a small hill down the Cash Canyon Road and pulled up to a plot of land filled with tall trees and direct access to the majestic Tennessee River as the sun hid behind the hills in the distance.

"Welcome!" Alex greeted them, standing underneath a string of lights strung between one quite impressive Motorhome and three school buses, painted white and refurbished into RV versions of houses on wheels, while a little dog with a wild set of puffy hair wagged its tail beside him.

"Good evening, Detective Stepka," Jade waved at him.

"Call me Alex!" He waved back. "We are far from work. And we are all friends here!"

"He's right," Rigel nodded and came around the pickup so Jade would feel more comfortable when she met the rest of his friends. "And his dog Rocko can attest to that."

"Rocko?" Jade looked at Rigel, with a bit of amusement in her eyes but also a lot of shyness.

"Yes, Rocko." Rigel grinned and leaned down to pet the dog as it ran to greet him and then ran back to Alex.

"Hi Jade! Nice to meet You!" Maria and Kasia waved at her from across the bonfire that lit up the area almost as brightly as the strings of lights.

"Nice to meet You as well!" Jade greeted them, feeling self-conscious until Rigel placed his hand at her back.

'Thank You...'

Jade smiled self-consciously at him, and her smile became more confident when he nodded, as if he understood her.

"Where's Sebastian? And Marek and Julia? I see Marek's car is here," Rigel looked around for his best friend, Maria's twin brother, and his wife.

"They are in Marek's RV. Something's up with the speaker, and they are trying to fix it," Alex chuckled.

"I told Marek not to overspend on his newest toy speaker, but some men never listen," Rigel shook his head and smirked just as the sound of noticeably Polish music blasted from one of the RVs. "Yup, that's Marek."

"Hey, Happyski!" Sebastian shouted at Rigel as he came out of Marek's RV and saw they arrived. "Hi, You must be Jade!"

"Hey, Lipa!" Rigel waved at his best friend.

"Thank You for allowing me to come along," Jade inclined her head.

"Nonsense! Rigel's friend is our friend!" Kasia came around the bonfire and embraced Jade as a man over six feet tall came out of the RV that was blasting the music and stopped on the last of the stair steps, staring straight at Jade and Rigel. Jade assumed it was because of her and immediately tensed up. Rigel felt it and moved his hand from her back to embrace her at her waist.

"Happyski..." the man staring at Rigel narrowed his eyes.

"Evening, sunshine." Rigel greeted Marek with the biggest smile on his face.

"Nice of You to come so late." Marek jumped off the RV's last step and made his way toward Jade and Rigel.

"Thanks, sunshine!" Rigel smiled even wider.

"Are You sure it was a good idea for me to come here with You?" Jade whispered so only Rigel heard her.

"Definitely," Rigel winked at her. "And don't worry. Marek is just a bit sad - and by sad I mean jealous - that I rented this pickup truck."

"Why?" Jade narrowed her eyes on him.

"I guess some egos cannot handle being second-best," he smirked and clicked his tongue.

"Very funny, Happyski. I see You finally got Yourself some respectable wheels," Marek walked up to the 2021 Ram 1500 TRX Rigel rented since his beloved car was shot at and was now stuck at the Chicago Police Department Auto Pound, serving as evidence.

"What can I say? Some men can handle big boy toys, and others cannot," Rigel mocked him, and both men laughed wholeheartedly.

"I guess You are right," Marek patted Rigel's back and turned to Jade. "Glad You made it. Nice to meet You, I'm Marek. And that's my better half, Julia."

"Hi Jade!" Julia waved at her as she walked over with a tray of cups. "Would You like some coffee?"

"Did Alex make it?" Jade asked politely and caused everyone to bellow out a loud laugh, much to her surprise. Everyone, except for Alex.

"Ah, welcome to the group," Marek grinned and shook his head lightly. "You'll fit right in."

"I hope so," Jade inclined her head.

"I know so," Rigel leaned in, whispering to her ear, fully aware his friends gave one another an all-telling look…

≈ Chapter 15 ≈

Fate's quite the fickle. Some would agree, some would disagree, and some would swear by it. Not because they accepted Fate's odd sense of humor, but because they understood the cards of life could not be reshuffled - they could only be accepted and played best to one's abilities.

Jade understood that. From a very young age. She was born in Guarujá, a coastal town near São Paulo. Though the place she called home looked like a paradise, growing up in a poor family did not allow her to experience all the town and its amenities had to offer. Her parents loved each other. They also loved Jade and her twin sister. And even though they did not have much, they had each other. Until Jade's father refused to take a bribe from the local Law Enforcement and vowed to stand on the right side of justice.

Those thoughts flooded Jade's mind as she sat in a chair facing the Tennessee River, late on Thanksgiving Thursday night. She watched as the bright reflection of the moon glistened in the water as the gentle lights of the stars danced across the night sky. She listened to the cheerful tunes of the music as it flowed through the air from Marek's RV. It was still prominent, but Marek lowered the volume for dinner. They may have been far from home, but traditions ran deep in Rigel's friends' veins. Jade felt grateful to him for bringing her along, but she could not get past the feeling that her family no longer felt as close-knit as it did before her father lost his life.

"I miss mine, too," Rigel said softly as he appeared behind Jade, startling her quite a bit. He heard her thoughts, and kept away for as long as he could, giving her enough space to sit away from the crowd gathered by the bonfire.

"Who?" Jade looked up and did not know how to hide the fact he caught her off guard.

"My parents." He walked up closer, looked down at her for a moment, then turned his eyes toward the reflection of the moon in the Tennessee River.

"Did they pass away long ago?" She asked shyly, touched that he felt comfortable enough to share his thoughts with her.

"Long enough for the pain to go away, not nearly long enough for the sorrow to do the same," he sighed. "Mind if I join You?"

"Please," she pointed to the empty chair beside her.

"Thank You."

"Did they pass away at the same time? Or years apart?"

"Together. At the same time. Maybe that is why it hurts so much. Grieving for one parent is hard enough. But two? It hits You in the gut twice as painfully."

"I am sorry You had to go through that." She meant it. Just as she meant to comfort him with the gentle touch of her hand as she caressed his hand. And even though she retrieved her hand quickly, the trace of her gentle touch left a tingling sensation on Rigel's hand far longer than she could have imagined.

"I appreciate it." He looked at the spot where her hand touched his and referred to that undeniable spark of touch rather than to her words.

"How old were You when they passed away?" Jade continued, and somehow realized talking to someone about a similar sense of sorrow calmed her aching heart.

"I was 19," he replied and sighed. "We found out about their passing less than a week before my brother's 21st birthday. You can imagine why he took it much harder than I did."

"You have a brother?" She asked, intrigued.

"Yes," he nodded, and had no idea why he shared the information with her. Or why he thought he could trust her with the real information about his family.

"I have an older sister," she turned a bit more toward him and supported her hand on the chair's armrest.

"You do?"

"Yes," she chuckled. "Jasper is my twin sister."

"There are two of *You*?"

"Never!" Jade laughed. "We are as different from each other as possible. Polar opposites."

"Interesting. But does she speak her mind the way You do?"

"And then some!" Jade waved a hand. "Jasper may be a few hours older, but she always treated me as if there was at least a year's difference between us."

"A few hours?" Rigel narrowed his eyes on her. "Isn't that a bit of time? For a twin birth?"

"Yes, Detective," she tipped her head toward him. "Believe it or not, I am the reason why I believe in the kindness of others."

"What do You mean?" Rigel turned toward her as well.

"My mother gave birth to us in our home. Our family was poor, and my parents did not have time - or money - to take my mother to the hospital. My sister was born first, and she came to this world quickly. It was a bit more complicated with me," Jade began to explain, and Rigel could not help but notice the way she lit up when she spoke about her family. How much more relaxed she seemed. How much more at ease her mind seemed to be.

"A bit more complicated? You?" he laughed. "I never would have guessed."

"You sound like Aunt Aline," Jade pointed at him.

"Goodness, now that's scary," he laughed again and raised his hands.

"I will be sure to tell her that."

"Don't!"

"Are You afraid of Aunt Aline?"

"Nope. Alsatian seems like he can smell a coward, though," he chuckled, suddenly hearing Sebastian's taunting thoughts.

'Look who's falling in love? And remember what You told me - SHE'S THE ONE...'

"I am going to grab something to eat. Would You like something?" Rigel rose to his feet and tried to make it look as casual as possible, though Jade noticed the change in his eyes right before he rose from the chair.

"Thank You, I am fine."

"Alright. I'll be right back," he inclined his head, and walked away contemplating whether to read Jade's thoughts or not as she watched him. He chose not to. It would not do him any good, considering Sebastian's wicked sense of humor and poor sense of timing. It also would make him feel as if he was invading her privacy. He only hoped Jade would not feel lonely or left out.

She did not. A few minutes after Rigel walked away, Kasia approached Jade with two cups of freshly brewed tea.

"It is a beautiful night, isn't it?" Kasia smiled sincerely and offered one of the cups to Jade. "I brought You some tea. I thought You might like some."

"Thank You," Jade accepted the cup of tea. "Would You like to sit down?"

"Very much. Thank You," Kasia patted her shoulder in a sisterly manner and sat beside her. "How do You like it here?"

"This is the first time I have ever left Chicago, and I must say this place captured my heart. It feels so calming and peaceful."

"I know what You mean. We searched for a piece of land like this for years," Kasia agreed. "We saw this place and we just knew it was the one."

"You seem like a close-knit family," Jade said with a bit of admiration.

"You may say on some level we are. Marek and Maria are twins."

"Really?" Jade replied with wonder and looked back at the group of friends gathered around the bonfire. Julie was dancing with Alex, Maria was dancing with her twin brother, and Rocko rested comfortably on Maria's chair. She involuntarily searched for Rigel. She found him speaking with Sebastian. He may have been speaking with his best friend, but... he kept his piercing gaze on her. She could see it even from afar. "I have a twin sister, but I doubt she would choose to spend time with me the way You all do."

"You have a twin sister?" Kasia asked and touched Jade's hand in a way that made Jade feel welcomed.

"Yes. Her name is Jasper."

"Jasper and Jade. Just like Maria and Marek!" Kasia beamed with excitement. "Are You the older twin? Or the younger one?"

"Jasper is older. She used to boss me around, but always got angry because I found ways of putting my foot down."

"Marek is older by 15 minutes. He tries to boss Maria around, but it always falls short of its mark because Maria does not need a Detective husband to come to her aid," Kasia leaned in, whispering the last words.

"Is Rigel a part of Your family as well?" Jade asked and hoped Kasia did not mind it.

"He is, though not in a way You may think," Kasia said in a softer tone of voice.

"What do You mean?"

"Rigel and Sebastian's brother Eryk enrolled in the Police Academy together. That's how we met. Then Rigel, Eryk, and Alex joined the Task Force together. Rigel and Eryk were partners for a couple of years until..." Kasia paused and looked back at Rigel.

"Until?" Jade inquired, unaware the answer would forever change the way she looked at Rigel.

"Until Eryk was gunned down," Kasia fell silent for a moment. "He died on Rigel's birthday, and Rigel never forgave himself for it."

"Why would he blame himself for that?"

"Rigel and the boys decided to go out that night. Eryk cancelled at the last moment, telling Rigel he was assigned a last-minute case he could not back out of. Rigel had a gut feeling something was wrong, but Eryk convinced him to enjoy his birthday. Rigel called Eryk the next day and went to his house because Eryk did not answer." Saying so, Kasia reached for Jade's hand and placed it atop Jade's. "That's when Rigel found Eryk, but it was too late."

"Rigel found him?" Jade whispered and covered her mouth with her free hand, feeling a sudden connection with Rigel. A connection she knew she would not be able to dismiss.

"Yes," Kasia nodded. "Rigel blames himself for Eryk's death. He never got over the thought that if he had convinced Eryk to go out with them, or if he went to his house sooner, Eryk wouldn't have died."

"But it wasn't his fault." Jade all but jumped when she felt a sensation of a warm blanket on her shoulders. She looked up and rose to her feet not because she saw Rigel standing right behind her, but because she saw the thunder in his eyes.

"Who's fault?" Rigel asked, having heard their conversation even from afar.

"It wasn't Your fault Eryk lost his life," Kasia explained and rose from her chair, aware it was best to leave Rigel and Jade alone.

"I see." Rigel followed Kasia with his eyes as she made her way back to the bonfire.

"Please don't be mad at her," Jade reached for his arm. He did not pull back. He couldn't. For good or for bad, he just couldn't.

"I am not mad at her."

"Are You mad at me?"

"No." He said in short, not because he did not mean it, but because he could not move past his reaction to the fact his heart rate sped up faster the longer Jade held onto his arm...

≈ **Chapter 16** ≈

Jade awoke to the light of gentle rays of the morning sun peeking through the window in the little bedroom at the back of the RV. It was early, but she had to admit the absence of bustling sounds of Chicago's population going about their morning routines allowed her to sleep better than she had in years. She felt refreshed, though not altogether guilt-free. Why? Because Rigel instructed her to sleep on the bed in the little bedroom while he insisted on sleeping on the little pullout couch at the front of his RV.

Was sleeping on that couch comfortable for him? Of course not, and Jade was aware of it. The little pullout couch could hardly accommodate a man of six feet tall. But he insisted, and Jade was convinced Rigel hadn't come across many people in his life who were able to change his mind. She also wondered if he applied the same principle to all the women he became close to. Or ones he chose to steer clear of.

With that thought on mind, Jade rose from the bed, made it as neatly as she could, and went to see if Rigel was as uncomfortable as she assumed he would have been. She opened the bedroom door, and... found the couch empty. She checked the bathroom. He was gone. And he left the RV without waking her up. That made her feel more awkward than if he had woken her up with sweet caresses. But the moment the thought ran through her mind, Jade shook it off.

Why on earth would he wake her up? And why on earth would he even consider offering to her anything beyond the friendly gesture of bringing her along? After all, the only reason he asked her to come to Tennessee was so he could make sure she was safe. They shared a few head-spinning kisses, but that was all. She was just a witness to him, nothing more. And nothing would change that.

So, she decided to go about the morning as if nothing happened. Truth be told, nothing did. And since she was alone, she was able to let her guard down. She turned on her favorite music on her phone, set the coffee maker, and took a quick shower. Somewhere between the moment she turned on the sleek and modern rain shower head and the moment last drops of water hit her skin, she started to sing and swoon to the rhythm of the music. She left the bathroom and sighed happily when the aroma of freshly brewed coffee hit her senses. And she began to smile. Sincerely and wholeheartedly. She was a grown woman, enjoying time alone. Away from her mother. Away from her suspicious and overprotective Aunt Aline.

She tiptoed toward the coffee maker, danced a little in front of it, and removed the towel off her wet hair. She fluffed her wet tresses, smiled into the cup of black and undeniably aromatic coffee, and... puffed out air because a call had come through on her phone, ending the music. She looked at the phone and was not surprised to see a photograph of Aunt Aline with Alsatian sitting beside her staring right at Jade.

"Good morning, Aunt Aline." Jade smiled and brought the cup of coffee to her lips to hide the grimace adorning her face.

"Good morning." Aunt Aline greeted her niece with eyes narrowed with suspicion. "Why did You pick up?"

"Because... You called me?"

"Why are You up so early?"

"Because I always wake up this early?"

"But You have a day off?" Aunt Aline continued while Alsatian growled as if he agreed with his master.

"So do You, Aunt Aline. Why are You up so early?"

"Because I can."

"And I cannot? Why can't I?"

"Because You could make enough sound to wake the Detective up," Aunt Aline responded in a scolding tone of voice.

"He already woke up," Jade said casually, but almost spit up the sip of coffee she sipped a moment before because Aunt Aline brought the phone close to her face. So close Jade was able to see the irises in her aunt's eyes.

"And You know this HOW?!?" Aunt Aline shouted so loud Alsatian dropped to the floor, covering his ears with his paws.

"Because he is not here," Jade moved her shoulders up and down.

"Eliana! Come here right now!" Aunt Aline shouted at her sister-in-law even louder than she did at her niece.

"What is it, Aline?" Eliana Alistair rushed to Aline's side.

"Your daughter is staying in the same room with that... Detective!"

"Yes, I know." Eliana nodded calmly. "And it is not a room. It is an RV."

"And You allow this?!?"

"Yes," Eliana smiled into the phone's camera. "Hi, Jade."

"Hi mom," Jade saluted her with a cup of her coffee.

" Hi mom?!?" Aunt Aline all but choked on air. "How can You allow this?!?"

"Because I love her, and because I trust her," Eliana explained with confidence.

"I trust her, too," Rigel chimed in suddenly as he opened the door to the RV.

"Good morning, Detective." Eliana greeted him as Rigel closed the RV's door and approached Jade. He stood right behind her and smiled from ear to ear.

"Good morning, ma'am. Good morning, Aunt Aline."

"Aunt Aline?" Jade's Aunt growled, unable to hide her indignation.

"Yes," Rigel grinned even wider. "Jade met my friends. They became her friends. So, to make her feel more comfortable it is only logical I refer to You as Aunt Aline."

"How...?!?" Aunt Aline began to speak but was cut off by Eliana.

"How kind of You to do so," Eliana smirked. "I am sure Your friends made my Jade feel welcomed."

"They did," Jade agreed.

"They really did. We are all friends here, Aunt Aline," Rigel winked at her and looked down at Jade, gesturing toward the cup of coffee she held in her hand. "Can I get some of that? It smells divine."

"You mean my coffee? Or the shampoo?" Jade asked, a bit startled he considered paying her a compliment on her coffee. Or worse, on her shampoo.

"Both," he inclined his head as if trying to take in the fresh scent of her just-washed hair, but reached for the cup of coffee, and took it from Jade's hand, aware yet again of the way the stroke of her skin against his made him feel.

"But I drank from it already," Jade admitted, surprised, and watched as Rigel gulped up the entire cup.

"You have no idea how it tastes after I had to drink Alex's coffee," he beamed with pleasure, and looked down to her lips while setting the cup down on the counter.

"Alex's coffee?" Jade whispered, forgetting her mother and Aunt Aline could see them.

"Yes," he nodded, his eyes locked on Jade's lips. "Though, I'd gulp up cupful of his coffee just to taste Yours."

"Can You believe him?!?" Aunt Aline exclaimed, causing Rigel and her niece to look at the phone.

"I can," Eliana sent her daughter a loving look. "I trust You two will behave."

"Yes, ma'am," Jade and Rigel nodded in unison.

"Good," Eliana nodded and ended the call.

"Morning," Rigel smiled at Jade and decided to refill the cup with more coffee.

"Morning." She tried to move but failed because of the way he blocked her while refilling the cup. She swallowed hard as he leaned in to set the coffee maker pot down.

'Oh, he smells divine...'

"I do." He noted, sending her a smug half-grin.

"What?" She blinked, petrified at the thought the man standing before her really might read minds.

"The coffee. I do believe it smells good," he explained and bit his lip to stop the smirk he knew would come next.

"Just the coffee?"

"And Your shampoo, too. It smells divine."

"My shampoo?" She blinked. "Divine?"

"Definitely." Rigel clicked his tongue while making his way back toward the hooks on the door. He took the jacket off, ensuring to turn his back so she could not see his smirk that came anyway.

"Rigel?" She asked and hoped she sounded more confident than she felt.

"Yes?" He turned and saw a shadow of sadness in her eyes, even from where he stood.

"Are You sure it was okay for You to sleep on the couch? I feel bad about it."

"I am sure. You are my guest here," he said matter-of-factly, but decided to add more to it because he read her thoughts of self-doubt. "I gave my word to the Chief that I will keep You safe. I plan to live up to my word."

"And You don't mind me invading Your private space or meeting Your friends?"

"Jade Alistair, You invaded much more than my private space," he admitted with such intensity in his gaze it caused the skin at the nape of her neck to tingle as he walked past her to the bedroom to change his shirt...

≈ **Chapter 17** ≈

When it rained, it poured. And maybe that wasn't such a bad thing? After all, the downpour continued throughout the day allowing Rigel, Jade, and his friends to spend time to unwind, relax, and simply enjoy each other's company.

As for Rigel, he enjoyed it on a whole other level, dismissing Sebastian and Alex's mischievous looks. Quite frankly, he stopped paying attention to them before long. Why? Because for the first time since they began coming to Tennessee, he no longer felt like the odd one out. He was a part of the group, he felt the connection between them all, but Sebastian had Kasia, Alex had Maria, Marek had Julia, and he had... the kind of void in his heart he never would have admitted to. Jade changed that. In ways not even Sebastian or Alex would have understood. Whether he was ready for it or not.

They made breakfast together, in Sebastian's Motorhome, which was better equipped than the other three refurbished RVs. The 2020 Prevost Motorhome stood out against the other refurbished RVs, but that was a seamless detail to everyone. They worked together, laughed together, watched a couple of movies together, ate and cleaned together as if they had done so countless times. And they made Jade feel like she was one of them already. That both pleased Rigel and... bothered him on a deeper level.

"Looks like the rain finally passed. Who's up for a little bonfire?" Marek clasped his hands together.

"That soaked firewood won't burn for another week," Alex pointed toward the stack of wood near the bonfire as he looked out the window. "It won't dry up before it gets dark."

"Worry not, my friend. There's a gas station that sells firewood not far from here. I can go buy it and get back in no time in my sweet ride," Marek wiggled his eyebrows at Alex.

"That's a cute way of referring to Your little Ram," Rigel flashed his pearly whites at Marek.

"Look who's talking?" Marek bellowed out a laugh. "You wouldn't have rented out the TRX if my Ram hadn't impressed You in the first place."

"May be so, but at least I chose one with horsepower," Rigel smirked at Marek in a cocky way.

"Do they always speak this way to each other?" Jade leaned in and whispered the question to Kasia's.

"Always. It's cute to watch," Kasia smiled, and caught the way Rigel looked at them. She sent him a smile as well and watched as the tough and buff Detective cleared his throat, perplexed. "That's really cute to watch."

"Alright. I'm going to get the wood. Who's coming with me?" Marek walked toward the hooks beside the door, grabbing his jacket.

"I'm in," Sebastian announced. "Someone has to make sure Your Ram knows how to get back here before nightfall."

"You're lucky I am good at pretending I don't hear certain things," Marek narrowed his eyes on him.

"You're also good at driving under the speed limit," Rigel chuckled and saluted Marek with the bottle of his favorite Polish beer in his hand.

"Not as good as some of us are at pretending not to see what's right under their nose," Marek sent Rigel a witty grin, and made sure Jade did not hear him. Since she did not, he sent Rigel another look and left with Sebastian, only to return a good hour later. He may have taken his time, but he did not return empty-handed by any means.

"You're never going to guess what happened," Marek beamed with excitement as he walked into the Motorhome.

"You and Sebastian had to walk back from the gas station because the Ram broke?" Rigel responded with a chuckle.

"Maybe if we had taken Your pickup," Marek dismissed his friend's witty comment.

"Good one," Alex grinned as he sat beside Jade at the little kitchenette table and tried to teach her the best ways to brew all kinds of coffees from around the world. "But what really happened?"

"The gas station ran out of firewood because everyone in the area and their mama bought it before we arrived," Marek began his tale.

"So, You didn't bring any?" Alex asked, resigned.

" We brought enough firewood to last until Sunday!" Marek grinned, proud of himself.

"But You said the gas station ran out of firewood?" Jade asked, intrigued.

"Yes, but we ran into an older farmer on our way back. His pickup broke down, and he looked like he could use some help. So, we helped him," Marek continued.

"That was nice of You," Maria praised her twin brother.

"You know me, I always help out however I can," Marek all but patted himself on his own shoulder.

"Sure, You do." Rigel smirked with sarcasm.

"Fine. It was all Sebastian's idea." Marek rolled his eyes at Rigel as others laughed. "I agreed because the man said he couldn't pay us but could offer us all the firewood we could carry. And not just any firewood. Dry firewood."

"Always the businessman," Rigel saluted Marek.

"You know me," Marek nodded. "But the man also gave us something we couldn't say no to."

"What?" Jade wondered out loud.

"This." Sebastian walked in and closed the door behind him. What he held in his hand brought a smile to Jade's face - and a suspicious look to Rigel's.

"Let me guess, the man twisted Your arm to take it?" Rigel asked in a skeptical tone of voice.

"No such thing. It was us who begged him for it," Sebastian replied, and Rigel knew he meant it. "We cleaned it up a bit, but it seems to be in good shape."

"I see." Rigel rose from the couch, albeit reluctantly.

Jade watched as the man she began to admire walked over to his best friend. He passed his beer bottle to Marek and reached for the acoustic guitar in Sebastian's hand. She watched, as if in slow motion, as Rigel picked up the guitar, ran his fingers along the edge of the guitar's neck and rich autumn brown body and sighed.

"Does Rigel like guitars?" Jade leaned in and whispered to Alex without taking her eyes off Rigel.

"I'll say. That's his weakness," Alex whispered back.

"He has a weakness?" Jade wondered, whispering more to herself than to Alex.

"It would appear so," Alex answered her question with words, but it was the silent answer in his mind *'Aside from You, Jade?'* that caused Rigel to string the key notes off tune while attempting to decipher the state of the guitar.

"I couldn't leave her in that shed, brother." Sebastian patted Rigel's back.

"This is a Vintage Gibson 1962 Hummingbird acoustic guitar," Rigel whispered so quietly Sebastian barely heard it.

"If You say so." Sebastian replied as his smile grew.

"She's old." Rigel could not hide how touched he was. "And she's beautiful."

"She's Yours. But You'll have to play it to keep it."

"Friends, bonfire, guitar? That's a no brainer." Rigel smiled so wide his dimples showed.

"Does he know how to play the guitar?" Jade asked and rested her chin on her hand as she leaned on it.

"Does he ever?!?" Alex exclaimed, sending praises about Rigel's talent to high heavens. "He plays Country music, Polish music, and can learn a new melody in a heartbeat. That's his talent."

"Can You play something for us?" Jade asked Rigel, but the sound of that last word hit him on a different level. It hit him hard. So much so, that he miscalculated the distance between the beer bottle he took back from Marek and his... lips.

The beer spilled on his shirt and pants, causing Rigel to swear under his breath. He saw Sebastian's all-telling reaction and contemplated growling at him. The only thing saving Rigel from feeling even more embarrassed than he already did was the fact his back was turned toward everyone else.

"I'll play once we set up the bonfire." He passed the guitar back to Sebastian and grabbed his jacket. "I need to change. I will be right back."

'I shouldn't have asked. Now he's mad at me...'

Those words rang loud and vividly clear in Rigel's mind. Knowing Jade felt guilty about asking an innocent question angered him even more. He swore as he walked to his RV, and a couple more times once he went inside. Since he knew the temper twisting his gut into knots would not go away, he decided to take a quick shower. A cold shower. An ice-cold shower.

The moment he left Sebastian's Motorhome, Jade felt as if she made a mistake that would not be easy to repair. She felt guilty. She felt sad. So sad that she barely heard the ring of her phone. Alex nudged her shoulder, and joked that maybe it was Rigel calling her to ask her to come to his RV. He meant it as a joke, but she took it as anything but. Luckily it wasn't Rigel. It was Aunt Aline.

"Good afternoon, Aunt Aline," Jade straightened up as she greeted her aunt.

"Good afternoon, to You." Aunt Aline nodded as she sat on the couch with Alsatian sitting right beside her. "Are You alone with that... man?"

"No." Jade shook her head.

"Good afternoon, Aunt Aline!" Everyone in Sebastian's Motorhome greeted her cheerfully.

"Hello." Aunt Aline raised her eyebrows as a faint trace of smile appeared on her face when Jade turned the phone around so she could see everyone. The smile on Aunt Aline's face disappeared in an instant when Jade turned the phone back toward herself. "Where is he?"

"He?" Jade asked, causing Sebastian to chuckle.

"The Detective guy?" Aunt Aline asked bluntly.

"He went to change his clothes," Jade answered calmly.

"How do You know that?" Aunt Aline narrowed her eyes with suspicion. "And why did he need to change his clothes?"

"He spilled some beer on his shirt," Jade replied and moved her phone away from her face as Aunt Aline brought the phone right up to her face.

"He drinks on the job?!?" Aunt Aline exclaimed in a judgmental tone of voice, causing Sebastian to chuckle again.

"No, Aunt Aline. Rigel is not on the job. This is his time off. And he is allowed to drink beer," Jade defended Rigel and rose from the kitchenette table, feeling utterly embarrassed.

"He is on the job. He is Your Detective. He took You and swore to keep You safe. He is not protecting You now. This means You are not safe," Aunt Aline all but growled the words out, and caused Rocko to start barking at her, much to Sebastian's amusement.

"Aunt Aline, that was not nice to say." Jade could feel her cheeks burning up. She went to grab her jacket and turned toward the door. "If You'll excuse me, I will speak with Aunt Aline and will be right back."

"Bye, Aunt Aline," the group of friends bid farewell to her while Sebastian continued to grin.

"Aunt Aline, that was mean," Jade scolded her on the way to Rigel's RV.

"That was not mean," Aunt Aline countered. "It was the right thing to say."

"Aunt Aline..." Jade shook her head as she walked inside the RV, closing the door shut.

"Jade, I don't like that this man is there with You. But more than that I don't like that he ISN'T there," Aunt Aline shook her head with disapproval. "He said he would be there, and he is not."

"That is not true," Jade denied the accusation, and sighed a big sigh of relief when Aunt Aline received an incoming call, ending their conversation.

It was a sigh of a completely different sort that escaped Jade's lips the moment Rigel opened the bathroom's door. He was barefoot, with hot steam filling the crammed space of the bathroom he walked out of, as if in slow motion. He wore jeans, again unbuttoned at the top just as he did the night she went to his house. And his bare chest showed undeniable signs of the shower he had just taken...

≈ **Chapter 18** ≈

Rigel stopped dead in his tracks. The moment he opened the bathroom door and saw Jade staring right at him surprised him even more than receiving the acoustic guitar from Sebastian. A guitar he always hoped to hold in his hands one day. Why? Because for a man who could read thoughts, he failed to hear Jade's, even though she stood on the other side of a few sheets of plywood.

That... in turn... caused him to smile. Whether or not she was aware that he was smiling at his own reaction, and not solely at seeing her.

"I... I did not follow You," Jade tried to come up with an excuse for being in the RV even though her brain fried its circuits in order to come up with words to make up that entire sentence.

"I did not say You did." Rigel raised his eyebrow without moving an inch.

"Oh." She said in short, not having blinked since the moment she looked at him. "Well, I did not."

"Alright."

"You're wet."

"I took a quick shower," he responded matter-of-factly and felt better with every passing second. Suddenly, going with the flow of how he felt about her seemed better than beating himself up for it.

"With water?" She asked and finally blinked for the first time since she locked eyes with him.

"That's... generally the idea." He bit his lip and knew if he grinned right now, he might come to regret it later. Then again, if he grinned right now, he may end up ruffling her feathers. So, he smiled. From ear to ear.

"I did not mean to make You angry," she said with remorse.

"You did not." The smile on his face disappeared in the blink of an eye. He realized she said those words without thinking about them. They weren't rehearsed. They were sincere. And they came from her heart. He decided to go with his gut. Looking at her with a gaze that pierced through layers of her comfort zones, he walked slowly toward her.

"Rigel," she said quietly, unable to command her vocal cords to create any sound other than a mere whisper.

"Jade," he said just as quietly, and just as affected by what he saw in her eyes.

"I am sorry I asked You to play the guitar," she whispered as he backed her up against the closet door.

"Never apologize for asking me to play the guitar," he whispered in reply and placed his hands beside her, above her head. She felt trapped, but then again, she didn't because his arms rested above her on the closet door - giving her a path to move if she needed one. The fact that he was shirtless, and his hair was still silky wet from the shower was a trap but of a completely different sort. "It's my passion."

'Passion...'

She repeated after him in her thoughts. "Playing the guitar is Your passion?"

"Among a few other things." The fact she stood before him vulnerable and defenseless pulled at him in ways no confident woman ever did. Or could.

"Then why did You get mad at me?"

"I did not get mad at You. I got mad at Alex."

"Alex? Why?"

"Because..." Rigel began to respond but paused because he did not know what to say. Would he tell her the truth? Should he? He was not ready to reveal it to her just yet. After all, how could someone own up to reading minds and hearts? No, he was not ready for that. Neither was she. What then? What should he say? Lie? Evade the truth? He neither condoned lies, nor did he prefer them over the truth. So, he sighed, and was about to answer whatever came to his mind, when suddenly Jade reached out toward him, and stopped her hand just before touching his ribs right beside his heart.

"Have You been shot?" That question got to him even more than her vulnerability did. The concern in it. The fear in it. The worry for his well-being.

"Oh," he took his eyes off her and looked down to the spot where her fingers almost touched his scar. "Shot, stabbed, You name it."

"Rigel...." She said his name with so much feeling that he almost kissed her.

"Hey, it comes with the territory. You don't exactly get to kick back and relax in Chicago P.D.," he tried to sound amusing, but it backfired in the sweetest way.

"How did it happen?" She asked and conquered her fear of reaching for him. She touched the scar left behind by the bullet that pierced his skin. And immediately retrieved her hand, afraid, because he sucked in air.

"Don't. Don't pull back, please." He reached for Jade's hand, pleading for her not to hide from whatever feelings were growing between them, and he heard the all-familiar words.

'She's the one...'

"Could You tell me how You were shot?" She did not retrieve her hand. She let him hold it as he guided her fingers across the scar. Though she was startled, she felt braver because he allowed her to reach for the scar.

"This one happened the first year on the job. The idiot thought he could outrun justice. Turns out he couldn't," he spoke slowly, unsure why he felt so affected by someone he just met. "And this one happened a week after I got back to active duty."

"How many times were You shot?" She whispered as Rigel guided her hand a bit higher on his chest, but to the opposite side of his rib cage.

"Four."

"Four?" She shot him a look that cut through layers he built up around his heart.

"And stabbed about three." He turned around slowly so she could see the scars on his back.

"About three?" She repeated, tracing her fingers along the five long scars near his waist. "There are five scars here."

"Three. Five. Who's counting?" He tried to smile but frowned because she retracted her hand.

"You are so strong. And so brave."

"I don't feel that way right now."

"Why?"

"Because of You."

"You don't feel strong or brave because of me?"

"Yes. It is the weakness You bring out in me that makes me a stronger person. A person I want to be when You are beside me, and when You are not."

"What do You mean?" She narrowed her eyes on him just as she linked the fingers of her hands together, self-conscious.

"You make me weak and strong at the same time." He cupped her face, standing barely an inch away. "I understand You may not feel the same way. But I can no longer deny how I feel about You. Do You want to know why I got mad out there?"

"Why?" She asked, with her fingers still linked together between them.

"Because Alex pointed out that You are my weakness." He did not lie to her. He could not. Because it mattered.

'I am Your weakness...?'

"Am I?"

"Take a guess," he said dangerously close to her lips. He did not kiss her. He lingered for what seemed like forever right there, right by her lips, neither touching nor pulling away. He told himself he was testing her, but in reality, he was testing his own ability to stand against the desire to crush her lips.

"And You got mad at Alex for that? Why?" She tried to remain calm and gauged that asking a question would steady her racing pulse. She was wrong.

"Because he figured it out before I did." Saying so, Rigel tipped his forehead to hers ever so slowly, and closed his eyes. He had never done so in his life, and the gesture added even more meaning to what he felt for her.

"Did he figure out You make me weak in my knees?" She asked shyly and reached to cover his hands with hers.

"Do I?" He tipped his head back.

"Yes, whether I can admit it out loud or not," Jade smiled and caressed the back of his hands with her thumbs. "Do You want to know something I may not be brave enough to share once this moment passes?"

"Tell me."

"Do You want to know what I wished for the day I first came by Your precinct?"

"What did You wish for?" He asked, fully aware of the answer.

"I wished for You to take a sip of Alex's coffee. If You would have done that, I swore to myself I would find a way to kiss You," she declared, hoping she did not make a fool of herself.

"I wish You hadn't said that."

"Oh." She sighed, saddened by his words. "Then I wish for that instead."

"Don't." He shook his head. "I am glad You told me. I just feel sorry for my stomach now."

"Why?"

"Because I will never pass up on that ill-tasting mud coffee from now on. I promise You that," he whispered into her ear and took them both on a journey their lips could not have gotten enough of…

≈ Chapter 19 ≈

Just as he promised, Rigel played the guitar while everyone gathered around the bonfire once the sun decided to take a rest, and the moon lit up the sky. It was something he loved. It was something he cherished. It was something too dear to his heart to let go of.

Whether he played melodies of Country songs, or Polish melodies he may not have known all the words to, the sounds created by his skilled fingers caressing the strings of the guitar soothed his rugged and restless side. There was something indescribable in the way he could bring life to the music flowing from his heart. And from the looks of it, Jade felt the same way.

They sat around the bonfire well into the night, covered with blankets to kept them as warm on the outside as Rigel's songs and the atmosphere of the evening kept them warm on the inside. Rigel felt so at peace even Sebastian had to admit he saw a change in his best friend. Whoever Jade was or would turn out to be in Rigel's future, he would be grateful to her for offering these moments to Rigel. Forever.

"Why the long face?" Rigel asked Sebastian as he finished playing a tune about love and loss.

"Nights like these are far too rare." Sebastian sighed heavily, sipping on the beer bottle in his hand.

"Isn't that the truth." Marek nodded in agreement.

"Rigel's guitar makes all the difference - compared to the rusty sounds of some speakers," Alex grinned as he sat beside Rigel.

"Thanks, partner." Rigel clicked his tongue and clinked his beer bottle against Alex's in a sign of comradery.

"It's true." Kasia agreed with Alex and looked at Rigel from across the bonfire flames. "There is something that changes the night air when You play. It stays with You in memories."

"Thank You," Rigel saluted her by tipping the beer bottle lightly against his forehead and made her smile.

"When did You learn how to play?" Jade asked Rigel as she sat between Sebastian and Kasia and watched him intently across the bonfire.

"Ages ago," he smiled but she saw undertones of sadness in his eyes.

"I noticed You play Polish melodies, but You don't sing them?" Jade wondered out loud.

"That's right, Detective." Rigel smirked, giving into an urge to play the guitar a bit more quietly.

"I'm not the..." Jade responded, recalling their original argument. She stopped herself and smiled. "Very funny."

"Isn't she the linguist intern?" Alex narrowed his eyebrows.

"Yes." Rigel chuckled.

"Don't You speak Polish?" Jade tipped her head.

"Why? Just because of my last name?" Rigel asked in a judgmental tone of voice.

"No. Yes."

"Typical." Rigel shook his head.

"Don't be fooled by his teddy bear cuteness," Marek advised Jade and pointed toward Rigel with his beer. "Happyski knows how to speak Polish. He's just not man enough to speak it."

"*Spadaj,**" Rigel replied to Marek and flashed his pearly whites at him.

"Don't tell him to get lost. It's nearly midnight," Jade fired back at Marek, and watched as all heads turned her way.

<u>Polish</u> -**Get lost**

"You speak Polish?" Alex asked, impressed.

"I'm not surprised. She's a linguist after all." Rigel nodded.

"I'm going to grab something to eat. Would You like anything?" Kasia turned to Jade.

"No, thank You." Jade waved her hand, feeling a bit lonely once Kasia walked away. Though not for long, because Sebastian decided to grill her about feelings she may or may not have toward Rigel. He wouldn't have been the best friend that he was if he didn't.

"Are You enjoying Your time here? With us?" Sebastian leaned toward her a bit but made sure to look casual about it so Rigel wouldn't figure out what he was doing.

"Yes, very much," Jade beamed at him with happiness.

"How about Rigel?" Sebastian asked bluntly. He thought he was smart enough to out-wit her. He was wrong.

"Is Rigel enjoying his time here with You?" Jade replied in a way that made Rigel smile from afar. Sebastian may have been a smooth talker, but Rigel wasn't born yesterday. He knew exactly what Sebastian was up to, so he decided to listen in on the conversation. "You would need to ask him about it."

"No, that's not what I meant," Sebastian puffed out air.

"Oh? Then what did You mean?" Jade leaned back in her chair and cuddled into the blanket.

"I meant to ask if You were glad he brought You here so far from Chicago?"

"Very much," Jade replied in short. "The TRX is a great pickup truck. The ride here was very pleasurable."

"That's not what I meant," Sebastian blinked at her, and wondered if he asked the wrong questions, or if he asked them in the wrong way.

"Oh? Did You then mean to ask if there is something more between us than the strict Detective-witness relation?" She asked bluntly, causing Rigel to bite his lip so they wouldn't know he was eavesdropping on their conversation.

"Well, um, that would be... a yes."

"Rigel is someone important to me. But I can only speak about my side of that answer." Jade said sincerely. "As for Rigel's side of that answer, You have to ask him about it."

'Damn, she's smart...'

Sebastian thought, impressed.

"You got that right." Rigel meant to respond to Sebastian's thoughts. And Sebastian figured it out. Jade didn't, and assumed he was speaking to her.

"I hope I didn't say anything wrong?" She frowned, worried.

"You did not. And maybe I should not have asked You, but Rigel is like a brother to me. He has my back, I have his." Saying so, Sebastian sat back in his chair and polished off the rest of the beer in his bottle.

"Would You mind if I asked You a question?" Jade fought with herself but decided she needed to feel brave if she wanted to someday mean more to Rigel than she thought she did now.

"Not at all. Ask."

"Did... Rigel fall for many women in the past?" She was scared to ask. But she had to ask. She took feelings seriously. And she hoped Rigel did as well.

"No."

"Oh."

"He only fell for one woman in his life." Sebastian whispered, but he knew Rigel heard his thoughts.

"Oh." Jade sighed, unsure if that answer scared her or eased her worry.

"She died a couple of years ago," Sebastian added, and knew to trudge cautiously when it came to his best friend's feelings.

"He must have taken it very hard," Jade said quietly.

"You have no idea." Sebastian turned to Jade and patted her hand gently. "That man has a heart that never felt the kind of love he deserves to feel. The kind of love that would fill the dark places of his heart. The kind of love that would make him believe he is a good man."

'He is a good man...'

Jade's words replayed over and over in Rigel's mind for the rest of the evening. He knew what Sebastian did, or at least what he attempted to do. And he did not blame his best friend for it. He only hoped Jade meant what she said.

As the evening ended and they all decided to retire to their RVs, Rigel stayed behind to ensure the bonfire burned out. Jade also stayed behind to keep him company. She folded the blankets, cleaned up the picnic table, all the while humming one of the ballads Rigel played on the guitar.

"You liked it?" Rigel asked when he heard her humming.

"Yes. You have such amazing gift. Why do You hide it?"

"That's... a bit of an overstatement," he paused, taken off guard by her words.

"It is not. Some people are born with gifts bestowed upon them by the heavens above but they choose to hide them, afraid of being judged or not accepted by those around them. Your gift makes You who You are," she spoke in such a way it twisted his gut. He was speechless. He also realized he was... slowly falling in love and did not know whether she would accept it.

"Can we take a walk?"

"Alright," she beamed when he took hold of her hand and guided her toward the shore of the Tennessee River.

'She's the one...'

"I get that," he replied to the thoughts that came to him and grit his teeth the moment he realized he said it out loud.

"Is everything okay?" Jade narrowed her eyes on him the moment he stopped near the water's edge and turned to her.

"Yes. No. I don't know," he babbled and felt perplexed about it. "I don't know what to do."

"Why?" She reached for his cheek. "Is it me? I thought You said in the RV that You have feelings for me. Did that change?"

"No. And that is why I don't know what to do," he sighed heavily. "Actually, I do. But it won't be easy."

"What won't be easy?" She tried to retrieve her hand, but he held onto it, and brought it to his chest, making it possible for her to feel his heartbeat.

"I never asked to be taken off a case. I may have to now."

"Why?"

"Because I cannot be personally vested in a case."

"Are You... personally vested?"

"That's not even a question." He said nothing more. He lowered his lips to hers and kept them there. For as long as he could.

'There are so many sides to You...'

He heard Jade's thoughts when she slowly opened her eyes and noticed how captivating his reflection looked in the light of the moon on one side, and in the light given off by the dwindling bonfire on the other.

"You are so easy on the lips, Detective."

"Eyes."

"Eyes?"

"I think You meant to say I am easy on the eyes."

"Oh. That, too," she giggled, and the sound twisted knots in his gut. "Whatever You like."

"That is a very dangerous statement, Jade Alistair."

"I've been in danger with You before. I don't mind it if You are next to me," she whispered and brought his lips down to hers.

"Wicked woman, I know You don't mind danger... You create it."

"Is that bad?"

"Not bad. Never bad. But undeniably dangerous," he replied and forced himself to ease away from the embrace. "You have no idea how powerful You are. No idea how strong and mighty. You pack a punch."

"I do?"

"You do." He caressed her cheek. Even though everything in his mind told him to pull away out of fear of everything his heart went through in the past, he lingered on for a heartbeat longer. "Let's head inside. We have a long day ahead tomorrow."

"Do we?"

"We do." He reached for her hand again, and smiled as they walked toward the RV with the familiar words on his mind, which somehow no longer scared him as much as they did before...

≈ **Chapter 20** ≈

Lookout Mountain seemed like the perfect place to choose for a day that would live in Jade's memory for years to come. Rigel thought it would make her smile. It did. He hoped she would like it, but he did not anticipate she would come to appreciate him so much more because of this gesture. But more than anything, he underestimated the impact the day would bring to whatever was growing between them.

And it started in the most innocent way....

"Good morning, Detective." Jade grinned from ear to ear as the delicate rays of the sun caressed her face. She sat on the bed in the little bedroom, and waved at Rigel sitting on the little pull-out couch on the opposite side of the RV. He wouldn't have admitted to her, but he watched as she slept for a considerably long time until she woke up.

"Good morning." Rigel brought the almost-empty coffee cup in the air. The caffeine in the coffee didn't raise his energy nearly as much as the first smile of the day Jade offered to him.

"You slept well, I presume?" She smirked, laying down on her stomach, and propped her chin on the palms of her hands.

"Yup." He nodded, aware she did not believe him.

"I still say You should take the bed. That little pull-out couch was not designed for someone Your size."

"You got that right," Rigel sent her a cocky smirk, but knew the meaning of the words would go unnoticed right over her head. That proved more alluring than if she had been trying to flirt with him.

"So, why do You insist on sleeping on it?"

"While I do agree with You that there are better... things I could sleep on, there is no way I would let You sleep here." Saying so, he patted the couch's cushion. Little by little, her safety was taking on a more serious meaning.

"Why? This is Your RV. And I am just a guest," Jade wondered out loud and innocently ran a hand through her long hair, oblivious to the sparks that flashed in his eyes.

"This is my RV." Rigel rose from the couch, crossed over to the bedroom and crouched beside the bed, in front of her. "But You are not a 'just' of anything. You will never be 'just' of anything."

"Oh," she whispered quietly as he leaned over to kiss her, but stopped merely an inch away, staring at her lips.

"Ready for an adventure?" He had a day trip planned for them but debated whether to forgo those plans altogether and spend it on watching a marathon of movies he knew he would pay no attention to.

"What sort of adventure?" She asked, with her eyes locked on his lips.

"Dangerous."

"Dangerous?"

"Very dangerous."

"Very dangerous?"

"Very, very... dangerous."

"What could be so dangerous?"

"Ruby Falls, the Incline Railway, Rock City..." Rigel rose to his feet, removing the shirt he slept in. "We are in Chattanooga, after all."

"I wouldn't call that dangerous."

'Now THAT'S dangerous...'

"Like what You see?" Rigel paused halfway to the bathroom, turning slowly, amused by her thoughts at seeing his bare back.

"No. Yes." She corrected herself and rose from bed so he would not see her burning cheeks. "You play with fire, Detective."

"Could be. But fire can either consume You or keep You warm, especially if it's slow burning."

"Or it can fry Your brain circuits if You don't know how to hold onto the match the right way." She said as confidently as she possibly could with her head held high after removing her shirt and walked past him to the bathroom wearing a sporty camisole that left him dry-mouthed, then locked the door behind her.

"You're definitely wicked." Rigel whispered under his breath, but she heard him.

"Thank You!" She said through the closed door

Though Jade may have smiled to herself because she realized she ruffled Rigel's feathers more than he ruffled hers, it was Rigel who got the last laugh. Or rather, the last grin. A very confident, and quite accomplished grin. Why? Because he showed Jade he cared about her as a person, not just in the passionate or physical sense. He showed her he cared about what she had to say, think, or hope for, and not just about the way their inner desire pulled them toward one another.

They visited the Ruby Falls first. Jade admitted that standing inside the tallest and deepest underground waterfall in the United States made her feel... small yet special at the same time. The aura of the place, the history of it, the colors and hues illuminating the waterfall, and the sounds that filled the winding cave made her smile. It also made it possible for Rigel to reach for her hand in a way she accepted as natural.

'She's the one...'

Did he hear the words he had heard before? Definitely. Was he learning to accept them? Yes, though getting used to the idea he may have found someone who had feelings for him did not negate - or eliminate - the reality of the fact he possessed certain gifts not everyone would have been willing to accept. Nor did it rid him of the burden of his family's past. But the longer he thought about it, Jade was beginning to sense a change in the way he related to her.

"Is everything all right?" Jade's question struck him as quite intuitive. They walked around the Rock City Gardens, its narrow passages, its deep and bottomless chasms, its intricate rock steps leading through the paths of lower and upper walkways, its mysterious red doorways, and even opted for the path of the Swing-A-Long Bridge per Rigel's suggestion. And yet, Jade paid as much attention to his point of view as she did to hers.

"Yes," Rigel replied but felt that since he relied heavily on trust and honesty, he owed as much to Jade. "Actually, my thoughts seem occupied by You."

"Me? Why me?"

"We came to Chattanooga to get Your mind off Chicago. I wanted to show You around, but instead we spent most of the time on our little patch of land." Saying so, Rigel stopped in front of the suspiciously narrow rocky entryway to the Needle's Eye passage ahead of them.

"I am grateful to You and Your friends for allowing me to come here with You. And I appreciate You planned this little day trip," Jade let go of his hand and walked up closer toward the entrance to the pathway, which appeared to match its name. "I have seen more today than I have seen since the day we arrived from São Paulo with my mother and Aunt Aline."

"That name scares me more than the cramped rocky canyon walls ahead of us," he shivered.

"Don't tell me a brave man like You is afraid of a woman half his size?" Jade could not hide her amusement.

"Size has nothing to do with it. I have no doubt Your Aunt would single-handedly wipe away crime in Chicago if she ever became the Mayor. Her haunting gaze can pierce through walls," Rigel mimicked Aunt Aline's spine-chilling stare as they made it to the other side of the Needle's Eye and made Jade laugh.

"Maybe that's why she never married? Men are just too afraid of her."

"Hey, You said it. I did not."

"Maybe not, but the look on Your face says it all."

"No such thing," Rigel disagreed. "I was simply worried my broad and buff shoulders wouldn't fit through the tight squeeze of that opening."

"Then why did You choose this path through the gardens?"

"For this." He nodded toward the view in front of them. The expression on Jade's face was more than enough to make him feel accomplished, and he did not feel the need to read her thoughts to figure out whether she liked what she saw.

"Rigel..." She covered her mouth with her hand.

"What do You think? Beats the desk job view?" He led her toward the sign in the middle of the terrace with the panoramic view from the Lookout Mountain. "This, my dear jewel, is the Rock City Point. You can see seven states at once from here: Tennessee, Virginia, South Carolina, North Carolina, Georgia, Kentucky, and Alabama."

"What did You say?" Jade looked up at him.

"You can see seven states at once by simply standing here: Tennessee, Virginia, South Carolina, North Carolina, Georgia, Kentucky and Alabama," he repeated the names of the states the arrows engraved in the sign pointed to.

"No, not that," she shook her head.

"Oh? Then what?"

"You called me Your jewel," she whispered, overcome with emotions.

"I did. Because that's who You are to me," he said in a deep voice. He brought her close and looked deeply into her eyes while dark clouds began to slowly roll in far in the distance...

≈ Chapter 21 ≈

Being tough in the field wasn't a walk in the park. But it was something Rigel mastered almost to perfection. He was brave. He was raw. He was confident all the way to the smallest cells of his body. And yet, he felt helpless, inadequate, and above all vulnerable while a pair of shy, vividly honest, and just as vulnerable eyes looked into his eyes.

Did he have a past, albeit long ago but one, nonetheless? He did. Was he proud of punishing those who broke the law? Not always. Did ridding the world of evil criminals justify his actions as an assassin years before he became a Police Officer and eventually a Detective? Perhaps. At least his siblings believed so. But for Rigel, that was not enough. He wanted more out of life. Why? Because as time passed, he realized that loneliness affected him more than being scared of not coming back alive from his shift.

But then, there was Jade. A woman who was a contradiction. Shy on one hand, and brave enough to shield him with her own body when they were shot at. Bashfully denying having feelings for him yet smiling from ear to ear as she twisted knots in his gut by simply looking at him. Even if she didn't know about it.

"Are You trying to make me not want to return to work on Monday?" Jade wondered as her hand cupped Rigel's bearded cheek.

"No such thing." He smiled and sent her his best flirtatious smirk. "I merely planned on convincing You to extend our stay here a bit longer."

"Isn't that the same thing?" Jade chuckled.

"Not by a long shot."

"Oh, really?"

"Of course." He responded in an undeniably flirtatious tone of voice. "I never tried to make You change Your mind. I planned for it."

"Is that why the look in Your eyes is more captivating than the view of the seven states over that railing?"

"You think my eyes are captivating?"

"That's one way of describing them. Though, I admit calling in sick on Monday would require a bit more... convincing."

"How's this?" He whispered, overcoming a deep fear of kissing her out in the public, and lowered his lips to hers.

"Rigel?" She sighed against his lips with such indecision after the kiss ended that it caused him to contemplate whether to read her thoughts. He opted against it, because whatever was on her mind was heavy enough to cause her to speak out about it. He did not want to lose that level of trust, or worse - he did not want her to figure out that he really could read her mind. This wasn't the time nor place for it.

"Yes, Jade?"

"Will... You still think of me the same way You do now when we return to Chicago?"

"Damn..." he said bluntly, taken aback by the sincerity of her words. He'd dealt with female confidence, vanity, and self-conceit. But never with this level of humility. And, quite frankly, he wasn't sure if he was man enough to accept it.

"I'm sorry, I shouldn't have asked." She pulled away with a clear understanding she was not the type of a woman Rigel was interested in for the long term.

"No, Jade, don't!" He reached for her with as much desperation in his words as in his arms when he embraced her.

"I understand I am not the kind of woman You prefer to have a serious relationship with. And I appreciate You being honest about it." She looked away because she wasn't brave enough to look at him.

"Jade Alistair, You are one stubborn woman!" Rigel raised his voice, unsure why he did so. Was it desperation? Was it anguish? Was it a hopeless plea for her not to close her heart?

"I may be, but that is no reason to raise Your voice at me. I have dealt with authoritativeness and narcissism, neither of which sit well with me," she stopped pulling away and instead stood her ground. "I will not deny having feelings for You, however I have too much self-worth to allow You to shout at me."

"I..." he paused, unsure of himself, and so far out of his comfort zone he wouldn't even know where to look for it. "You don't understand."

"Detective, I may be inexperienced when it comes to relationships, and that is on me. I am sure Your track record when it comes to women far exceeds the number of men I have allowed to come into my life. However, I..." she would have kept going but he interrupted her.

"Got me all figured out, don't You?" He straightened up, feeling more and more timorous.

"Tough, buff, rough, and definitely worthy of the badge You carry around." Jade looked right into his eyes and fought an inner battle to find the courage not to cry. "Tell me, Detective, do You bring all Your witnesses to Chattanooga?"

"I have never brought any woman, let alone a witness, to Chattanooga," he said as stoically as he could.

"And why would I believe You?" She shot up her chin so fearlessly he could not stop himself from lowering his gaze down to it, then back up to her eyes.

"Because... because... You scare me," he whispered, finally admitting out loud what his heart felt inside.

"I am not some to be feared," Jade scoffed at the oddity of that statement.

"I beg to differ."

"You expect me to believe someone like You could be scared of someone like me?"

"That is as honest an admission as I will ever make in my entire life."

'Don't believe him. He will never accept You for who You are. You will never be his. He will never be truly Yours, Jade. Never...'

Those words rang so loud in his mind he nearly shouted at her to stop. He didn't know what to do. He didn't know what NOT to do. And the indecision sent a surge of fear through his veins.

"I don't think I have enough in me to stand before You right now and listen to all of this. Would You please take me back to the RV?" Jade clenched her fists to direct her emotions into the palms of her hands and away from her eyes, which were on the brink of losing the battle against her tears.

"I won't. At least not just yet."

"And why not?" She replied, anticipating an angry response. What she received instead weakened her knees.

"You scare me, Jade. Right down to my heart."

"Why, Rigel? Why?" Jade shook her head. "Give me one reason, ONE."

"Because before I met You, I thought I would spend the rest of my life in loneliness," he said bluntly. "I don't know how to deal with the fact You are strong enough to look me in the eye and not reject me."

"What?"

"I may be tough. I may be buff. Damn it, I am rough, and not just around the edges. There are things about me that scare people off. And being rejected because of who I am hurts in a way that is too hard to explain," he said in one breath, and took a few steps away.

"What kind of a woman would reject You?"

"One that knew who I am." He gazed back at her and saw she stood right behind him. "I don't open easily, Jade."

"Who does, Detective Happyski?" She laid a hand on his shoulder. "You have Your past, I have mine. Who doesn't? The real question isn't whether I scare You or not, though."

"No? Then what is the real question?"

"The real question begs an answer to the aspect of the future, not the past."

"What do You mean?" He turned to her, forgetting about his own ability to read minds.

"Well," she reached for his face, cupping it. "Would You prefer to beat Yourself up over Your past, or be grateful for the future You chose by letting go of Your fear?"

"Please don't reject me," he whispered right before he lowered his lips to hers.

"Then don't push me away." She laid her head on his chest.

"I won't. I'd be too afraid to face tomorrow without Your hand holding mine."

"But what will we do back in Chicago? Aren't there regulations against Detectives flirting with witnesses?" She asked and yelped as he whirled them around.

"I'll give You flirting," Rigel laughed with mischief.

"Promise?"

"Detective's honor," he flashed his pearly whites as the sound of thunder reached them from afar.

"What should do once we get back home?" She wrapped her arms around his waist under his unzipped leather jacket.

"How about we play it by the ear?"

"Don't You mean to say we should play it by the guitar?"

"That, too, Ms. Linguist. That, too." He laughed but cut it short as another round of thunder shook the air. "I guess the Incline Railway will have to wait until next time. We should head back to the truck."

"Do You think we have time to stop by a gift shop? I promised mother and Aunt Aline I would bring them souvenirs," Jade wondered as they began to make their way toward the exit of the Rock City Gardens.

"I doubt Aunt Aline will accept a Truck Stop magnet?" He smirked at the thought of Aunt Aline's sour face grimace.

"Of course, she wouldn't. She is a very particular woman."

"I'll say," he laughed. "C'mon, I know this quaint little shop in St. Elmo, at the foot of the mountain. I am sure You will be able to pick something out for them."

"Thank You, Detective Hunky," she grinned from ear to ear and almost ran into Rigel because he stopped abruptly.

"Detective Hunky?"

"Detective Happyski's okay, but I can't call You Detective Hunky? Hypocrite..." Jade shot up her chin again and passed him by but yelped when he pulled her back against his body.

"Call me whatever You want, but these rocks are my witness if You raise that chin up at me again, I won't need Alex's coffee as an excuse to kiss You," he all but growled.

"Understood." Jade saluted him playfully while still pressed against his body, sending a dozen jolts to his gut.

"Hungry?"

"Of course, I'm hungry!" She agreed in a heartbeat. "Are there any places around here that serve onion bagels?"

"I cannot believe You said that. I'll find such a place even if I spend the next two hours searching for it," he leaned in to kiss her until her knees buckled, and rushed them toward the exit in hopes of getting to the truck before the rain arrived...

≈ **Chapter 22** ≈

Though the rain came as expected, it brought out the unexpectedly humorous side of Jade. She smiled as the first drops of rain fell upon her cheeks. She giggled as the rain drops morphed into the kind of rain that could only be admired from a cozy couch inside a warmly heated RV. And she laughed, utterly amused, as Rigel rushed them toward the truck parked on one of the St. Elmo's side streets. Why? Because the brave Detective Hunky swore under his breath. Over and over. Much to her delight.

Rigel swore no less as they arrived at their camp site and ran from the truck to the RV. The fact he dropped the keys and had to crouch down to retrieve them from the muddy ground didn't help either. In fact, it made it even worse. Much, much worse. All the while Jade continued to poke fun of his sour mood.

"Would You stop it?" Rigel puffed out air as he tried to clean the dirt off the key before he was able to finally shove it into the lock of the RV's door.

"Stop what? The rain feels amazing!" Jade exclaimed with a happy grin and looked up to the sky so that the raindrops falling upon it forced her to close her eyes.

"You have got to be kidding me! You LIKE this weather?!?" Rigel hissed out and pulled her inside the RV.

"Why did You do that?"

"It's November. It's raining. And it's cold outside," he tried to make her understand his point of view. He failed.

"You are such a grumpy grouch," Jade pointed at him and tried to remove her fitted leather jacket that was stuck on her arms because of the material's soaked condition. "I bet You hate snow, too."

"I live in Chicago, I have no choice," he growled. "I hate the snow. I hate the slush. I hate the cold."

"Well, now I'm cold. You shouldn't have said that," she responded in a sulking tone of voice while continuing to attempt to remove the soaked jacket.

"Serves You right! You shouldn't have spent all that time out in the rain!" He tried to help her with the jacket and managed to get one sleeve off her arm.

"You shouldn't have made me wait so long for You! I thought men didn't like shopping, but You took Your sweet time," she replied with so much sarcasm in her voice it caused Rigel to narrow his eyes on her. "What on earth could have been so important it justified me getting rained on?"

"Something." He shot her a thunderous glance.

"Something?"

"Yes." He grit his teeth. "Something important."

"A man of a few words." She rolled her eyes, wincing when Rigel freed her other arm from the tightly fitting and wet jacket. "Savage!"

"Don't call me that." He hissed out slowly with more resentment than fury. He hated that word. Hated it. The last time he heard that word directed at him it rolled out of the lips of the woman he thought he could trust. Right before she ripped the heart out of his chest by calling him a deceiver and inhuman. And that... hurt the most.

"Why? Don't tell me Detective Hunky has a weak side?" She mocked him, unaware of how much he was hurting inside.

"Tell Yourself whatever You want, but NEVER call me that." The gaze he sent her raised the hair at the back of her neck. She thought of taking a step back, but something told her what Rigel needed was not retreat, but rather a confrontation of whatever pain gripped at him inside. She walked up toward him, so close she had to look straight up to look into his eyes, bringing her hand up to caress his cheek.

"Rigel Brzozakiewiczowicz, You are not weak." Though she whispered those words, she did so with confidence, and would have continued if he hadn't grabbed her shoulders and pulled her against his soaked wet chest.

"This time I am..." he replied with fire in his words and in his eyes, right before he conquered her lips. He didn't just crush them. That would have been an understatement. No. He conquered them. Time and again. The whirl of emotions, desires, and passion that burst within them proved unavoidable. A cupped cheek against a cupped cheek. His hand in her hair dripping from rain, against hers in his hair dripping from rain. Sigh against breathless sigh.

They turned, around and around, hitting their knees against the couch and thighs against the kitchenette countertop. By the time Jade's back hit against the closet door, she was shirtless and so out of her comfort zone the only thing she could do was to trust him. And he felt that, down to his core.

'You're built like a Stallion...'

If his lips weren't pressed against hers, Rigel was certain he would have burst out laughing at the thoughts that kept coming at him from Jade's unsuspecting mind.

'I was right! Holy pecs!'

Hearing that caused him to lose his balance. Who wouldn't have? Especially because he heard it the moment he removed his wet shirt and threw it somewhere toward the kitchenette area. The shirt landed in the sink, and his... arse landed against the bathroom door's doorknob. He swore to high heavens and released her momentarily.

"Face the melody, Rigel. You may be more skilled with a guitar in Your hands than with a woman," Jade smirked.

"It's 'face the music', and I believe this is an insult I will not take lightly."

"Oh," Jade yelped as he picked her up and swung the bathroom door wide open.

"But don't worry," he whispered the moment he walked under the rain shower with her legs wrapped around his waist and stood her down on the shower floor, slowly turning on hot water. "We'll make our own melody."

He didn't know what got to him more: the fact Jade didn't wince as the stream of hot water hit her bare back, or the fact she stood on her toes and reached to kiss his neck. One kiss after another, she left a trail of kisses from one side of his neck to the other. He sighed, picking her up again.

His head spun, his heart pounded, and he could not tell whether they spun under the rain shower or the RV spun around them. Each caress led to a new inch of her skin he had not known a moment ago. Each touch she allowed herself to give to him reached the part of him he didn't know was yearning for touch. Until...

'Please, be gentle...'

He froze. In motion, in breath, in thought. He tipped his head back slowly, with streams of water and clouds of steam all around them. He couldn't dismiss her thoughts. Not because he didn't care about her passion and feelings for him, but because he did.

"Jade, are You...?" He whispered, shaken by what he realized.

"I may not be as experienced as the women You have been with." She eased herself away from him, embarrassed.

"Jade, don't." Instead of pulling her toward him, he extended his hand, hoping she would accept it. "You matter to me because of who You are and not just on the outside. Your heart matters and Your feelings matter."

"And... THIS doesn't matter?"

"It does, but not in the way You might think." He cupped her face and turned off the water. "This.... THIS makes You all the more precious."

"I wish I could believe You."

"Believe me. And, believe me, we will return to THIS topic when the time comes for You to be comfortable with it," he gestured in a circle motion with his index finger between them.

"You are not mad?"

"I wouldn't use the word 'mad'." He led her out of the bathroom. "C'mon, let's change out of these soaking jeans before we catch a cold, and let me show You something."

"Alright."

Once they changed into dry clothes, the rain stopped. Rigel ran to the pickup truck to retrieve something he told her he left inside the truck so it would not get rained on.

"Here, this is for You." He walked back inside the RV carrying an oversized box.

"When did You get it?" Jade accepted the gift, surprised.

"I bought it when You went shopping for those souvenirs. I hid it in the truck before You returned," he explained, following her into the little bedroom.

"If You finished Your shopping before I did, why did You make me wait for You?" She wondered out loud and set the box on the bed.

"I had to get a cheesy magnet for Aunt Aline," he winked at her and passed the magnet to her.

"Wicked man!" She laughed. The laughter was cut short, though, because it morphed into a gasp when she lifted the lid off the box to reveal a tulle dress of dark jade green with multiple layers.

"I've been told the top tulle part of the dress converts to different styles, so You could choose the way You would like to wear it." He sat on the edge of the bed, hoping she would accept the gift. "Do You like it?"

"Do I? It's wonderful!" Her words made him grin as much as the joy he read in her thoughts did. But then, she paused and looked at him. "I have something for You as well."

"You do?" His surprise doubled because he realized he was beginning to read her thoughts less and less.

"Yes," she rushed out of the room, holding the dress, and returned with a little box tied with a little jade ribbon. "I know the size of this box is incomparable to the one You gifted to me, but I hope You like it."

"Sometimes size doesn't matter."

"I'll try to remember that one." She clicked her tongue and watched as Rigel untied the little jade ribbon around the box and removed the lid. "I was told it is one of a kind."

Rigel looked at her with a piercing gaze and took out the hand-crafted coffee mug with a handle that looked like an acoustic guitar, overcome with gratitude, and touched beyond words by her gesture. "Those words apply to more than just this mug."

"Do You mean it?"

"I wouldn't have said it if I didn't mean it." He rose from the bed, walked up to her, and wrapped his arms around her.

"You are a wonderful man."

"Do You mean it?"

"I wouldn't have said it if I didn't." She flashed her grin, causing him to laugh, but then tipped her head back and narrowed her eyebrows. "But where will I wear such a dress?"

"Funny You ask. You'll wear it next weekend."

"Next weekend?" She replied, surprised.

"Yes. We're going to meet the President of the United States, but it's a secret," he leaned in and whispered the last part slowly into her ear…

≈ **Chapter 23** ≈

The last morning in Chattanooga brought on a sense of contentment in Rigel he could not hide. There was a new sense of peace he exuded from within, a new level of serenity that was undeniable. Alex saw it. Marek saw it. Sebastian saw it as well. Whether Rigel liked it or not.

While the women busied themselves with preparing breakfast in Julia and Marek's RV, the men packed up belongings they brought on the trip back to their trucks and cleaned the area so they would be ready to leave for Chicago soon after breakfast while Rocko ran around them enjoying the last moments before the long drive. It was the perfect opportunity, in Marek's opinion, to grill Rigel over the fact the tough Detective fell for a woman so fast, so deep, and so completely.

"I am glad we could have made this trip a reality. Life flies by too quickly in Chicago," Marek smiled innocently as he picked up suitcases onto the back of his pickup truck, moving them toward the front of the truck's bed and under the bed cover.

"Tell me about it." Alex nodded in agreement, packing Maria's five suitcases, and one of his. "Though I wonder how long it will take us to fall back into the usual rhythm of everyday life."

"Some of us may not want to," Marek wiggled his eyebrows and nodded in Rigel's direction, causing Sebastian to burst out laughing, much to Alex's confusion.

"What is that supposed to mean?" Alex wondered.

"Yes, sunshine, what is that supposed to mean?" Rigel leaned back against the front bumper of his packed up pickup truck.

"For a Detective, You aren't too keen on details," Marek grinned mischievously.

"What is THAT supposed to mean?" Rigel asked in a more serious tone of voice.

"Whatever You want it to mean, sunshine. But... I have never seen that look in Your eyes before. It's cute."

"I don't know what You mean," Rigel shook his head.

"You don't, but we do. It doesn't come often. Heck, it only comes once in a life for some of us," Marek continued, more and more amused.

"And what sort of a look is that?" Rigel cocked an eyebrow.

"The kind of a look when You know deep down You're a goner," Marek chuckled.

"I'm not a goner," Rigel asserted.

"Sure, You are. And You denying it is even cuter," Marek chuckled again and nodded toward Sebastian who leaned against his pickup truck. "Am I right?"

"Definitely. It's cute to see that look in Your eyes Happyski," Sebastian sent his best friend a witty look.

"Whatever." Rigel moved his shoulders up and down but decided to inquire more about what his friends were accusing him of. "The look in my eyes did not change."

"Not since we got here," Alex chimed in at the perfect moment. "Well, technically not since Jade brought You a box of those onion bagels."

"Again, nothing changed." Rigel tried to make it seem he didn't just realize what his friends had in mind.

"Fine." Marek walked over to Rigel, leaned back on the bumper beside him, and wrapped his arm around Rigel's back in a brotherly way. "Say Jade's name."

"What?" Rigel chuckled nervously.

"You heard me, Happyski. Say Jade's name," Marek repeated.

"Jade," Rigel said, subconsciously smiling from within, which, of course, became apparent as corners of his mouth came up in a smile he was unable to stop.

"I rest my case," Marek went back to packing items onto the back of his pickup.

"Shit." Rigel murmured. He did have feelings for Jade he was not afraid to admit to himself and Jade. But he wasn't ready to reveal them to his friends. "Is it seriously that obvious?"

"Seriously," Sebastian clicked his tongue and crossed over to his best friend, patting Rigel's back in a not-so-gentle way. "I am glad it finally happened to You."

"You said it like it's a sentence," Rigel countered.

"On the contrary, my friend," Sebastian smirked. "Though, it is a sentence. And I hope it's a life sentence without parole."

"That's not funny."

"I didn't mean for it to be funny," Sebastian smiled sincerely at Rigel.

"Marek, can You come and do something about this speaker? We cannot hear the music again!" Julie shouted at her husband with a smile on her face as Maria stood behind her, shaking her head.

"You said You bought a top-of-the-line speaker! Was that one on sale?" Maria teased her twin brother.

"It is top-of-the-line! And it wasn't on sale!" Marek brooded over his twin sister's accusation. "C'mon Alex, I'll make sure that the speaker works. And You make sure to keep Your wife from insulting me while I do it."

"Twins." Alex shook his head, laughing, and followed Marek, leaving Rigel, Sebastian, and Rocko to finish packing the trucks.

"He's right, You know?" Sebastian decided to pick up on the topic which Marek started.

"About that speaker? I doubt it, though it does sort of look like a top-of-the-line one," Rigel laughed under his breath.

"No. He's right about Jade. Or, about Your feelings for her to be more precise."

"Is it really that obvious?"

"More than You think."

"When did it happen?" Rigel whispered so only the two of them heard it.

"No one really knows." Sebastian moved his shoulders up and down. "All I know is that from the moment I figured out I fell in love with Kasia, I never looked back. She is my everything."

"From the moment You... fell in love?" Rigel whispered, this time more to himself than in response to Sebastian's statement.

"Yes. That look in Your eyes? That isn't infatuation, buddy. That look comes from somewhere much deeper. It comes from Your heart - and there is only one reason for it."

"Double damn. You're right," Rigel sighed. "So now I guess there are two things I have to do."

"What are they?" Sebastian raised his eyebrow.

"I guess I have to request to be taken off the case. I cannot solve the case and protect Jade when I have feelings for her. It would jeopardize the case," Rigel rubbed his chin.

"What's the other thing?"

"I have to tell her who I am. All of it. Before it goes any further. As much as it scares me."

"Then I guess it's good that it scares You."

"And why is it good?" Rigel asked, surprised by his best friend's words.

"Because that's when You know it's real," Sebastian nudged Rigel. Suddenly, frowned because Rocko started barking.

"What is it, Rocko?" Rigel wondered. "You never bark. What's wrong?"

"Maybe he saw a squirrel?" Sebastian chuckled, but since Rocko continued to bark, both men looked in the direction in which the dog was looking right before it took off.

'Son of a...!'

Rigel heard the words in his mind. He heard them, and it twisted his gut. They weren't alone. And, what made it worse, he didn't realize it sooner.

"Someone's out there Sebastian! Be careful!" Rigel shouted as Sebastian ran beside him. He didn't have his gun with him, and that made him worry for his best friend's life.

"Damn it!" Sebastian yelled out as whoever they were running after ran between the trees and hopped in a white sedan, speeding off.

"Damn it is right!" Rigel hissed out.

"Who do You think it was?" Sebastian tried to catch his breath and bent down to pet Rocko's head. "Good boy, Rocko! Good boy!"

"Whoever it was, they didn't come all this way for sightseeing. There's nothing here except the trees and us," Rigel grit his teeth and swore.

"How long do You think he stood there?" Sebastian straightened out and looked back at their campsite.

"That's not the point. I am more interested in how he knew where to find us? Or rather, where to find Jade?" Rigel swore once more and gestured for them to head back to where the mystery intruder stood when they first saw him. "Let's see if he left anything behind."

"Driver's license, if we're lucky," Sebastian growled and followed his friend and Rocko to the spot where the man stood a moment ago.

"Well..." Rigel said out loud and crouched down to examine several little piles of cigarette butts. "Damn it. Whoever that guy was, he must have watched us for days. These piles are all soaked from the rain. But his pile is dry, most likely from today."

"Son of a..." Sebastian began to speak but Rigel interrupted him.

"That's exactly what he thought when I looked at him," Rigel rose to his feet.

"So that means he came here with a purpose. And he came here because of Jade."

"Damn it," Rigel fisted his hands and nodded. "Let's get a few of these cigarette butts so I can ask the lab to run a DNA test to see if they can find anything. Can You go back to the RV and get me a few plastic bags?"

"You bet," Sebastian agreed, but paused. "Hey, Rigel? Maybe it's best we don't mention it to the others? You know how they would react. Especially Jade."

"You're right," Rigel nodded.

"But You also know what You have to do now, right?" Sebastian sighed, aware of the inevitable and how that would make Rigel feel.

"Unfortunately," Rigel sighed with full understanding he would have to reach out to his brothers…

≈ Chapter 24 ≈

Friday. The day which usually signified maximized effort and twice as much concentration. And this time, it was so much more than that to Rigel. Why? Because by the end of the day he would have done what he had never done in all his life, during all of his career as a Police Officer. He was going to ask to be taken off the case that began with the serendipitous meeting between him and Jade.

Staring at the empty mug with an acoustic guitar-shaped handle beside the monitor on his desk at the precinct, Rigel was lost in his thoughts about the unsolved Police Officers' murders. Did he want to solve the case? And not just this one but, all of the unsolved cases secretly piled up at his desk that only Nicholetta knew about? Yes, a loud and indisputable yes. However... He believed in the letter of the law. He'd witnessed too many times where the law was broken, battered, and crushed under the foot of those who disregarded it. So, he knew what he had to do. Even if it meant surrendering the reigns to the murder case at the Mayor's Office and handing it over to someone else.

Were the murders linked? Of course. He knew it in his mind and in his gut. After all, the repeated and presumably solved murders on Police Officers weren't a coincidence. Not to him. The men in uniform who lost their lives weren't new to the force. They were seasoned cops. And he wasn't going to allow another one of his colleagues to be checked off as a victim of a simple robbery. Not this time. NOT. THIS. TIME.

Even though prior murders of the Police Officers were labeled as robberies-gone-wrong and dismissed as unfortunate, Rigel knew the Mayor's Office murder case was going to change that. Regardless of whether he led the investigation or not. As such, he needed the case to be as streamlined and as clean to prosecute as possible. There was an invisible link between the murders. There had to be. And something told him he was getting close to finding the first piece of the puzzle. He would just have to choose what to do with it. Or when to reveal it...

"More coffee?" Alex's unexpected question shook Rigel back to reality.

"That depends," Rigel replied without looking up from the file containing documentation surrounding the murder at the City Hall.

"What does it depend on, Happyski?" Alex sat on the edge of Rigel's desk and extended his arm with the spare cup of his famously infamous coffee toward Rigel.

"On whether it was delivered here or made by You," Rigel sighed heavily but managed to grin at his partner.

"Ouch," Alex retrieved the offered coffee cup. "You didn't mind my coffee in Chattanooga?"

"That's because Maria made up for it with her onion bagels," Rigel's grin widened briefly at the thought of the taste of Maria's homemade bagels. "It's obvious You married her for her amazing cooking skills, but I still wonder to this day what she married You for?"

"She married me for my great looks and my mad coffee skills," Alex announced with pride but frowned when those around them burst out in laughter.

"Don't worry, they only laughed at Your coffee reference," Rigel chuckled, feeling better momentarily. He rose to his feet, gathered the files on his desk, and patted Alex's arm. "I'm sure Your coffee skills will improve someday."

"That was rude, Happyski!" Alex called out after his partner, who was on his way to Nicholetta's office.

"What can I say, Stepka? I like honesty," Rigel opened his arms wide and flashed his pearly whites.

"That doesn't always work in Your favor!" Alex called out after him.

"Perhaps, but neither does lying," Rigel clicked his tongue, turned around, and stopped by Nicholetta's office door.

"What is it, Happyski? If You came to ask if You can skip the President's Gala tomorrow, the answer is no. Mayor Lucchese requested Your presence there," Nicholetta said grimly as she sat behind her desk.

"I agreed to go, but last time I checked my job description didn't include any mention of being at Lucchese's personal disposal."

"And You would be right. However, the President and the First Lady will be there, and the Mayor wants to ensure all safety measures are taken in case there is a threat," Nicholetta responded with stoic calmness.

"I doubt anyone would bother with the Mayor as a target if he'll be in the room with J.J. Monroe," Rigel chuckled, amused to say the least.

"I would reconsider that statement," Nicholetta shook her head. "The Mayor is the Mayor, and I would think You may have heard about the threats on the President's life in the recent past?"

"I... may have heard something about that."

"Then You will agree the President's Gala will benefit from Your benevolent presence."

"I did agree to go, didn't I?"

"Yes," Nicholetta nodded. "So, why the visit to my office right before the end of the shift? If You want to ask me again for a budget for the tuxedo rental for tomorrow night, the answer is still a NO."

"I got that covered from all the lucky pennies I picked up on the graveyard shifts," Rigel chuckled but the smile did not reach his eyes, which Nicholetta always recognized as a sign of bad news when it came to her best Detective.

"It's all about the pleasantries with You, Happyski," Nicholetta nodded in silent agreement. "Come in and close the door."

"I hate black tie events." Rigel closed the door, sat down in the chair opposite Nicholetta.

"Maybe so, but I bet trading Your weathered leather jacket for a fitted suit might get You some female fans," Nicholetta tipped her head to the side and narrowed her eyes on Rigel when he did not flash his trademark grin at her. "All right, Detective Brzozakiewiczowicz. What is it?"

"It scares me when say my last name," Rigel straightened in the chair.

"It scares me when You have that stoic distant look in Your eyes," Nicholetta sighed. "What's wrong?"

"I wouldn't say that something's wrong. But..." He handed the top file he carried with him to Nicholetta containing the case of the murder at the Mayor's Office.

"Don't tell me You solved it?" She raised her eyebrows and leaned forward to accept the file.

"Not exactly."

"No? But You did make progress in the case?"

"You might say that."

"What does that mean?" Nicholetta took her glasses off and linked her fingers together.

"Well... I decided to look at the cases from a different angle. I didn't look for the suspect. I looked at the murder victims themselves and who they were."

"Did You find anything that could possibly link the cases?" Nicholetta looked toward the door to ensure they were closed.

"You might say that."

"Repeat those words again and I'll make You wear a tuxedo for a week," she grinned. "Now, what did You find?"

"All the men, starting with the first murder years ago, were Police Officers with at least ten years of experience on the force. They were from the wealthy city precincts. They were all gunned down at night, during the graveyard shift, but on their night off. With no witnesses around. And the murders occurred in within their precincts limits, ruling out any cross-precinct jurisdiction investigations," he continued.

"Anything else?" Nicholetta raised her eyebrow, impressed, and sat back in her chair.

"They were experienced cops, Chief. Experienced. But when they died, neither one of them reached for their Glocks pistols. Not one. Their guns were still in the holsters."

"Which means?" Nicholetta asked but knew the answer down in her gut.

"Which means they knew the shooter - or shooters. And, what's more important and crucial to the cases, they all trusted the bad guys," Rigel stood, dropped the files on the chair, placing his hands at the hips.

"Bad guys? So, You think there are more than one?"

"The more I looked at the reports, the more evident it appeared there were two shooters, and two reasons for those shots."

"Why do You say that?" She closed the file in front of her, intrigued by Rigel's theory.

"I believe the three shots fired at these victims' chests were meant to kill them. They were all +P bullets, which means these murders couldn't have been simple robberies. If someone was trying to rob them, they would have used the cheapest bullets out there. Not these ones. Moreover, in each case the three shots were fired in close proximity to one another, which means whoever pulled the trigger knew what he was doing, and he was skilled."

"Assassin?" Nicholetta raised her eyebrows.

"No such thing," Rigel shook his head in denial. He would never admit to Nicholetta how he knew that, but that wasn't the way assassins worked. It simply wasn't.

"All right. What about the shots to the head?" Nicholetta opened the file and searched for the description of the fourth shot.

"That is my main point of contention and driving force for my argument of two shooters. All these reports indicate all the bullets were fired from one gun, and that they were all the same. They were not. Not to me. The photographs of the shell casings and bullets retrieved from the victims leave no doubt in my mind they were fired from two different guns. Even if the reports were written to omit that part. And there is one more thing," Rigel looked at her with intensity in his eyes. "I am convinced whoever shot at Jade and me is involved in these cases and is the person who executed the shots to the head on these guys."

"And You think it's Lucky?" Nicholetta closed the file again.

"Yes. I don't believe in coincidences. Nor do I believe in blind luck," he leaned forward on the chair's back. "Lucky made a mistake coming over Jade's house. He made another mistake shooting at us."

"Us?" Nicholetta narrowed her eyes on him because she heard the way he said the last word and realized instantly why she noticed a change in Rigel ever since he returned from Chattanooga.

"I... Yes." He walked over to her side and crouched down so he could whisper. "You know I believe in law, Chief."

"Yes," she agreed, anticipating what he was about to say.

"I am close to cracking this case. That's why I cannot jeopardize it," he paused. "I need to ask to be taken off the case."

"Rigel, I..." She began to answer but found that a few words would fit the sudden turn of events. "Why?"

"Because if this case gets cracked wide open, and we find these SOBs, there can be nothing undermining the evidence," he stood up and went back to lean against his chair.

"And what could possibly undermine it?" Nicholetta countered his argument.

"Me falling in love with the witness," he said quietly, knowing he could trust the Chief...

≈ **Chapter 25** ≈

Saturday evenings were meant for laid back moments. Beer in hand. Or a smooth whiskey drink. And friends gathered around the living room table or a bonfire. They were NOT meant for fitted tuxedos, uncomfortable shoes, or the stiff air filling rooms full of false smiles and empty words coming from those who Rigel never would have met if he hadn't been forced to attend the President's Gala at one of Chicago's most posh hotels.

Then again, he would have come to the hotel anyway, but not in a tuxedo. And definitely NOT because the Mayor requested his presence. There were, after all, back door entrances and secret pass codes. But such as it was, Detective Brzozakiewiczowicz had no other choice. He had to attend the Gala the Mayor Lucchese threw in honor of President J.J. Monroe and First Lady Eleonor Monroe. That - Rigel swore to himself - was the only consolation prize. Well, technically it wasn't the only one. After all, having friends in so-called high places enabled him to add a PLUS ONE to his invitation.

Would they cause a few heads to turn at the Gala? Rigel was certain of it. He gauged the evening with Jade by his side was going to prove quite interesting. Just how interesting? Even he could not have predicted how much. Not just for others, but most importantly for the two of them...

"Good evening, Detective," Aunt Aline's gentle voice caught Rigel by surprise. She opened the door to her house even before Rigel reached for the doorbell, leaving the screen door closed. Even more surprising, though, was the way Alsatian stood beside Aunt Aline and wagged his tail at Rigel, as if he was welcoming an old friend.

"Good... evening, ma'am," Rigel nodded with respect.

"What happened to Aunt Aline?" She immediately narrowed her eyes. "I thought Your loudmouth group of unreformed friends - with You at the forefront - decided to refer to me by my designation and name?"

"My apologies," Rigel inclined his head out of fear and respect. "May I come in, Aunt Aline?"

"I thought You were going to stand there in the snow," Aunt Aline flashed her wicked grin and made a welcoming gesture toward him.

"That thought... did cross my mind," Rigel smiled cautiously but took a swift step back and almost slipped on the snow-covered stairs when she opened the screen door and Alsatian jumped at him. However, instead of barking, the German Shepherd continued to wag his tail and waited for Rigel to... pet him.

"Good boy," Aunt Aline called the dog back. "Heel, Alsatian, we should not make Jade wait too long."

"Thank You," Rigel offered her a hesitant smile and walked inside.

"Good evening, Detective." Jade's mother welcomed him with a gentle smile as she stood behind the kitchen island and sipped on coffee.

"Good evening, ma'am," he replied politely and looked back at Aunt Aline because she chuckled under her breath.

'Kiss-up...'

He couldn't tell what amused him more: Aunt Aline's unexpectedly warm greeting at the door, or her mischievous thought just now.

"Jade will be ready in a moment," Eliana shook her head at Aunt Aline's chuckle, unaware of her sister-in-law's thoughts and looked back at Rigel. "Would You like some coffee?"

"Yes, I would very much appreciate it. I doubt there will be any good coffee served at the Gala." Saying so, Rigel unbuttoned his knee-length coat revealing the perfectly fitted tuxedo and a crisp white shirt, with the black tie completing the look. He walked toward the kitchen island and sat on one of the barstools.

"Now that's impressive," Aunt Aline raised her eyebrows. "You clean up nice for a Detective."

"Thank You, I think..." Rigel inclined his head at Aunt Aline, thrown off by the sudden change in her behavior.

"You sure do, Detective," Jade's delicate voice caused Rigel to turn his gaze from Aunt Aline toward the door to Jade's bedroom. In it, he saw a woman who stopped the air flow to his lungs, and blood supply to his heart. He was certain his knees would have buckled if he had been standing when he saw her.

"You look pulchritudinous," Rigel whispered, taken with the way Jade looked in the tulle jade dress he bought for her on a whim of a gut feeling in the little vintage boutique in Chattanooga.

"What a flat compliment," Aunt Aline rolled her eyes.

"It was anything but flat, Aunt Aline," Jade replied to her Aunt without taking her eyes off Rigel. She may have considered him to be handsome before, but there was something enigmatic about the way he looked. "If anyone deserves such a veracious compliment, Detective, it is You."

"Do You know what they meant?" Aunt Aline asked Eliana and shook her head.

"No, but I am sure they do," Eliana passed the cup of freshly brewed coffee to Rigel, amused because she had to nudge him to even notice the cup in front of him.

"I didn't know You were going to wear a tuxedo?" Jade finally blinked, unable to take her eyes off Rigel. She walked up to the kitchen island, placed her hand on the countertop and balanced herself while slipping into thin and sleek black high heels that caused Rigel's mouth to run dry despite the hot coffee he was drinking.

"I was going to wear jeans, but the invitation did call for 'Black Tie and White Gloves'. As much as it pains me, I'd rather blend in than stand out. Though, I doubt we'll be able to blend in with You looking the way You do."

"Please tell me that is a good thing?" Jade paused with one of the shoes in her hand, too conscious of her reflection in the mirror just a moment ago.

"My dear, it is a very good thing," Eliana smiled.

"Oh," Jade nodded and looked at Rigel. "Shall we go?"

"Or maybe we can skip the whole thing and go for onion bagels?" Rigel waved his hand.

"Yes!" Jade beamed up at him.

"I wish," he chuckled. "Alright, let's go."

"What if the snow intensifies?" Aunt Aline asked suddenly, narrowing her eyes on Rigel.

"This is Chicago. The snow always intensifies at first, but ends up yielding half of the forecasted amount," he noted.

"What if it doesn't?" She responded in a way that caused Alsatian to growl. Rigel bit his lip to prevent a smirk from coming because Aunt Aline turned back into her suspicious and overprotective self.

"They have rooms at the hotel where the Gala will be held, Aline. I am sure Rigel will be able to figure something out. He's a grown man," Eliana scolded her sister-in-law.

"That's what I'm afraid of," Aunt Aline replied and pointed at Rigel. "You get separate rooms. You hear me?"

"Aunt Aline!" Jade scolded her. "Rigel is not that type of a man!"

"No?" Aunt Aline sized Rigel up and down. "You spend a weekend away from us with this man, and suddenly You trust him with Your life? What about Your dignity?"

"Aunt Aline," Rigel stood from the barstool and spoke as politely as he could. "I don't know what sort of men You may have dealt with in Your life, but I respect Jade. I also respect the fact she has her boundaries and stands by them. If You were wondering, nothing happened in Chattanooga. As to whether Jade can trust me with her life - or with her dignity - that is not and will not be a question in my mind. Ever."

"Nor in mine, Detective." Eliana inclined her head. There were aspects of the man standing before her she felt strongly about, but she knew this was not the place nor time to speak of them. Especially not in front of her sister-in-law. "I hope You will take care of Jade tonight. She feels overwhelmed in big crowds. Especially since one of the attendees at the Gala will be the President of the United States himself."

"She won't have to worry about feeling overwhelmed with him in the room. J.J. Monroe is a good man. Nonetheless, I will stand by her side, especially in front of the President."

"There will be a lot of people at the Gala. You don't think he'll know we will be there, right?" Jade asked and looked at him with worry.

"Jade, I don't see a way he won't know with You dressed this way," he chuckled but saw her eyes growing wider with even more worry. "Then again, he'll have to go through me if he'll want to dance with You."

"What?!?" Jade exclaimed.

"That was a joke, Jade," Eliana chuckled. "You better leave now, before she changes her mind."

"Can I?" Jade looked at Rigel with hope in her eyes.

"No," he laughed and helped her with her coat.

"Hey, it didn't hurt to ask."

"No, it didn't," Rigel laughed again. It did not hurt to ask. But with the way she glowed in the vintage jade tulle gown, there was no mistake in his mind Jade wasn't going to blend it. She was going to illuminate the evening by simply being herself. And he counted on it. More than he was willing to admit to himself when they left Aunt Aline's house.

As they approached the destination for the Gala, Rigel looked at the woman sitting beside him in his car and wondered how she would react to meeting the charismatic J.J. Monroe and the first Lady Eleonor Monroe. Then again, he wondered how they would react to meeting her…

≈ Chapter 26 ≈

Arriving at the President's Gala turned Jade's stomach. Truth be told, she agreed to accompany Rigel to his assignment at the request of the Mayor. But she thought they would stay in the background, behind the scenes. Most importantly, she thought wearing the tulle jade dress was a mere formality so they would not attract attention. After all, all eyes would be turned toward Mayor Lucchese, the President of the United States, and the First Lady.

Or, so she thought...

Standing at the entrance of the grand hotel where the Gala was to take place also turned Rigel's stomach, but for completely different reasons. He hated Black Tie events. He hated White Gloves events. Hated them. But there was a reason why he agreed to attend the Gala, and it had nothing to do with the Mayor. Even if the Mayor thought he held the upper hand over Rigel.

While Detective Rigel Brzozakiewiczowicz was a man who refused to see the validity in pretending anything, Rigel Alistair saw benefits in it - he would not have become the assassin that he was if he didn't. The more Rigel thought about the case, the more his gut feeling pushed him toward the notion that whoever stood behind the linked murders of high rank Police Officers was someone of influence in the city of Chicago. As such, Rigel figured a little game of chess with the attendees of the Gala was exactly what he needed to survive the next few hours and possibly come across a clue that would help him solve the unsolved cases...

"Do You think it was a good idea for me to come along with You?" Jade stopped, frozen with fear, as she exited Rigel's rented 2021 Ram 1500 TRX and saw the string of limousines waiting in line.

"I would say it was one of the best ideas I had in years," Rigel replied with confidence and a light smile as he surrendered the truck's keys to the valley driver.

"Then why do I feel so bad about it?" Jade stared at the woman who exited the limousine behind her. The woman wore gold from head to toe, and her hair looked like it had been styled for hours.

"You don't feel bad. You feel overqualified, my jewel," Rigel smiled at her, and knew referring to her by the nickname he liked to call her by would snap her out of her state of mind.

"I like when You call me that," Jade looked back at him and released an enormous bout of fear.

"Then I shall refer to You that way all night long," he tilted his head and took hold of her hand as he led her toward the hotel's main entrance.

'She's the one...'

Hearing those words again calmed Rigel more than he thought he needed it. Jade may have felt scared to come with him, but he felt ill to his stomach because of the atmosphere that he knew would await them. He attended his share of similar events back in the days of his assassin life. And he hated them all. He always felt sick to his stomach after attending them. His talent to read people's thoughts helped in his... trade. However, it proved more of a curse than a blessing at such events because of the darkness hiding in the minds of those whose hands he would come to shake. And it always took him days to rid his mind, and gut, of the dark energy of those who he cared not to remember from those events.

"Good evening, Sir. Ma'am." The young security woman greeted them with a wide smile as fake and cold as her pretended sincerity. "May I see Your invitations?"

"Here You go," Rigel took out the envelope from the inner pocket of his coat and passed it to the security woman.

"May I have Your names?" The woman asked as she took out the invitation from the envelope.

"Rigel Brzozakiewiczowicz and Jade Alistair," Rigel said calmly.

"The invitation lists only Your name, Sir," the security woman narrowed her eyes on Jade, causing instant knots of fear in her stomach. And since Rigel still held her hand, he felt the jolt of her fear as well.

"Please check Your system. The invitation was mailed out and then it was modified to include Ms. Alistair's name," he said calmly but firmly.

The moment the security woman typed Rigel's name into the system, one of the Secret Service agents appeared right behind her. "Detective Brzozakiewiczowicz and his guest of honor may proceed."

"Yes, Sir." The security woman almost curtsied to the Secret Service agent and inclined her head to Rigel while returning the invitation to him. "Enjoy the evening, Sir. Ma'am."

"Thank You," Rigel answered the security woman. He placed the invitation back into the inside pocket of his coat, sending a barely noticeable smirk to the Secret Service agent, who reciprocated the almost invisible gesture before disappearing.

"Who was that?" Jade whispered into Rigel's ear as they passed through the main doors into the hotel's main hallway.

"A good angel," Rigel winked at her as another young security woman approached them.

"Good evening, Sir. Ma'am. Please surrender Your coats and follow the signs to the Grand Ballroom. Please remember to put on the white gloves before entering the grand ballroom. If You did not bring any, we would be more than happy to provide them to You."

"Thank You very much. We have brought our own," Rigel grinned at the security woman and pulled out two sets of gloves from the pocket of the lapel on the inside of his knee-length coat.

"You've come prepared?" Jade raised her eyebrow when he passed a pair of long white satin gloves to her.

"Let's say tonight's requirement of white gloves works in favor of many," he smirked and placed the white gloves on his hands. "It may feel odd to You at first, and it is definitely something You don't see nowadays, but it is something that I am willing to abide by when the necessity calls for it."

"Why?" Jade asked, amused at his sudden philosophical statement.

"Because it matters," he whispered and left the rest unsaid.

"Detective Brzozakiewiczowicz?" Mayor's surprised tone of voice caused Jade to turn her head and direct her gaze from Rigel to Mayor Lucchese. "Jade?"

"Good evening, Mayor," Jade smiled shyly, and could have sworn her employer choked on air while saying her name. She just didn't know why.

"Mayor." Rigel greeted Vincent Lucchese with a dry tone.

"Good evening," Vincent Lucchese greeted them in the same dry tone of voice as Rigel's. "I did not know You were invited, Jade. Interns usually are not invited to these sorts of events, given the gravity of the Gala."

"She was invited. Just not by You," Rigel said stoically and kept his simmering temper at bay. The Mayor didn't realize it, but Jade certainly did.

"I see." Vincent Lucchese narrowed his eyes on Rigel as if he did not acknowledge Jade at all. If there was anything he hated more than being unaware of things, it was being upstaged. Especially by Rigel. "Enjoy the evening."

"I am sure we will." Rigel retorted firmly and led Jade toward the Grand Ballroom.

"So, You hate him?" Jade asked Rigel without looking back at her boss.

"The feeling is mutual, Jade. And it goes far beyond that basic human emotion," he explained as they made their way to their table.

"Why do You hate him?"

"This is not the time or place to go into details, but since You asked..." Rigel paused for a moment. "I was involved with his sister. Years ago."

"Oh," was all Jade could say because her throat locked up. She suddenly felt insecure, self-conscious, and inadequate. Above all, she realized Rigel was out of her league. He was not only the best Detective on Chicago's most prominent Task Forces, but now she found out he dated the Mayor's sister. She felt like leaving without turning back, without looking back.

The change in Jade's eyes did not go unnoticed to Rigel. He felt the urge to comfort her but did not know how. He leaned in and whispered words he thought would comfort her, but instead they made her feel even more self-conscious. "Camilla passed away years ago."

'But You would have still been with her if she were alive...?'

Though Rigel did not hear her words, preoccupied by looking for someone in the crowd gathered at the Gala, someone else did. Someone Jade never would have suspected...

≈ **Chapter 27** ≈

Sitting at the table by the windows overlooking the breathtaking view of Lake Michigan basked in the glory of the full moon, Jade tried to appear as though she was enjoying herself. But tried as she might, she could not maintain her smile for too long. She was bad at pretending, and even worse at small talk with men and women who judged her for the simple fact of looking better than they did.

From the moment they walked into the grand ballroom, Jade could not help but feel that people were looking at her. And she was right. But not because they thought she did not fit in due to her simple upbringing or her background. Oh, no. Everyone stared at her because she glowed in the vintage tulle jade dress. Where every woman in the grand ballroom drowned in jewels and diamonds from head to toe, Jade wore no jewelry at all aside from a delicate bracelet she always wore. And that... only made her stand out even more.

She may have thought it was a bad thing. She may have thought that the women in the room would make Rigel take notice of them. But she was wrong. Very, very wrong. He sat beside her. He held her hand in his. And he did not take his eyes off her. Not even during the Mayor's over pompous and dry speech welcoming the President of the United States and the First Lady. Much to Jade's surprise, the only time Rigel did look away from her was when the Presidential Pair walked into the room.

"You look tense?" Rigel moved his chair a bit closer to Jade's and wrapped his arm around her.

"Of course, I am tense," Jade whispered into his ear as the Mayor continued his speech consisting of multiple mentions overemphasizing the fact this was the only Gala the First Lady Eleonor Monroe had come to attend from the moment the world learned of her existence. "I feel so out of place. I don't even know how I am still breathing."

"I can find other things that may affect Your ability to breathe," Rigel whispered into her ear and gently ran the contour of her ear with the tip of his nose, sending bolts of unexpected desire through her body.

"Detective, how could You make me think about something like that in a place like this?" Jade turned to him and came dangerously close to his lips.

"But... I did make You think about something other than a place like this, didn't I?" He offered her a cocky grin, which caused her to look at his lips.

"Wicked man," she chuckled lightly and sighed.

"When it comes to You? Always," he winked and repeated the gesture he made with the tip of his nose, but this time did so with his thumb, followed by placing a strand of her hair behind her ear.

"You should not do that here."

"Oh?" Rigel opened his eyes wider and decided to send his thumb on a journey down the back of her neck, down her shoulder, all the way down her arm, ending the journey by the elbow. "You're right. Doing it... all the way there was a much better idea."

"Rigel, this is not helping." She could not stop her lips from forming an amused grin, much to the judgmental gazes of those seated at their table.

"Don't worry, my jewel. Soon the music will start and those staring at us will stare at the pairs on the dance floor, judging them," he whispered to Jade before straightening up in his chair. "But at least the food shouldn't be too bad. I hope."

And, surprisingly, it was not. As time passed, Rigel ensured to keep Jade's mind preoccupied with their food, their smiles, and their comments that allowed her to ease the ball of nerves in the pit of her stomach. It worked wonderfully, until the moment Rigel advised her that he needed to use the bathroom. She immediately rose from the table along with him.

With no other choice but to walk with her, Rigel directed their footsteps toward the high tables set along the wall near the luxuriously stocked bar. He ordered them a set of drinks, and asked Jade to keep watch over his whiskey. This way, she would keep her mind on his drink, and not on the fact that he would be gone from her side. It seemed like a good idea, until the Mayor decided to disturb her peace - with a leggy blonde beauty in a red-hot gown who appeared to be glued to his arm.

"I see that... Detective blew You off already?" Vincent Lucchese caught Jade by surprise. "You should have known better than to accept anything from that... bloke."

"Rigel went to the bathroom. He will return soon," Jade replied politely, nervous and utterly self-conscious because of the way Mayor's companion kept sizing her up and down.

"I thought You were less gullible, Jade." The Mayor plastered on a fake smile and kept it for a longer while because a few of the President's Secret Service men walked by. "You are a linguist, Jade. You should know when a man lies to You."

"I have no reason to believe Rigel would lie to me," Jade spoke as calmly as she could and counted seconds in her head so that she could look more at ease.

"That man is as unpleasant as half the men in uniform, but I may be biased. It seems odd he would consider bringing You along. I ordered him to come because I wanted to be sure I was protected. I would not have bothered if I knew he would spend more time paying attention to You than to my safety."

"I assure You, Sir, he does not pay more attention to me," Jade shook her head and caused the Mayor's companion to laugh.

The Mayor laughed as well, only to stop abruptly. "Camilla figured that out as well, but it was too late."

"I am sorry, Ma'am," Jade inclined her head at the woman beside the Mayor, thinking he was referring to his companion.

"Oh. No, dear." The woman tipped her head back, laughing in an unladylike manner. "Rigel is way below my standards. Vincent was referring to his sister."

"Oh?" Jade raised her eyebrow at the woman's double standard statement which seemed to go over the woman's own head but did not go unnoticed by the Mayor. He retracted his arm from the woman at once.

"Camilla is no longer with us because of that... poor excuse of a man," the Mayor hissed the words through his teeth and leaned in to ensure no one else but Jade heard him. "You stay away from him. He will never be good enough for anyone. He'll end up in a lonely dark place with no one to turn to."

"I believe You may be overstepping Your boundaries, Lucchese," Rigel's ice-cold tone matched the thunderous look in his eyes as he stepped up behind Jade and wrapped his arm around her. The way she leaned into him told him just how frightened she was by the Mayor's words. He swore under his breath and was about to offer stronger words to the Mayor when a figure appeared behind the Mayor's back that caused Rigel to straighten up.

"I believe You may be overstepping Your boundaries, Mayor," the man behind Vincent Lucchese's back repeated Rigel's words in a similar ice-cold tone of voice. Rigel watched with sweet pleasure as the Mayor swore - out loud - and turned around to respond to the unfortunate man who dared to insult him in public the same way Rigel did, only to realize it was the President of the United States of America himself.

"Pres.... President Monroe," the Mayor choked on his words as his mouth ran dry.

"Mayor Lucchese." J.J. Monroe smiled but all the Mayor saw was authority and disapproval in the President's eyes. "Is this the way You treat all guests attending events hosted by You?"

"No, Mr. President." Lucchese responded, sweating bullets.

"I see. Is this the way You treat Your employees, then?" The President tilted his head to the side.

"No, Mr. President." The Mayor shook his head with even more fear, which intensified as two Secret Service agents stepped up behind the President's back.

"I thought so." J.J. Monroe adjusted his stance, smiling from ear to ear, and patted the Mayor's arm so hard the Mayor took a step to the side. "I hope Ms. Alistair will remember this evening for its grand atmosphere and not for some poorly worded comments."

"I hope so as well, Mr. President," the Mayor replied as his face turned from pale to burgundy red. His face turned back to pale once again as J.J. Monroe extended his hand toward Jade, paying no attention whatsoever to the Mayor's blonde companion.

"I do believe I have not seen You on the dance floor as of yet this evening, Ms. Alistair?" J.J. grinned lightly at Jade but his grin grew to a full-blown smile when he looked at Rigel. "Am I right, Detective Brzozakiewiczowicz?"

'You like her...'

J.J.'s thoughts rang loud and clear in Rigel's mind. He grit his teeth and agreed with the President because he valued honesty - and their friendship. "Yes, Mr. President."

"I am afraid I am not a very good dancer, Mr. President," Jade curtsied at J.J. but since he kept his hand extended her way, she looked to Rigel for guidance.

"I am sure the Detective would permit me to lead You to Your first dance of the night," J.J. sent Rigel an all-telling look when Jade glanced at Rigel for guidance once more.

'Well, double damn. She likes You, too...'

"Yes, Mr. President." Rigel agreed again.

"Yes, Mr. President." Jade repeated Rigel's words, unaware of their unspoken conversation, and begged the heavens above for strength to keep up with a man like J.J. Monroe.

'All right, Happyski. Let's find out just how much she likes You. Because if I am right, You've found Yourself a keeper...'

"Yes, Mr. President." Rigel inclined his head at J.J.'s mischievous thoughts, and watched as the woman being led onto the dance floor by the President of the United States of America himself kept looking back at him...

≈ Chapter 28 ≈

With eyes searching for Rigel each time J.J. Monroe twirled her around the dance floor, Jade found herself stuck in a situation not even Aunt Aline would have believed. She was a small-town girl, from a country far from the riches and opportunities available in the United States of America. She was as shy as a mouse, and even more frightened than anyone else could have assumed. And yet, there she was, dancing in the middle of the Grand Ballroom dance floor with the President of the United States himself.

She held onto J.J. Monroe as hard as she could. Not because she wanted to make sure she wasn't dreaming. She did so for dear life. She had gone so far out of her comfort zone just to agree to accompany Rigel to the Gala. She wore the vintage tulle jade dress - a dress in which she virtually flew around the dance floor compliments of the President's suave dance moves. And much to her surprise, the man who held her hand was more interested in what she had to say as opposed to worrying about the gossiping crowd gathered around them.

"So, Ms. Alistair, I hope that poor excuse of a buffoon doesn't give You trouble on a daily basis?" J.J. asked a presumably innocent question and hoped Jade would relax enough for him to learn a thing or two about her feelings for his brother-in-law.

"Oh, no, Mr. President." Jade shook her head as they swayed to the gentle melody. "Rigel isn't really that big of a buffoon."

"Heavens, no!" J.J. bellowed out a hearty laugh, causing Rigel to narrow his eyes on them. "I was referring to the Mayor, but I think You may have just sparked my curiosity as to what Detective Happyski could have done to make You think of him in such a way."

"Rigel?" Jade asked shyly as her cheeks began to turn into darker shades of red. "He is a very good man."

"Is he now?" J.J. grew more serious. He raised his eyebrow and shot a direct look Rigel's way, allowing Rigel to read his thoughts loud and clear.

'She likes You, Detective. Points for You...'

"We may have met under unfortunate circumstances, but I am glad our paths have crossed," Jade spoke softly and decided that it may have been best to keep her thoughts on Rigel rather than on the fact she was dancing with the President.

"And does he behave as a gentleman should?" J.J. offered her a polite smile.

"Very much, Sir. Even if Aunt Aline doesn't believe him," Jade said before she could stop herself, and then scolded herself for saying too much.

"Who is Aunt Aline?"

"She is my father's sister. She moved to the States with my mother and myself when my father passed away. She is quite suspicious of Rigel."

"She is quite suspicious of Rigel? I like Your Aunt already," J.J. smiled, looking straight at Rigel again.

'Getting grilled by the family? I wonder how You feel about that, Happyski? Points for Aunt Aline...'

"Oh, Aunt Aline isn't too bad. She trusts him, even after we were shot at. She is grateful to him because he saved me," Jade said and paused with fear in her eyes. "I am so sorry, Mr. President. You did not need to hear about that."

"On the contrary, Ms. Alistair." J.J. shook his head, but something changed in the tone of his voice. "As the head of the country, it is my duty to be aware of everything that goes on around here."

"Even in Chicago?" Jade raised her eyebrows.

"Even here, Jade," J.J. inclined his head. "May I call You Jade? Titles feel too formal for me."

"Yes, Mr. President."

"Call me J.J. After all, Detective Happyski is a dear friend of mine."

"I am afraid I may not have the courage to call You by Your first name, Sir. I can barely gather enough courage not to fall or stumble right now," she admitted honestly.

"Alright," J.J. nodded. "Mr. President it is. For now. But the offer stands if You ever find the courage to call me by my name. I think Rigel would like that."

"Thank You, Mr. President," Jade smiled, relieved.

"Now, tell me more about the time You both were shot at?" J.J. turned them around so that he was facing Rigel.

"As You wish, Sir." Jade almost curtsied before him, which luckily went unnoticed due to the dress she wore and the fact that J.J. twirled her around. "Someone keeps following me. Rigel believes this person had something to do with the murder of the Police Officer discovered at the Mayor's Office."

"Interesting." J.J. said quietly and looked briefly at Rigel.

"Well, it isn't all that interesting when You think about it. You have gone through so much this past year that it is insignificant. But, there was this one time when I was scared, so I called Rigel to feel safer," she tried to explain but paused briefly at the recollection of the day they were shot at.

"You feel safer around Rigel?"

"Yes, Sir."

"Interesting." J.J. noted, sending another casual look Rigel's way.

'She likes You and she feels safe with You by her side. Double damn points for You...'

"Well, I do feel safer with him near me. And he does matter to me. That's why I pushed him out of the way when someone shot at us," Jade explained and suddenly realized just how strongly she felt about Rigel.

"You... pushed him out of the way?" J.J. paused just as the melody ended, masking his reaction.

"Yes, Sir," Jade whispered, unsure of what to do because they stood still in the middle of the dance floor. "Thank You for the dance, Mr. President."

"It was my pleasure." J.J. shook himself out of the astonished feeling that overcame him. "Let me walk You back to Detective Happyski."

"Thank You, Mr. President." She smiled with gratitude. "Do You think the First Lady was okay with me dancing with You?"

"I assure You she did not mind it one bit. As a matter of fact, she is grateful to You for putting up with my mediocre dance moves," J.J. chuckled and led her off the dance floor in the direction where Rigel stood beside the fuming Mayor.

"Sir, Your dance moves are not mediocre?" Jade looked up at J.J. and could hardly believe he referred to himself in such a term.

"That's what I keep telling him, but he insists my dance moves are superior to his," said a gentle voice from behind Jade's back. She turned around, startled, and almost fainted.

"Mrs. President," Jade managed to mumble in the direction of the First Lady who stood right behind her with her eyes locked on Jade. The midnight blue tulle dress with multiple intricate layers and her long braid cascading down one of the shoulders made Luna look like a vision. Her lack of jewelry aside from the wedding ring and a delicate diamond crescent moon pendant made the dress stand out even more.

"Please, call me Eleonor. Formal titles feel too... formal for me," Luna greeted Jade with a sincere smile.

"It is an honor to meet You, Ma'am," Jade replied and could not shake off the feeling that Luna looked not only into her eyes, but much deeper.

"Likewise." Luna inclined her head and slowly turned her gaze from Jade to Rigel. "Detective Happyski, would You please introduce Your guest?"

"With pleasure, Ma'am," Rigel flashed his cocky grin at Luna, fully aware referring to her that way sealed his unfortunate Fate for being scolded for it later. But he hoped that luck was on his side. "Please allow me to introduce to You my guest... Ms. Jade Alistair."

Rigel paused on purpose. He was aware of the way Luna would react. J.J. was aware of it as well. Well aware of it. That was why they wanted to prolong the meeting of the two women for as long as it was possible. Not because of Jade's feelings. But because of Luna's.

Luna blinked. Then blinked again. The rest of the world - or the room for that matter - did not exist for the next split seconds of time. Jade watched with fear in her eyes as the First Lady smiled faintly at her at, only to look up at Rigel, then at the President, to finally lean against her husband's arm. She did not say anything. She could not. And Rigel knew why. He also knew they needed to cover Luna's reaction with something which would make others take notice of that instead of the First Lady's current state. He looked at J.J. and realized J.J. thought of the same exact thing.

"It was a pleasure to meet You, Ms. Alistair. I hope Detective Happyski knows how lucky he is to have a woman like You by his side," J.J. spoke a bit louder than he would have liked as he embraced Luna and tried to figure out how to cause a diversion.

'Rigel, help!'

"Thank You, Mr. President." Rigel nodded at J.J. and uttered the first thing that came to his mind. "That is why I hope Jade would someday agree to marry me."

"What?" Jade shot a look at Rigel, almost causing him to take a step back.

"What?" J.J. blinked a couple of times, impressed by Rigel's quick thinking – or rather lack thereof.

"What?" Mayor Lucchese choked on air once again that evening.

"What?" Luna stood upright again, blinking herself into a state where she appeared to have regained full consciousness.

"That's right." Rigel nodded, panicked in a way not even Luna would have understood. She tried to read her brother's mind, but his mind went blank. Completely. And the only thing he could see, hear, or feel was Jade standing in front of him. Shocked as much as the rest of the room…

≈ **Chapter 29** ≈

The blank stare Rigel directed at Jade cut the air supply in her lungs. The evening went from stressful to electrifying to downright inconceivable. To say Jade felt uncomfortable as all eyes pierced through her, including J.J. Monroe's, would have been an understatement. Even the President himself was shocked to hear Rigel's admission.

And, to be honest, Jade wondered if Rigel was just as shocked as everyone else gathered around them. He stared at her. He wasn't looking at her, he only... stared. She was beginning to suspect he would soon faint or drop to his knees because he stopped breathing altogether.

Unsure of herself, and of what to do, Jade took her eyes off Rigel and looked at J.J. for help. That caused her head to spin. How could she describe in any conceivable terms she was hoping to receive help from the President of the United States when she had just met him? But, somehow, J.J. seemed to understand her without a single spoken word. He nodded gently and spoke up as if on the most rehearsed and practiced queue.

"Well, in that case I do wish You all the luck in the world, Detective." J.J. took a decisive step forward and patted Rigel's arm. He did so out of concern, even though it appeared as a mere formality to the rest of the world.

"Thank You, Mr. President." Jade smiled as wide as she could under the circumstances, linking her arm through his.

"I must say this comes as a bit of a surprise, Detective. Albeit, a pleasant surprise." Luna inclined her head. "Congratulations to You both."

"Thank You." Jade curtsied in response, unable to come up with any other way to reply to the First Lady.

"If You will excuse us, First Lady and I have a rather important call we have to make," J.J. spoke up and decided it was best to leave while Luna was still able to do so.

"It was a pleasure to meet You," Jade smiled faintly as the First Couple left the grand ballroom. She looked at Rigel. He looked down at her with the same blank stare. "Thank You for that rather elaborate declaration of Your feelings, Detective. Maybe we could speak about it a bit some other time?"

"Of course," Rigel moved as if on auto pilot. He was about to ask Jade to take a walk back to their table once the First Couple left the room, when the young hotel representative who advised them of the Gala's white gloves policy approached them.

"Detective, there is someone who wishes to speak with You. It is an urgent matter. Would You please come with me?"

"Do You know who could ask to speak with You?" Jade inquired out of concern.

"No clue," Rigel cut his response short. He knew who asked to see him, but instead of debating on the matter in front of everyone - including the suspicious Mayor himself - Rigel, took hold of Jade's hand, and gestured for her to follow him. "Let's go."

"This way, Sir." The hotel representative pointed them toward an elevator off to the side, leading up to the private penthouse suites.

"Rigel, are You sure You can trust whoever asked to see You?" Jade tugged at the sleeve of his perfectly fitted tuxedo.

"Yes," Rigel looked at her with... humor in his eyes. The sudden change in his stance surprised her.

"Should... I trust them?"

"Without a doubt," he leaned in and kissed the top of her head, surprising her even more with the display of affection.

"So, do You know who wants to speak with You?"

"Oh, yeah."

"Can You please tell me who it is?" Jade narrowed her eyebrows at his limited and elusive answers as the elevator door opened.

"My sister..." Rigel whispered and rushed to embrace the woman standing no more than a foot away from the elevator's door.

"Your... Your... who?" Jade blinked, trying to wrap her head around the image of the man she was falling in love with sharing a sincere embrace with the First Lady of the United States of America.

"Oh, hi Jade!" J.J. leaned out from behind Luna and greeted her in the most natural way.

"Hi..." Jade replied inaudibly, waving slowly at the President.

"Detective." P. Amber saluted Rigel in an informal way as he walked past the private elevator door, inclining his head at Jade. "Ms. Alistair."

"Sir." Jade repeated the slow hand wave gesture at P. Amber, recognizing him as the Secret Service agent who assisted them at the entrance to the hotel.

"I've missed You, baby sister!" Rigel exclaimed and continued to embrace Luna.

"We spoke last night, remember?" Luna tipped her head back to get a better look at her big brother. "Your memory sucks for a Detective."

"And Your manners suck for a First Lady," Rigel teased her back. "Do use more formal words if You're going to insult me."

"Ah, I've missed You!" Luna laughed and embraced him again.

"Speaking of manners, I seem to forget mine," Rigel loosened their embrace, extending a hand toward Jade. "Luna, this is Jade. Jade, this is my sister Luna."

"Pleasure to meet You." Jade curtsied before Luna for the second time that night.

"So, You're my future sister-in-law?" Luna chuckled and extended her hand toward Jade.

"I... I..." Jade mumbled. "To be honest, I am not sure why Rigel said that."

"I know why." J.J. chimed in and took a sip of his cold and smooth whiskey drink.

"Oh?" Jade raised her eyebrows.

"You pushed Rigel out of harm's way," J.J. said bluntly. "Men fall for women who save their lives."

"They do?" Jade replied, surprised.

"Did You?" Luna narrowed her eyes on Jade, only to direct her gaze at Rigel in the end. "Did she?"

"Um... Yes, though I am not sure how he found out about it," Rigel replied a bit bothered.

"My future sister-in-law told me," J.J. flashed his pearly whites at Rigel. "What can I say? I'm a smooth dancer."

"And not a mediocre one at all," Jade tried to sound confident, and smiled when J.J. understood her train of thought and bellowed out a laugh.

"See?" J.J. grinned. "I, too, have my talents."

"I never said You didn't," Luna laughed, but touched the side of her stomach.

"I am sorry about the way we met," Jade advised Luna because she felt guilty and all-too-conscious about the way Luna reacted to meeting her.

"Oh, sweet Jade, please do not apologize for it," Luna took hold of Jade's other hand, not only because she read Jade's thoughts but also because she felt guilty about making Jade feel that way. "I am very happy we met. My brother is very dear to me, and I am glad he finally found someone."

"I doubt Rigel knew what he said back there," Jade shook her head. "We just met. There must have been another reason why he said what he said."

"There was." J.J. crossed over to Luna, placing his hand at her belly. "We were worried about Luna's condition. But that does not discredit Rigel's proposal."

"Does that mean...?" Jade retrieved her hands slowly, worried about Luna's condition even more.

"Yes," Rigel smiled at his sister. "Luna is great at finding ways to cover up that growing beach ball and her inner glow, but she took the risk of coming to visit me."

"So, You did not come to Chicago at the invitation of the Mayor?" Jade looked at the Presidential Pair.

"Heavens, no!" J.J. laughed. "That buffoon is so into himself he barely noticed us. Dancing with You was the perfect opportunity to remind him who everyone at the Gala came to see."

"But why didn't the First Lady dance? After all, You two look beautiful together?" Jade asked them.

"I get dizzy on my feet. I may be tough, but this little gentleman demands as much rest as possible," Luna smirked and patted her belly.

"So, it will be a boy?" Jade smiled from ear to ear.

"Yup," J.J. nodded proudly.

"For now, we call him 'Seven'," Rigel chuckled.

"Why 'Seven'?" Jade tipped her head to the side.

"Tom picked it, and it stuck," Luna smirked.

"Is Tom Your nephew?" Jade asked Luna, unable to stop herself.

"No!" Rigel and Luna laughed in unison.

"Tom is our big brother," Luna added after a moment.

"You did mention having an older brother," Jade looked at Rigel. "But You did not mention having a sister?"

"That's because I don't exist," Luna inclined her head toward Jade. She trusted Rigel. Since he trusted Jade, she decided to trust Jade as well.

"I am not sure what You mean?" Jade frowned.

"Well, I do exist as Eleonor Monroe," Luna leaned against J.J. and embraced him. "But the person I was before I married J.J. no longer exists."

"I see," Jade nodded.

"Do You want to know why I reacted the way I did when Rigel revealed Your name?" Luna asked Jade.

"Yes, it would mean a lot to me," Jade replied with honesty.

"My real name is Luna Alistair. Jade Alistair was our mother," Luna said softly and placed her hand on her husband's shoulder for support, both physical and emotional…

≈ Chapter 30 ≈

Leaning back against the countertop of the grand island in the luxuriously decorated kitchen of the Presidential suite, Rigel twirled a glass of the smooth whiskey on the rocks in his hand and smiled to himself. Maybe, just maybe, Saturday evenings were meant for laid back moments after all. Maybe they were meant for family time, gathered in a living room, sincere laughs and memories meant to be cherished for years to come. And maybe... he was experiencing just that.

He sighed, silently enough for no one else to notice. Among the Secret Service agents going about their usual business, among other trusted staff that accompanied the Presidential Pair on the First Lady's first official trip outside of Washington D.C., there was his family. The family he missed so very much.

Though he never admitted to anyone, he did miss his family. He missed being a part of it, he missed his siblings, he missed his parents. In a way he could not put into words. Life crushed them all the day they learned of their parents' passing, and each Alistair sibling reacted to it in their own way. Tom revolted, Caelum disappeared, Perseus sought refuge deep in the mountains, Rasalas chose to devote his life to what he did best, Gunay switched from identity to identity, Luna transformed from a young girl to a woman virtually overnight.

As for him? Rigel chose to... close his heart because keeping it open proved too painful.

"You know, extensive overthinking has been proven to fry one's brain cells." J.J. leaned back against the countertop of the kitchen island beside Rigel.

"Says who?" Rigel replied to his brother-in-law without taking his eyes off the two women sitting on the sofa across the room from them.

"Says Your sister." J.J. brought his glass filled with whiskey on ice to his lips.

"Figures."

"I worry about You, brother."

"And why would You say that?"

"For a man who reads minds, You cannot see what Jade thinks when it comes to You." J.J.'s words caused Rigel to look at him.

"I don't know what You're talking about," Rigel took a sip of his drink.

"You don't?" J.J. tipped his head to the side. "Maybe so. But I've been where You are now. I know it's scary."

"I don't know what You're talking about," Rigel repeated himself and took another sip of his drink.

"Sure, You don't." J.J. shook his head, amused, and all-too aware of how Rigel felt. And he did not need to pretend to read minds to know so. "I fell in love with Your sister when I no longer believed love could happen to me. Feeling that way scared me down to the core. But what scared me more was the fear that it took too long for me to figure it out. That Luna might have disappeared from my life before I got a chance to ask her to stay by my side forever."

"You have a hell of a way to convey what You think," Rigel looked into his almost-empty whiskey glass.

"Nope. And Leo would agree I suck at it," J.J. smirked. "But I learned to speak up about the way I feel."

"I wonder why?" Rigel sent him a level look.

"Because I realized I would lose Luna if I kept my feelings for her to myself," J.J. paused for a moment. "Rigel, I was fortunate to have found love twice in my life. I loved Aurora's mother. But I realized what love really meant when I came face to face with the fact I might lose Your sister. I hope You and Jade find the kind of love Luna and I share. And I hope You will never have to beg the heavens above for Jade to live like I did when Luna was shot."

"Monroe, I..." Rigel wanted to speak, but his throat locked up.

"Alistair, I will never be able to repay You for the kindness You showed me when You told me where to find Luna," J.J. paused and looked down into his drink. When he looked up, Rigel saw nothing but sincerity in J.J.'s eyes. "I see the way You look at Jade. She is a special kind of a woman. If she wasn't, You would not have trusted her enough to bring her up here tonight. If You have feelings for her, don't wait to tell her about it. She may not be brave enough to wait that long."

"And Leo says You don't know how to prepare a speech on the go," Rigel chuckled nervously.

"That's because Leo's better at it. He'll make a damn good President this coming election," J.J. clicked his tongue and nodded in agreement. "As for Jade. She now knows who we are to You, and how much we mean to You. You need to figure out who she is to You, because the way I see it - You already know how much she means to You."

"Double damn."

"Got that right," J.J. patted Rigel's shoulder.

"I sure am glad Luna picked a good guy for a husband," Rigel clinked his glass against J.J.'s.

"You and me both, brother," J.J. saluted Rigel with his glass and drank the remaining whiskey in. "Let's see how badly the ladies gossiped about us."

"We did not," Luna spoke up too soon, making it obvious to both men she had been listening to their conversation.

"Sure, You didn't," Rigel chuckled and went to sit beside Jade.

"We did not." Luna mocked Rigel's response and leaned against J.J. when he sat behind her. "Well, not too much."

"Thank You for Your honesty," Rigel flashed his pearly whites at her.

"If You must know, we were speaking about Jade and her family. You, big brother, were nothing but an honorable mention during our conversation," Luna replied with a mischievous smirk.

"Ouch," Rigel grimaced.

"A much-deserved ouch," Luna smiled victoriously. "But Jade did mention Your hidden talents."

"Did she?" Rigel looked into Jade's eyes as she looked back at him. He smiled because he saw how intimidated she felt while sitting beside Luna and J.J., yet she tried her best to remain calm. He moved closer so she could lean against him if she needed to. That gesture made Jade feel more comfortable, and it did not go unnoticed to J.J. and Luna. "And what hidden talents do I possess?"

"Playing guitar, for instance." Luna wiggled her eyebrows at her brother. Jade took it as a sign of a sisterly love on Luna's part, but it was anything but innocent because Luna conveyed to Rigel how she felt about her presumed future sister-in-law. And she did so in her thoughts, where neither J.J. nor Jade could hear them.

'She is a keeper! I am so glad for You!'

"Sure." Rigel nodded and grit his teeth because he could not respond to Luna in a different manner since he did not want to make others aware of their silent conversation.

"Being a linguist is very impressive, I must say." Luna paid a compliment to Jade, and looked at Rigel.

'Is playing a guitar Your silly way to impress her?'

"I agree, it is quite impressive." Rigel replied and caused Luna to let out a laugh. Luna meant it as a response to Rigel's silent joke, but Jade felt self-conscious about her profession. Luna realized what she had done and immediately scolded Rigel for it.

'Not nice, Happyski! Don't play on words!'

"I bet knowing so many languages makes You a bit of an expert in Your field," Luna continued to speak to Jade despite feeling embarrassed.

'Oh, she IS an expert in the field of tongues and linguistics. Trust me!'

Rigel's mischievous thoughts caused Luna to laugh again. The fact he continued to wiggle his eyebrows did not help at all.

"Thank You," Jade inclined her head and looked at Rigel. She realized he had been making faces behind her back and narrowed her eyes on him. "Were You making fun of me all this time?"

"No," Rigel opened his eyes wider and shook his head.

"Should I call You by Your last name to make You fess up to the truth?" Jade scolded him.

'She knows You and Your honesty soft spot already! You're a goner!'

J.J.'s loud and clear thoughts caused Rigel to look at his brother-in-law. "I've heard that before."

"But I've never said that before?" Jade tilted her head.

"My apologies," Rigel replied to her and wished, just this once, for J.J. to have possessed the ability to read minds. If he did, Rigel would have been more than happy to tell J.J. how he felt about him at that very moment.

"Anyway," Luna chimed in after she figured out what was going on between both men. "Jade, You started to tell me how brave my brother was when he saved You from flying bullets?"

"She saved me," Rigel spoke up before Jade did.

"It wasn't important who saved who," Jade looked up at Rigel in a way that revealed to Luna how strong Jade's feelings were for her brother. "What's important is that Rigel did not get hurt."

"Well, like I said before Jade, men fall for women who save their lives," J.J. said matter-of-factly and kissed Luna's shoulder in a caring way. "So, technically, Rigel's impromptu proposal downstairs may have been a prelude to what's coming next."

"J.J. Monroe, it is not up to You to get these two to stand before the altar," Luna shook her head and patted her husband's hand.

"Before the... altar?" Jade blinked, surprised. "You cannot possibly think Rigel meant what he said earlier tonight?"

"Maybe?" J.J. grinned.

"Rigel?" Jade looked back at Rigel. "Now, hold Your chickens!"

"Chickens?" Luna and J.J. asked in unison and looked at each other.

"Horses," Rigel let out an amused laugh.

"Horses?" Luna and J.J. asked in unison, again, and looked at each other once more.

"Horses? What about horses?" Jade narrowed her eyebrows.

"You meant to say 'hold Your horses'. It's horses, not chickens, Jade." Rigel laughed, shook his head, and looked at J.J. and Luna's facial expressions. "She's a linguist."

"Huh." J.J. and Luna glanced at each other in silent understanding.

'You get her jokes? Oh, You definitely are a goner!'

J.J. congratulated himself on his rather exceptionally cognitive deduction of Rigel's state of mind, until he looked at his brother-in-law. And then, he understood why Rigel did not reply to his jab. Rigel didn't have a comeback not because he couldn't find the right words to reply. He simply took J.J.'s words to heart, and agreed with him...

≈ Chapter 31 ≈

Saying goodbye to Luna and his brother-in-law dampened Rigel's spirit. He knew J.J. was on a mission to support Vice President Leo Madison's run for the Presidential seat in the upcoming election. He also knew Luna accompanied J.J. on his visit to Chicago only because she missed her brother. And he knew how much it took for Luna to overcome her fear of appearing in the public.

But that wasn't all. Although he had known J.J. Monroe for a short time, Rigel accepted him as family. Without question, and not later, when Luna forgave J.J. for breaking her heart but from the day they met. J.J. was an honest man. Trustworthy. He had a good heart. And he was very much in love with Luna. That's why Rigel accepted him. He accepted the fact his baby sister opened her heart to someone. He accepted the fact that in doing so she showed more guts than all the Alistair brothers put together. And he hoped if it happened to Luna, it may, someday, happen to him.

And it did. Despite the fear twisting his gut.

Jade Alistair was a woman he never expected to meet. Likewise, she was a woman who did not pursue him. Nor was she a woman who hung on his every word. She did not. And the more he thought about it, the more he was beginning to see he was the one who pursued her. Whether he was ready for it or not.

"And that is why I sided with Tom and his brilliant plan," J.J. smiled from ear to ear, embracing Luna, as they stood and waited for the elevator door when Rigel and Jade were about to leave the Presidential suite.

"I already told You NO," Luna jabbed at her husband's ribs.

"But You must admit it's a brilliant plan," J.J. wiggled his eyebrows.

"No," Luna chuckled.

"Rigel, it is a brilliant plan, isn't it?" J.J. looked to his brother-in-law for support in the matter at hand.

"No." Rigel shook his head with amusement. "Not unless You follow this pregnancy with triplets or twins."

"Having twins is not that uncommon," Jade chimed in, feeling more and more comfortable in the company of the President and the First Lady. "I'm a twin."

"And Rigel's a triplet," J.J. pointed triumphantly at Rigel.

"Are You? I thought You said You only had an older brother," Jade tipped her head up at Rigel. "I've met Luna. So that's three. Do You have more siblings?"

"There's seven of us," Luna beamed at Jade.

"Seven?" Jade repeated slowly.

"What?" Luna looked at Rigel in a teasing way when he narrowed his eyes on her. "She's in the circle of trust. She should know what she's getting herself into."

"Luna," Rigel said her name, but feared saying anything more. He needed time to reveal the entire truth to Jade. And this wasn't the time nor place for it.

"I say seven IS a good number to count toward," J.J. spoke up, having realized the way Rigel was feeling.

"Well, let's see if this one resembles me or You, and then we'll talk," Luna patted her belly and they all looked toward the elevator door which opened.

"Thank You for visiting Chicago and for allowing me to meet You," Jade extended her hand toward Luna, who accepted it without any hesitation.

"Hey, don't thank us. Thank Rigel. He doesn't call in a favor unless it's important. And it looks like this time it was important," J.J. winked at Rigel. "Let that buffoon boss of Yours wonder how You were able to attend the Gala. If he keeps asking, tell him J.J. Monroe heard about Your exceptional dance skills, and he just had to get You on the roster."

"Thank You," Jade smiled shyly. "And You have my word I will not speak of this meeting or who You are to anyone."

"I know." Luna smiled and squeezed Jade's hand she was still holding. "The baby and I can feel it."

"You can?" Jade raised her eyebrows. "He can?"

"Yes," Rigel said mysteriously and crossed over to embrace Luna.

"It was really good to see You, Detective." Saying so, Luna leaned into Rigel's embrace and held onto him for a longer while. When she looked up, Jade saw tears in her eyes. "I will miss You."

"I know," Rigel sighed, noticing her teary eyes.

"But I won't miss these pregnancy hormones!" Luna exclaimed and wiped her tears away.

"Tell me about it!" J.J. chuckled and winced when Luna sucker-punched him.

"Didn't You say You want more kids?" Rigel teased him.

"Hey, it was Tom's idea, not mine," J.J. laughed.

"And how did he come up with seven?" Jade asked and watched as J.J. cut his laughter short and looked at Luna.

"No idea," the Presidential Pair said in unison.

"Interesting." Rigel raised his eyebrow.

"Not at all," Luna replied to her brother and embraced him one last time. "Promise me You'll visit soon."

"We will," Rigel replied before he could stop himself, and somehow did not feel regretful about it. "See You around, blue eyes."

"Blue eyes?" Jade looked up at Rigel, cognizant of the fact J.J. had hazel eyes.

"That's an inside joke," J.J. smiled and patted Rigel's shoulder. "It really was good to see You, brother."

"You, too." Rigel nodded and wrapped his arm around Jade's back, embracing her as if he had done so countless times.

"Double damn," J.J. smiled at Rigel.

"Double damn," Rigel repeated it and guided Jade toward the open elevator. "See You soon."

"Promise?" Luna smiled at him, and Rigel could hear her heavy sigh long after the elevator door closed.

"You are very fortunate to have a family like that," Jade leaned into the embrace Rigel continued as they rode down in the elevator. "Not everyone is this fortunate."

"What do You mean?" Rigel looked into her eyes, worried about the sudden sadness he heard in the tone of her voice. He intended to ask her about the way she felt when the elevator door opened to reveal Mayor Lucchese's fuming face.

"Where the hell have You been, Happyski?" The Mayor hissed through his teeth, almost spitting in Rigel's face.

"The name's Detective Brzozakiewiczowicz," Rigel kept his cool and spoke calmly, but Jade could feel the way his arm tensed up while wrapped behind her back. "I don't believe I owe You an explanation for my whereabouts when I'm off the clock, Mayor."

"Like hell, You're not!" The Mayor raised his voice loud enough for other Gala patrons gathered near the elevator to notice. "You're still on the clock!"

"I don't think so." Rigel tipped his head to the side, debating whether to read the Mayor's thoughts. He decided not to - for the Mayor's own good.

"Rigel didn't do anything wrong, Sir." Jade tried to defend Rigel, much to the Mayor's disapproval.

"You stay out of it." The enraged gaze in the Mayor's eyes scared Jade more than the tone of his voice. "I don't know who You bribed to come here with him, but it was a mistake. I ordered Happyski to attend the Gala for my protection, not to show off his momentary fling trophy."

"Never refer to Jade that way again." Rigel stepped up to the Mayor so swiftly, and so close to his face the man took a step back. "As for Your sudden interest in my work ethic, I am no longer on the clock."

"Like hell, You're not..." The Mayor repeated his own words, this time whispering them through his clenched teeth.

"I'm off the case, Lucchese. And I am not Your personal bodyguard," Rigel said calmly. "And whoever I choose to meet with on my own time is none of Your business."

"Is there a problem?" P. Amber's ice-cold voice startled Mayor Lucchese.

"No," the Mayor shook his head and took a step back from Rigel.

"The President had been notified of Your ill-timed argument, Mayor. He asked for the matter to be resolved immediately." P. Amber narrowed his eyes on the Mayor and sent an almost undetectable nod Rigel's way.

"Please send my sincere apologies to the President and the First Lady, and inform them we are leaving," Rigel advised P. Amber and took hold of Jade's hand.

"You cannot leave," the Mayor warned Rigel, paying no attention to P. Amber.

"Relax, Lucchese." Rigel leaned in toward the Mayor and made sure P. Amber heard what he had to say. "Your ego may be inflated, but with the President of the United States in the building, I doubt anyone would bother to come after You."

"You have no right to speak to me this way," the Mayor grit his teeth at Rigel.

"Likewise," Rigel straightened and directed his and Jade's footsteps toward the reception area to retrieve their coats.

They left the Gala at once. They left in silence. And drove in silence, until Rigel halted the truck's tires to a screeching stop on the side street in front of Chicago's Cloud Gate, now deserted in the middle of the night. Despite the heavily falling snow, Rigel needed to walk his fuming temper off. And he needed to do so before his anger got the better of him...

≈ Chapter 32 ≈

Anger was not the answer. It never was. Rigel was aware of it for years. He witnessed it daily, and he knew losing one's temper meant one was unable to control the situation on all other levels. Even if the situation itself seemed out of control. But he was at a loss for words.

His dislike of Vincent Lucchese began the moment they met. Rigel understood being protective over one's sister. Heavens knew, he understood it. However, Vincent Lucchese made up his mind about Rigel even before they met. Status, class, and upbringing mattered to Lucchese more than his sister's feelings. When Camilla Lucchese introduced Rigel to her big brother, it took Rigel one look at Vincent to figure out they would not see eye-to-eye. And it wasn't because Vincent judged Rigel for being who he was. Vincent judged him for not being the man he should have been - he was not influential enough for his sister.

That didn't hurt Rigel. The way he saw it, those who judged others for having low standards usually lacked them themselves. What hurt Rigel was the fact Camilla decided to side with Vincent one day. That day closed a chapter in Rigel's life which pertained to trusting someone, loving someone in one-of-a-kind way, or even hoping for that kind of a connection with someone.

It all changed the moment he realized he had feelings for Jade. It sickened him to think Lucchese had the audacity to insult Jade. Worst of all, in the company of P. Amber and everyone gathered near them - and loud enough for J.J. and

Luna to hear of his insults. That level of disgust with the Mayor triggered Rigel's temper. So much so, that he felt the urge to walk it off. Because if he hadn't, he knew he would eventually end up taking the anger out on Jade. And it would cause him to hate himself for it in the end.

"I am sorry," Jade whispered quietly, standing behind Rigel after he finally decided to stop his fast-paced flounce few feet away from the Cloud Gate's grand mirror-like monument structure.

"Sorry? Why would You feel the need to apologize?" Rigel half-turned toward her, though he still faced the monument.

"I..." she paused and turned away from him, facing the streetlamps of the Magnificent Mile illuminating her face. Somehow, speaking to him with her back against his, not looking at his face, made her feel more confident. "You wouldn't have gotten yelled at if I had not come along with You."

"And I would not have realized how much You mean to me if I hadn't had the guts to ask You to come with me tonight," he said before he could stop himself.

"That is not a good way of changing the subject, Detective."

"I did not change the subject," Rigel replied and instead of turning toward her completely, chose to look up and searched for their reflection in the snow-covered mirror surface of the Cloud Gate. He narrowed his eyes and smiled lightly because he saw the little images of their silhouettes among the reflections of the dark building and yellowish glows of the streetlights.

"You did change the subject," Jade countered his response and winced as the soft large snowflakes falling gently from the sky fell upon her cheeks. "I did not think coming with You tonight would have angered the Mayor so much. That makes me feel twice as guilty."

"Can we not speak about that... piss-poor thickheaded ignoramus? My gut won't stand it," Rigel clenched his jaw. "He should not have insulted You. You didn't do anything wrong."

"And neither did You." Jade closed her eyes and realized she was beginning to feel angry - and that sort of feeling was new to her.

"Why are You angry?"

"How do You know I just felt that?" Jade opened her eyes and looked back at him without turning around fully just yet.

"I... saw it in Your facial expression," he replied quickly, mad at himself because he let his guard down and read her thoughts unconsciously again, just as he did the day Jade visited his precinct for the first time.

"But You were not looking at me?"

"I was." Rigel replied in short. He was panicking. Was he panicking? Yes, he was. Was he ready to reveal the truth to her? No, he wasn't. Not yet. Not just yet. "I... saw Your face in the Cloud Gate."

"Only a man with superpowers could see the faces in the Bean from this far," Jade chuckled and turned around. "You can't see us from this far. Don't You know the Bean was designed so You see everything else but not Yourself from this distance?"

"That... is a novel idea," he looked down and saw her standing beside him. The dimmed light of the night worked to his benefit because she did not notice the way his gaze changed at the notion of her referring to superpowers. He reached for her hand, now bare of the white satin glove, and smiled.

'She's the one...'

Jade looked down at their joined hands and then up, into his eyes. "Why are You smiling?"

He did not answer. Instead, he linked their fingers together and took a slow step toward the monument. Then another. And another.

"See? What did I tell You?" Jade said with sarcasm as they made their slow journey up the snow-covered sidewalk.

"Don't worry. Let's just keep walking," he grinned. They walked all the way up to the monument, stopping no more than an arm's length away from it. Their smiling faces looked back at them in the darkness illuminated by the light yellowish glow of the streetlamps.

"I did not realize how tall You are," she whispered more to herself.

"Must be the hair and the raised collar of the coat," Rigel chuckled, but grew serious. "That dress of Yours makes You look like a vision from another time and place."

"You want to hear something funny?" She felt a bit self-conscious and wanted to retrieve her hand to hug herself, but Rigel only tightened the grip on her hand.

"Tell me." He turned to her. His gut twisted because of the way she had to look up just to look into his eyes. The snow falling softly around them added an aura of mystery and the kind of desire he was no longer able to deny.

"When I saw myself in the mirror, wearing the dress, with the hair brushed to the side, I wished we could have been going to an empty ballroom, somewhere in the past long ago, instead of a Gala full of pretentious buffoons."

"I'll be sure to tell J.J. what You think of him," Rigel flashed his cocky grin.

"No!" She exclaimed, embarrassed. "That's not what I meant. Your brother-in-law is a wonderful man."

"I'll be sure to tell Luna what You think of her husband."

"No! That is not what I meant, either!" Jade shook her head, feeling awkward and scared, which was something he easily read in her eyes. "I don't consider him wonderful!"

"Oh?" Rigel's grin disappeared. "Is there... anyone You would consider wonderful?"

"No," she shook her head.

"Oh?"

"But there is someone I would consider unforgettable."

"And who is that?" He took a fraction of a step closer and wrapped his arm around her waist, still holding onto her other hand. He moved their joined hands behind her back, embracing her with both arms.

"The only man who wasn't afraid to see me for who I am," she whispered with the gleam of love in her eyes. She rose on her toes and kissed him.

The kiss shocked him as much as her words did. How many times had he hoped to say those words, exactly those words, to someone who would see him for who he was and accept him for who he was? All of him? The good and the bad?

"Jade... Jade Alistair..." he pried his lips away from hers, fully aware of how wretchedly painful it felt. His head spun, but it was no comparison to the way his heart pounded within his chest.

"Mhm?" She murmured, trying her best to catch her breath.

"If You could be anyone in the world, anyone, who would You be?"

'Yours...'

She did not answer the question out loud. She tried, but the moment that thought came to her, her throat locked up. She closed her eyes and looked down.

"Jade?" He whispered her name. And only that. The thought that locked up her throat also struck at his throat. And at his gut. And at his heart.

"Yes?"

"You want to hear something? But I am afraid it will not be funny."

"You are afraid?"

"It would take a linguist to twist my words around," he tipped his head, amused. "Yes, I am afraid of what I am about to say to You."

"What could a man like You be afraid to say?" Though she asked, she felt the answer before he offered it. And she realized why saying it out loud scared him. Hearing it out loud scared her as well.

"I love You Jade... I love You Jade Alistair," he whispered, hoping she would accept him for the man he was…

≈ Chapter 33 ≈

The silence that fell upon them gripped at Rigel's heart. He let his guard down. He opened his heart in a way he never did in his life, not even with Camilla Lucchese. Compared to the strength of his feelings for Jade, whatever he felt for Camilla seemed less significant than her brother's cynicism. That was as evident to him as it was fearsome.

Had he faced fear in the past? Yes. He had seen fear and grew accustomed to it as both an assassin and as a Police Officer, and conquered it with the confidence that ran through his veins. But as a man? That kind of fear struck him hard and stripped him bare of all his confidence. Why? Because he knew Jade's response would carry with it irreversible consequences, whichever way she would have decided to respond.

So, he waited. And waited. And as the undeniable signs of trepidation began to pull at his heartstrings, he heard it. Not from her lips, but from somewhere much deeper. Somewhere, where it mattered the most. Somewhere, where honesty left no room for doubt, indecision, or lies.

'I love You, Rigel. More than You know...'

He no longer waited for her lips to repeat what laid in her heart. She didn't need to. She did not have to. For a man with the ability to read what laid in people's hearts, to feel the depth of Jade's feelings for him almost forced tears in his eyes. The intensity, but more importantly the honesty of it, sent a wave of emotions from her heart, through their joined hands, right into his heart. He could not encompass all the feelings he felt at that moment. He could not describe it. He could not even speak up.

Unsure of herself, and afraid of the prolonged pause of silence between them, Jade laid the palm of her other hand on his chest. She could feel his heart pounding underneath it. She heard his heart batter within his chest before. But not this way. Not his loud. Even though the coat Rigel wore was thick, she could still hear his heartbeat. And she realized she was the one who caused his heart to quicken its pace.

"Rigel," Jade whispered, taking a deep breath. "I..."

"I know..." he breathed and lowered his lips to hers. The moment their lips met, he wanted to cup her face with both of his hands. But Jade tightened the grip on their linked hands, resting at the back of her waist. And he knew. He finally knew with unquestionable certainty that the words he heard when he took hold of her hand the day they met were his words, his own heart's admission. Not hers. That's why they sounded different. Because they came from deep within his own soul.

'She's the one...'

'She's the one...'

'She's the one...'

That thought repeated itself over and over in his mind. So much so, that he smiled for a moment, with her lips crushed against hers, though he did not stop the kiss. He couldn't. He didn't dare.

As their lips journeyed alongside their hearts, so did their feet. Unaware, and completely lost in each other, they began to sway. Side to side. Gently and unconsciously. After a while, they began to turn in circles, unknowingly allowing their bodies to move to the soundless melody their hearts set the pace to. They turned, around, and around, and around through the delicate layer of the freshly fallen snow. They danced ever so slowly underneath the Cloud Gate, underneath its mirror surface, from the Michigan Avenue side toward the side facing the Millennium Park.

"You sure take a breath away, Detective," Jade whispered as her head laid pressed against his chest after the kiss ended.

"I would say back at You, but I think You would just argue again that You are not a Detective."

"Something tells me You like to argue with me," she raised her head.

"That is unavoidable. Your mind works in a peculiar way."

"Peculiar? In what way?"

"In a way that twists my gut." He brushed a strand of her hair behind her ear. The soft large snowflakes in her hair added to her beauty. There was a part of him that wanted to wipe the snowflakes away, but the part of him that loved the way she looked refused to deny the snowflakes the chance of melting in her hair. And the way the moonlight caressed her face now as opposed to the streetlamps they left behind on the other side of the Cloud Gate added a level of surreal beauty Rigel had never come across in his life.

"I cause You indigestion?"

"Heavens, no!" Rigel bellowed out a laugh that echoed through the snowy night air. "How come You always twist my words?"

"I thought I twisted Your gut. Now I twist Your words? You are a confusing man, Rigel Brzozakiewiczowicz."

"Jade, I..." he grew much more serious. He wanted to tell her the truth. About his past. About his family. About who he was long ago. All of it, and all in one breath. But the sudden fear gripped at his heart. How would he find the courage? How would he find the right words? How would he confess what he had been hiding for so long? "You matter to me, Jade. I can see I matter to You as well."

"It does not take a Detective to figure out how I feel about You," she raised her hand to his cheek, and then looked in the direction of the monument. "Have You ever touched Your hand to the Cloud Gate?"

"What?"

"I have lived in Chicago for about two years now, but I never found the time to visit this place before. I always wanted to try it." Saying so, she released the grip on their joined hands, walked up to the monument and reached to touch it. She giggled at the piercing ice-cold sensation underneath the palm of her hand.

"Why would You want to touch it?" Rigel wondered, standing where he stood.

"It is tradition," Jade looked back at him, with her hand still pressed against the mirror-like surface. "It's like visiting France and eating frog legs."

"I'll keep that in mind." Rigel shrugged, recalling his brother's love for frog legs, and then grinned because he recalled J.J. Monroe's disgust whenever they brought up the notion of eating them. And because he smiled, he decided to join Jade. He walked up to the monument, and stood right behind her, placing his hand beside hers.

"You have big hands."

"That's right," he smirked. "Men tend to think size matters. It does, in my case."

"I'll keep that in mind," she laughed when he tickled the back of her neck with his other hand. She wanted to say more, but she saw the way he looked at her in their reflection in the Cloud Gate. There was something in his eyes. Something she never saw before. She felt the sudden change in the air, and it had nothing to do with the gentle breeze flowing underneath the monument. She looked down at her gown and realized it had been soaked almost up to her knees because of the snow that continued to fall as well as the layer of melted snow they danced through. "My goodness, how long have we been here?"

"Long enough to realize I may get in trouble with Aunt Aline if I bring You home in a dress that's soaked with snow," Rigel shrugged at the thought of Aunt Aline's angry face. "Then again, I may fear Alsatian's bite just as much as Your Aunt's bark."

"What if... she wouldn't find out about the state of my dress?"

"Those are some direct words, especially for a linguist. Are You sure You meant what You said?"

"Yes," she said in a trembling voice.

"Jade, I..." he paused. "I need You to be sure. There would be no turning back. I am a man of my word, but I also know I won't be able to stop..."

"I am sure." She placed her hand on his cheek. "I trust You."

And she showed him how honest she was with both of her statements. She was sure. She was sure of her feelings for him and of the way she hoped to be held by him. She also knew she trusted him. And that made the difference between the courage to stay by his side versus the fear of what awaited her at home if she dared to change her mind...

≈ **Chapter 34** ≈

They made it to Rigel's rented pickup truck in a seemingly civilized manner. Holding hands, brushing the snow off Jade's gown every so often, smiling from time to time, all the while the gleam in their eyes proved how much they cared about each other.

They drove through the deserted streets leading out of the Downtown area and leading toward the direction of Rigel's home. Again, in a seemingly civilized manner. Rigel tried his best to control whatever was going on in his mind, gut, heart, and everywhere else. He thanked heavens above Jade did not possess a gift for reading people's thoughts. Otherwise, she may not have thought of him as civilized, or restrained, for that matter.

Jade, for her part, thought the same exact thing. With one distinct difference. Rigel heard every thought of hers. Each. And. Every. Thought. All of it. What began as a restraint to keep his growing desire for the woman sitting beside him at bay, soon morphed into his growing... fascination with her thought process and the way she debated over the choice she made not to return to Aunt Aline's house for the night...

'Jade, You are shaking! Stop shaking...!'

"Are You cold?" Rigel asked, no more than three traffic lights away from his house.

"Why?" She looked at him, as if surprised at his question.

"You are shaking," he replied, making it a matter of utmost importance to keep up a stoic face.

'What will he think of You? Just say it's because of the snow!'

"Oh, I am fine, maybe it's the...."

"Must be the snow. Do You want me to turn the heat up?" He asked and bit his lip to prevent the coming smirk.

'What?!?'

"Oh, no, no. I am fine. It's hot enough in here," she replied, and then realized how it sounded.

"It is?"

'It is! No! That's not what I meant! Oh, for heaven's sake, it is!'

"Oh, it is just fine," she smiled and grit her teeth to stop herself from saying anything more foolish, or worse - out loud.

"Are You nervous?"

'Duh! Who wouldn't be?!? Wouldn't You be?!? Of course, You wouldn't!?! It's You, after all!!!'

"No." She whispered through her teeth while pretending to smile.

"Alright." He nodded and looked out the window as they made it onto his street. And then, he heard her... growling at herself. He looked back in one swift move, unable to dismiss that little detail. "Did You... just growl?"

"No," she shook her head.

'Yes!'

"No?" He repeated after her.

"No." She denied it again.

'Fine, Yes! Yes!! Yes!!! Can't a woman growl in peace?!?'

"Jade Alistair, if a woman wants to growl, at herself or otherwise, it is her business," he could not resist. He just couldn't. "But if You do, at least own up to it."

"Fine!" She exclaimed when the truck came to a halt as Rigel parked it.

"Fine," he whispered under his nose, amused, and watched as Jade opened her door and... fell out of it into the little snowbank because she locked her eyes on him and did not look down when she set foot out of the car.

"Double damn!" Jade hissed out through her teeth and tried to rise from the snow, only to fall into it again because of the length of her tulle dress.

"You spend one evening with J.J. and You pick up his line?" He laughed and did not bother to hide it. He exited the truck, came around to help her, but realized she was fuming with a temper like her Aunt Aline, and as such, it was safer for him not to ask if she needed help.

"I most certainly did not spend an evening with that man!" Jade finally stood up, brushed the snow off her dress, and walked past him toward the front door of his house. "And I don't use someone's pickup lines!"

"Pickup lines?" Rigel raised his eyebrows. "I am afraid You misunderstood me, Ms. Alistair."

"Wouldn't be the first time!" She exclaimed and stomped up the staircase leading up to the door, while holding up her snow-soaked and now dirty dress.

"No, but this would..." he whirled her around and crushed her lips with such speed she didn't know if Rigel opened the front door or if they flew right through it. There was no patience in this kiss. Only urgency, desire, and the kind of yearning she could never have imagined.

'Who on earth kisses like THAT?!?'

Jade's thoughts clouded his mind as his lips left a trail down her neck. She tipped her head back, but then reached for his face and brought his lips back to hers.

"I do." He whispered against her lips, unaware Jade hadn't asked the question out loud.

Shocked, she opened her eyes and thought the first thing that came to her mind.

'I wonder if Alex's coffee tastes as bad as everyone says it does...'

"You think of Alex's coffee at a moment like THIS?!?" Rigel pried his lips away from hers.

"Rigel?" She froze from sheer shock and disbelief.

"What?!?"

"You... You really can read minds?"

"What?" He responded, shocked and surprised.

"You just read my mind," she said slowly, and watched as fear appeared in his eyes.

"Why would You say that?" He released her from embrace, pretending to check if he closed the front door.

"I thought of Alex's coffee. And You scolded me for it."

"Well, of course I did," he replied, nervous. "Anyone who says about his coffee deserves a good scolding."

"But I *thought* about it - I did not *say* it out loud," she brought her hands together, linking her fingers. The fragility of her demeanor, the shyness of it shook him. And it only meant one thing. The time had come for him to admit who he was, to reveal the truth. All of it.

"I..." he decided not to come any closer just yet. "You're right."

"I'm..." she choked up. "You... You really can hear my thoughts?"

"I'm afraid so."

"Why would You be afraid?" She narrowed her eyes on him.

"It is more of a burden than a blessing, Jade." He moved his shoulders up and down, resigned.

"I understand," she nodded. And then, she realized what his admission really meant. She raised her hands and covered her mouth. "Did You read my thoughts?"

"Yes," he nodded, afraid and aware he would have to accept it if she wanted to leave.

"You mean... all this time?"

"Yup."

"Like, all of them since the day we met?"

"Pretty much." He took a sip of water from the glass in his hand.

"You... You heard everything?" She tried to steady her breath. "Even the part about Alex's coffee at the precinct?"

"Why do You think I gulped up that muddy concoction that day?" He offered her half a smile.

"Did..." she swallowed hard. "Did You... hear me in the truck on the way here, too?!?"

"Mhm," he clicked his tongue. "Hey, I would get nervous, too. Especially since it really was hot in the truck."

"You ARE a wicked man, Rigel Brzozakiewiczowicz!" Jade scolded him, unaware that there was more. So much more.

"Rigel Alistair..." He stated calmly yet with barely the confidence needed to admit it all.

"Alistair?"

"My real name is Rigel Alistair. It's not Brzozakiewiczowicz. Luna didn't just reveal her name to You. It wasn't just her and my mother's last name. It's my last name as well," he explained quietly and sighed, waiting for a response from her. Any response. But she just stood there, staring at him. "And I used to be an assassin."

"Used... to... be?" Jade repeated the words among moments of prolonged pause.

"Yes. My siblings and I became assassins to avenge our parents' deaths. They were murdered for what they believed in. We tried our best to figure out who stood behind it, we still do, but I realized I needed more out of life." He set the glass on the kitchen island countertop and closed his eyes. Truth hurt. Rejection hurt even more. But what hurt the most was the disappointment that came with the realization he was too broken, too complicated, and too damaged to matter to someone else.

Then again...

"I love You, Rigel Alistair..."

The words he heard shocked his heart just as much as the sight of loving eyes that belonged to the woman standing right in front of him, reaching up to caress his cheek...

≈ Chapter 35 ≈

"Can You repeat what You just said?" Rigel needed to hear the words to be certain, if only once more, because his heart pounded both in his chest and in his ears.

"Should I do it with my thoughts? Or with my lips?" Jade smiled with so much love in her eyes that repeating her admission would have been unnecessary.

"Whichever You prefer."

"I love You, Rigel Alistair..." She crossed over to him, rose on her toes and kissed him, as gently as she could because somehow she felt he needed to be kissed in such a way. "I love You. I love You for the man You are now, for the man You were in the past, and for the man You will become in the future."

"Do You mean that?"

"I do. You can read my mind if You have any doubt in my words."

"Ouch."

"Can I ask You a question?"

"Ask."

"Your parents. How did they die?" She needed to know. For her own sake, but she felt speaking about it now mattered to Rigel as well.

"Well," he rubbed at his beard. He leaned back against the kitchen counter, crossing his arms at his chest. "We know they were murdered. We learned they were ambushed, and they died protecting and shielding each other."

"Rigel..." Jade brought her hands up and covered her lips, overcome with sorrow and compassion.

"You know what hurts the most about it? Aside from the obvious fact they were betrayed?"

"What?"

"Their bodies were never discovered. We couldn't even give them the proper burial they deserved because spies don't exist." Saying so, he turned around and leaned on the counter, closing his eyes because the last image of seeing his parents alive came to his mind.

"Spies?" Jade repeated after him. "As in, secret spies?"

"Not just secret spies," Rigel shook his head and looked grimly her way. "The kind of secret spies who worked with the government to uncover double agents."

"Did they... lose their lives because they were going to uncover those who worked against the country?" She continued to whisper, suddenly afraid to speak any louder.

"No, they lost their lives because they succeeded. But in doing so, they tugged at the deepest strings within the country and the government itself. Those who were discovered weren't ready - or prepared - to go down."

"They died at the hands of those who... hired them?" She didn't want to say it. Saying so out loud somehow made it sound even worse.

"More or less," Rigel lowered his head again. "But whoever did this failed to acknowledge one thing. Or rather, seven."

"You mean...?"

"Yup," he said bluntly with his head still down, and closed his eyes. "People forget that those who work undercover have families, that they have children, that they have lives just like the rest of humanity."

"And You think You can avenge Your parents' murders?" She asked and took a step toward him.

"Maybe not avenge - after all if we did that then we would be no better than those who did this to them," Rigel opened his eyes and noticed she stood right beside him. "But we've vowed we would figure out who stood behind the order. We owe it to them."

"Would You believe me if I told You when I said I loved You a moment ago, the amount of that love just doubled in size now?"

"It did?" Rigel looked from her eyes to her hand resting on his shoulder, then back up to her eyes. "Why?"

"Do You want to know why Aunt Aline is the way she is toward You?"

"Just me? Or men in general?"

"You, men, law enforcement."

"Why?" Jade's words intrigued him.

"My father was murdered in the name of so-called justice by those who were supposed to be upholding the law back where I am from," she took a deep breath. "Yours isn't the only family looking for answers, Rigel Alistair."

"Jade," he straightened his back. "How come I could never read that in Your mind?"

"Because I trained it to blank out the images I have lived with from the day my father died."

"Is that... why Your mind went blank the day we met?"

"Yes," she nodded. "Seeing that poor man lying on the floor breathless, motionless, lifeless, brought back the memory of seeing my father getting shot."

"Wait," he turned to her now and gripped at her arms. "You mean to tell me You saw Your father getting killed?"

"Mhm," she waves of tears flooded her eyes. "My family heard the shots. But I saw it all. They thought I didn't see anything because I was the last one to run out of the house. But they did not realize the reason why I rushed last to my father's lifeless body lying in the street in front of our house was because I saw everything from my bedroom window."

"Oh, Jade." He brought her close and wrapped his arms around her. She trembled, she sobbed, she reached out for him in a way that felt so natural to them both. They stood holding each other for a long time. Not because she needed it, but because they both needed it. As painful as it was to admit, Rigel understood then and there that the threads of their lives somehow connected in that moment. Whatever they went through in their past crushed both of their hearts, and it left them broken. But, as serendipitous as it may seem, life offered them a chance to piece their hearts and lives back together by finding each other. Whether they were ready to accept it or not.

"The day someone fired shots at us at my house wasn't the first time I saw the red laser dot being pointed at someone," she tried to speak calmly, but the sobs denied her that luxury. "Seeing it pointed at Your back scared me more than I will ever be able to put into words. The images of those red dots pointed at my father in the darkness of the night, under the faint light of the streetlamps in front of our house etched themselves in my mind. It took me a long time to overcome the nightmares that kept coming back. They still do from time to time."

"Is that why You tossed and turned at night in Chattanooga?"

"You watched me sleep?" She looked up and had to tip her head back to look into his eyes because of the closeness of their embrace.

"I tend not to sleep on the watch."

"All work? No rest or play?"

"Well, it wasn't all work..."

"I'm cold," she shivered suddenly. His gentle caress calmed her down enough to finally acknowledge the state of her dress.

"I'll keep You warm." Saying so, he deepened his embrace to make sure she felt safer and warmer.

"That is a novel idea, but something tells me we'll both catch a cold if I stay in this soaked dress any longer," she giggled and held the skirt of her dress up. "And we need to do something about these stains. Aunt Aline is a stickler to details."

"Right," he looked down and realized the bottom of his tuxedo trousers were in no better condition. "Let's get these off."

"What?!?" Jade exclaimed. "Rigel Alistair, I've heard You are a pretty direct man, but I hoped for a little bit of a romance before...."

"Ouch," he winced and gripped at his chest. "I don't think anyone's ego could survive such a blunt insult."

"I meant what I meant." Jade tipped her nose at him.

"And I said what I said," he mocked her while removing his tuxedo jacket, handing it to her. "Here, go to the bathroom and change into one of the spare shirts I keep in the towel closet. You can use the jacket if You still feel cold."

"Are You sure it does not need to be dry cleaned?" Jade accepted the tuxedo jacket and found it hard not to acknowledge the way he looked in the perfectly fitted white shirt.

'Heavens, help me...'

"First of all, we should be okay with the wash if I set it to Delicate. And second of all, I heard that," he sent her a smug grin.

"Not fair," she pointed at him. "And that half-smirk of Yours should come with a warning label."

"It does." He winked triumphantly and blew her a kiss on the way to the mud room to look for a laundry detergent that would cause the least amount of damage to the tulle dress. He felt even better when Jade growled at him for the second time that evening while closing the bathroom door behind her.

But the last laugh, or rather the last half-smirk, belonged to Jade the moment she emerged from the bathroom wearing his tuxedo jacket - and barely anything more…

≈ Chapter 36 ≈

Either the time stopped, or a second meant to follow its predecessor forgot the purpose for its existence. Looking at Jade, clad in the tuxedo jacket he loathed all evening long now forced him to acknowledge the fact that... he would end up keeping the rented jacket regardless of its cost. After all, the jacket fit Jade as if it was made for the sole intention of covering her curves.

He could have sworn all air supply escaped from his lungs as his throat locked up. And it did not end there. His dry mouth was the least of his problems. Complete lack of restraint was. The emotions and reactions he always knew how to keep at bay, whether as an assassin or a Detective, now betrayed him. His eyes locked on Jade as if she were the most dangerous target. And technically, she was, but for reasons he could not verbalize.

Then again...

"Heavens help me." He said, unaware he did so out loud and not in his mind.

"I heard that," Jade smirked as sparks of mischievous humor flashed in her eyes.

"What?" Rigel blinked, struck with the same amount of fear he ridiculed Jade for not long ago. "You can read my thoughts?"

"No." Jade shook her head slowly as her smirk grew into a full-blown grin. "But judging by what You just said, reading Your thoughts would have probably produced matching results."

"I didn't say anything," Rigel denied her allegation.

"We'll go with that, Detective," Jade bit her lower lip to prevent the coming chuckle and handed the tulle dress to Rigel. She doubled down on that bite when Rigel took the jade tulle dress from her and froze as if his mind suffered a major malfunction.

"Those are some legs," he said the moment he moved the dress further away from her exposing her bare legs, again unaware he did so out loud.

"They do go higher than the hem of the jacket," Jade announced sarcastically and wrapped the open jacket around her waist, covering it but exposing more of her thighs in the process.

"What?" Rigel blinked again, swallowing hard.

"My legs. Your jacket." She chuckled now, unable to keep a straight face any longer.

"What about my jacket?"

"What about my legs?"

"They go on for miles."

"I assure You someone with my height couldn't possibly own up to miles of long legs."

"Sometimes size matters, sometimes it's irrelevant in order to pack a punch, Ms. Alistair," he shot her a piercing gaze, raising the hair at the small of her neck.

"Were You referring to me? Or to Yourself?"

"Let us agree that Your question was never asked," he said with every intention of the words, and grit his teeth. "Either I've just gone blind, or I didn't see a shirt under that jacket?"

"You've run out of shirts," she moved her shoulders up and down and suddenly felt awkward. And undeniably uncomfortable in her own shy skin. "Don't worry, Detective. I don't have any intention of seducing You. Nor do I know how to act in a situation such as the one we seem to have found ourselves in."

"Why would You say that?" He leaned back against the washing machine, thrown off by her admission as well as the timing of it.

"I see the way You look at me right now. I assure You, I don't know how to do what You accuse me of in Your mind." Saying so, she hugged herself and walked into the kitchen, leaving him behind with a dumbfounded look on his face.

"And You have no right to accuse me of something that did not cross my mind at all," Rigel replied with a bit of a temper. He threw the dress into the washing machine in one swift move and walked to the kitchen.

It surprised him to find Jade sitting on the barstool by the kitchen island. She looked strong and confident when she walked away from him a moment ago. But the woman he saw appeared to be anything but that. She looked fragile and more affected by her bashfulness than she was leading him to believe. Somehow that image of her got to him. He smiled lightly to himself because it dawned on him how Jade's vulnerability and frailty only made her more attractive and more precious to him.

There was an unspoken calmness about her. And he realized why she moved his heart in a way he was unable to dismiss. She allowed him to see that part of her, the broken and unguarded part in which he saw... himself.

"I won't hold it against You if You'll want to drive me home after the dress dries," Jade said quietly and gathered whatever was left of her courage to be able to look at him. Her heart ached inside, and she felt as if she made a mistake thinking she could match up against someone like Rigel. Now she realized she wouldn't. Feelings were one thing, but the thought of intimacy was another, especially with him.

"You might not, but I would." He stood by the refrigerator, with arms crossed at his chest, and wondered what caused the change in her so quickly.

"Why would You? I am not capable of whatever it was You were hoping to achieve or accomplish tonight."

"That is a bit judgmental. Don't I get to have a say in what I hope for?" He tipped his head to the side and debated whether to read Jade's mind or whether to walk up to her to take hold of her hand. He opted for the latter because pride was not the issue here - their future was. The moment that thought crossed his mind, he grew serious because he knew what that meant.

"You do. Of course, You do," she nodded as knots tightened in her stomach. "But sometimes hope fails, and disappointment sets in."

"You preach to the choir." He chuckled, involuntarily, at the brutal accuracy of her statement. "Tell me, Jade, have You ever been in love?"

"Once," she whispered and dared not to add that she was looking at the only man she had ever fallen for.

Even though he asked the question, hearing Jade had fallen in love before jabbed at his heart. Some were more fortunate than others, he thought. "Did it matter how experienced or how direct that man was?"

"No."

"Then what mattered?" He crossed over to her side of the kitchen island and leaned on it next to where Jade sat.

"It mattered how I felt with him by my side."

"And how did You feel?"

"I felt safe, protected, wanted..."

"Jade, this is not a precinct MUST HAVE list," he shook his head and stood up straight. "How did You feel?"

"Needed." She whispered with sincerity. "And accepted for the person I am."

"And do You think this... guy could have changed his mind because You thought of Yourself as inadequate in any way?" Saying it sucked. But he had a point to prove to her.

"No," she replied with signs of tears in her eyes. "At least I hope he won't."

"You hope he won't?" He raised his eyebrows. "Do You still have feelings for him?"

"Yes."

That was not the way he hoped the evening would turn out. Certainly, not the way he hoped she would answer. "Is that why You reacted the way You did a moment ago?"

"Yes."

"Jade..." He tried to say more, but his gut turned. Could she really have fooled him so much? Could she have led him on for so long? "If You still love him, I won't stand in Your way."

"What?" Jade raised her eyebrows. "For a Detective, and a mind reader, Your cognitive skills are worse than my... verbal skills," she chuckled unexpectedly. "Could someone really misunderstand me this much?"

"It would appear so." He tried to decide if he should bring her close or tug at her hair. "You are a universe of misunderstandings, Jade. Don't ever change that about You."

"I'm sorry," she inclined her head but dared not to rise from the barstool. There was so much she wished she could share with him, so much she wished he would understand.

"What are You apologizing for? For having the courage to be vulnerable and honest?"

"You don't play fair, Rigel Alistair."

"I have no intention of playing with You or Your feelings. Believe me."

"Believe You?"

"Yes. Believe me and trust Yourself with whatever happens next. Believe me and trust Yourself with whatever will come afterwards."

"I'm not very good at these things," she whispered with a trembling voice as she stood from the barstool and wrapped her arms around his waist.

"Jade, don't dismiss Your abilities when it comes to something You haven't yet experienced with me," he cupped her face and looked so deep into her eyes that fear no longer found any room in her heart. Nor in his....

≈ **Chapter 37** ≈

A wise person once said the route to the path yet undiscovered begins with a single step. The first step. The most important and crucial step. Why? Because that decision leaves behind the boundaries of one's comfort zone. Jade felt that exact way as she decided to trust herself and followed Rigel up the stairs of his home.

Holding his hand, she knew Rigel was aware of how she felt. It seemed like a scary concept, but it helped her somehow to know that in a way she was in charge of the situation. Rigel did not rush her. He guided her one milestone of a step at a time. One pounding beat of a heart at a time. As they reached the top of the staircase, Jade realized it wasn't so much fearsome as it was... metamorphic. Why? Because it dawned on her Rigel believed he could trust her enough to show her the side of him many weren't privileged to. And that made the difference between retracting back to her comfort zone and staying where she knew Rigel needed her.

"So, does this place look lonely to You?" Rigel asked as they stood at the foot of the second story open floor plan of his house.

"That is just about the most lame and primitive pick-up line I have ever heard. It's bad, even for someone like You."

"What?" Rigel almost snapped his neck looking at her. "That was not a pick-up line."

"No?"

"Of course not," he denied with undertones of panic in his voice. "Besides, we are past the stage of pick-up lines."

"Then why did You ask me if this place looked lonely?"

"Do You remember the day we met? You showed up at my house and told me point blank my house looked lonely," Rigel tried to explain himself.

'Oh, right.... Those pecs and the unbuttoned jeans....'

"I... remember," she said and was about to ask why he smiled wickedly even before she spoke up, when she realized he read her thoughts. "Stop that."

"Stop what? Stop reading Your thoughts?" He sent her a mischievous half-wink. "Or stop smiling like a man who figured out he most likely fell in love the moment he opened the door and found a woman he never saw coming."

"You did not see me coming because I didn't tell You I would come by that night."

"That's not what I meant," he laughed, tipping his head back, and cupped her face with both hands. "And to think I fell in love with You before I knew how much more there was to You."

"Is that another pick-up line? Because if it is, You sure learn quickly," Jade smiled affectionately, and chuckled when Rigel growled at her witty assertion.

"I assure You, Jade, if my undeniable charm didn't work on You until now, no pick-up line would have, either." He lowered his lips to hers, ever so slowly, and only skimmed her lips with barely a touch. He knew what he was doing. He raised his head back and saw her eyes were still closed, as if in anticipation of the kiss that was to come but never did. "Now, that's an Alistair's take on a pick-up line, if I ever had one."

"Wicked, wicked man, is what You are, Detective," Jade whispered and licked her lips as if she was desperate to taste whatever skim of lips he offered to her. Rigel watched with silent amazement as she pressed her lips together and rose on her toes, trying to kiss him. He smiled triumphantly to himself and closed his eyes, waiting for her lips to crush his - and waited in vain. He opened his eyes to find Jade grinning from ear to ear. "Though, wickedly inexperienced, I should add. But who would listen to a linguist?"

"That... was clever. Remarkable, surprising, and alluring. But, be forewarned, karma is best served in the most unexpected of ways," he whispered and crushed Jade's lips with such passion she went placid against his chest, all but melting against it.

'Oh... my... taste buds....'

Jade's thoughts caused Rigel to pause momentarily. Worse yet, it caused him to grin, in the middle of the kiss, with his lips pressed against hers. She interrupted the kiss and took a decisive step back, placing hands at her hips. "That was rude!"

"No, that was enlightening," Rigel flashed his pearly whites in a purely cocky way. He winked at her and pointed at the wide-open tuxedo jacket which revealed a considerable amount of her skin. "But THAT's rude."

"In which way exactly?"

"In the most direct kind of way," he chuckled and decided it was best to put some momentary distance between them. He wanted Jade to feel comfortable, not just with him, but in his house as well. In his entire house. And this included his upstairs master bedroom. "But we'll get back to that soon."

"Mhm," she murmured.

"So, what do You think?" Rigel spread his arms a bit, allowing her a chance to look around the room.

"It's poorly lit," Jade said bluntly, unable to overlook the fact that although the second story open floor plan of Rigel's bedroom stretched the entire length of the house, it consisted of seven lamps, two tall vintage ones at each side of the king size bed, and five smaller lamps spread about the room, also vintage, matching the style of the minimalist decorum. There was no ceiling light, no recessed lighting, and not one main switch controlling all the lamps.

"I like poorly lit spaces."

"And vintage lamps."

"Not just lamps," he pointed to the Vintage Gibson 1962 Hummingbird acoustic guitar in the corner of the room.

"I see You bought a stand for the guitar?" She grinned at the memory of the evening they spent in Chattanooga sitting beside the bonfire listening to the melody created by his talented hands.

"I had the stand. It was a birthday gift from Eryk, Sebastian's brother," he said and grew quiet. "It stood empty for a long time."

"Did he...?" Jade wanted to ask but her throat locked up. Luckily, it took Rigel no time to figure out what she intended to ask.

"Yes. He gave it to me the day he died," Rigel inclined his head. "Eryk was a keen introvert with a sharp eye for detail. He wasn't born with any special skills or gifts like I was, but he could look at You and he would figure out what made You tick and what fueled Your hobbies and interests. I remember walking into the precinct and seeing this hideously wrapped contraption on my desk. He was a good friend but sucked at gift wrapping as much as Alex sucks at brewing coffee."

"It must mean a lot to You."

"It does." It dawned on him Jade was the first person, and quite frankly the only person he was not ashamed to admit it - or afraid to do so. Not even his siblings knew it. "After Eryk died I could not look at it, nor could I bring myself to throw it out. It was the only thing I received that day. The only present. He was the kind of guy who remembered Your birthday, and the birthdays of Your wife, husband, kids, and Your in-laws. Hell, he even remembered the day Our Chief adopted her dog from the pound. Winston received a new collar one year later to the date. Eryk called it Winston's doggieversary."

"Was he Your best friend?" Jade asked and walked cautiously from the guitar stand toward the plain vintage wooden desk alongside one of the walls. It was void of any papers, pens, staplers, aside from one small vintage lamp. She ran her hand across the top of the desk and gauged the desk must have served as a piece of decor as opposed to it serving its intended purpose. Though it appeared to be clean, it looked unused for weeks, if not months.

"He was. It still hurts when I think he died on my birthday. That guitar stand will always remind me of the day he lost his life," Rigel grit his teeth and leaned against one of the bare walls. "I should have listened to my gut. I should have gone with him wherever it was he was going to. He would have still been alive."

"Or You both would have died, and we never would have met," Jade replied with sadness in her voice. "I know how You feel about Eryk's passing. I have spent countless nights crying over the regret of not rushing to my father's side when the men who shot him came to see him. I believed for a long time I could have saved him. But it was a child's blind faith in her abilities."

"I... never thought of it that way," he rubbed at his beard.

"Did Eryk know about Your identity and ability to read minds?" She crossed over to him with her hands linked in front of her, making sure the tuxedo jacket stayed closed.

"He did not. Only Sebastian and now You are aware of it," he responded, feeling the sudden change in the air between them. There was something in Jade's eyes he did not see before. Something that twisted his stomach into knots. Something... unfamiliar.

"Can I ask You a question?" Though she felt self-conscious, she realized something while looking around the room.

"Ask."

"Why are there no photographs in Your house? "

"I don't know about You, but I've read somewhere that it's customary for a bunch of assassin siblings to try to hide their faces and identities - and their connections to each other."

"I may have read a thing or two about it. But that wasn't the reason for my question. Why aren't there any photographs of You? Not even one?"

"You really are keen on details, Detective Alistair," Rigel smirked and reached to caress her cheek. "Do You want to know why I don't have any photographs here or downstairs?"

"Yes. I wouldn't have asked if I didn't want to hear an answer," she took a step forward. "And I am not Detective Alistair, You are."

"All right, Ms. Linguist," he clicked his tongue. "The reason why there aren't any photographs around here is because if there were, every photograph would remind me how lonely and alone I feel."

"Not anymore," she wrapped her arms around him and made him believe in her words...

≈ **Chapter 38** ≈

The air around them kept spinning. Likewise, the surge of love filling Jade's heart caused it to spin cartwheels within her chest. She felt as if her heart grew with every beat of it. As impossible as it was, she really did feel that way. After all, how could her heart withstand all the emotions filling it to its brim?

She was aware she fell in love with the mysterious Rigel Brzozakiewiczowicz. Correction. She fell in love with Rigel Alistair. A maverick. A Detective. A... former assassin. He was all of that, and so much more. So inexplicably more...

"If I could come up with a music note for every heartbeat of Yours that drums within my mind right now, it would be enough to play an endless melody on that guitar for the rest of my life," Rigel tried to speak between breaths he so desperately fought to catch, while supporting himself on elbows alongside of her.

"That is a serious declaration, Detective," Jade smiled gently and caressed Rigel's hair which had fallen across his forehead.

"I've already proposed to You tonight. Consider this to be part of the fine print," he wiggled his eyebrows and kissed her.

" Someday You'll have to step it up a notch, and then what will You do?"

"I'll get the President to officiate over our marriage ceremony," Rigel chuckled, glad she chuckled as well, and kissed her once more. "He did mention it tonight."

"He mentioned a few other things."

"Oh? Like what?"

"He said that men fall for women who save them."

"Yeah. J.J. is a smart guy. My baby sister sure found a good man."

"Did she save him, too? I thought she only saved the President's daughter during the televised funeral for him?"

"She did. That's how they met," Rigel responded, kissing her again, and again, and again, until she raised her hand and held it against his chest.

"You know, I am trying to enjoy a moment of a civilized conversation here, but You are not helping."

"And I am trying to enjoy a moment - civilized or otherwise. And.... You.... Are.... Not.... Helping...," Rigel whispered back, kissing her between each of the last words he spoke.

"I should berate You for it, Detective. But I do have to admit You are a good kisser."

"Good? Just good?"

"All right. Let's agree You are a skilled Alistair."

"Skilled Alistair. I like that!" He announced triumphantly, running his tongue along his lips in a flirtatious way.

"You know, when You lick Your lips, You saturate Your own ego, Alistair.".

"Keep talking this way, and I'll have to put You on house arrest."

"That will not be possible. Aunt Aline would never allow it. Then again, she could come here and stay with us." She laughed, even more so when Rigel's eyes grew wider with fear.

"Forget I ever mentioned it."

"Done," Jade nodded and kissed him. She meant it as a light, gentle kiss. But he deepened the kiss. It grew more passionate. More demanding. Until she began to gasp for air. She tried to breathe, but he cupped her cheek with one hand, and rolled them again, with his other hand resting now underneath her. She laid on her back again, pressed between the sheets and him.

She gasped for air again, more and more aware of how difficult it was to breathe.

"Rigel...," she whispered against his lips, but did not get his attention. So, she decided to take a different approach.

'1... 2... 3... 4... 5... 6... 7....'

"Why are You counting? Was it that good?"

"I wouldn't say so," Jade rolled her eyes, amused. "Anyway, how could counting be linked to...?"

"Oh, it could. Believe me." Rigel cleared his throat, taking her statement as a direct jab at his ego. "Let me show You what 7 feels like...."

And he did. But in doing so, Rigel failed to foresee how much his understanding of what a relationship should or could be. Jade didn't take. She gave. She offered. And the more she offered of herself, the more Rigel longed to offer to her in return. What they shared went far beyond the physical attraction.

"How come You waited all this time to shine the light on Your... skills?" Rigel breathed heavily as his heart pounded uncontrollably with Jade resting in his arms. It never crossed his mind before meeting Jade someone yearned to be cuddled securely long after reaching... number 7.

"I assure You, Detective Happyski, I have no skills You could be referring to at this moment."

"If those weren't skills, I fear the day You'll gain some."

"You would blame me in a moment like this for Your inability to keep up?" She grinned in a smug way only to yelp when he turned them around. He pulled the covers above them, kissing her in pitch-black darkness.

"You couldn't possibly assume I would leave this sort of slander unanswered, would You? I'll have us counting 7 times 7 if I have to."

"If You think You can," she tried to sound mischievous, but Rigel noticed her voice began to tremble.

"What is it?" The question brought back a smile to Jade's face, even if a faint one. Since he asked, she took it as a sign Rigel valued her privacy. Just because he could, it did not automatically mean he would resort to reading her mind. And, somehow, it made what she had to say even more significant.

"You are a man of many layers. There are so many wonderful depths to You people don't see. You keep them buried. You keep them hidden," she spoke softly and slowly because it mattered that she said everything she needed to say. "Why me, Rigel? Why reveal them to me? What makes me different?"

"Because You're real." He replied with the kind of sincerity that begged for no light to reveal how honest he was. And it mattered to him more that he said it in pitch darkness. This way he trusted his other senses, relying on what Jade felt for him as opposed to being guided by the tone of their voices.

"There are many women who would show You how real they could be just to be able to spend time with a man like You. You cannot tell me You never noticed it."

"I... may have noticed it once, or twice." Rigel paused, debating whether to mention his past relationship with the Mayor's sister. "It isn't about showing how real someone could be with me. It's about feeling that they are."

"How so?".

"Life isn't about show & tell moments. Life is about feeling needed and accepted."

"Were You hurt in the past?" She asked but did not wait for an answer. "The Mayor's sister? Was she the reason why You closed Your heart?"

"Yes," he admitted. "Do You recall the way I reacted when You said I was savage?"

"Yes, I called You Detective Hunky that day, too."

"Permission granted to call me that. Anytime, any day," he grew serious again. "Sebastian was right, back in Chattanooga. I took it hard when Camilla lost her life. But he didn't know the whole story."

"The whole story?"

"He knows Camilla broke up with me. But he thinks she did so because I told her about my ability to read minds." He sighed, heavy with the burden of the memories and of his own past. "He doesn't know she reduced me to a ruthless nobody when I told her who I really was."

"How could she leave You after learning more about who You are as a person?" Jade shook her head. She often wondered why people dismissed honesty. Why they dismissed someone's leap of faith? Why they discarded open hearts yearning for love?

"Poetic notions of love aren't common these days, Jade," he clenched his jaw and turned to lay on his back, throwing the cover down, uncovering them.

"Maybe they should be?" She turned to him, laying her head on his chest. "It took me a long time to make peace with my father's passing. It took me an even longer time to understand how my mother was able to go on without my father holding her hand. But when we decided to move to Chicago, she told me something that made me understand life a little more."

"And what was that?"

"Love heals from within. It helps us survive the hardest of days. Once You find the kind of love that allows You to be who You are so You can grow and make the world a better place, time is irrelevant. Whether You spend a year or a decade with that person, their love will stay in You forever. Just like the rhythm of their heartbeat because at one point it matched Yours," she whispered and kissed the spot right above his heart.

"The universe speaks through Your words, Jade Alistair," he breathed the air out and kissed the top of her head.

"Those are my mother's words, but I'll gladly accept the compliment. I am a linguist, after all."

"You are more than that. So much more...." Suddenly Rigel sat up, causing Jade to sit up along with him.

"Is everything alright?"

"Indeed, it is." he brought her into his lap. "But we have a problem."

"What?"

"Your dress is stuck in the washer. Someone needs to throw it in the dryer. I don't want to leave the bed any more than You do. So, I suggest a challenge might help determine the poor soul who would be forced to make their way downstairs to take care of that."

"What challenge do You propose?"

"A counting challenge. First one to make it to 7 loses and must throw the dress in the dryer."

"Challenge accepted, though You might lose rather quickly. I have faith in Your skills."

And though she yelped rather loudly, surprised by Rigel's swift moves, it was nothing compared to the petrified yelp that escaped her lips as she decided to adjust the stand of the lamp flickering its faint light atop Rigel's barely used desk on her way down to the washer and dryer after losing the challenge. Not because the light of the lamp burned out, but because six hidden monitors appeared from inside the wall above the desk and lit up the moment Jade turned the lamp off...

≈ Chapter 39 ≈

Jade panicked. To say the least. She blinked. And blinked again. Although, she wasn't sure whether she did or not. She held her breath for what seemed like an eternity. Blinded by the bright lights coming from the six monitors that appeared from out of nowhere from behind the wall and began to turn on one by one, she didn't know if she should run, duck, or faint.

To make matters worse, the monitors didn't just turn on, they began to display strange numbers running from one side of the screen to another, with different numbers displayed on each of the respective six monitors. Then, the numbers turned into names of cities spread around the globe. And then... the names of the cities disappeared only to be replaced with faces of six extremely good-looking men looking at her. RIGHT at her.

As for Rigel, he sat in the middle of the king size bed among disheveled sheets, blankets, and pillows and watched with silent consternation at what was happening right before his eyes, as if each passing second of what just transpired belonged to a different part of a script that was just too impossible to believe.

Having lost the bet and forced to take the tulle dress from the washing machine to the dryer, Jade rose from the bed, and decided she would feel more comfortable if she wore something on her way down the stairs. Rigel mentioned the house was better protected than the White House itself so she should not have to worry about being seen, dressed or otherwise. But since her conscience and self-doubt knew better, she grabbed the white shirt Rigel wore under the tuxedo earlier that evening. She smiled to herself because the shirt still smelled of Rigel's masculine scent mixed with his cologne. Smitten, she left the shirt unbuttoned and fluffed her long raven hair in a momentary boost of confidence because of the way the shirt hugged her curves.

And then, much to Rigel's surprise and her own horror, Jade decided to walk over to the empty desk beside the wall on her way out. Since the small vintage lamp on the desk began to flicker, she reached to turn it off. That seemingly innocent gesture inadvertently initiated a sequence of steps resulting in the most unconventional introduction to the Alistair assassin family Jade could have ever experienced.

"Hi, Jade." J.J. Monroe's amused smile scared Jade more than the initial shock that sent a jolt of sheer panic through her. She was so shocked she did not even notice heavy duty metal blinds covering up the two windows at the ends of the upstairs master bedroom, making the room even darker than it was a moment ago.

"Hi, Sir." Jade waved back in the same slow and petrified manner she waved at him in the Presidential Suite during the Gala.

"He gets the Royal Treatment, and we get the cold shoulder?" A man in one of the other monitors chuckled and shook his head.

"I don't know, Rasalas. It looks like someone else got the Royal Treatment," Perseus shook his head and smiled wider as the other brothers laughed – with exception of one of them. Jade didn't know why, but she felt most conscious of the silent man's presence. He did not speak. He did not blink. He did not move.

"Alright, gentlemen. This is not a way to make a good first impression," Rigel scolded them, still sitting in the bed.

"But this is?" All the brothers replied in unison, pointing at the monitor and thereby at Jade and the way she looked in his shirt, except for the one who kept silent even now. J.J. decided to keep quiet this time, which proved beneficial because Luna appeared right behind him.

"Don't mind them, Jade. Some men wouldn't know what good manners were if they were slapped with them sideways and in broad daylight," Luna greeted Jade with a sincere smile.

"Hi there," Rigel greeted Luna.

"Hi there, Your Royal Highness," Luna wiggled her eyebrows. "Why don't You man up and join in on the conversation?"

"Will do,," Rigel saluted his sister but directed his gaze at Jade. "Come here, Jade."

"Why?" Jade looked back at him and tried to figure out if her knees would feel steady enough for her to move.

"Yes, sunshine. Why?" Gunay repeated Jade's question with a full-blown grin.

"No reason in particular," Rigel replied with undertones of impatience and reluctance to share what he was about to ask Jade with the rest of his family. "Jade, please?"

"Yes, Jade, please!" A chorus of his siblings, except for the same brother who continued to remain silent, exclaimed in unison after realizing in an instant that Rigel begged for her assistance out of bare necessity. A quite bare necessity.

'Oh, for the love of...!'

"They can read Your thoughts, too," Rigel advised Jade in a not-so-silent way, fully aware it was best to warn her now about the Alistair trait they all shared.

"They can?" Jade stopped dead in her tracks, halfway to the bed, and looked back at the monitors, shocked even more than a moment ago. "You can?"

"Yes, with the exception of blue eyes over there," one of the brothers replied, pointing in the direction of J.J. and Luna's monitor.

"Thanks for the reminder, Fin Boy," J.J. clicked his tongue at his brother-in-law's jab.

"Anytime," Caelum said dryly, but couldn't hide his smirk.

"Why did You refer to the President as 'blue eyes'? Rigel mentioned it was an inside joke?" Jade looked back at everyone after passing a pair of jeans to Rigel, making sure she blocked him so others would not see him.

"It is an inside joke." J.J. replied before Caelum did so.

"Basically, some of us cannot read thoughts if blue contact lenses come into play," Caelum shrugged at a not-so-pleasant memory of the day his sister flirted with J.J. whilst they wore costumes Caelum wished he had never seen in his life.

"Would that work on You?" Jade looked up at Rigel and caused him to wrap his arm around her as they walked up closer toward the monitors together.

"No." He leaned in and kissed the side of her head, making it possible to whisper into her ear. "You may want to button up that shirt."

"My goodness!" Jade exclaimed, covering up immediately, totally embarrassed.

"Don't worry, Jade. And don't mind my brothers. It doesn't look bad at all. It looks like a solid 7 to me," Luna beamed with joy.

"You heard our 7?!?" Jade brought her hands to cover up the ruby red color of her cheeks.

"She didn't, but I did," the brother who kept silent until that moment finally spoke up.

"Tom, be nice," Rigel shook his head.

"He's right, Tom." Luna scolded her big brother. "Besides, You both are not the only ones with aspirations pertaining to the lucky number 7."

"What?" Jade and Rigel looked at Luna.

"It's an inside joke," Luna and J.J. chuckled, and kissed after pausing to look at one another.

"Don't remind me," Tom shrugged. "However, You did shout so loud I just had to make the call to see what was wrong."

"I didn't shout?" Jade denied the allegation.

"You didn't, but he did." Tom replied grimly and narrowed his eyes on Rigel.

"He didn't shout, either?" Jade looked up at the man embracing her as he stood behind her.

"I may have shouted once... or twice," Rigel cut his response short.

"Or 7," Tom replied with dry humor.

"7? Does that mean You lost the challenge, not me?" Jade wondered.

"What challenge?" Rasalas asked, intrigued.

"There was no challenge. She's a linguist, and she's talented. That's all," Rigel pointed at Jade, holding in a chuckle.

"I see." Tom moved his gaze from Rigel onto Jade and decided to say nothing more.

"And 7 happens to be a lucky number for many," Luna winked at Jade, making Jade feel better. "So, like I said, be nice Tom. Besides, You haven't even been properly introduced to our future sister-in-law yet."

"Future sister-in-law?" The brothers, apart from Tom, exclaimed at once, while Caelum opened his eyes wide at Luna's comment.

"You work fast, brother," Caelum shook his head at how fast another one of his siblings fell victim to love.

"Shut up." Rigel grit his teeth, feeling protective over Jade.

"Please be nice to Your brother," Jade looked up at Rigel again, and then back at the monitor displaying Caelum's grinning face. "We needed a distraction to keep everyone's eyes off Luna when she felt dizzy at the Gala. And Rigel distracted everyone when he somewhat proposed to me."

"You somewhat proposed?" The brothers replied as if they choked on air, apart from Tom. He kept silent. He did not blink. He just stared at Jade.

"I did," Rigel nodded, feeling more and more comfortable with the idea.

"Why did You need a distraction to keep everyone's eyes off Luna at the Gala?" Tom looked at Jade with eyes that pierced her soul. She did not know why, but she felt Tom was different from his other siblings. More reserved, and somehow more... filled with sorrow.

"Because, gentlemen, the woman You see in Rigel's arms has a very unique aspect about her," Luna spoke softly, and tried to calm Jade.

"And what is that?" Caelum asked intrigued by Luna's words and the fact Rigel chose to keep Jade's existence from them.

"Her name," Luna said quietly.

"And what is her name?" Caelum asked, aware of her first name, but totally unprepared for the rest of it.

"Ladies first, Fin Boy," Luna flashed a wide grin. "Jade, these are the remaining Alistair brothers: Rasalas, Caelum, Perseus, Gunay, and the silently brooding one is Tom."

"It is a pleasure to meet You, gentlemen." Jade reached for Rigel's hand, linking their fingers as his arms rested around her waist.

'She's the one...'

"It definitely qualifies as pleasure," Rigel winked at the men in the monitors, while smiling at the words he heard in his mind, hoping what he said wouldn't get him in trouble with Jade. It did.

"Did You just twist words on a linguist?" Jade raised her eyebrows and felt a thud in her heart when he first kissed her forehead.

"You do it all the time." He kissed the top of her head again before looking back at his siblings and one very happy President.

"She does?" J.J. wondered out loud, grateful to see his favorite brother-in-law found courage to reveal his feelings to Jade.

"She does. You'll find out soon enough." Rigel embraced the woman in his arms with love and affection but sent an all-telling smirk J.J.'s way.

"What's Your full name, Jade?" Tom spoke with such intensity Jade almost jumped.

"My name is Jade Alistair," she whispered shyly, unsure if she preferred Luna's worrisome reaction to her name over the thunderous look Tom shot her way, giving her goosebumps she was unable to hide...

≈ Chapter 40 ≈

If it wasn't for the fact Jade stood in front of him, reminding Rigel of her existence, he would have forgotten about pleasantries and manners. Not because the unexpected call from Tom interrupted their intimate evening he and Jade shared up until that moment, resulting in a conversation Jade wished she could have experienced under more... pleasant circumstances. No. It wasn't the call that raised Rigel's temper. It was the man who initiated it.

Rigel knew revealing Jade's full name would affect his siblings. Luna's reaction to meeting Jade was a perfect example of it. That was why Rigel kept it a secret for as long as he could. Truth be told, he called Tom the day he and Jade returned from Chattanooga. He didn't call his oldest brother to chit chat, nor did he call to confess his feelings for someone. He called Tom because of the cigarette buts that were found not far from their camp site thanks to one rowdy and overconfident pup. And because of the nagging feeling in his gut.

But, for reasons Rigel was vividly conscious of, he did not disclose Jade's name to his brother. Not her full name, to be exact. And now Tom realized why. Much to the discomfort of both men.

"No way!" Rasalas exclaimed in his deeply throaty voice. "Is Your name really Jade Alistair?!?"

"I am afraid so." Jade replied, more timid than she did at the Presidential penthouse after Luna revealed the significance of her name.

"Way to go, Happyski!" Perseus sided with Rasalas. "Did You use Your Detective connections to search for her?"

"No!" Rigel replied too eagerly, which caused Jade to almost snap her neck as she looked up at him.

"He didn't," Tom said quietly.

"Thanks." Rigel nodded.

"So, then, how did You meet? How did it start?" Gunay inquired, intrigued by Rigel's protective stance when it came to Jade. It spoke volumes about his feelings for her, even if she wasn't fully aware of it.

"It started with a murder," Rigel replied with an ice-cold tone of voice.

"No way!" Rasalas clasped his hands with a loud thud and leaned in closer toward the monitor. "Don't tell me You were told to take her out, but You fell in love instead?!?"

"No!" Jade denied it, turning to Rigel. "That only happens in the movies."

"It happens more often than You think," J.J. kissed the top of Luna's head.

"Obviously." Caelum rolled his eyes.

"Really?" Jade raised her eyebrows in disbelief.

"Really," Caelum shivered, smiling, nonetheless.

"Remember when I said men fall for women who save them?" J.J. grinned and winked at Jade.

"Yes, Mr. President."

"Does she know who we are?" Gunay asked bluntly.

"Yes," Rigel replied with honesty.

"Alright. But does she know what we do?" Gunay modified his question.

"Yes. And some of us no longer do it," Rigel noted firmly.

"Alright," Gunay nodded, accepting his brother's explanation. "And can we trust her?"

"We can." Tom announced matter-of-factly, and by doing so gained a lifetime friend in Jade.

"Thank You, Tom." Jade could have sworn something changed in his eyes. Something unexplainable, yet impossible to overlook.

"Don't mention it," Tom nodded and leaned back in his chair. He did not smile, but even Rigel noticed the change in his demeanor. "And the name's Vega. It's reserved only for friends."

"Thank You, Vega," Jade smiled sincerely, and right out of her heart, which in turn was something Tom could not overlook.

"How come she gets to call You 'Vega' and I'm still on 'Tom' terms?" J.J. asked in a sulking tone of voice.

"Because You forced me to reconsider the significance of 7 rifles," Tom smirked at J.J. and watched as the Presidential Pair looked at each other with horror in their eyes. "And that was when You were still on boyfriend non-boyfriend terms."

"Double damn," J.J. swallowed hard.

"You like to say that a lot?" Jade grinned and realized she felt comfortable in the current company, as unbelievable as it may seem. Maybe it was the ease with which the President spoke with a group of assassins as if they came from similar backgrounds? Maybe it was the sincerity with which those joining in on the conversation cared about one another. Or maybe it was the way everyone accepted her for the person she was.

"He does say that a lot." Rigel smiled and tightened his embrace around Jade's waist.

"And I am afraid little 'Seven' will be a talker like his father," Luna patted her belly, which looked a bit more prominent than it did earlier in the evening at the Gala.

"He's a talker already," Tom grinned while he stretched his arms above his head and then ran his hands through his hair.

"You can hear him?" Jade asked before she could stop herself. She wasn't sure if she did the right thing, but Tom smiled at her question.

"Tom's definitely the most gifted one of us," Rigel noted.

"Are You?" Jade raised her eyebrow, intrigued.

"You may say that." Tom grinned, foreseeing what Jade's question may have been. "Though, I doubt Aunt Aline would have been more skeptical of me because of it."

"You... know about Aunt Aline?" Jade blinked, impressed.

"I do." Tom inclined his head.

"Who's Aunt Aline?" Caelum wondered.

"Jade's father's sister," Tom said without a shred of doubt.

"She's scarier than the cell guards at our precinct," Rigel shrugged.

"And she's already suspicious of Rigel." J.J. smirked.

"How do You know?" Rigel turned his gaze to his brother-in-law.

"Jade told me on the dance floor." J.J. flashed his pearly whites. "I learned quite a lot during that dance."

"What else did You learn?" Jade tried to recall the conversation.

"Nothing." J.J. and Rigel said in unison.

"Are You sure?" Jade looked up at Rigel.

"Yes." Again, J.J. and Rigel said in unison.

"That sounded rehearsed," Jade frowned.

"It wasn't," J.J. and Rigel said in unison for the third time in the row.

"We'll go with that," Perseus chuckled. "Anyway, I should be going. It's the middle of the night for You, but it's already a late morning for me."

"Perseus is right," J.J. agreed. "And we should be landing in D.C. soon. I'm glad we didn't stay in Chicago for the night. I wouldn't stomach having breakfast with Lucchese."

"You had to spend time with that useless buffoon?" Rasalas stopped swinging back and forth in his chair.

"Worse, Rigel defended Jade from him," J.J. grit his teeth.

"What?" Rasalas leaned in toward the monitor again.

"It's a long story," Jade tried to intervene. "And not important."

"That's not how I saw it," J.J. was about to say more when the pilot announced through the speakers the Air Force One would be landing soon. "Alright kids, we'll talk soon."

"It was nice to speak with You again Luna. Mr. President," Jade waved at their monitor.

"Don't You 'President' me. It's J.J. and don't You forget it," J.J. grinned.

"It was nice to speak with You J.J.," Jade smiled shyly as the Alistair siblings chuckled.

"Talk to You soon," Rigel bid them farewell and waited until J.J. and Luna's monitor turned off in preparation for landing. He turned his gaze toward the other monitors and didn't move for a good couple of minutes.

"Rigel?" Jade asked after a longer pause of silence. "Is everything alright?"

"No. Yes. It will be." Rigel spoke mysteriously. "My apologies, it was rude of us to communicate this way in Your presence."

"You were... communicating?" Jade responded cautiously.

"Yes, we were." He offered her a faint smile. "Would You excuse us for a moment? We need to discuss something."

"Of course," she nodded and looked at the men in the monitors. "If You will excuse me, I will go downstairs for a while. I need to make sure my dress dries by morning."

"What happened to the dress?" Gunay grinned in a cocky and purely masculine way. "Happyski, You beast."

"No!" Jade exclaimed and shook her head. "I fell in the snow and Rigel offered his shirt to me while the dress dried."

"And THAT's why You're wearing his shirt. Inside out. In his bedroom. In dim light," Gunay said not-so-subtly.

"What?!?" Jade looked down in sheer horror. And noticed, too late for her own good, that she did in fact wear the shirt inside out. With stitching as visible as her ruby red cheeks. And she could not stop herself from thinking the thought that came to her mind – and traveled to all the Alistair brothers' minds.

'Oh, for the love of...!'

"Happyski, You beast." Rigel repeated Gunay's words and bellowed out a laugh.

"But I am telling the truth!" Jade replied with a temper.

"So are they." Tom said with an amused gleam in his eyes.

"That was not nice. Correct, but not nice," Rigel smirked and winced when Jade sent him an ominously piercing gaze, sending a chill down his spine.

"Goodnight, gentlemen. It was nice to meet You," Jade puffed out air, smiled at the Alistair brothers, and did not wait for their response. She left the room and turned the shirt inside out the moment her foot stepped over the threshold. Rigel saw what she did, and that sent another chill down his spine, albeit of a different sort.

"All right, boys. I have a favor of You to ask...." Saying so, Rigel fell silent. He had something urgent to say. And what he had to say was too important and too worrisome for Jade to have overheard. His gut feeling was dead sure of it...

≈ Chapter 41 ≈

For someone who thought of laundry as a gruesome chore, the excuse to perform that mundane task, or at least the time needed to do it, allowed Jade to vent her fuming temper. She was mad. She was furious. And she only had herself to blame. Not only for deciding to turn off the lamp on Rigel's desk as it flickered in the dim light of his bedroom, but for wearing his shirt inside-out as she met the rest of his siblings.

Well, if she wanted to make a lasting first impression on the family of the man she had fallen in love with, she succeeded. And what a first impression it was! She did not know what was worse: her appearance, the fact she got caught red-handed by his siblings - plus one very amused President, or the fact she found out they all possessed the ability to read thoughts.

How?!? HOW on earth could she be confident enough to have a future with a man whose family was capable of knowing what occupied her mind?!? She paused suddenly, with the wet bundle of tulle in many shades of dark jade no longer resembling a dress in her hands. Was she foolish enough to think she could hope for a future with Rigel? Was she foolish enough to think his family would accept her after the unfortunate display of her empty-headed nature?

"You're not empty-headed. Neither is the nature of Your actions," Rigel's low tone of voice scared Jade to the point that she jumped and dropped the wet bundle of tulle down to the floor. She turned around and caught her breath. He stood there, in the doorway, leaning against the threshold, shirtless. Wearing nothing more than the pair of jeans she had passed to him during the video call with his siblings.

"How did You get here?!?" Jade exclaimed, startled by his presence, appearance, and the fact he clearly read her thoughts.

"Well, my parents met, fell in love, then Tom was born, then Rasalas, then myself, then Caelum, then..."

"I asked how You got here, not how You got here."

"Isn't that the same thing?" Rigel raised his eyebrow.

"No."

"Then in that case, I came down the stairs and spent the last couple of minutes admiring You," he spoke slowly because his heart paced a mile a minute. How could he explain he was admiring her bare legs as much as her train of thought? Then again...

"There's nothing to admire," Jade replied bluntly and reached to pick the dress up off the floor.

"I beg to differ."

"I don't," she retorted, shoving the dress into the dryer.

"Ever heard of the expression that beauty is in the eye of the beholder?" Rigel crossed his arms at his chest and watched as Jade selected several buttons on the dryer machine without checking which ones she pushed.

"May I be so bold as to suggest this expression is irrelevant if You look the way You look?"

"Ouch."

"It's the truth," Jade grit her teeth and walked out of the laundry room and into the kitchen without turning the dryer on. She walked right past him and did not bother to wait if he would move or not.

'It shouldn't hurt You, of all people...'

"Why not?"

"Did You read my mind again, just like they could?"

"Reading Your mind was acceptable before, but not anymore, huh?" He clicked his tongue, hurt as well, and reached to turn the dryer on. He paused briefly, placed his hands on the dryer, and closed his eyes. He wasn't surprised at the way Jade acted after she met his siblings. He was afraid.

"It was acceptable when I thought You were the only one who could read my thoughts. Now there are seven of You," Jade exhaled and went to turn the kettle on.

"And that makes it acceptable to blame us for being born the way we were?"

"No! And I never said that!" She shook her head without looking at him. Instead, she reached for two mugs from the kitchen cabinet and for the tea essence in one of the metal containers on the counter.

"Maybe it was so obvious You did not have to?" He leaned against the refrigerator, with arms crossed at his shirtless chest.

"Was it as obvious to You as the fact I felt shy and self-conscious in the company of Your family?" She turned and jumped for the second time because he stood right in front of her, barely an inch away.

"Perhaps it was as obvious as the fact they accepted You for who You are the moment they met You without judging You for not being able to read minds?" He placed his hands in the pockets of his jeans. He knew he had to, otherwise he would reach for her, and that wasn't the type of... connection they needed right now. "Do You think You could spare them the same courtesy and accept them for who they are?

"That was totally uncalled for. How can You stand there and accuse me of not accepting You all?" She pointed her finger at his chest. "I felt so inadequate because I cannot read minds."

"I'll be sure to tell J.J. Monroe You just referred to him as inadequate," he replied, and hoped she would find the humor in his comparison. She did. Though not in a way he assumed.

"No! That's not what I meant! J.J. Monroe is superior to others!"

"So, now he's superior to me?"

"No! That's not what I meant!" Jade puffed out air.

"Do You really think Luna considered his... abilities or inadequacies when she fell in love with him?" The absurdity of that argument was too hard for him to comprehend.

"Well, not the way You say it..." Jade ran out of steam. Now all that was left in her heart was the fear she really was not good enough for him.

"Why did You get mad at me?" Rigel reached and cupped her face, unable to prevent it. He wanted to shake the nonsense out of her. He wanted to make her understand how much she meant to him. He wanted to convey how he felt inside, watching as she moved around his kitchen as if she already belonged there.

And then... he saw the change in her eyes. It was silent. It was unspoken. It was overwhelming for someone who read minds.

"Because... You need someone better than me." She covered her eyes with her hands and dared not to look at him. The honesty of that admission cut through her heart.

"I could say the same thing to You."

"Yeah, right." She looked at him after hearing his words and saw her reflection in his eyes glistening with what appeared to be signs of tears. "How could anyone be better than You?"

"I... could ask You the same thing with reference to Your own self-doubt." He looked deeper into her eyes. "Jade, please don't pull away because I am different from others. I don't think my heart would survive being rejected for that reason. Not again."

"Why would You think I was contemplating rejecting You? I was referring to myself when I said what I said. Do You remember when I told You in Chattanooga that You have many layers? You do. But You should not think of them as something that would keep someone away. Those layers make You who You are, especially the hidden ones."

"You're the one to talk?" The slow smile that appeared on his face began to calm her down. And because it did, it calmed him down as well.

"Rigel, Your parents died for this country. You and Your siblings fight for justice. Even Your brother-in-law is a just man. How on earth can I ever compare to that?" There, she said it. She wasn't afraid of his family's ability to read minds. She was afraid of never being able to fit in.

"Your father chose to stand up to corruption and injustice and paid the ultimate price for it. You agreed to bear witness to the crime that was committed in cold blood. Heck, Your Aunt Aline is so adamant about protecting righteousness she could wipe out crime in Chicagoland if she became the Mayor. I said it about her before, and I say it again. How's that for starters?"

"For starters?" She whispered, barely able to speak. "Rigel, what's left?"

"What's left?" "He repeated her question and wiped away the tears that came to her eyes. "What's left is the fact You weren't afraid to open Your heart to a man who's been hiding who he really is for all of his life."

"Rigel..." She choked up. She could not speak. She wanted to reveal how she felt at that moment. But she couldn't. So, she did what she could, with the little spark of courage that lit up in her heart.

She reached to embrace him, kiss after kiss. They danced, turning around and around, and moved to the silent melody that matched the melody of their hearts when they danced in the moonlight under the Cloud Gate earlier that night. They didn't reach the bedroom for a long while. After all, kitchen islands proved sturdy enough, from what Rigel had learned from his brother-in-law. And what proved most crucial through all the night was the fact Jade gained enough courage she no longer doubted their love, their future, and the strength of their joined hands.

That was a good thing because their joined front would soon be tested. The next day Rigel dropped Jade off at home. She was forced to wear his clothes, because of Fate's fickle sense of humor, and the fact vintage tulle dresses didn't mix well with the added heat setting of one particularly sworn-at dryer.

And that was only the beginning...

≈ **Chapter 42** ≈

Bravery. Rigel was born with it in his blood. His parents instilled it in his mind, and he cultivated it throughout his life, whether as an assassin, as a Police Officer, and as a Detective with the Special Task Force. It was as much a part of him as his dislike for Alex's coffee. And yet, he felt like a coward whenever he had to deal with one very particular person. Aunt Aline...

The mere thought of her name turned his stomach. And it had nothing to do with Alsatian. Rigel was fond of dogs. Dogs were a great judge of people's character. Truth be told, Alsatian was loyal to Aunt Aline's command, but this only meant she knew how to rule over animals as well. And that magnified Rigel's fear and respect for Jade's Aunt to the second power.

As such, his and Jade's bravery was tested as he dropped her off at Aunt Aline's home on the late Sunday morning following the most eventful 24 hours. The fact Jade spent the night at his house was undeniable. The fact she had to borrow his clothes to get back home was even more self-evident. And they were certain the shrunken vintage tulle jade dress would be the least of their problems.

Much to their surprise, Aunt Aline wasn't home upon their arrival. They breathed a sigh of relief, especially when Jade's mother opened the door with a smirk and a silent shake of her head. So, they got off easy. Right? Not exactly, because Rigel knew with certainty that somehow, someway, Aunt Aline would still find a way to scold him and Jade for their not-so-secret misdeeds. And he was right.

The following day felt like the longest Monday ever. Waiting for his shift to end proved to be a real trial of Rigel's will. He finished going over the mundane task of reviewing cases he had on his desk, added paper to all the printers at the precinct - twice, made coffee in the coffee maker four times - forgetting he had done so, and... drank Alex's muddy concoction of a coffee three times by mistake. That didn't matter. Going over to see Jade as soon as his shift ended did. He missed her. And he didn't bother to hide the fact his grin grew wider and wider the closer he got to Aunt Aline's house.

His grin disappeared the moment Aunt Aline opened the door. Leaving the glass screen door closed, as usual.

"Oh, it's You." Aunt Aline greeted Rigel with an obviously annoyed look in her eyes.

"Good evening, Aunt Aline," he almost bowed before her. He felt dumb instantly. Even Alsatian had no problem figuring it out and tilted his head to the side.

"You came back already?" Aunt Aline asked bluntly. She believed in honesty as opposed to petty politeness.

"Yes." He nodded, almost bowing again, and grit his teeth the moment he realized it. "May I speak with Jade?"

"No." Aunt Aline crossed her arms at her chest.

"Alright," Rigel replied, deciding to bite his lower lip and modifying his question instead of responding in a way cocky way. He knew better. And he was raised better than that. "May I speak with Jade, please?"

"No." Aunt Aline said more firmly, and Alsatian matched her stance.

"Why?"

"Because she's not home."

"She hasn't returned yet? She finished working almost an hour ago?" He said more to himself. Although a sliver of worry crossed his mind, he realized he hadn't told her he would come by. He wanted it to be a surprise. As such, he decided to keep the thoughts of concern to himself. "May I come inside and wait for her? It is a bit chilly today."

"On one condition," Aunt Aline took a decisive step closer toward the closed glass screen door.

"And what would that be?"

"You tell me what happened to my niece's dress?" she asked slowly, raising the hair at the back of his neck.

"Jade fell in the snow."

"Jade fell in the snow?"

"Yes."

"Where did she fall?" Aunt Aline narrowed her eyes.

"In... front of my house," he replied as a nerve pinched at the nape of his neck. Was it possible to feel more afraid of Aunt Aline with every passing second? Yes. It was...

"What was she doing in front of Your house?" Aunt Aline may have asked that question without moving an inch, but Alsatian picked up on his master's tone of voice. The dog's growl sent a cold sweat down Rigel's spine.

"Aline Alistair, that is quite enough." Eliana appeared behind her sister-in-law with a stern look on her face.

"I asked the Detective a question," Aunt Aline pointed at Rigel through the closed glass screen door. "He should be man enough to answer it."

"I am." Rigel straightened up and sent a piercing gaze Aunt Aline's way. "I love Jade. I respect her boundaries. And I proposed to her last night."

"You what?" Aunt Aline's jaw dropped, and Rigel couldn't have felt any better about it.

"He proposed to Jade last night," Eliana said in a gentle tone of voice and opened the doors for Rigel. He walked inside with his head held high, pausing momentarily as he passed by Aunt Aline and her trusted canine.

"If You don't believe me, ask the President of the United States to verify it. I am sure he would love to speak with You about it." Oh, that felt good! Indescribably good! He decided instantly that he owed J.J. Monroe a glass of whiskey on ice for that one! Heck, he'd make it a bottle!

"Please forgive my sister-in-law. Aline has a peculiar way of showing affection," Eliana gestured for Rigel to sit down by the kitchen island.

"That was a show of affection?" Rigel raised his eyebrow sarcastically. "How does she show disapproval?"

"You wouldn't want to find out," Eliana leaned in toward Rigel and whispered as if she was sharing the world's biggest secret. "Besides, Jade already explained to us what happened to the tulle dress. Though, she did not mention the proposal part."

"If You knew what happened to the dress, then why grill me over it?" He looked Aunt Aline's way.

"To make sure both sides of the story match." Aunt Aline flashed him a wide emotionless grin, which disappeared as fast as it appeared.

"I see." He nodded and decided Aunt Aline just scored an enormous amount of appreciation in his mind. Family always came first, and Aunt Aline knew it.

"Jade returned home wearing hideous clothes. Couldn't You give her something better to wear?" Aunt Aline walked into the kitchen area, poured a cup of coffee, and passed it to Rigel. He didn't know whether to accept it or pass on it in fear of it being poisoned.

"I like my clothes, thank You very much." He flashed the same kind of cocky emotionless grin mimicking Aunt Aline's grin and chose to accept the coffee. Her coffee couldn't have tasted any worse than Alex's. "Besides, I do not have many clothes that would fit Jade."

"You could have at least given her better socks," Aunt Aline said sarcastically.

"What's wrong with my socks?" Rigel tilted his head to the side. "I like the socks I gave Jade."

"They look old and worn out," Aunt Aline chuckled.

"Well, I got them on my first day on the job as a Detective on the Task Force." He explained in his defense.

"And You kept them all this time? Why?" Aunt Aline shook her head in disapproval.

"Because I like them," he moved his shoulders.

"So, You are a keeper?" Aunt Aline countered his words.

"I see who Jade gets her linguistic skills from," Rigel responded, amused to say the least, but raised the cup of coffee to his lips to hide his smirk.

"Aline, could You leave us for a moment? There is something I need to discuss with Rigel. In private." Eliana's words twisted knots in Rigel's stomach.

Aunt Aline nodded, and disappeared from the room without a single word. Rigel didn't know if he should be glad or... afraid. He looked back at Eliana and watched as she came around the kitchen island. She sat beside him on the barstool holding a cup of coffee in her hand.

"I hope I can speak with You about Jade before she returns," Eliana spoke calmly but with intention. Rigel saw it in her eyes and felt it in the tone of her voice.

"Of course."

"I am not sure where to start, so I may as well start at the beginning. Did Jade tell You she has a twin sister?"

"She did. I believe she said her sister's name is Jasper?" Rigel rubbed at his beard as if he was trying to recall the details Jade shared with him about her family. "She also told me her father was killed."

"I see You two are closer than I may have assumed," Eliana raised her eyes, both surprised and pleased. "In that case what I have to say will be much easier to share with You, and that much more important."

"Jade matters to me. I want her to know she can trust me to keep her safe. I want You to know it, too."

"That is good to hear," Eliana smiled. "Did Jade ever tell You the story of how she and her twin sister were born?"

"She said Jasper was born first, and there was a complication when it came to her birth, that something went wrong." He understood what it meant. He himself was a triplet, and the notion of a multiple birth was close to his heart.

"Saying something went wrong would have been an understatement," Eliana took a long pause and sipped her coffee. "I lost a lot of blood when Jasper was born. And I mean a lot. By the time Jade was ready to come into this world I was drained, exhausted, and I technically bled out. I lost consciousness. My husband, Pedro, went out onto the streets of São Paulo in search of someone who could help before I lost my life, and Jade's as well."

"I am sorry."

"Aline is a hard woman to understand, but I wouldn't be alive today if it wasn't for her - in every sense of the word. She kept me alive until my husband returned with a wonderful couple who delivered Jade via emergency c-section."

"Wait, Jade was born via c-section? At home?" If he thought being interrogated by Aunt Aline was scary, he was wrong. Hearing the woman he fell in love with almost died the day she was born caused the kind of a scary cold sweat he could not even describe.

"Yes. If it wasn't for the woman who delivered Jade, we wouldn't have survived. That is why we named Jade after the woman who saved her." Eliana took another long pause. "I tend to repay kindness with kindness. That is why I trusted Fate when I saw Jade fell in love with You. You seem to understand her the way my husband understood me."

"May I ask how he died?" He had to ask. He just had to. He learned so much about Jade's father's passing from her, but he felt he needed to hear Eliana's side of the story.

"Pedro was a good man. He was an honest man. He would speak less and do more. He never judged people. And he believed in Fate. That was why he went searching for help the day Jasper and Jade were born. He didn't leave in panic, he left believing that the people who would cross his path were meant to cross it." She sighed heavily and wiped away her tears. "The day Pedro was killed was the darkest day of my life. Of our lives. He lost his life because he refused to lead the corrupted Law Enforcement to Jade and Richard Alistair. To the people who saved Jade's and my lives."

"What do You mean?" Rigel straightened up, stricken by a sudden realization that shot through his mind. There was no way. No way on the green earth Jade was alive because his mother could have helped bring her into this world? It was impossibly impossible! Could his parents have travelled so far around the globe and never tell their children they ever set foot in South America? Could they have been involved with their government work when he and his siblings were young? Could it have anything to do with their deaths years later? Could it have anything to do with Jade's father's death?

"I am afraid I cannot share any more with You. I already may have said too much. I wouldn't be able to live with myself if anything happened to You because of me," Eliana wiped more tears away, and laid her tear-soaked hand on top of his hand. The surge of sorrow bleeding out of Eliana's mind that struck him was staggering. He wanted to say something. Anything.

But... he received a call from Alex, which he sent to voice message.

Much to his such surprise, the missed call was followed by a text message reading: 'URGENT!!!!!'. He called Alex back, and almost fell off the barstool because of the thrust of thoughts rushing through Alex's mind.

"You better get to the precinct, ASAP," Alex's voice sounded more ominous than his thoughts.

"What is it?" Rigel asked, but already knew it had something to do with Jade. He heard it in Alex's thoughts and felt it in the pit of his stomach.

"Jade's been arrested for the murder of the officer at the Mayor's Office."

"WHAT!?!?!" Rigel stood from the barstool and rushed toward the door, sending Eliana an all-telling look, shutting the front door behind him. "Who's bringing her in?!?"

"I am. I thought You should know about it before the news gets out," Alex almost whispered, aware Jade could hear him from the backseat of his car.

"News?!?" Rigel hissed through his teeth as he flew down the flight of stairs, toward his car. Suddenly, he stopped dead in his tracks because he heard a faint thought not far from where he stood. He ended the phone call at once and ran in the opposite direction from which the unexpected thought came from. Not because he was scared, but because he knew what he was doing. He wasn't running away. He was running around the houses, to catch the coward who came by Aunt Aline's house to spy on them.

"Lucky Knuckles. Why am I NOT surprised to see You?" Rigel clenched his jaw as he grabbed the man hiding behind one of the cars, lifting him off the ground with such force that one of Lucky's shoes never made it off the ground...

≈ Chapter 43 ≈

Rigel swore. Out loud, in his mind, and all the way down in his gut. He should have known. He should have! Seeing Lucky spying on Jade right in front of her Aunt's house infuriated him. He swore not only at Lucky, but also at his own inability to foresee it.

And because he didn't, his guilt added another level to his already fuming temper.

"What are You doing here, Lucky?" Rigel lowered the man down, but not enough for him to touch the ground. He was dangling up in the air, with Rigel's furious face not even an inch away from his.

"I... Detective... I'm begging You, don't hurt me!" Lucky shouted, gasping for air between words, and yelped as Rigel shook him.

"Raise Your voice again, and You won't get a chance to beg for anything," Rigel snarled at him. "I know how to make You disappear a hundred different ways, and make it look like You've gone on vacation."

"Sorry," Lucky whispered, swallowing hard.

"Better." Rigel tightened the grip on Lucky's jacket. "Now, let me ask You again, what are You doing here? And don't lie."

"Why would I lie?" Lucky tried to sound shocked, but it did not work in his favor.

"Do You need a reminder why we've become such frequent acquaintances back in the day?"

"No!" Lucky shouted again and raised his arms up in surrender. "No... no reminder is needed!"

"Didn't I tell You not to raise Your voice?" Rigel brought him even closer. The last thing he needed was for Aunt Aline, Alsatian, or Eliana to hear Lucky's shouting right in front of their house. "Don't. Make. That. Mistake. Again."

"Got it..." Lucky reached to caress Rigel's jacket, as if wiping dust off it. "A man like You should know I am sincere in my words."

"Hardly," Rigel snarled with an ice-cold stare. "Now, spill it."

"If I talk, You have to give me Your word no one finds out You got the information from me."

"Let's find out if the information is worth my word, and then I'll think about it," Rigel set the man down. "But let me warn You first. If You even consider running away right now, I will shoot You and You'll die on the spot. If You somehow survive, then whoever You work for will know we talked, and You'll die anyway. So, let that sink in before You choose to go that route."

"Detective Happyski, I would never run from You."

"Don't lie, Lucky." Rigel took a swift step forward and narrowed his eyes on Lucky as the man winced.

"Fine, I would never run from You *again*," Lucky paled. "I know how it ends, and it ain't pretty."

"Got that right," Rigel caressed the man's jacket, mimicking the way Lucky caressed his jacket a moment ago.

"Fine." Lucky rubbed at his unshaved chin. "I was told to spy on You, not on the clumsy dimwit You fell for."

"What?" Rigel raised his eyebrows. That... was something he never saw coming. "You were not spying on Jade?"

"No. Whatever her name is." Lucky cleared his throat because of the way Rigel looked at him. "My boss didn't care for her. You're the one on his radar."

"If that was the case, why did You follow her to her house the day we met You?"

"You got it all wrong." Lucky reached for a cigarette in the front lapel of his jacket. "I was paid to follow You. But I lost You. My boss doesn't tolerate failure. So, I looked for information regarding the intern. I figured sooner or later she would go to meet You. And I guess I got lucky that day - You came to meet her."

"You're lying." Rigel hissed through his teeth, but he found no inner monologue inside Lucky's mind which would have existed if the man had been lying.

"Am I?" Lucky lit up the cigarette and puffed out a cloud of smoke that smelled like a nasty cheap version of a poorly rolled up street tobacco. "Tell me, Detective, didn't it bother You in the least bit why I shot at Your little intern house only once? Why didn't I come back to finish the job? She's driven home alone countless times."

"So, You admit You shot at us that night?" Rigel couldn't decide whether he was astonished by the fact Lucky was foolish enough to admit he committed that crime, or whether he was astonished by the fact Lucky's explanation made sense.

"I shot at You, Detective, not at both of You..." Lucky clicked his tongue and felt superior to Rigel for a moment.

"Well, You missed." Rigel narrowed his eyebrows, bothered and furious at himself for not figuring it out sooner.

"That's because I wasn't aiming to kill You, per se. Anyway, it was good I missed. My boss was furious when he found out someone shot at Your little intern and almost killed You in the process. Naturally, I did not tell him it was me," Lucky puffed out another cloud of smoke. "But believe me, I never saw him more enraged."

"Why?" Rigel asked bluntly, recalling Jade's words that whoever was shooting at them was aiming at him, not at her, because of their height difference.

"The man I work for has it in for cops. Since You're one of the top ones, You're on his radar. Which means he wants to finish You off himself - You know, ego issues can be a nasty thing," Lucky shook his head. "I got lucky because I didn't kill You."

"You got lucky?"

"Though, I did screw up in Chattanooga."

"I had a hunch it was You," Rigel chuckled. Gut feelings aside, he was willing to bet his entire arsenal of guns he kept hidden in the basement of his home on Lucky being the idiot who left the cigarette buts behind near their campsite in Chattanooga.

"Well, at least You chose a place with a warmer climate. I would not have followed You to Alaska," Lucky snorted sarcastically.

"At least." Rigel replied, amused, and laid his hands on Lucky's shoulders. "Now, tell me who You work for, and we will part ways on amicable terms."

"I cannot." Lucky said grimly. "You and I both know how quickly loose tongues become dead tongues."

"Better than You think." Rigel uttered. "But You have to give me something. A clue, a hint, anything."

"I don't think that would be possible, Detective. I like my life. More importantly, I'd like to continue enjoying more of it." Crushing the cigarette but, Lucky looked up and realized Rigel retrieved his hands back to his pockets.

"Same here, Lucky. Same here," Rigel sighed heavily. "Look, if Your boss is as powerful as You think, and as fearsome as You say, then it won't matter whether You tell me his identity. I'm a walking dead man in Your book anyway."

"Huh," Lucky scratched the back of his neck and debated what to do.

"You have to give me something. Anything." Rigel hoped Lucky would forgo the bad guy's code of conduct. If not verbally, then at least in his thoughts. He concentrated on all the thoughts rushing through Lucky's minds. And he wasn't disappointed.

'City Hall's Rooftop Garden...'

"What?" Rigel asked before he could stop himself.

"I didn't say anything," Lucky denied opening his mouth.

"Lucky...?"

"Fine! Check the City Hall again," Lucky said loud enough for Rigel to reach for the man's jacket. "Whatever You do, don't look in obvious places. Look where those who do the dirty work hide tools of their trade."

"What does that mean?"

"You're the Detective, You figure it out," Lucky mocked him. "Anyway, I've gotta bail. You can bring me in for Your intern's little home remodel assistance if You can find me."

"I will find You, Lucky."

"Sure thing. Just remember who followed who tonight," Lucky grinned wickedly and turned to leave. "Watch Your back, Detective."

"Back at You, Knuckles," Rigel responded and shook his head while trying to process everything he just heard from Lucky, when the man stopped, and turned around to face Rigel. Rigel reached for his gun, but Lucky just raised his eyebrow at the gesture.

"I'm not dumb enough to shoot You now. We both know You'd turn me into Swiss Cheese before I would blink," he tipped his head to the side.

"Then what is it?" Rigel took a few steps forward to show Lucky he wasn't in the mood for charades.

"Make sure Your little intern stays in jail. She's safe as long as she's there. She sparked my boss's interest when he figured out You got the hots for her," Lucky said nonchalantly before turning around. He disappeared into the night, leaving Rigel with a bone-chilling cold sweat running down his back....

≈ Chapter 44 ≈

Jade was innocent! He was going to move heaven and earth to prove it. There wasn't a shred of doubt in Rigel's mind about her innocence. There also wasn't a shred of doubt in his mind that whoever did this to Jade had connections high up the food chain at the Police Department. Really high up.

It took Rigel no time to get to the precinct. He parked the pickup truck in front of the precinct's door. With a screech of the tires. With a cloud of smoke. With a loud echoing thud of the driver's door when it closed, thrusted by the full force of his swing.

Rigel walked inside and made his way straight to the holding cells. He did not speak with anyone. He did not look at anyone. He did not even bother to check if Alex already arrived with Jade. He knew they had. He heard Jade's fearful thoughts. And he swore to himself that whoever did this to her would pay. One way or another.

He was about to turn the last corner of the hallway before the part of the building leading up to the holding cells, when Nicholetta Stormstrong walked right into him as she, too, turned the corner from the opposite side. She looked up with such unspoked authority, that it forced him to take a step back.

"Detective Brzozakiewiczowicz?" Nicholetta greeted him coldly by his last name. His formal last name. Not by his nickname, nor by his first name. That raised a half a dozen more red flags in his already exasperated mind. He wanted to swear and scream of great injustice right into her face. But this was neither the place nor the time for it. So, he just fisted his hands, shoved them into the pockets of his jeans, and clenched his jaw.

"Chief." He nodded and she could see he was trying to control his temper. "What the hell is going on here?"

"I should ask You the same thing," she whispered slowly in a way that exuded authority and took a step toward him, closing the distance between them. "My office. Now."

Rigel nodded in a silent gesture of subordination and followed his superior's orders. Clenching his jaw, he walked behind Nicholetta, passing his colleagues. They all stared at him, shocked by the recent turn of events. Gossip sure travelled faster than truth. He blocked their thoughts to save his sanity, shaking his head at the speed in which everyone judged him without bothering to verify if the accusations against Jade were true. He waited until they made it to Nicholetta's office before speaking up again.

"Where's Alex?" He asked while closing the door behind him, trying to make small talk before the door closed even though he knew where Alex was.

"He's assisting with Ms. Alistair's processing. Looks like she will spend the night in the holding cell." Saying so, Nicholetta walked over to the blinds hanging in the door and glass walls of her office, and turned to close them, one by one, making sure no one would see or hear their conversation. "Sit down, Rigel."

"I'd rather stand."

"I'd rather You didn't," she said firmly. "It would be best if You were sitting for what I have to say."

"Why didn't anyone call me before Jade was arrested?" He asked bluntly, choosing to stand for the time being.

"Because You're no longer on the case, remember?"

"Jade's innocent."

"That is not what concerns me." Nicholetta paused as she passed by him on the way to her chair.

"Shouldn't it? She did not kill that Police Officer," he hissed out, no longer able to control his temper.

"I see." Nicholetta frowned. "Rigel, she's being accused of all those murders on Police Officers, not just this one."

"What!?!" Rigel shouted, aware of how it would appear to those on the other side of the glass walls. "You cannot be serious!?!"

"I'm afraid so." Nicholetta pointed to the chair on the other side of her desk. "Sit down. We have to discuss a few things."

"Like hell, we do, Chief." Rigel swore loud enough for Nicholetta to hear it, but sat down anyway.

"Now, first thing's first. Did You tell anyone You were working on all these unsolved murders cases?" She pointed to the stack of files that looked eerily similar to the ones he locked inside his desk before leaving work on Friday.

"No. Alex doesn't know about them, either. You were the only one who knew about them."

"Alright," she nodded. "Second thing. Does this mean You might have the original files locked somewhere?"

"What?" He asked, confused. "Why would You ask if I had the original files if the files You are pointing at are the... originals?"

"Because I don't believe they are."

"Why would You say that?"

"Because the files on my desk do not seem to match the files You brought in the day we first spoke about them," she said quietly, leaning forward over the desk. "As a matter of fact, I know they don't."

"Chief..." he moved his chair closer and leaned forward as well. "Do You know how it sounds?"

"Unfortunately, I do. I also know what it means." Nicholetta growled at the clear notion of her implications. "Someone inside the precinct falsified legal documentation to implicate Ms. Alistair. They want to discredit her."

"No, Chief. They want to discredit me."

"Not everything is about You, Detective."

"This one might be."

"Alright." She nodded. "Why do You think so?"

"I... may have had a friendly run-in with Knuckles right after Alex called me about Jade's arrest," he rubbed at his beard.

"You may have?" Nicholetta chuckled, surprised. "This gets more interesting each time I blink. And why did Your friend consider revealing this information to You?"

"Because people tend to be honest when their feet dangle above the ground."

"Huh." Nicholetta raised her eyebrow, not surprised after all. "And what did You learn during Your... friendly run-in with Lucky?"

"That his boss gave serious consideration to Yours truly as his next target." Somehow saying it didn't sound as amusing to him as it did when Lucky said it.

"And why does Lucky think his boss considers You to be his target?" She leaned back in the chair and crossed her arms at her chest.

"Because apparently he has a thing for cops. It's an ego thing. And because I am one of the best. That's Lucky's words, not mine," Rigel added, pointing at her.

"You are one of the best." She sighed. "Does this mean I should put two men on You in case Lucky's boss tries to come after You?"

"No. But putting two men on Jade wouldn't hurt." Those words caused another wave of worry he was not accustomed to. Sure, he worried about his sister's well-being over the years, but this was different. Jade wasn't an assassin. She wasn't taught self-defense. She couldn't endure the pressure like Luna did.

"Right. This brings us back to Ms. Alistair and her involvement with You." Nicholetta cleared her throat and reached into one of the drawers in her desk, pulling out a yellow manila envelope. She passed the envelope to Rigel and waited until he opened the envelope. "It appears You have a secret admirer. Or, rather, a fan."

"Son of a..." Rigel swore out loud after retrieving photographs depicting him and Jade during their trip to Chattanooga from the envelope. Namely, from their day trip to Lookout Mountain. He looked at one photograph after another, and his stomach turned. Not because the photographs were taken from a close distance, but because they depicted moments when he and Jade let their guard down while embracing, holding hands, and kissing.

"Do You want to know what bothers me the most about the contents of this envelope?" Nicholetta leaned in again and tapped at the envelope that now laid empty on her desk while he held the photographs in his hands.

"The fact I suck at protecting witnesses since I did not realize we were being watched?"

"No. Well, kind of. Since You mentioned it," she rubbed her forehead. "What bothers me is the fact I received this right after You left the office on Friday - before anyone knew You asked me in private to be removed from the case."

"Son of a..."

"I know. Someone is trying hard to undermine Your and Your judgement. Influencing the witness? Tampering with the evidence? You name it." She hated it, but she knew what it looked like. And she just figured why.

"I would never do that, Chief..."

"Rigel, I need to ask You a question. I need You to be honest with me. No lies. No half-truths. No bull crap." She searched for one of the files in the stack on her desk. She pulled the file out of the stack and placed it between them. "Did You ever tamper with the file report pertaining to the murder at the Mayor's Office?"

"I never tempered with any of the reports," he said with anger.

"Alright," she inclined her head, acknowledging his response. "Did You ever temper with any of the evidence?"

"No!" He raised his voice. "I would never do that!"

"Understood," she took her glasses off. "Can You explain to me, then, the significance of a single green thread? Or why it wasn't included in the evidence in Your original report but it mentioned in it now?"

"A single green thread?" Rigel said more to himself, feeling a sudden sharp pinch of a nerve at the small of his neck.

"Was there, or wasn't there a single green thread on the list of the evidence?" That question was asked in a formal way, from a superior's point of view, not from a private point of view. And Rigel understood the significance of the difference between the two. He sighed, took a deep breath, and realized the enemy of justice may not have necessarily come from outside the Police Force, but from within.

"There wasn't one on the list of evidence, but there was one at the crime scene when I first arrived at the Mayor's office," he admitted with full comprehension of what it implied...

≈ **Chapter 45** ≈

The silence that fell upon the room after Rigel confirmed the existence of the single green thread felt like the longest pause in the history of all pauses. The temper he felt a moment ago was replaced by something of a completely different nature. And it wasn't fear. It was helplessness.

For a man with a past as dark as it was mysterious, Rigel knew how to handle pressure. He knew how to handle ruthlessness. But he did not expect he would come to the necessity of handling helplessness - not in his own precinct. And certainly not because of tampered evidence by one of his own colleagues.

And then, there was Nicholetta Stormstrong herself. She was a stern woman. A strict woman. A woman who always had his back because she trusted the man who was once assigned to work for her and who never broke trust. Until now...

"Would You mind repeating what You just said?" Nicholetta spoke calmly, albeit with a clenched jaw.

"When I first arrived at the Mayor's office, I noticed there was a single green thread at the crime scene," Rigel repeated his words with heaviness that laid on his heart. He screwed up. Big time. And he knew it.

"Where exactly did You see that thread?" Nicholetta asked, reserving the judgement for her best Detective until she heard everything, and took out her notepad to write down his side of the story. She was furious on the inside, but she did not get to where she was by showing emotions.

"In the man's right hand."

"Are You certain?"

"Yes. The victim laid on his right side, with the back of his right hand against the carpet. The single green thread laid in the palm of his hand."

"Possible indication of struggle?"

"Could be, but more likely an unintentional outcome of a struggle," he moved his shoulders. "Jade saw the thread at the crime scene as well."

"Did she?" Nicholetta paused her hand's writing motion at half of a written word.

"Yes."

It bothered Nicholetta that Rigel did not mention the single green thread to her or in the report. It also bothered her he did not think to tell her their only witness - and now suspect - saw it, too. "And when did she tell You about it?"

"The night of the murder."

"Then, why didn't You mention it in Your report?"

"Because it wasn't among the evidence brought back from the crime scene." Her question unnerved him. Not because she questioned it, but because she was right. "And... because I forgot about it until Jade reminded me of it later."

"You forgot?" Nicholetta raised her eyebrow.

"Yes."

"What made You forget it? Or should I ask... who?"

"Let's say that question was not asked."

"Interesting."

"What's interesting is the fact that by the time Jade returned to the room where she found the victim after I interrogated her that night, the thread made its way from the man's hand onto the carpet beside the body," he took a deep breath to add to the importance of the point he was trying to make. "But what's most interesting is that Jade saw it when she retrieved her laptop from the Mayor's Office, but it disappeared when by the time I walked back to that room myself."

"And You are certain neither You nor Ms. Alistair touched the body?"

"Certain." He was convinced Jade had not touched the body, but more than that he was convinced she would not have taken the single green thread. Not after she went out of her way to tell him about it. "Permission to speak off the record?"

Nicholetta narrowed her eyes. The man sitting in front of her was one of very few individuals she would have trusted with her life. Not because he was skilled, but because of his integrity. As such, she offered him the benefit of doubt. If he believed in Jade's innocence, he must have had a good reason. "Granted."

"Jade's father was murdered before her eyes by corrupt Policemen. She took it hard. That sort of trauma stays with You. There isn't a cell in my body that would ever believe she could have done this. Or any of these murders for that matter. She freezes when she sees a gun. She would not be able to hold one, let alone point one at someone."

"Alright. Let's assume we'll go with Your version of the story and the possibility of her being innocent," Nicholetta cleared her throat, impressed that he already knew the quiet Ms. Intern on such a personal level. "There are a number of things we need to go over."

"Such as?" Asking the question not only calmed him down, but it also convinced him his superior really did believe in justice. And she believed him. Rigel watched as she wrote a set of numbers down the page in a column.

"Well, for starters, where do You think the single green thread came from?" Nicholetta not only asked the question, but also wrote it down by the Number (1) bullet on her notepad.

"Beats me. It sure did not fit the crime scene. Jade thought so, too," he crossed his arms at his chest and leaned back in his chair.

"Alright. Next question: who could have taken it?"

"Owens or Slingman. The night guards. Though, my bet's on Owens. That guy is a dipshit," he shook his head, recalling Owens's inapt sense of tactless attitude.

"Moving on...." Nicholetta smirked but the smirk disappeared from her face as soon as it appeared. "The victim. Time of death was established as sometime in the early morning hours on Friday. Since the cleaning crew cleaned the Mayor's office before leaving, how did the body end up where it did?"

"Are we sure they cleaned it?"

"They were questioned, and they all indicated they did."

"But did they really?" Rigel tipped his head to the side on a gut hunch. "It was no secret the Mayor left to visit his family on Thursday. Why clean the room again a day later if no one bothered to mess it up?"

"Are You implying they all lied?" That was a notion she was not yet ready to accept. Nor dismiss, for that matter.

"Am I implying they were all paid or threatened to lie?" He twisted the words and bit his lower lip to prevent a smile from coming when he noticed Nicholetta wrote that question down as one of the bullets on the notepad.

"Next question. Or rather, an unexplained aspect of the crime. The victim was found in the Mayor's Office. But there wasn't enough of a blood stain on the carpet to suggest he was killed there. There was no blood pattern to suggest the shot to the head was fired there, either. So, if the Police Officer wasn't shot there, then where? And why go through so much trouble bringing the body there anyway? Why not kill him in the alley in the back of the building?"

"Those are all separate questions, Chief," he pointed out, and this time did not bother to hide his smile when Nicholetta erased the questions she wrote down and corrected them into separate bullets.

"All right, wise guy. Let's say the victim was killed somewhere else on the City Hall premises. How could the body have been moved into the Mayor's office?"

"Easily, if two men carried it."

"Not without being recorded on surveillance."

"Perhaps, if the surveillance hadn't been down for maintenance that day," Rigel clicked his tongue. "Those pesky things always seem to be down at the right moment."

"You said it, not me," she concurred. "But it still leaves the question as to why it was moved there? Why there, of all places?"

"Believe me, Chief. I've gone over all those questions hundreds of times." Rigel rose from his chair, placing his hands in the pockets of his jeans. "There are only two explanations that make sense to me: either whoever wanted to get rid of the body stumbled upon Jade in the office and had to dump the body somewhere, with the Mayor's office being the closest. Or... the body was there all along for the entire day, hidden somewhere, and they got scared when they realized Jade was still working after hours."

"Which brings us back to Ms. Alistair..."

"What about her?"

"I am not sure if Alex told You, but when he went to the Mayor's Office with the warrant for her arrest, they searched her desk. Rigel, they found the single green thread as well as the supposed murder weapon in her desk," she said cautiously, fully aware of the way he would react.

"Excuse me?" He turned toward her, placing his hands atop her desk. "They found what? And where?"

"Alex found the single green thread along with the gun used to shoot at all the victims' heads inside Your intern's desk. If Your theory of Jade being framed checks out, I assume the bullet signatures from that gun will match the ones from all the prior cases. That's why she's being accused of all these murders. And if the story about her father being killed by Policemen is true, she does not stand a chance against the allegations in all these murder cases," she spoke grimly and placed the pen down on the notepad. "Rigel, if she's innocent, someone has done a hell of a lot of legwork and must have gone to great lengths to frame her."

"They did. And she IS innocent," he straightened up, fully intending to prove his beloved was not guilty...

≈ **Chapter 46** ≈

After a week of brainstorming, gritting his teeth, and pacing back and forth around his house, among other things, Rigel was ready to head back to the precinct with the kind of an adrenaline rush that only came whenever he made a vital crack in the case. Why? Because, indeed, he had...

To everyone at the precinct, including Alex, it was apparent Rigel was ordered to take time off. To clear his head. To cool off. To... steer clear from the press demanding his response to the allegations he was somehow involved in the murders of the Police Officers because of his relationship with Jade. After all, his attendance at the Presidential Gala with Jade at his side did not go unnoticed.

Was he involved with Jade? Of course! He would never, EVER, deny it. But, as Nicholetta pointed out, his presence at the precinct would cause Jade more harm than good. So, he left the precinct with a heavy heart after being told he could not even see his beloved. Although, he did not leave empty handed. Or rather, without being told to continue his work on the case he asked to be removed from.

Per Nicholetta's instructions, he did not contact Alex about the status of the case, aside from brief daily calls to see how Jade was handling the situation. He also refrained from visiting her to prevent making matters worse for her. It pained him to think she was locked up for crimes she had not committed. For a week now. But that realization also came with another –Jade was safe as long as long as she remained locked behind bars.

Whether Lucky was telling the truth or not, it unnerved Rigel to think whoever stood behind the murders now directed their attention to Jade. He could not risk that being true. He simply could not. So, he did not even pause for a single heartbeat when Nicholetta asked him to continue to secretly work on the case - as well as all the other cases - from the vicinity of his home. To follow his gut. To follow the leads. Any leads.

And he did just that.

One very early morning, under the cover of the night and a heavy snowfall, after speaking with his tech-savvy brother Perseus to ensure all the surveillance cameras outside the City Hall were disabled, Rigel climbed the outside stairway on the inner part of the building. The climb was steep and unpleasantly unsafe due to its exposed surface of the stairs. But it also offered him the opportunity to get to the top of the City Hall unnoticed. After all, he needed to follow the nagging hunch at the pit of his stomach that the Rooftop Garden was the one place they missed while investigating the crime scene at the Mayor's Office. That hunch only became more prominent after his... unconventional conversation with Lucky Knuckles.

Equipped with night vision equipment, which could detect blood, sweat, and all other traceable evidence left by humans, Rigel searched the place for close to an hour. But the sun began to rise, and the dawn of the new day came to warn him that he did not have much time. He circled the Rooftop twice. He walked back, forth, in between the little aisles and pathways of the garden's sections, now reduced to lifeless beds of shrubs, sticks, and frozen ground usual for December weather. He knew he had to leave because City Hall workers would be arriving soon at the building, and he did not want to get caught. Ney, he COULDN'T get caught.

He was close to giving up. Hunch or no hunch. Almost a month passed since the crime had been committed at the Mayor's Office. Even if something did happen up on the Garden Rooftop, the weather itself became the killer's most unlikely ally. Rain, snow, high wind in between Chicago's skyscrapers. It all played in the killer's favor. Killers' favor - Rigel corrected himself.

Any sign of struggle would have been gone by now. Suddenly, the moment he thought of it, Lucky's words came to his mind.

"Look where those who do the dirty work hide tools of their trade." Whispering those words sent a bolt of enlightenment through his mind. Dirty work. Tools of the trade. Gardeners. The gardening shed.

He looked around with a sense of urgency. The rising sun proved both a blessing and a burden to him. He removed the night vision equipment but knew if he did not find anything within the next five minutes he would have to head back. He ran around the corners of the Rooftop and the massive air conditioning units. There was no gardening shed. None whatsoever. He swore to himself and kicked the ground. Unbeknownst to him, his foot kicked a rock that had rolled off the garden's gravel path. The rock... hit a metal door in one of the walls.

The void sound of the rock hitting the door echoed through the freezing morning air. Rigel walked up toward the door and tried to open it. It was locked, understandably so. But could a locked door stop a seasoned assassin? Rigel smirked, somehow feeling better because his past proved good for something. Indeed, it had. The door unlocked with ease, fully aware it was no match against an Alistair's skill and experience.

Sighing heavily right before turning the door's knob, Rigel nodded to himself and opened the door. And... swore at the sight which came to his view.

With the sunlight behind his back peeking into the room, Rigel stood still and looked at what he could only describe as a crime scene. The original crime scene. There were signs of struggle. Obvious ones. He pulled out his phone and began recording. Evidence, whether limited or not, could always be removed before he would signal for Nicholetta to obtain a search warrant for the place. So, he recorded everything. And that meant everything. Down to the smallest detail.

The dried-up blood on the floor and the walls.

The blood pattern indicating where the Police Officer was first shot in the chest.

Likewise, the blood pattern where the man had been shoved against the ground and shot in the head.

The tools that had been thrown around, convinced Rigel the man who lost his life did not go down without a fight.

The bloodied shoeprints - three different sizes.

"Lucky, the unlucky, and the... mastermind?"

Rigel zoomed in on the different shoeprints and their patterns. Though all the blood stains now dried due the rigid and harsh conditions of the place, looking at the shoeprints seemed as if he was looking at a still photograph of the crime scene that was undisturbed because no one tended to the garden in the winter.

And then... Rigel paused. He swore. And swore again. There was no chance in all lifetimes... None! Could it really have been so simple? So freaking simple?!? Directing the phone's camera, Rigel zoomed in at the corner of the little room.

"Son of a...."

There it was. In the corner, laying on the ground under a few gardening tools, covered with dust. A torn up green tie.

"There's Your sign of struggle," Rigel said to himself under his breath, feeling an indescribable sense of relief.

Ending the video recording at once, Rigel walked out of the room, leaving the scene undisturbed. He locked the room, and left, convinced that the proof of Jade's innocence had just been found. They just needed to be smart about it.

He made two calls on his way home. One to Nicholetta, telling her all about what he found so she could request a search warrant for the Rooftop Garden, and one private call. And smiled to himself when he ended both calls.

That smile disappeared the moment he arrived home and made his way up to his bedroom, activating the hidden monitors system.

"What's up, Happyski?" Perseus greeted his brother with a not-so-amused look in his eyes.

"It's good to see You, too."

"Found something useful, I, see?" Perseus grinned lightly.

"Something. Watch this." Saying so, Rigel hooked up his telephone to the equipment hidden inside his seemingly plain desk. The video he recorded in the morning downloaded into their shared library for his siblings to be able to view it.

"Cracked the case, did You now?" Tom's ominously cold tone of voice caused both brothers to raise their eyebrows as he joined the call.

"Maybe not cracked it, but made definite progress," Rigel replied with conviction.

"Or, an irreversible setback," Tom said to himself, always keen on the whole picture and not on particular details.

"Why do You say that?" Rigel grew worried, forgetting about the way he felt a moment ago. It did not bother him that Tom refuted his discovery, but that his brother was usually right about those kinds of hunches.

"You sent this video to Your Chief." Tom said bluntly.

"Yes," Rigel nodded.

"She can be trusted, but devices seldom can. Your video message could have been intercepted," Tom said, blunt as before.

"He's right." Perseus nodded in agreement.

"He's right about what?" Caelum joined the conversation from J.J. and Luna Monroe's Boston residence.

"About You taking Your sweet time in the shower, Fin Boy," Perseus snorted at his brother's appearance in a lavish bright yellow floor-length towel wrapped around his waist.

"Good looks take time," Caelum flashed his pearly whites.

"They sure do," Perseus mocked the unkempt state of his brother's living quarters.

"Alright, boys," Tom scolded them. "Caelum, watch the video Rigel just uploaded. Gunay and Rasalas are on assignments. You might want to speak with J.J. and fill him in. Luna hasn't taken the recent turn of events too well, so we'll make sure she gets the much-needed rest for now."

"You really pulled a fast one at the Gala," Caelum tried not to sound judgmental as he watched the video Rigel uploaded to their system's library. "Not to mention after the Gala...."

"Shut up," Rigel clenched his jaw. "I may have attracted unwanted attention not only my way, but Jade's as well."

"What?" Caelum and Perseus asked in unison while Tom remained silent.

"Whoever murdered all those Police Officers decided that Yours Truly fits the profile of the next victim. And Jade's right behind me – or beside me, I'm afraid."

"Damn," Caelum clenched his jaw.

"Double damn," Perseus added. "Alright, how soon do You need us to get there?"

"Caelum and I will come. You need to work on surveillance in the buildings surrounding the City Hall, and inside it. See if

You can trace a pattern between the victim and the City Hall. See who he visited there. See how often." Tom directed his words at Perseus. "And keep looking for possible links connecting men who were shot."

"I've already tried, and bent over backwards," Rigel advised his brothers. "There are three things linking them. They were high level Police Officers who died within their own precinct's borders. They died from the same weapons based on the bullet signatures. And they trusted whoever shot at them enough not to reach for their weapon before it was too late."

"There's one more thing linking them," Tom added dryly.

"What's that?" Rigel raised his eyebrow. He knew his eldest brother, and Tom never pointed things out unless it was necessary.

"One very unlucky Lucky Knuckles," Tom said with an ice-cold piercing gaze that was undeniably thunderous…

≈ Chapter 47 ≈

There were many things Rigel felt grateful for when it came to his brother Tom. Or rather, Vega Alistair to be exact. He was the brother the rest of Alistair siblings looked up to, even if neither one would admit to it out loud. And not only because he was the oldest.

Tom was the least talkative, least exuberant, and least optimistic of all seven siblings. But he was the most skilled of all of them. There was something mysteriously superior about him that his siblings accepted and respected.

Though Tom always indicated he could not foresee the future, his so-called hunches always proved accurate and undeniably precise. They were never wrong. And no one knew that better than Rigel himself.

"How do You know about Lucky?" Rigel asked but shook his head, aware of how foolish it sounded. So, he rephrased the question. "What can You tell us about Lucky in all of this?"

"His luck does not match his name because of the choices he continues to make," Tom said stoically.

"Make Your bed and lay in it?" Caelum asked bluntly, already feeling sorry for whoever the man was.

"You could say that," Tom nodded. "He's a criminal with a shred of conscience. There may come a point where that will come to our aid."

"But it won't come without a price. I know Lucky." Rigel decided to change his clothes before heading back to the precinct. He took his shirt off and walked into his closet to retrieve his favorite dark blue shirt.

"True, but who pays the price isn't always up to us," Tom whispered ominously.

"Then we have to make sure Jade won't be the one paying it," Rigel said in a raised voice from the closet, making sure he spoke loud enough for his brothers to hear him. He paused suddenly, seeing the white shirt Jade wore the last time the monitors had been turned on. He grinned involuntarily at the memory of her frightened reaction at seeing his family, then closed his eyes and clutched his fists at the thought of what she must have been wearing now in the holding cell at the precinct. If there was any consolation price in all of this, it was the fact Nicholetta gave him her word Jade would not be moved from their precinct.

"We'll make sure she doesn't, Happyski," Caelum called out to his brother when Rigel hadn't emerged from the closet for a while.

"I won't rest until she's free and cleared of all the charges. They will pay for this," Rigel answer back and returned to stand in front of the monitors.

"There is always a price to pay when justice is crippled by greed," Tom said quietly.

"But it sucks that too often those who pay the price are innocent," Perseus chimed in as he kept zooming in and out of the video Rigel uploaded.

"Not always," Tom said mysteriously and caused the other brothers to narrow their eyes on him because he never spoke in such a way.

"What do You mean?" Caelum wondered, unsure if Tom was speaking about Lucky, their parents, or something different altogether.

"Justice pays the price, but crime doesn't pay forward either," Tom stood from the chair. "I'll be leaving shortly. These darn currents shouldn't be too much of an issue, but You never know once I get to the Mississippi River. You couldn't have dropped anchor in Florida, couldn't You?"

"That's Rasalas's playground. Besides, if I did, I never would have met Jade or her family..." Rigel moved his shoulders to mask the fact he may have said something he did not wish to reveal to his brothers. Not yet.

"How long will it take You to get to Rigel?" Tom asked Caelum as he packed his waterproof backpack and other waterproof gear.

"Twelve hours, give or take. Depends on whether I stop for sightseeing," Caelum flashed his pearly whites. "I could always swim my way to You."

"Don't." Tom and Rigel both warned him in unison, and immediately narrowed their eyes on each other.

"Tom?" Rigel walked up toward the desk and leaned on it.

"Rigel?" Tom replied but did not bother to look at the monitor, nor did he bother to stop packing.

"What are You not telling us?"

"There isn't anything to tell. Or not tell. Fin Boy just shouldn't waste time on getting to You," Tom paused then and looked at the monitor, turning halfway toward it.

"I hate to quote J.J. Monroe when I don't have to, but those words don't sound positive," Caelum said grimly.

"Double damn, I know. And I feel the same way, Fin Boy," Rigel nodded, feeling sick at the pit of his stomach. "Tom, if You know something, anything, You have to tell me."

"Make sure she stays locked up at the precinct. That's all I know. I swear," Tom said as calmly as he could, and meant it.

"Damn," Rigel whispered.

"Yeah, double that," Tom whispered back.

"Double double damn," Caelum adjusted his towel.

"Hate to be a party pooper, and hate breaking up Your little J.J. Monroe fan club, but I think I found something interesting," Perseus chimed in and reminded the rest he was still a part of the conversation.

"What is it?" Rigel turned his gaze toward Perseus's monitor, as did the others.

"How many different shoe prints would You say You've found in that little hole-in-the-wall up on the City Hall Rooftop?" Perseus leaned back in his chair.

"I counted three," Rigel said, recalling the different shoe prints patterns he noticed at the crime scene he discovered.

"Try four. Though, one of them appeared much less frequently than the others. Possibly visited the place only once," Perseus noted and linked his outstretched hands behind his back.

"The victim?" Rigel tipped his head to the side and placed his hands at the hips.

"No. Another person," Perseus disagreed, proud of his advanced tech scanners and software.

"This means someone else knew about that room. Someone who knows what happened," Caelum noted.

"Someone who's too scared to talk," Rigel uttered.

"Or too greedy to do so," Tom said slowly.

"What?" Rigel hissed out.

"You might want to let Your Chief know there might have been another perpetrator, or an accomplice," Perseus explained his finding in plain words.

"Son of a..." Rigel swore and hit his fist against the top of the desk.

"Easy, Detective. You first must convince Your boss she needs to investigate that crime scene," Caelum pointed out.

"I am sure I can convince Nicholetta," Rigel smirked and remembered he left the light on in the closet. He walked back to turn the light off and noticed the acoustic guitar in the corner of the room displayed on the guitar stand given to him by his late partner and Sebastian's brother. His gut twisted into knots that were almost unbearable. Not only for Jade but for Eryk's sake. He was right to request to be removed from the case. He was too invested and involved in the case now, and too much was at stake. "I can't shake the feeling that whoever is behind these murders had something to do with Eryk's death. I owe it to Eryk to make sure they rot in prison for lifetimes to come."

"I'm with You on that one, brother. But don't do anything foolish before I get there," Caelum leaned in. He knew Rigel, his nature, and his unwavering sense of righteousness. He also knew once Rigel decided to go after the bad guy, no hell or high water would be able to stop him.

"Thanks for Your concern, Fin Boy," Rigel winked at him.

"He means it," warned him.

"I know," Caelum grinned.

"No." Tom shook his head. "I agree with You. Rigel, don't do anything foolish before we get there. Or at least until Fin Boy gets there."

"That won't be an issue. Jade's safe. I'm heading back to the precinct right now to speak with Nicholetta about the video I recorded. See You soon." Rigel saluted his brothers in a gesture of saying goodbye, and Perseus and Caelum ended their calls. But Tom did not.

"Rigel..." Tom's tone of voice got to Rigel more than the fact his brother did not sign off the call when the others did.

"I suspected You were going to stay on for longer to warn me not to go 'All Alistair' on the bad guys."

"You should know better than to go 'All Alistair' on anyone in broad daylight," Tom stood in his signature pose, with feet firmly on the ground and arms crossed at his chest. "But that's not why I wanted to talk to You."

"Oh? Then why?"

"Make sure Jade does not leave the precinct."

"Why? What do You know? What aren't You telling me?"

"It's more like what You aren't telling me..."

"If it's about my feelings for Jade, then I have nothing to hide. I love her."

"Love her. That's fine. But I was referring to the way Jade's father was murdered. Or rather, why..." Tom switched the weight of his body from one leg to the other.

"I... How do You know about that?"

"I read feelings. And it goes much deeper than that, Detective Hunky," Tom sighed. "Whether it was serendipity or a more meaningful virtue of Fate that caused Your paths to cross, You meeting Jade set in motion something we may not be ready for."

"I will not give up on her, and I won't leave her," Rigel fisted his hand.

"I would never ask You to do that. She is the key to our past as much as the path to Your future. Not only Yours. That's why You must protect her at all cost," Tom said in one breath. His heart ached all the way down to its very depths. He could not explain to Rigel what he felt at that moment. He would not even know where to begin.

"You scare me when You talk like that," Rigel straightened up, feeling even worse than he did a moment ago.

"I would not say it if it wasn't important," Tom sighed and walked up to turn the monitor off. "It shouldn't take Caelum long to get to You. I hope to see You soon. All of You."

"I'll hold You to that," Rigel pointed at his brother.

"Do that - on Your and Jade's end as well. And make sure she does not leave that holding cell." Tom pointed back at him and switched the monitor off.

The cold sweat that rolled down Rigel's back after hearing what Tom said rolled down his back in waves the moment he arrived at the precinct only to be told Jade had been released from custody and left with the Mayor of Chicago, who personally vouched for her safety…

≈ **Chapter 48** ≈

The shock of fear, despair, and rage rushing through Rigel's veins felt paralyzing. For a moment he did not know whether to punch the Police Officer who informed him of Jade's release from custody, or whether to scream out Nicholetta's name with such anger she would hold no doubt in her heart as to the depth of betrayal he felt.

With no choice but to conceal his true feelings, with the last resort of keeping up appearances in front of everyone around him, Rigel rushed to Nicholetta's Office. He did not shout. Not just yet. He was saving it for the moment the door to her Office would shut behind him. He walked with such force and blind fury in his eyes that those who stood in his way simply stepped back out of fear of being thrown back.

He was mad. He was hurt. He was enraged, desperately afraid for Jade's life. And he knew he would not be able to stop himself from throwing it all in Nicholetta's face. Except...

She wasn't in her Office. So, he stopped abruptly and looked around. His heart pounded so fiercely that he had a hard time hearing Alex calling out to him. And it did not help at all when Alex approached him and repeated his question.

"Happyski, I asked what You're doing here?" The concern on Alex's face matched the tone of his voice.

"I have to speak with Nicholetta," Rigel hissed out as calmly as he could.

"She rushed out to speak with the judge about a search warrant. She received some classified information and left right away," Alex explained and tried to calm his partner down.

"What information?" Rigel asked, fully aware he sent the information to Nicholetta.

"She didn't say. She just told me it was classified."

"Who signed off on Jade's release if she left?" Rigel placed a hand on Alex's shoulder. He tried his best to whisper, but restraint wasn't his strong side.

"Nicholetta did. Before she left," Alex whispered and grit his teeth to prevent a wince when Rigel squeezed his shoulder.

"She signed off on the release herself?" Rigel tried to speak even more quietly. "Did it not make her wonder why Lucchese came personally to ask for her release?"

"Of course, it did not," Alex inclined his head. "He's the Mayor."

"From where I'm standing, he's a whole lot more than just the Mayor. A whole lot worse than that." Rigel clenched his jaw and looked Alex dead in his eyes.

"You don't mean...?" Alex swallowed hard.

"Don't I?"

"Son of a..."

"Got that right," Rigel growled and released the grip on Alex's shoulder. "We need to find Lucchese, and we need to do it fast."

"The Mayor's car is still in the parking lot," Barb, the receptionist, said as she passed them on the way to the kitchen area to refill her coffee cup.

"He's still here?" Rigel shot her a piercing gaze.

"That's what it looks like," Barb nodded and resumed walking toward the kitchen area.

"How long ago was Jade released? How long ago did they leave?" Rigel asked, too urgently for others not to have noticed.

"About half an hour ago? Give or take a minute?" Alex replied and began to understand the urgency behind Rigel's concern. Or rather, the reason for it.

"Grab Your jacket. We have to go now!" Rigel pointed toward Alex's jacket, urging Alex to pick up his pace.

They hurried out of the precinct, running toward the parking lot behind the building. Rigel swore, more than once, at the slush of snow mixed with dirty pavement and gravel of the parking lot ground. He wanted to run, rush, to possess the kind of speed his sister was capable of. He wanted to find Jade, Lucchese, and his car. But as he turned the corner of the building and saw the Mayor's car still parked in the spot Lucchese apparently parked in, Rigel paused, frozen not out of rage, but out of fear. Why? Because the sight of a pair of legs lying beside the car nearly caused his knees to buckle.

"Holy shit!" Alex swore for probably the first time in his entire life as he looked in the direction of the Mayor's car.

"Holy shit is right!" Rigel exclaimed more to himself and began shouting Jade's name as they ran toward the car. "Jade! Jade! Jade!"

"How the hell are we going to explain this to Nicholetta?!?" Alex shouted and stopped mere inches from the body laying between the Mayor's car and a Police Squad car next to it. Since Rigel got to the body first, it left little room for Alex to crouch down beside it as well.

"Help me turn him over!" Rigel scolded his partner.

"Oh, damn!" Alex shouted and felt sick to his stomach the moment they turned the body over... only to reveal it was the Mayor himself.

"Double that!" Rigel almost hit Alex out of anger. "Wipe off that shitty pale grimace off Your face! Call the ambulance! He's still breathing!"

"Rigel..." The Mayor's faint whisper sounded almost silent.

"Don't talk, Vincent. You're alive, let's keep it that way," Rigel spoke frantically and realized the Mayor was shot three times in the chest. "Damn it!"

"The ambulance is on its way! Hang in there, Mayor!" Alex removed his jacket and covered the Mayor to keep him warm.

"Rigel... Jade..." Vincent Lucchese coughed with each breath he took. "You have to... save her...."

"This wouldn't have happened if You left her inside that cell!" Rigel shouted, unable to stop the guilt and despair from coming up to the surface.

"They... found out... You were onto them...." Vincent whispered in between coughing.

"They? Who? How?" Rigel asked, feeling the cold sweat rolling down his back again.

"The Gala... they saw Jade with You... They got scared. And then panicked today when You... went to the... Rooftop..." the Mayor whispered helplessly.

"What?!?" Rigel shouted more at himself than at the Mayor. "Who?!? Who's behind all this?!?"

"Owens... the City Hall Security Guard and... Lucky? I think he said his name was... Lucky?" Vincent replied and began to close his eyes.

"No! Don't close them Lucchese! Stay awake!" Rigel almost shook him. "How do You know Lucky? When did You meet him?"

"Owens... received a visit from this.... guy this morning. I saw them... talking when I came to the City Hall. I... demanded he would tell... me his name." Saying so, the Mayor grit his teeth and began to reach for Rigel's hand. Rigel grabbed it. And swore deep down inside.

"Son of a..." Rigel was unable to stop himself. By grabbing the Mayor's hand, he finally read his mind. All of it. Down to its deepest abyss. And... he realized in that very heartbeat that Vincent Lucchese may have been a tyrant and a nasty person, but he wasn't the murderer nor the mastermind behind the murders.

"Rigel... after Owens shot me... he grabbed Jade. They sped off...." the Mayor coughed and winced from pain as they heard the siren sound of the approaching ambulance. "Lucky...."

"What about Lucky?!?" Rigel begged him frantically. "And don't call me Rigel. It's scary. After all of this is over, and You recover, go back to calling my Happyski."

"That... guy wouldn't... wouldn't... shoot me like Owens demanded. He... fired the shot, but at the pavement. He... said..." Vincent coughed more and more, but the way he held Rigel's hand left no doubt in Rigel's mind he would make it through.

"What did he say?" Rigel asked as the ambulance pulled up right behind them.

"He said... Chattanooga. They were... taking Jade to... Chattanooga," Vincent uttered and grit his teeth as the paramedics switched places with Rigel and Alex.

"Got it," Rigel nodded toward the Mayor in an unspoken gesture of understanding and... appreciation. They may have hated each other, but Rigel realized Vincent's feelings for him came from a point of view of a brother's love for his sister, and that, THAT, was something Rigel understood all too well.

"We have to call Nicholetta," Alex called out after Rigel as they made their way toward Rigel's pickup truck.

"Let's get in the car first. There are a few choice words I have to exchange with her, and it's best that unwanted ears won't hear them," Rigel hissed out and looked in the direction of the precinct, where most of his colleagues rushed out to see what was going on.

"Are You going to yell at Nicholetta?" Alex asked and shivered from the cold as they entered Rigel's car.

"I know better than to yell at Nicholetta," Rigel hissed out, reaching behind the passenger seat to retrieve one of his spare jackets and passed it to Alex.

"Sure. You were about to yell at her at the precinct," Alex snarled at his partner and dialed Nicholetta's phone number.

"I learn fast," Rigel turned the pickup toward the expressway with a screech of tires.

"Yeah, right. I'll learn how to brew a decent cup of coffee before I agree with You on that one," Alex shook his head and appreciated the warm feeling of Rigel's jacket, though he could not get past the fact he looked like a child in the oversized jacket. He looked at the phone, shaking his head. "She's not picking up."

"Call her again! And call Sebastian and Marek!" Rigel scolded his partner, having already communicated with his two brothers, wherever they may have been…

≈ Chapter 49 ≈

All the days and nights spent in his past livelihood as an assassin could not have prepared Rigel for the real test of his character. Fear used to mean nothing. Danger used to mean nothing. But now? Now all his fears morphed together with the threat of danger he was not able to overcome.

He made the trip to Chattanooga countless times. He knew which roads to take, where to cut through the traffic, which shortcuts to choose over the main roads. But now, Rigel knew he was racing against time. And with nearly nine hours to go, they had no time to spare. Were Owens and Lucky Knuckles headed to Chattanooga with Jade as their hostage? Rigel made damn sure of it before leaving Chicago. What good was the Alistair trait and gift of reading minds if they could not have used it to their advantage? Having communicated with Tom, even when he fought against the underwater currents on his way to the United States, Rigel was reassured by his eldest brother that Lucky had not lied. They were headed to Chattanooga. But the question remained why?

Though, it wasn't the only question on Rigel's mind as he drove out of Chicago with Alex in the passenger seat. The other question troubling Rigel's mind pertained to Nicholetta Stormstrong. Or rather, lack of any communication on her part.

"We left the precinct nearly an hour ago. Why isn't she answering?" Alex wondered out loud while looking intently at his cell phone. "Can't she see how urgent this is?"

"She better have a good explanation for not picking up," Rigel gripped the steering wheel as he cut between cars on the highway at the speed which Alex began to associate with the queasy feeling of being seasick, carsick, and motion sick. "I understand court houses and their damn 'no cell phones' Policy, but how long does it take to get a search warrant?"

"As long as it takes?" Alex bit his tongue when Rigel sent him an ice-cold stare.

"Call her again," Rigel called out to his partner after another failed attempt, but before Alex was able to do so, he received a call, whose name on the caller ID surprised him, and not in a good way.

"The precinct?" Alex said out loud, and his words formed a bad feeling in Rigel's gut. "Oh, man, I hope the Mayor's alright."

"Then don't hope. Just pick it up,"

"Barb...? What is it?" Alex accepted the call, and his grim face twisted additional knots in Rigel's gut.

"What is it?"

"That's not possible!" Alex raised his voice, turning to Rigel. "What is it?!?"

"Nicholetta..." Alex began to speak but his throat locked up.

"Give me the phone!" Rigel hissed out and reached for the phone, but Alex moved it out of his reach.

"Nicholetta's been shot. She's at the hospital," Alex said as calmly as he could, but the fear for their Chief was all too visible in his eyes and mind.

"What?!?" Rigel shouted and involuntarily pressed on the gas pedal, causing the pickup to speed up. The pickup wavered in between the lanes, which forced Rigel to reduce the speed to regain control of it. "What do You mean she's been shot?!?"

"Stop shouting so I can hear Barb," Alex warned him. "Go on, Barb."

Rigel didn't know if he was more furious at Barb for not calling him with that information, at Alex for not turning the speaker voice option on the phone so he could hear Barb as well, or at himself for not figuring out he could have put Nicholetta's life in danger as well – just as Tom hinted during their last conversation.

"Alright. I'll call You later to check in on Nicholetta's condition. Thanks, Barb," Alex ended the call and swore out loud.

"Stop swearing. It looks bad on You." Rigel looked at Alex after he fell silent. "Well, what happened?"

"Nicholetta was shot," Alex said, irritated and mad.

"You already said that!" Rigel puffed out air and patted his partner's shoulder in a not-so-delicate way. "Snap out of it. We don't have time to turn this pickup around to go back to Chicago so I can ask Barb where she's been shot."

"Right," Alex nodded, then shook his head to think more clearly. "Nicholetta was shot in the courthouse garage."

"Damn it!" Rigel hit the steering wheel with his fist.

"That's not all," Alex sent him a grim look.

"Then speak!" Rigel shouted, forgetting about his skill of reading minds amid everything that was going.

"She... was apparently shot by the judge she was going to see about the search warrant," Alex advised him but paused, looking at Rigel.

"Damn!" Rigel hit the steering wheel with his fist for the second time.

"That's not all," Alex dropped the phone into one of the beverage holders between them.

"Well?" Rigel puffed out air. "Care to share?"

"Barb said she reviewed the precinct surveillance footage at the precinct to see if she could find out what car Owens and Lucky drove off with Jade. She found the car, but she found more than what she was looking for." Alex rubbed his eyes. Everything he thought he knew about his job and those he worked with was falling apart right before his eyes. "Barb said one of the cameras recorded Phryners from the Evidence Room making two phone calls right after Nicholetta left. And then... the recording showed him greeting Owens in the parking lot while Lucky sat in the car when Vincent Lucchese was about to walk out of the precinct with Jade."

"You've got to be kidding me?!?" Rigel yelled. "The records guy?!? No freaking wonder!"

"Don't worry. They got Phryners. A couple of Detectives punched the daylights out of him and threw him in a holding cell. He..." Alex swallowed hard. He didn't know whether he wanted to share the information with Rigel or punch him instead. He chose to offer his partner the benefit of a doubt before judging him. "Phryners admitted to calling the judge. He warned the judge before Nicholetta arrived at the courthouse. That's why the judge waited for her in the courthouse garage."

"Son of a..." Rigel shook his head. "That's why they were always one step ahead all these years!"

"The judge thought he was taking care of their coverup, but security guards saw him firing the gun at Nicholetta. He's in custody, pretty beat up as well," Alex said, looking out the window.

"How's Nicholetta?" Rigel asked, feeling worried and guilty beyond words. "Did Barb say anything about her condition?"

"She was unconscious, but not in critical condition. That's all they've been told."

"That's good," Rigel breathed a momentary sigh of relief.

"Rigel? How did You know about the search warrant? How come You weren't surprised Nicholetta went to see the judge? How come I didn't know about any of it when I'm the one on the case?" Alex's words twisted knots of different sorts in Rigel's stomach.

"I... Nicholetta asked me to continue working on the case. On all of the cases." He sighed heavily and knew how much his words hurt Alex, even without reading his thoughts.

"What do You mean on all of the cases?"

"You know about the cases where Police Officers supposedly got shot and killed during robberies?"

"Yes," Alex nodded slowly. "You mean those cases are linked to the murder at the Mayor's Office?!? All of them?!?"

"Yes and no," Rigel swerved swiftly to switch highways as he cut through traffic.

"Care to unpack it for me?"

"The cases are linked. Same ammo. Same suspect. Well, same suspects to be exact. But no, the murder did not occur at the Mayor's Office. That Police Officer was killed on the City Hall's Rooftop."

"Are You kidding me?!?" Alex raised his voice, which almost never happened. "Have You ever looked up the definition of partnership?!? What about trust?!? What about sharing information?!? What about loyalty?!?"

"I... I'm sorry," Rigel said remorsefully. "I had a hunch when I saw the bullet wounds on the latest victim. So, I brought it up to Nicholetta. She asked me to look into the murders. Well, technically she asked me to continue looking into them. There was just too much of a coincidence between these cases the way I saw it."

"And never, EVER, did it cross Your mind to share this with me, Happyski?" Alex gave into the urge of punching Rigel's shoulder. "Why did You keep all this to Yourself?"

"I lost one partner. I sure as hell wasn't going to lose another one," Rigel said quietly. "I really am sorry, Alex. You have to believe me."

"Believe You? It's a bit hypocritical, don't You think?" Alex chuckled with resentment.

"You're right. But the day we lost Eryk haunts me every day," Rigel sent a sorrowful gaze Alex's way. "Vincent requesting for me to take the lead may have been a wicked fickle finger of Fate. Who knows. But the moment it dawned on me all these murders on Police Officers may be linked somehow, I promised myself there won't be another murder like that. This string of murders on Police Officers will end with me, one way or another."

"That's deep. Real deep, Happyski," Alex patted his arm. It was hard to stay mad at a man like Rigel, especially when he spoke with words that came from his heart. "Now, step on it. You not only have Jade to worry about. Think what Marek will say if he gets to Chattanooga before us."

"That wasn't funny," Rigel shook his head, as both men knew that what awaited them in Chattanooga was gravely serious. So serious it would affect their lives forever...

≈ **Chapter 50** ≈

By the time they arrived in Chattanooga, Rigel figured out a few very important things. He was in love with Jade and made peace with it in a way only a man content with his feelings could. That truth was as self-evident as the fear for her life. He also calmed down enough to be able to think straight again. Acting on impulse rarely produced expected results, and he was aware of it. He also knew Owens needed to be stopped – before he harmed Jade.

Grateful for his band of brothers, whether linked with him by blood or by friendship, Rigel parked the pickup truck a couple of miles away from their campsite. He communicated with Tom once again, before exiting the main roads, and made sure Owens and Lucky took Jade to the location of their Chattanooga campsite, and nowhere else. It both sickened him and calmed him down to know that Owens directed their car to the exact location of their campsite.

Much to the disadvantage of the bad guys, Rigel and his friends knew that piece of land like the backs of their hands. And since Tom reassured Rigel that Jade's thoughts screamed so loud repeating Rigel's name he would not have any problem hearing her from the moon, he was certain they did go to the campsite, and that although Jade was tied down, she was alive and otherwise unharmed. Tom also indicated they arrived at the campsite not long before Rigel got there as well. As such, Rigel knew he had to park far enough from the campsite for Owens to remain unaware of their presence.

It surprised Rigel, and impressed him as well, to see when Marek pulled up in his pickup truck moments after Rigel parked his on the side of the road. It was getting dark, and Rigel knew they could not drive up with their headlights on. They needed the element of surprise if they wanted to save Jade. That was the most important thing - to all of them.

"I have to hand it to You for getting here so fast." Rigel greeted Sebastian and Marek, patting both men's backs in a brotherly gesture. "If the circumstances were different, I would have even said I'm officially impressed by what You baby truck can do."

"I'll carve that in my doorstep mat," Marek offered him a faint grin.

"You're sure they came to the campsite?" Sebastian said quietly when Alex and Marek walked to the back of Marek's car to retrieve the backpacks Marek brought with him.

"Yes. But I could not figure out why. It appears Owens acted spontaneously when he kidnapped Jade," Rigel replied grimly.

"So, it seems. But drive all the way out here?" Sebastian shook his head.

"Whatever his reason for it, he didn't want witnesses. There's no one out here for a couple of miles each way." Just thinking about it turned Rigel's gut. He chose not to think of the reasons, but only one came to his mind.

"Did that idiot really shoot the Mayor?" Sebastian rubbed at his beard.

"Yes. Three shots in the chest," Rigel gestured with his fingers in the fading light of the setting sun.

"Seriously?" Sebastian grit his teeth. "He isn't just an idiot. He's an idiot with a death wish."

"His accomplice shot my boss, so..." Rigel added, but paused when Sebastian shot an angry gaze his way.

"Seriously?" Sebastian clenched his jaw. "Where the hell are the Security Guards when You need them?"

"Well, Owens is a Security Guard. Though, I doubt he'll be allowed back at the City Hall after this. So, I guess he *was* a Security Guard," Rigel frowned.

"What?" Sebastian and Marek replied in unison as the other men returned with the backpacks.

"Owens was a Security Guard at the City Hall. He had the perfect view and front row seat to everything and everyone who visited the building," Rigel spoke in an ice-cold tone of voice.

"And it looks like he joined forces with the idiot judge who shot our Chief," Alex pointed out.

"What?!?" Sebastian and Marek raised their voices and immediately realized they should not have done so.

"Yup. Owens was always a dipshit. So was Lucky Knuckles, but I didn't suspect a judge to be involved in all of this," Rigel shrugged. "Damn it, I wonder if they've been working together since the first murder of all those Police Officers."

"There's a bad guy named Lucky Knuckles?" Marek cocked his eyebrows.

"He's bad, all right. He's a part of it, but he also told the Mayor where they were taking Jade," Rigel inclined his head Marek's way.

"You don't think he did so intentionally, do You?" Sebastian wondered while searching through the backpack Marek handed to him. "Do You think he wanted You to come after them to finish You off?"

"No. I've known Lucky back in the days on the Police Force. He wouldn't do that," Rigel rejected the idea and accepted the backpack from Marek.

"Rigel, if he's involved with this Owens guy, and if this Owens guy hates Law Enforcement, is it possible Lucky may have something to do with Eryk's death?" Though Sebastian asked the question unaware that the multiple murders on Police Officers were linked, his question caused a wave of guilt in Rigel's mind. And in his gut. And in his heart.

"Son of a..." Alex swore before Rigel did.

"Sebastian, I..." Rigel clenched his jaw. He swore at himself for not bringing Lucky in for questioning all the countless times he ran into him. If he knew. If he only knew. If he decided to read Lucky's mind deeply enough to pick up on those bits and pieces of information Lucky guarded so well, all those Police Officers may have still been alive. Eryk may have still been alive.

"Rigel, it's alright." Sebastian patted his best friend's shoulder. One look at Rigel, and he saw in Rigel's eyes what they both felt in their hearts. "Don't beat Yourself up for it. What's been done, has been done. Eryk's gone. It wasn't Your fault."

"That's right, Happyski," Marek nudged Rigel and adjusted the bulletproof vest he removed from his backpack. "I miss Eryk. He was a good man. But we have an important task to take care of on this mission. Reminiscing about the past won't help us."

"Mission?" Alex countered his brother-in-law's statement.

"That's right," Marek adjusted the straps of Alex's bulletproof vest. "Call it a mission. Treat it like a mission. Succeed in completing it, just like a mission."

"You must miss Your days in the Special Forces, but I could be wrong," Alex teased Marek.

"The Army doesn't leave Your blood just because You no longer wear the uniform," Marek flashed his pearly whites at Alex, though he did so to get back at him and not out of amusement.

"You look more manly when You talk like that," Rigel grinned at Marek while removing his jacket to put on the bulletproof vest, only to cover it up again with the jacket.

"I don't need to look more manly. I've reached maximum human capacity for it," Marek smirked at Rigel.

"Alright, boys. And Mr. Masculinity," Rigel nodded at Marek. He looked at Sebastian to make sure his best friend was wearing the bulletproof vest. "Whatever happens, we have to make sure Jade comes out of this alive. Whatever the cost."

"What about Owens? And this guy... Lucky?" Marek asked as they were getting ready to leave their pickup trucks behind.

"Owens is the mastermind behind all of this. I'd snap him like a twig with my bare hands, but there would be poetic justice in making sure he survives and goes to prison. Criminals are partial to Law Enforcement, but they are even more partial to those who kill Law Enforcement Officers. He wouldn't last the night if he ever went behind bars." Rigel said in one breath as they placed night vision and surveillance glasses on their heads so they wouldn't need to search for them in darkness.

"What about Lucky?" Sebastian wondered with a temper simmering under his skin.

"We... have a reason to believe he may have been involved in Eryk's murder. Whatever happens to him, happens. But if we can spare him, I am sure they would take into consideration that he technically helped us when the Mayor was shot," Rigel moved his shoulders up and down.

"I'm sure," Sebastian nodded but went back to Marek's pickup, opened the passenger door, and retrieved his axe.

"Was that really necessary?" Alex speculated.

"Yes." Sebastian raised his favorite axe to look at it in the last rays of the setting sun. "You shoot Your guns, and I swing my axe."

"And what, engraving it added flying magic to it?" Marek chuckled, perfectly aware the guns he brought for them stood a better chance against the bad guys.

"No," Sebastian grinned. "I don't need toys to feel confident about my abilities against some gun wielding thugs. My hands are skilled enough to hold an axe and I know what I'm doing. Plus, You throw an axe and it's silent. You shoot and no silencer will ever muffle the shot completely."

"He does have a point," Rigel nodded in agreement with his best friend's train of thought, patting the handle of the axe. "It's no guitar, but we may use its own melody to our advantage."

"Exactly," Sebastian responded with the full confidence of a Polish Highlander.

"Let's go save Your woman, Happyski." Marek's stern words reminded them about the reality of the situation. "First You compliment my car, then You compliment Sebastian's choice of weapon. Let's leave before You lose Your mind completely and compliment Alex's coffee."

"Hey!" Alex brooded.

"What?" Marek turned to Alex.

"Fine," Alex uttered. "I'm not ready for that day either. I'd rather be the best of the worst."

"Alright," Rigel asserted. "Sebastian, turn on the lights at the campsite. Let them think it was a result of the sun going down, and not of us coming after them."

"On it." Sebastian pulled out his cell phone and activated the lights placed at the corners of the campsite as well as the strings of lights strung between the four parked campers.

"Thank You for doing this for Jade, and for me," Rigel made sure their bulletproof vests were secured. "And for Eryk."

"For Eryk," Sebastian inclined his head, swinging his axe over his shoulder.

"And for Nicholetta," Rigel sent Alex a confident look. Alex knew that look. He'd seen it before. And he knew his partner always made the bad guys pay when that piercing gaze appeared in Rigel's eyes…

≈ **Chapter 51** ≈

The nightfall worked in their favor. As did the knowledge of the grounds surrounding the campsite. It felt unfathomable to Rigel that the one place on the surface of the earth that felt like a safe haven to him now signified his fear for Jade's life.

He loved Jade. He was in love with her – and yes, to him those two aspects were different yet intimately intertwined with one another.

He feared for her life.

The moment they came up on the hill overlooking the campsite, they crouched down to the ground. Though they wore the night vision goggles, which allowed them to see the unseen, Rigel preferred to scan the area without them. He focused on every detail, knowing the smallest details were as important as the big picture. Especially, since Tom was stuck somewhere in the waters of the Gulf of Mexico near Florida, and Caelum was still making his way up the Tennessee River.

"The night vision goggles work only if You wear them on Your nose, Happyski," Marek nudged Rigel, pointing toward the goggles on top of Rigel's head.

"Seeing what Owens sees will help us. At least when it comes to figuring out the best way to get to Jade." Rigel pointed out.

"The best way to get to her would be from the Tennessee River, but neither one of us would be so bold as to try that approach," Marek scanned the area for signs of movement.

"You're right... on both accounts," Rigel nodded in agreement. He almost smirked at the thought of Caelum coming up to their location from the riverside. The question remained, however, as to when his brother would make an appearance.

"I see their car, but where are they?" Alex nudged his partner, crouching beside him. "Marek, I thought these gadgets were supposed to pick up movement and heat sources?"

"They do." Marek replied flatly, examining his phone displaying security features of the campsite.

"So why can't we see them?" Alex doubted Marek's words.

"They are either between the RV's or inside one of them," Marek sneered at Alex for implying his equipment wasn't working properly. "Plus, the lights at the campsite aren't helping us."

"You do have a point," Rigel agreed. "Sebastian, can You turn off the main corner lights and leave the strings of lights on?"

"On it." Sebastian nodded, but swore out loud.

"What is it?" Rigel asked, worried.

"Not on it. The lights won't turn off." Sebastian damned the application responsible for switching the lights off and on at the campsite. "Seriously? Now it decides to malfunction? Damn good-for-nothing technology."

"Don't blame technology. Blame the user," Marek mocked him.

" Let me remind You of Your faulty speaker," Sebastian mocked Marek back.

"At least I have one," Marek mimicked Sebastian's response in a sarcastic way.

"I don't need one. My RV is equipped with more stuff than what is necessary," Sebastian sent Marek a cocky grin.

"That's right," Alex chimed in, wincing when his brother-in-law looked at him.

"Let's deal with the bad guys, not with each other," Rigel scolded his friends. "Sebastian, how good are You with throwing that axe?"

"Better than some are with handling speakers," Sebastian replied and looked at Marek.

"Let's hope Your aim is as accurate as Your words," Marek retorted.

"Very funny." Sebastian's face turned into a smug smirk.

"What?" Marek raised his eyebrow.

"The circuit breaker box for the corner lights is next to Your RV. No wonder the app stopped working," Sebastian taunted him.

Marek was about to respond in a not-so-polite way, when they heard a breaking sound coming from one of the RVs. Namely, Rigel's RV.

"Jade..." Rigel whispered urgently under his breath and was about to leap into action when Alex grabbed onto him.

"Stay down," Alex hissed through his teeth while he held Rigel down. "We didn't come all this way for You to screw it all up now. You didn't want to call the Police, fine. You wanted us to handle it this way. So, let's handle it, and not screw up."

"Nice speech," Marek patted his brother-in-law's back.

"Nice or not, he's right," Rigel shook his head at his own reaction and admitted his partner had a point. "Sebastian, You and I will go around the RVs to see if You can throw that axe of Yours at the circuit breaker box. We can't walk up to it or shoot at it. Marek and Alex, You guys come around from the other side and see if You could get a good angle on Owens. I gauge he'll have Lucky guarding Jade. Men like him want to be in charge, but I doubt he'd do the dirty work himself. We take out Owens, and Lucky will surrender to save his own skin."

Once they separated, Rigel communicated with Tom. Caelum was close, closing in on their location. However, he was still too far for Rigel to be able to count on his help if he needed it now.

With Alex and Marek disappearing into the night, Rigel and Sebastian made their way far behind the RVs to the other side of the campsite. They located the circuit breaker box, and Sebastian was about to swing the axe in the air when Rigel caught sight of a movement between the RVs. He grabbed Sebastian's arm and held his breath.

There she was. Jade. His Jade! She was being led by Lucky out of his RV. Her clothes looked a bit disheveled. Her unbraided hair blew freely in the night breeze. Her hands were tied together. But she seemed unharmed otherwise. He could not hear what Lucky was telling her, but he could see Jade's reaction to the words. And it boiled his blood. Though, there was something else that boiled his blood even more. He read Jade's thoughts. Or at least he attempted to do so. Her mind was blank. Completely void of thoughts. Any thoughts whatsoever. This told him she blocked out all thoughts of fear, violence, and everything that was happening to her - and he knew why.

"Son of a..." The words Rigel whispered held more fear for Jade's life than his anger in them. They crouched down and watched from afar, hoping not to have been discovered just yet.

"Why do You think they broke into Your RV?" Sebastian leaned in closer toward Rigel.

"No clue." Rigel narrowed his eyes and concentrated on reading Lucky's thoughts. "Damn."

"What?"

"I just read Lucky's mind."

"And?"

"It's blank."

"What does that mean?" Sebastian turned his gaze to Lucky and Jade.

"It means they don't have a plan, or Owens doesn't trust Lucky enough to tell him what he planned for Jade. Neither of which is good for us," Rigel sighed heavily. And then, he whispered. "Tom..."

"He's here?"

"No. But he can help us." Rigel closed his eyes and communicated with Tom. He needed Tom's help. Namely, his unsurpassed ability to communicate with others. He did not need for Tom to arrive - he just needed Tom to let Jade know they were at the campsite in case she saw them so she would not shout their names.

"Rigel..." Sebastian nudged his best friend since Rigel kept his eyes closed for a longer while. "Rigel."

"What?" Rigel opened his eyes.

"What did You do?" Sebastian's question shot a jolt of fear through Rigel's heart. "I thought You didn't have the ability to communicate with Jade?"

"I don't. But Tom does." Rigel replied and watched as Jade's stance changed from that of a frightened victim with a blank stare into that of a woman not afraid to face whatever was coming. She straightened out, running the fingers of her tied hands through her hair as if she were trying to move strands of hair away from her eyes, but in reality, she searched the area for any sign of Rigel. She looked to the right, and then to the left. Suddenly, she paused. She saw him! She did! And the moment she did, she lowered her head back down, and resumed the stance of a victim, letting out a resigned sigh.

'You came...!'

That thought, that single thought, offered them both so much relief Rigel lost his balance for a moment and leaned toward Sebastian. But it wasn't a loss of balance caused by fear, it was one fueled by hope.

"Oh, she's good..." Rigel whispered under his breath.

"What are You talking about? She's crying." Sebastian scratched his head, confused.

"She is. But now she knows we're here. And she is aware of what it means."

"And what does it mean?"

"It means Your axe is about to fly," Rigel clicked his tongue and sent Sebastian his mischievous Alistair look, content in the fact he would soon hold Jade back in his arms again…

≈ Chapter 52 ≈

The only thing sweeter than watching Sebastian's axe flying through the night sky, with its sharp blade glistening in the moonlight, was the deaf sound of the axe hitting its target. The circuit breaker box burst into a bright cloud of firecracker sparks seconds before the corner lights went out around the campsite.

Owens swore to high heavens. So did Lucky, but for a totally different reason. Although, they both thought the same thing. They weren't alone. And that realization sent flames of enraged fury through Owens' bloodstream. His blood boiled at the mere thought of being discovered, of being followed, of being one step behind those who chose to come after him.

Rigel watched with gut-wrenching fear in the pit of his stomach as Owens walked over to Jade, grabbed onto her jacket, and shoved her toward the center of the campsite. They stopped next to the fire pit, right below the string of lights hanging above their head. And although Rigel's first instinct was to leap out of hiding and rush to them, he knew better than to do so. He had the advantage of Tom communicating with Jade, as well as Marek and Alex's presence on the other side of the RVs. He knew what he needed to do, as did his friends.

"Stay down. Don't let that Highlander blood get the better of You," Rigel whispered to Sebastian. If he didn't know any better, he would have sworn his best friend had Alistair blood running through his veins.

"You expect me to follow that order?"

"Yes. You've done Your part, and since You refused to take the gun from Marek, we cannot risk You getting hurt. I lost one Lipa partner, I'm not willing to lose his brother."

"That's deep, but I doubt it will hold me back." Sebastian replied with conviction, but he knew he would follow Rigel's request. "Keep that Alistair head low, and remember if all else fails, You are a mind reader. Use it to Your advantage."

"Thanks for the pep talk. It's good that You're here," Rigel's gaze softened.

"Hey, NO ONE messes with friends and family of a Polish Highlander and lives without regretting it," Sebastian nodded, deadly serious. "Now, go and get Jade. She's the one, remember?"

"Wiseass. She is. That, she is. And I'm going to make damn certain it stays that way."

Saying so, Rigel communicated with Tom to let Jade know he was about to make the move. She needed to know it and needed to be prepared to run to safety. Whatever happened next, whatever happened to him, Jade's well-being and life mattered more than his own.

Leaving Sebastian behind, Rigel made his way closer toward the RVs. He not only saw Owens better from where he stood now, hiding behind his RV, he also heard him as well.

"You think You're lucky someone cared about You enough to come here for You?" Owens held onto Jade's arm. "You're a goner. So's the dolt who decided to come after us."

Jade said nothing. She kept looking at him with a blank stare, unchanged ever since she regained consciousness halfway to Chattanooga.

"Boss, maybe the power blew out?" Lucky asked unconvinced, yet aware the Mayor may have indeed conveyed his secret message to Rigel.

"Like hell, it did! Use Your brain, Knuckles!" Owens scolded his accomplice, making it obvious what he thought of his own superiority over Lucky. "Is that You, Happyski?!? Show Yourself or I'll finish Your little trophy piece right now!"

"I would reconsider the way You speak of Jade if You want to come out of this alive." Rigel's ice-cold stoic tone of voice scared Owens more than his sudden appearance from behind the RV. It was something he immediately hated Rigel for – not as much the fact Rigel dared to show up, but the fact he startled him. Rigel picked up on it without missing a beat and decided to use it to his advantage. If Owens directed his rage at Rigel, he would pay less attention to Jade. "You made a big mistake going after Jade."

"Your words don't scare me. How did You know we came to Chattanooga?" Owens snarled with fury in his eyes.

"It wasn't hard to figure out once I realized what kind of a weakling stood behind the murders." Rigel spoke calmly, inching closer toward the center of the campsite, one cautious step at a time.

"Ha!" Owens exclaimed. "There's no way You could figure it out Yourself! You were always a dipshit!"

"You're the dipshit." Rigel countered his statement. "What kind of a self-respecting mastermind commits a crime on his own turf? The City Hall Rooftop? Really, Owens? Beginner's mistake if You ask me."

"You have no proof it was me!" Owens shouted, both panicked and furious, especially with Lucky since the crime scene wasn't cleaned – even though he demanded for Lucky to do so.

"Don't I?" Rigel flashed a cocky grin. "The single green thread with the victim's DNA that mysteriously found its way to Jade's desk at the Mayor's Office also appears to match the tie I found atop the Rooftop."

"Bullshit," Owens sneered, trying to mask the panic creeping up his spine. "I gauge it'll match perfectly against the shitty tulle dress Your little trophy piece wore the other night."

"Oh, You're good, Owens." Rigel pretended his grin disappeared.

"Damn right, I'm good!" Owens snarled wickedly.

"Too bad I have a receipt showing the dress was purchased well after the murder," Rigel smiled slowly as Owens' mind filled with mad desire for retaliation.

"Have You ever heard evidence can always be manipulated?" Owens waved the gun he held in the air.

"Have You ever heard crime never pays off?" Rigel grinned from ear to ear, reading thoughts of rage and panic rushing through Owens' mind.

"Says a cop without a conscience!" Owens shouted into the night sky, shoving Jade back and forth.

"I have a clean conscience, which is something You cannot vouch for Yourself." Rigel's words struck a chord somewhere deep in Owens' gut.

"You're a blind dolt, too full of Yourself to see You're not without flaws!"

"Is that so?" Rigel inclined his head, keeping his gaze on Owens, though his thoughts changed direction. Unbeknownst to Owens, and Lucky as well for that matter, Marek and Alex slowly circled behind the RVs from the riverside. Rigel saw the silhouettes of their shadows behind the trees. He decided to cackle nervously to ensure Owens kept his eyes on him. The benefit of surprise was still on their side, and he intended to keep it that way. "You're the one to talk."

"Am I? You wasted Camilla's life because You dumped her!" Owens yelled out and shook Jade. She looked up at him with a piercing gaze. But the gaze was not full of anger, it was full of confusion and worry. All because Jade realized who Owens was referring to.

"How dare You speak to me this way..." Rigel tried his best to keep his temper at bay. But the moment Owens brought up Camilla Lucchese's name, Rigel's emotions took over his sense of restraint.

"How? How?!? She's dead because of You!" Owens clenched his jaw.

"Camilla broke up with me. It was her decision. Her choice. The plane crash wasn't my fault. She got on that plane out of her own free will," Rigel said slowly. Oh, how painful it felt to speak of it right now? And with the man presumably responsible for the death of his partner all those years ago? And, in front of Jade of all people.

"I always took You for a lousy bastard. Now I know You are one. Camilla would have been alive if You hadn't broken her heart," Owens spit into the dried-up fire pit. "The way I see it, getting rid of Your intern will show You how it feels to lose the dearest thing to Your heart."

"Is that what this whole thing is about?" Rigel raised his eyebrows, struck by the vein absurdity of it all. "You thought You stood a chance with Camilla?"

"I DID stand a chance with her! But You showed up and she shoved me aside as if I didn't even exist," Owens shouted all his resentment out. It felt cleansing. It felt rectifying. It felt... powerful. And Rigel knew what it meant. Owens wasn't after justifying his actions any longer. He was after taking revenge.

"If Camilla didn't acknowledge You, she must have thought little of You," Rigel noted dryly, ensuring Owens directed his anger at him for as long as possible.

"It doesn't matter," Owens shoved Jade to stand in front of him while holding onto her. "Camilla's gone. Your intern will soon be gone, too."

"What's the hurry, Owens? You drove all this way to Chattanooga. Why finish Jade here?" Rigel asked, trying his hardest to read Owens' thoughts.

"Because making it look like You killed her for ruining Your life will be the best and sweetest form of payback!" Owens gestured for Lucky to point his gun at Rigel. "I shoot her, You shoot Happyski. It will look like murder-suicide! Poetic justice, isn't it?"

"Not on my watch!" Marek's stern words cut through the night air so unexpectedly Lucky almost dropped his gun. But it wasn't Marek's words that scared Lucky, it was Marek's gun pointed right at Lucky.

"Don't be stupid! Shoot Happyski!" Owens shouted at the top of his lungs. He panicked because he was suddenly losing ground and refused to go down without a fight.

"But boss...!" Lucky replied, afraid for his life. He was scared of Owens' rage, but he sure wasn't willing to end his earthly existence because of it.

"You dare undermine my command?!?" Owens shouted and shoved the gun at Jade's back. "If You don't shoot him now, I'll shoot her first, and then You!"

"Damn..." Lucky whispered. He shook his head, raising the hand that held the gun, and said quietly. "Sorry, Detective."

What followed next was the sound of a single shot that left its barrel. One shot. Only one. But it wouldn't be the last one...

≈ Chapter 53 ≈

The sound that filled the night air shook Jade's heart. She did not think the man both Rigel and Owens referred to as Lucky Knuckles could have pulled the trigger of the gun pointed at her beloved.

Did Lucky scare her the first time they met? Of course, he did. But he also, for some unknown reason, restrained himself from harming her any more than he had to. She hoped Lucky would have come to his senses. She hoped he would have turned the gun on Owens. She hoped he would have helped them.

He did not.

Lucky wasn't the worst of criminals. But he was a greedy one, and that was his downfall. He spent years on the dark side of the streets of Chicago not because he couldn't do any better. He knew he could, he just preferred the crooked easy way of making a living...

"No!" Jade's cry of despair echoed through the campsite louder than the sound of the shot being fired.

It was a cry for Rigel's life, and simultaneously a cry for her own as well because of what Owens said a moment ago. He was going to have Lucky kill Rigel, and he was going to kill her as well. She closed her eyes the moment she heard the trigger being pulled, refusing to look at Rigel being shot. Even if she would lose her life a heartbeat later, she would not give Owens the benefit of witnessing her beloved's death. She just wouldn't.

And perhaps, she truly wouldn't...

"What the hell was that?!?" Owens exclaimed, trying to comprehend what just happened.

"Self-defense." Marek responded matter-of-factly as Lucky's lifeless body fell to the ground.

"Rigel...?" Jade uttered in a fearful tone of voice, aware of Marek's presence but unaware of his uncanny skill of never missing his target. She opened her eyes at once and saw Rigel standing before her. Still alive. Alive!

"Who the hell are You?!?" Owens demanded, swinging his gun from Marek to Rigel, no longer pointing it at Jade. At least for the moment.

"He's the best Green Berets Commander the Polish Special Forces ever had in their ranks," Rigel smirked, proud to have a friend like Marek by his side.

"Son of a...!" Owens looked at Lucky's body lying on the ground.

"And then some," Rigel agreed, making sure he sounded cocky and calm. Seeing that Owens did not offer any response, Rigel turned his gaze to Jade. "Are You all right?"

"I am," Jade whispered quietly, still afraid but very much relieved to see Rigel had not been shot.

"Not for long!" Owens grabbed her arm and brought her closer, using her as a shield to protect himself.

"Your quarrel is with me, not with her. Let her go." Rigel attempted to reason with Owens, aware it most likely would not have worked. Then again, he just needed to buy them time until Caelum's arrival.

"There's no way she'll live after You shot Knuckles. If I go down, she's going down before me," Owens hissed out with blind fury in his eyes.

"Already planning on going down?" Rigel tipped his head to the side. "I thought You were a badass, not a sissy-ass dipshit without a backup plan."

"You think You're so wise, Happyski! You're not! Your life is finished, one way or another!" Owens took a step back, forcing Jade to take the step along with him. Rigel narrowed his eyes, not to see them better in the moonlight, but to read Owens' thoughts. He tipped his head to the other side, reassured, because Owens was still only aware of his and Marek's presence.

"Humor me for a moment, will You?" Rigel lowered his gun. He figured Owens did not foresee things going so wrong. He also figured if he played it calm, they stood a better chance against time. So, he forced his growing anger back and commanded his voice to come off as resigned. If Owens wanted to think he was in control, why not let him? "Since You're planning on killing me and Jade anyway, and Marek – *if* You're quick enough, can I ask You a question?"

"I don't think so." Owens snarled, but Rigel picked up on the curiosity growing in Owens' mind.

"Suit Yourself, but I thought masterminds liked to brag about their... accomplishments," Rigel grimaced. "You've got an audience here, one that won't be able to talk after tonight, so why not take advantage of that?"

"I hate You!" Owens fired back with passion.

"I'm pretty sure we've already established that," Marek chimed in, right after he noticed Rigel nodding his way, as if to let him know to lower his gun as well.

"Shut up!" Owens pointed the gun at Marek, and grit his teeth when Marek only raised his eyebrow with mocking amusement at his gesture. "I hate You! And everyone like You!"

"Is that so?" Rigel tipped his head.

"Yes. You cops are all the same! You swear to uphold the law, to protect the law, to praise it! But greed can become a nasty habit when it comes to those You love the most," Owens advised him with disgust.

"You... blackmailed the Police Officer I found at the Mayor's Office?" Jade asked with a shaking voice.

"Not just him," Owens shot her a thunderous look, which struck Jade as even more dangerous because of their proximity.

"Were there more?" She asked, immediately regretting asking the question because he snarled at her.

"Even if there were, it's my business!" Owens shouted at her, causing her shoulder to curve inwards out of fear. It took a great deal of willpower for Rigel not to rush toward them just then.

"Why did You kill Eryk?" Rigel asked bluntly, much to Owens' surprise.

"Lipa?" Owens scoffed. "That coward didn't know what was good for him."

"How so?" Rigel crossed his arms at his chest, showing Owens he lowered his guard down.

"It took me months to lure him out," Owens reminisced about the past, admiring the gleam of moonlight alongside the barrel of his gun. "When I did, he wouldn't even consider turning against You."

"Turning... against me?" Rigel whispered, feeling again the crushing sorrow he felt years ago following the death of his first partner on the Police Force.

"You would never consider going against the law. You're too damn clean, even for a cop. Knuckles told me countless times You could never be blackmailed – shit, there wasn't even anything to blackmail You with!" Owens shook his head. "I bet Your own family even considered You too damn virtuous!"

"I doubt it." Rigel replied, filled with agony.

Suddenly, Owens grew more serious. There was a change in his stance, in his attitude, and in his gaze, which Jade saw before Rigel and Marek did. "Once I lost Camilla, I vowed to bring You down. I tried everything. But no one could find any dirt on You, regardless of blackmail or a bribe. And then, they had the nerve to ask for more money! They asked ME to fork out more bribe dough! Damn greedy!"

"You killed those Police Officers to get to me?" A cold sweat rolled down Rigel's spine.

"Don't flatter Yourself!" Owens raised his voice. "Those douchebags served their purpose before Camilla died. But Lipa... He said he wouldn't betray the badge – or You."

"Eryk was a good man." Rigel grit his teeth, not only for the sake of his memories of his friend, but for Sebastian's sake as well. He knew Sebastian was listening, just as he knew Sebastian was the only one he chose to reveal his identity to. This - if anything - was the consolation in all of this. This, Rigel thought, was the only solace, that Eryk did not lose his life trying to protect his secret. But it did not ease the pain, even years later.

"Greed does not choose its victim, they choose it," Owens replied wickedly and began to move the gun slowly toward Jade's back.

"Possibly, but Phryners won't need to be bribed anymore," Rigel decided to switch into offense mode now. He sensed the growing irritation brewing in Owens. That needed to change, or at least change who it was directed at. He swore to himself Jade would survive. She had to! "Your careless accomplice got caught red-handed."

"Phryners was an idiot!" Owens bellowed out a distressing laugh, trying to mask the panic spreading uncontrollably through his body.

"I know. He was an easy catch, just like the judge You ordered to shoot Nicholetta Stormstrong," Rigel smiled slowly, even though he wanted to launch at Owens with his bare hand. Then again, seeing fear in his eyes did force Rigel to stand his ground. "Oh, You didn't know he got caught, too? Then I guess You probably didn't know the judge sang Your name out to the

Police Officers who arrested him. And, oh yes, he blamed You for blackmailing him."

"Son of a...!" Owens swore, and then... gripped at Jade's arm with double the force. Marek raised his gun at once, pointing it at Owens. Surprisingly, Rigel did not.

"Let her go, Owens," Rigel spoke as calmly as he could. "We both know You'll only be able to take one shot before Marek shoots You. You kill her – I live, and You die. And that's not what You're after."

"Shut up!" Owens shouted, moving Jade in a position to shield himself from Marek.

'Rigel, no! You must live! For Your family! For Luna!'

Jade's thoughts clouded his mind. They rang within his heart and sounded like the sweetest yet most sorrow filled melody in his soul.

"You want me to pay for Camilla's death. So be it. Killing me won't bring her back but killing Jade won't end Your sick vendetta either." Saying so, Rigel threw his gun to the ground and raises his hands into the air. And took a decisive step forward. Then another. And another.

"Rigel, don't!" Jade cried out. Her heart was breaking into pieces. And she was powerless to stop it.

"It's all right, Jade Alistair." Rigel looked at her with love, paying little attention to Owens standing behind her. "You've given me more than I ever deserved. And You deserve so much more than what being with me had put You through."

'You cannot speak this way! You cannot! I love You too much to allow You to lose Your life over mine!'

"Jade..." Rigel whispered, pausing at once because he was beginning to hear her intentions. "Don't..."

'I know... I now know why my father chose to defend justice the day he was killed. It was out of love - out of love for his family and for those who saved my life.'

"Jade..." Rigel whispered again.

'I love You.... I fell in love with You the moment You caught me when the chair rolled away the day we met. I saw Your soul in Your eyes. I heard Your heartbeat then - and I felt it every moment afterwards. I do not need to know how to read minds to understand what You feel for me. Knowing I mattered to You was enough...'

"Jade! Don't!" Rigel exclaimed with sheer fear ripping through his heart the moment Jade paused her thoughts. She leaped toward Rigel, attempting to shield him from any bullets Owens would surely fire his way.

A shot had been fired...

Then another...

And another...

The shrieking sound of agony roared high into the night sky. Owens fell to the ground, screaming with wild abandon from two gunshot wounds that penetrated both of his shoulders. He aimed at Rigel. He shot at Rigel, but the unexpected sound of something splashing in the water at the shoreline of the calm Tennessee River, right behind his back, startled him. So, he fired at Rigel, missing Jade by less than a hairline. The bullet missed her and hit Rigel - shooting through his right arm.

"Rigel!" Jade cried out, laying atop Rigel, trying her best to shield her beloved as Marek and Alex walked past Lucky Knuckles' lifeless body toward screaming Owens, with Sebastian not far behind them.

"Don't You ever try that again," Rigel whispered, wincing from pain, utterly relieved to be holding her back in his arms.

"Don't You ever try to tell me I cannot protect the man I love," Jade whispered and left a trail of kisses on Rigel's cheeks and lips, embracing him as gently as she could.

"Hey, don't I get a THANK YOU for showing up and saving the day?" Caelum's voice startled Alex and Marek, causing Rigel, Jade, and Sebastian to look his way with relief.

"About time, Fin Boy!" Rigel greeted his brother and continued to wince as Jade helped him stand up.

"Who are You?" Marek narrowed his eyes on the stranger emerging from the ice-cold Tennessee River water.

"He's Fin Boy," Rigel grinned and walked over to his brother.

"He's Fin Boy," Sebastian moved his shoulders and went to check up on Owens who kept looking at Alex.

"Why the hell did You shoot me twice?!?" Owens hissed out from pain.

"Guess I got lucky - no pun intended," Alex smirked at Marek while putting his gun back in its holster.

"You're way out of jurisdiction, Stepka!" Owens clenched his jaw. "I'll make sure to deny all allegations!"

"You really are a dipshit, Owens." Alex shook his head. " You shot the Mayor, You kidnapped Jade, You broke into the RVs, and You're trespassing on private property – OUR private property. We damn well have the right to defend this land. And sure as hell don't need any jurisdiction red tape for that."

"Damn right, You don't," Caelum added, not entirely proud of himself since his brother did end up getting shot.

"Double damn," Rigel smiled and wrapped his arms around Jade, forgetting about the pain in his arm.

"So, what's the plan now?" Marek asked as he rose to his feet after securing Owens' hands and feet.

"Let's get back to Chicago, let's throw this dipshit behind bars for lifetimes to come, and let's talk about that wedding," Rigel clicked his tongue while looking deeply into Jade's eyes, right before crushing her longing lips…

≈ Epilogue ≈

The snow, heavy and quite impressively falling since dawn, could dampen the spirit of any couple about to be wed. But not Rigel and Jade's. The snowflakes falling gently from the sky on December 28th added to the aura of the day. It reminded them of the day they let their guard down beside the Cloud Gate. It reminded them of the day they revealed their insecurities to each other. It reminded them of the day they whispered their I LOVE YOUs for the very first time in their lives.

If anyone would have told Rigel Alistair he would one day wed his beloved in the private residence of the President of the United States himself, he would have dismissed the notion as a cruel joke worthy of a rather painful punch to the gut. But, alas, Fate's fickle path led Rigel and his beloved Jade straight to J.J. Monroe's private residence in a quaint suburb of historic Boston.

Were those who knew Rigel surprised at his wild idea of getting married before the end of the year? Of course. Was J.J. Monroe surprised? No. After all, J.J. knew the moment he met the quiet and shy-as-a-mouse Jade Alistair that Rigel was a goner. And prolonging the inevitable was pointless.

Just as it was pointless for Jade to feel shy around the Alistair brothers. All of them...

"They sure make for one handsome Alistair pack, don't they?" Luna smiled at Jade as both women stood in the living room of the Monroe residence and watched from afar as Rigel's brothers mocked the elusive Detective Hunky for taking the plunge of lifetime.

"You mentioned there were seven of You. I understood what it meant, but I had no idea all Alistair men possessed the good-looking gene," Jade whispered to Luna, leaning closer toward her soon-to-be sister-in-law. The moment she whispered the words, all Alistair brothers stopped speaking at once and looked her way, much to her horror and consternation.

Luna looked her way, smirking from ear to ear. "You might as well forget about whispering. They can hear Your thoughts, You know?"

"Oh. Right," Jade blinked with fear in her eyes, and followed the initial response with a sincere chuckle when she noticed Rigel winking at her as he stood among his brothers. He held his gaze for a longer while. Not because he was amused with her reaction, but because he was entranced by the way Jade looked in a vintage off-white tulle dress with a pale jade sash tied around her waist.

As for Rigel himself? The black satin sling securing his wounded arm because it had not healed yet from being shot added to the mystery and reality of who Rigel Alistair was. He wore a tuxedo. The same tuxedo he wore the night of the Gala. More importantly, he wore the same crisp white fitted shirt Jade wore that night as well.

And they both knew why he kept that tuxedo...

"He looks good when he cleans up from those worn-out jeans," Luna spoke up after a while, hearing Jade's thoughts, aware of the way Jade must have felt. She was aware why her soon-to-be sister-in-law's heart trembled at the thought of marrying the man she had fallen for. After all, Luna married the effortlessly handsome J.J. Monroe in the same spot Jade and Rigel were about to be wed not too long ago.

"He looks just as good in those worn-out jeans," Jade replied without thinking, causing Luna to raise her eyebrow with amusement.

"I bet he does," Luna chuckled and sighed a happy motherly sigh as J.J.'s daughter Aurora ran into the room, rushing toward her.

"Can You believe how much our family has grown this year?" Aurora beamed with joy while embracing Luna. "I have You, all my uncles, baby Seven, and now Our family gets to grow even bigger with a new Aunt!"

"I am glad You approve of me." Jade inclined her head and smiled when Aurora flashed her wide grin at her, reminding Jade of J.J. Monroe's confident grin. "But You must remember I come with a full package – complete with my mother and Aunt Aline."

"I like Aunt Aline!" Aurora exclaimed happily, causing all Alistair men to look her way with an obvious disdain.

"I like Aunt Aline, too!" J.J. chimed in as he appeared right behind Luna, Jade, and Aurora, with Aunt Aline on his arm. They were both smirking. And they both held the same cocky and mischievous gaze in their eyes.

"You two seem to have teamed up pretty quick," Luna caressed her pregnant belly while holding onto Aurora's hand.

"I need all the help I can get when it comes to keeping a healthy balance on the non-Alistair side of the family," J.J. flashed his pearly whites, winking at Aunt Aline. Jade chuckled in an instant, deciding that she would stand on calmer ground with a man like J.J. Monroe as her brother-in-law. His ability to tame Aunt Aline was a bonus.

"I'd say You have Your work cut out for You if You want to maintain a healthy balance on the non-Alistair side of the family," Tom startled Jade with his cryptic response to J.J.'s statement. "Though, I reckon we'll be in good shape if You ever decide to count to seven."

"Do... You think having triplets is a genetic predisposition?" Jade asked Tom, hoping for an answer that would not have her holding her breath.

"I would bet on it. Especially with Rigel's... stamina. You might as well make peace with the idea You'll probably bring life to seven rascals years before J.J. and Luna will." Tom sent Jade a wise half-wink, causing her to swallow hard with trepidation.

"Why do You insist on the number seven?" Jade raised her eyebrow after the initial shock passed.

"Well," Tom looked directly at J.J., making sure to sound ominous. "There are certain aspects of love when counting all the way up to seven is worth the effort."

"Uncle Vega is right!" Aurora chirped happily and took hold of Tom's hand. His eyes changed immediately. His gaze softened, revealing the depth of love he was capable of, and the unspoken longing for something that would never come to pass in his life. And then, that gleam, that enigmatic spark in his eyes disappeared. But not before Jade caught a glimpse of it.

"Would You mind speaking with me in private?" Jade turned to Tom.

"What is it?" Tom narrowed his eyes.

"I would like to ask You something in private. And I was hoping You would agree," Jade bit her lower lip. Since Tom nodded, Jade excused them for a moment and guided Tom to the softly lit library with tall vintage-stained windows.

"Is everything alright? I pick up on emotions. And Yours are loud and intense right about now," Tom advised her in a calm yet direct tone of voice, choosing not to read her thoughts out of respect, though picking up on her emotions was unavoidable.

"Would You mind walking me down the aisle?" Jade asked quickly. She knew if she waited to say it slowly, she would have bit her tongue, changed the subject, and wouldn't have gathered the courage to ask him.

"Do You mean it?" He replied, touched beyond words. He was a stoic man, with a facade of restraint not many looked past. And yet, he felt an unspoken connection with Jade. There was a fragility to her mixed with courage, and Tom knew better than anyone how important it was to balance those two virtues. He could not pinpoint why, but he felt as if he was gaining a sister in Jade instead of losing a brother to her.

"Yes, I do mean it." Saying so, Jade linked her hands. "I lost my father years ago. You all lost Your parents. There is something about the way You care about Your siblings, about the way You took it upon Your shoulders to look after them. I know how that feels. My sister may be the older twin, but I am the responsible one, regardless of what she says."

"You heard me in Chattanooga, didn't You?" Tom smiled almost unnoticeably, understanding Jade perfectly.

"I did. Loud and clear," Jade nodded. "Especially when that man was about to shoot Rigel right before Caelum showed up."

"So, why didn't You listen when I told You to run to Caelum?"

"Would You have ran to safety? Or would You have rushed toward Your beloved with the faith that You could save them?"

Those words got to Tom. Not because he never cared for anyone the way Jade cared about his brother. Or, maybe because of it. Luna loved J.J. Monroe, but all Alistair siblings respected each other's boundaries and chose not to intervene in each other's lives unless it was a matter of life and death – or a matter of someone's thoughts calling out for attention. But Jade... She was not afraid of the courage needed to face life alongside an Alistair – much like J.J. Monroe did. It made Tom appreciate her in a brotherly way that was hard to describe. And because... she reminded him of his own mother and his parents' love for each other.

"It would be my honor to walk You down the aisle." Tom smiled with a soft gleam he seldom showed to others.

"There You are," Rigel stood in the doorway of the library with Jade's mother embracing his left arm due to his sling on his right arm. "We've been looking for You."

"Please forgive me. I wanted to ask Vega if he could walk me down the aisle. I felt too shy to do so in front of everyone." Jade smiled affectionately at her soon-to-be-husband. "He agreed."

"Is that so?" Rigel smirked.

"Yes, very much so." Tom nodded, sending his brother an all-telling look. "I could not say no to Jade. After all, how could one say no to love at first sight?"

"More like love at first catch." Jade grinned in a mocking way, shaking her head.

"Catch?" Tom looked at her, puzzled.

"Yes. Love at first catch," Jade replied matter-of-factly.

"Just agree with her," Rigel chuckled and winked at his beloved. "She's a linguist, after all."

"Isn't it a bit untraditional for the groom to see the bride before exchanging vows?" Aunt Aline appeared right behind Rigel, with J.J. towering over her with a mischievous grin which had not left his face all day long.

"There's nothing traditional about this family," Rigel replied to Aunt Aline, wincing the moment those words rolled off his tongue.

"Oh, there's no question about that," Aunt Aline narrowed her eyes on him. "I thought Your friends would have joined us today. Didn't You say they were Your family?"

"I did. They are," Rigel agreed wholeheartedly. And because they were, he needed to think of their safety, first and foremost. Especially Sebastian's. "But I also respect their right to lead their own lives. Besides, Alex is busy receiving all the medals and awards for saving the Mayor's life. Even Marek received an honorable mention."

"It was a good thing the Mayor survived," Eliana smiled sincerely.

"Yes, it was," Rigel agreed. "Who would have thought Alex and Vincent Lucchese would bond over the fact Alex offered his jacket to keep the Mayor warm after he'd been shot?"

"It must have been some jacket," J.J. chimed in.

"Apparently," Rigel chuckled, then grew serious and turned his gaze toward Jade. "Ready? It's time to make history, Mrs. Alistair."

"Don't You mean Mrs. Brzozakiewiczowicz?" Aunt Aline puffed out air sarcastically.

"Our last name is not Brzozakiewiczowicz. It's Alistair," Rigel replied slowly. He and Jade decided not to reveal the entire truth to Jade's family out of fear for their well-being, but he at least wanted to let them know Jade would honor her last name - his true last name. That was her wish, and her only bridal request. "And as such, Jade decided to keep the last name as Alistair."

However...

"Our last name is not Alistair," Eliana whispered cautiously, finally gathering enough courage to reveal the truth only Aunt Aline was aware of.

"What?" Jade asked, shocked to say the least.

"It's time You learned the truth, although I must say I hoped to reveal it to You under different circumstances," Eliana crossed to her daughter.

"If our last name is not Alistair, then what is it?" Jade turned her gaze from her mother to Aunt Aline.

"It's Alsatian," Aunt Aline revealed.

"Your last name is Alsatian?" Rigel raised his eyebrows. "It explains a lot."

"What does it explain?" Aunt Aline shot him a warning look.

"Nothing. Nothing at all," Rigel tipped his head back in fear.

"Jade, we named You after the woman who saved You, this much is true, but we also took on her last name as well – to divert danger away from her and her husband," Eliana explained and laid her hand on Jade's shoulder. "You and Jasper were born in São Paulo, but we fled to Guarujá for safety."

"Who was Jade Alistair?" Jade blinked, having a hard time understanding her mother's words.

"I think she was... our mother," Rigel walked up to her, taking hold of her hand.

"What?" Eliana shot him a surprised look. "What was Your father's name?"

"Richard," Tom swallowed hard.

"That's not possible." Eliana whispered, reaching for the long chain of a pendant she wore under her dress, pulling out a dainty pale jade heart-shaped pendant with intricate silver and gold leaves around it.

"J&R." Tom whispered as his throat locked up.

"Yes, how did You know?" Eliana frowned and turned the pendant over.

"I... I made this for our mother as my first attempt at being a silversmith. I was just a kid back then, but she loved it. She said she would never part with it unless it was a way of sending a message to us," Tom reached for the pendant. "J&R – Jade & Richard. The seven leaves around the heart signified seven of us."

"You mean to say Jade and I survived because of *Your* parents?" Eliana looked up at Tom.

"Yes," he nodded inaudibly, unable to speak.

"That explains why Your voice sounded so familiar to me the day I met You," Eliana turned to Rigel, placing a hand on his shoulder.

"Mom, do You know what this means?" Jade looked at Eliana with eyes filled with tears.

"Yes, it means Your lives were connected by Fate. Let us keep it that way." Eliana removed the pendant and placed it around Jade's neck. "J&R. Jade & Richard. And now Jade & Rigel. Rigel's mother gave this pendant to me years ago. It feels as if it was meant for You all along."

"I wish mother was here with us to see this," Rigel embraced Jade as she held the pendant in her hands.

"I wish she was here, too," Tom agreed.

"I am sure she will love to hear You have found this connection between our families," Aunt Aline interrupted the silence that had fallen upon the room.

"I am afraid it will not be possible. Our parents died years ago," Rigel replied in a way that caused Jade to embrace him with tenderness.

"Your mother did not die..." Eliana said with such conviction it twisted Tom's gut.

"How do You know?" Jade narrowed her eyebrows, sensing the growing intensity in Rigel.

"Because she did not. She's still alive. But she's been hiding for years because of who she really is," Aunt Aline added with emotion in her words.

"We know who she really is," Rigel advised Aunt Aline, exchanging silent looks with Tom and J.J. Monroe.

"We know, and we will not rest until we find her..." Jade declared, holding the pendant in one hand, and her beloved Rigel's hand in the other.

The moment Jade took hold of his hand, Rigel heard the words his heart whispered so many times before:

'She's the one...'

And perhaps she truly was the one – his love, his beloved, and the key to unlocking the secrets of the Alistair family's past...

≈ **TO BE CONTINUED** ≈

Thank You for taking the time to read the story that inspired my imagination and allowed me to pen the story on paper.

If You enjoyed it as much as I have enjoyed writing it, please feel welcomed to leave a review on the book's Amazon page.

Sincerely,
J.M. KÆ

Please feel free to visit my Author Website for more information about other published books.

www.joannakurczakwriting.com

- Now Available -

THE HIDDEN MERIT OF WEAKNESS

BOOK III OF THE ALISTAIR SAGA

J.M. KÆ

≈ Chapter 1 ≈

Venice. The romanticized city known to many as the Queen of the Adriatic, La Serenissima, the City of Bridges. It attracted many with its atmosphere, its scenery, and its dynamic. It was exactly what a man like Caelum Alistair preferred. He used to lead two separate lives – as Dottore Caelum Cesello in a local hospital by day, and as assassin Caelum Alistair by night. That all changed in the blink of an eye the day he was accused of an unethical crime he had not committed. But instead of fleeing from the city he had fallen in love with, he chose to stay. Why? Because a man who no longer existed did not have to answer to anyone.

He was born in a close-knit family. His bloodline linked him to those whose lives mattered to him. Yet being born into a family of secret agents made that bloodline link even more significant. And all the more burdensome. Even more so after Caelum's parents were murdered for exposing double agents while working undercover for the government of the United States of America. Or so the Alistair siblings were duped into believing.

Even though Caelum could hardly believe life could deal him yet another painful blow, finding out his parents' deaths were staged did just that. The fact Richard and Jade Alistair had not died when they supposedly did shocked all seven Alistair siblings. But there was so much more to it. And it had little to do with the fact they had learned the truth by sheer coincidence from his brother Rigel's brand-new mother-in-law. Then again, it had everything to do with it. Not because Eliana Alistair kept that information secret for a good part of her life, but because Caelum's parents did so themselves.

That notion gripped Caelum's heart with such an excruciating force it left little room in it for anything else. It also angered him. He felt betrayed. No. Not betrayed. He felt cheated. He felt... deceived by those whose loss hit him harder than anyone would have suspected. He may have been the middle child out of the seven Alistair siblings, he may have been the youngest of the triplet brothers, but he wasn't as tough as everyone always assumed...

Unable to control his simmering temper any longer, Caelum knew he had to leave his brother Rigel's wedding reception in Boston, USA. Wedding, or no wedding. He needed to get back home, back to Venice, back to his safe haven.

He respected his new sister-in-law Jade and her family. After all, if it wasn't for Jade, her mother Eliana, and her Aunt Aline, the Alistair siblings would never have learned the truth about their parents. But he could not stand among his siblings and those few guests gathered at the private wedding reception and pretend to remain calm while the dark cloud of indignation filled his heart and mind.

He went back to Venice. He did not waste time getting back home, hidden in the waters underneath the famed church of Santa Maria della Salute. He needed to cope with the shocking reality that his parents were alive, or at least his mother Jade Alistair was. He wanted, no.... he needed to be alone. He did not want to speak with anyone, see anyone, or be bothered by anyone. But as he arrived, he forgot one very important and unavoidable aspect of the City of Venice.

The grand all-night-long Venice New Years Eve fireworks display. He swore to himself. Then once more, even if it did not make him feel any better. *'Venice!'* He thought and shook his head, gritting his teeth. Then again, he chose to live where he did. It did not choose him. So, he swore one last time and decided to take a swim in the Grand Canal's dark waters. He took a long look at the New Years Eve fireworks filling out the night sky, when suddenly, he heard a child's cry. And it wasn't coming from above the surface of the water. It was coming from under the surface.

He brushed off the sound at first. He must have imagined it. Clearly, he must have. There was no possibility of a young child crying underwater. Not at this hour. And not deep under the buildings.

Then, again...

The child cried out once more. There was no doubt in Caelum's mind now that he heard it again. And again. The third time the child cried out moved Caelum to action. The Dottore's soft side of his heart won over the assassin's hardened side. His conscience nudged at his gut. He needed to help the child, and debating over what he should or should not do was pointless. A child needed his help, and he needed to find it. The faster, the better.

He closed his eyes and floated perfectly still. He listened to the waves and vibes of the water. Not many people knew that water was a powerful virtue. It spoke, it hummed, it carried within it the knowledge and memory of all the things it touched: buildings, boats, people...

He opened his eyes right away. He heard the child cry out one more time. He felt the waves carry the sound, but importantly, he felt the waves carry within them the location where the sound was coming from. He turned around and swam away from Santa Maria della Salute. Though the water may have seemed shallow at times, he took a shortcut and swam through the Rio di San Moise, down Rio de l'Barcaroli, Rio di San Luca to the other side of the Grand Canal. He barely blinked, and turned to Rio di San Polo, Rio De San Agostin, and ended up on the other side of the Grand Canal, pausing momentarily.

He heard the cry loud and clear now. The fifth and sixth cry raised the level of his fear for the child's well-being. He needed to find it, and he had no time to spare. He turned left, right, and smirked. He knew he was close. Unmistakably close. He turned to his left and swam as fast as he could. Though, not above the water, but under its surface. He swam deeper, and deeper, and... rushed above the surface the moment he made his way under one of the old vacant buildings.

There she was! The child, and... its mother. It surprised Caelum to see who the mother was. But more importantly, it surprised him that the child looked at him, stopped crying, and reached to grab his neck, with the clear intention of not letting go...

- Now Available -

MOUNTAIN DEEP

BOOK IV OF THE ALISTAIR SAGA

J.M. KÆ

≈ Chapter 1 ≈

Zakopane. The serene self-proclaimed winter capital of Poland. Stretching from its high mountain peaks ruling over the beautifully picturesque highlands down to the valleys and gorges hiding mysteries not yet discovered. This was the land that called out to Perseus Alistair. It called out to his reticent heart and introverted soul. He chose that region of Poland for a reason. He did so not out of necessity for solitude, but because he decided long ago that the life of a loner suited him. Why? He liked it - nay, he preferred it that way. Because his parents offered him a perfect example of two people who fell in love so deeply that they chose to defend their love over their lives.

He could not fathom yielding such power to someone else. The way he saw it, doing so would mean surrendering his basic need. A need for control. Control he could not foresee losing one quiet snowy morning, in the most unfathomable Twist-Of-Fate sort of way imaginable...

The day his life changed forever began as it usually did on a cold and wintery December day. December 24th to be exact. The snow, falling gently the night before, seized its soft gale to the first rays of the rising sun. Perseus loved that part of the day. The quietly simmering energy. The promise of a day not yet lived. The hours soon to come, full of possibilities. There was something to be said about the way the early morning rays of the sun caressed the crisp undisturbed snow. Perseus may have lived near the 'Ku Dziurze' Gorge, beside the mountain stream bearing the same name, in a narrow valley leading up to the

Gorge, but he loved the freedom the open mountain ranges offered him.

Was he an assassin? When the occasion called for it. Did he prefer to work alone? Very much so. His siblings referred to him as an unreformed mountain man, and the designation fit him to a 'T'. The only person whose existence he tolerated daily was the man who once saved his life. The man he thought of as his grandfather, if he ever had one...

"Morning," a raspy seasoned voice greeted Perseus while he stood by the kitchen window and watched the snow glistening in the morning sun rays along the banks of the narrow and rocky 'Ku Dziurze' stream flowing down the mountain near his hidden mountain cottage.

"Morning, Alan," Perseus replied, with his back turned toward the man. He raised his espresso cup filled with the jet-black liquid, as if he were saluting the man who had just walked in from the cold.

"It is a fine dawn to begin a much-deserved vacation, don't You think?" The voice appeared to soften as the man approached Perseus, though he paused by the antique clay stove when he saw the packed backpack beside the stove. "I see You've already packed for the journey. Good. I presume it should not take more than a couple of days to reach Isola Bella, even with the holiday traffic."

"My means of travel differ somewhat from the usual mode of transportation," Perseus smirked into his cup and turned toward the man. "And I would hardly call visiting Caelum a vacation."

"Oh?" The man raised his eyebrow, and a hint of wit in his short retort could not have gone unnoticed. Not to Perseus.

"The Alistairs are a sizable bunch. But You must agree that adding two more Alistairs into this world is quite admirable.

Especially at once," Perseus tipped his head while sipping on the espresso.

"I'll say," the man clicked his tongue. "To think falling in love would turn Caelum Alistair into a father material. And so soon."

"I saw it in his eyes when he saved Anya. Caelum has a big heart, even if he hides it so well. It just surprised me that he's welcoming twins on his first try," Perseus smirked in a purely Alistair cocky manner.

"He definitely gave J.J. Monroe and Rigel a run for their money. No wonder J.J. Spared no time with ensuring Aurora and little Seven will have a sibling so soon," Alan laughed. "Rigel better step up his game."

"Definitely. He already grew tired of Tom's teasing," Perseus shook his head. "Then again, with three Alistairs down, it's good that they put their minds to it. Better them and not me."

"Even the most stubborn loners fall eventually," Alan retorted as he poured more water into the kettle.

"Are You speaking about me? Or about You?" Perseus raised the cup Alan's way.

"Both. Years lived offer something to a man that You youngsters seldom strive for."

"Experience?" Perseus smiled with confidence.

"Wisdom, dear Perseus."

"That is true," Perseus noted. "That's why I prefer these walls, these mountains, and these snow-covered hills. Odd how tables of humanity have turned. Society today acts more savage than the wilderness itself."

"I'd be careful about the way You speak. I would not call it wilderness. Nature might turn the tables on You someday," Alan pointed at him with a teaspoon before piling up a hefty amount of freshly ground coffee onto it.

"Wisdom? Or experience?" Perseus smirked with amusement at both the gesture and the man's words.

"Both," Alan flashed his smile. "She might even play one on Your heart for referring to her as wilderness."

"I'm well aware of my secluded space and the secrets it hides. No woman will come here, that I assure You," Perseus flashed his smile in return. "And I have every faith in You watching my back to ensure it stays that way."

"As You wish," Alan shook his head and poured steaming water into his cup.

The men enjoyed a quiet breakfast worthy of mountain men. Perseus was about to rise from the kitchen table when his emergency phone rang. Both men looked at the phone in silence, exchanged looks, and knew what it meant.

"Don't tell me You're going to take that on Your day off?" Alan noted with hesitation.

"I'm afraid Tatra Volunteer Search and Rescue doesn't get days off," Perseus rose from the table, and went to answer the phone.

"Don't they know You're leaving?" Alan asked and gathered the plates and cups.

"I haven't left yet," Perseus moved his shoulders and picked up the phone. He stood, still, and listened to the dispatcher's information and instructions, after which he replied in a way Alan knew what would soon follow. "Understood. I'm on my way. I'll head there from here. I'll get there faster."

"How many?" Was all Alan asked.

"Four. A mother and her three sons. They never returned to their hotel last night."

"Last night?" Alan set the plates down, filled with worry. "In this weather? That doesn't amount to anything good."

"Exactly." Perseus agreed and walked out of the room only to return in full rescue gear.

"Watch Your steps out there."

"I always do," Perseus sent the man a quick smile. "I guess Caelum will have to wait a little longer for me."

"Oh? Look how that worked out for You?" The man grinned, but the grin disappeared. "You may not like kids too much, but I hope those You're leaving to find now are found unharmed."

"You and me both," Perseus retorted and zipped up his jacket before opening the front door.

The crisp morning mountain air filled his lungs and invigorated his mind. Perseus picked up a pace that allowed him maximum agility. He had come to know the Tatra mountains like the back of his hand, both the outside facade as well as the inner caves and the tunnel's connections. Especially the tunnel connections. Not many were aware of the tunnel network hidden within the mountains. But he was. And he owed that knowledge to Alan. He owed much more to the man, but he chose to accept it rather than dwell on it. Just as he chose to use those tunnels to move about the mountains as a volunteer to save those whose lives hung dangerously close to the edge of life itself.

This time was no different. A mother, and her three young sons. He was provided with their names, but not their backstory. And the backstory always fueled his drive to help those in need. He may have been a loner, but he soon began to find interest in learning about the stories, albeit the short versions, of those he rescued. It wasn't nosiness, nor did it carry an ulterior motive. He simply hoped to one day come across someone whose story may provide a hint that would lead him to finding the truth about his parents' passing.

With that thought far from his mind in this case, Perseus arrived at the destination indicated by the dispatcher. Since he exited one of the caves, he found himself at the bottom of a steep mountain cliff-like wall. He looked around and did not come across any sign of the family that got lost. He called the dispatcher and advised him of his arrival and location. The dispatcher noted the information and advised Perseus that the rescue helicopter was on its way, and for him to follow the side of the mountain.

Filled with determination, Perseus began to move forward, listening to even the smallest sound he could detect, both with his ears but most importantly with his mind. Not far from the cave's entrance, he heard a sound that caused him to pause. With his eyes closed, he concentrated on the silence around him. The snow, the mountain breeze, the way the air moved along the mountain. And he heard the sound again. No, he heard... a thought.

His heartbeat quickened its pace and his eyes opened at once. If he heard a thought, then those he was searching for must have been near. He closed his eyes again and listened. But what he heard cut through him with such shock he barely reacted as a man's body fell from the cliff of the mountain, landing right at his feet.

The sight of the lifeless body dismayed him, but it was the thoughts Perseus heard that left him speechless. And without a doubt about what he just witnessed...

'I can't believe father's dead because of me. Now there's no way to save mother...'

- Coming soon -

SPITEFUL CHARADES

BOOK IV OF THE ALISTAIR SAGA

J.M. KÆ

≈ Chapter 1 ≈

São Paulo. Rich in culture. Full of architectural wonders. Steeped in centuries-old traditions. City, which Gunay Alistair found to be the perfect cover for his life. His undercover life. Life of a nameless, always elusive, assassin living up to the reputation of the greatest con artist in history. And he firmly believed himself to be one without the slightest shred of a doubt.

Did he love being an assassin? Of course. Was he forced by Fate to choose this path of life and no other? Yes. But he always knew deep down he would have become one inevitably. Why? Because he loved it. The intrigue. The secrets. The secret missions. The thrill of it all.

Did he pity his targets? To some extent. Yet he reckoned it worked in everyone's favor because he only accepted assignments targeting the worst criminals, the worst offenders, the worst of the worst.

But he had a vice…

That vice was his family. His parents. His siblings. His past.

His parents were the main reason he became an assassin. His siblings were the reason he chose to move as far away from them as possible. His past was the reason he worked alone. Not because he ever failed at his job - he NEVER did. But because he failed as a man years ago. And his heart never forgave him for it…

"It really is such a pity to waste an entire trip on one business meeting." Gunay murmured as if to himself while pretending to savor the taste of stale champagne, dressed in a perfectly tailored high-end tuxedo. He was leaning against the column on a second-floor balcony with a crystal champagne flute in his hand. The rather mediocre bubbly did nothing for his taste buds, but it played its part as a prop. He held it up to his lips whenever he wanted to hide a disdained smirk. He turned it in his hand to appear interested in the atmosphere around him. He ran a finger up and down the length of the flute as a sign of allure to the few women he found worth his attention to pass the time. Bored, he looked across the grand ballroom and spotted the most ignored and most dolled-up woman in the venue.

'Show time...'

He thought, making his suave way down the marble staircase of Villa Milanese on the tropical island of Galapagos.

To those around him, he played it stoic and cool while flirting with the overly enthusiastic floozy whose only ambition in life was to collect millionaires, one way or another. In reality, though, Gunay scanned the room for the reason he attended the carouse. His next target.

"Yeah. I pity You," Roberto Sivrice, Gunay's security tech and best friend, whispered in the earpiece device with sarcasm.

"You should..."

Gunay's unimpressed tone amused Roberto. He knew perfectly well how much Gunay loathed cheap champagne, and loathed cheap millionaires even more. "A couple more hours, and You'll be relaxing down at the beach with Rasalas."

"Sounds amazing." Gunay smirked, unintentionally siding with something the flirtatious floozy said. Her long red hair, slicked back into an immobile braid, did nothing to accentuate her natural beauty. Neither did the white designer gown. Yet both were overshadowed by the dazzling jewelry she was practically drowning in.

"I know, handsome." The woman linked her hand through Gunay's arm and leaned in closer. "I knew the moment I saw You that You were the type of a man who knew how to appreciate the effort it takes to look this unforgettable."

"You would be correct." Gunay sent the woman a well-trained half grin. Women loved the gesture. He loved the effect it had on them.

"Is she really that unforgettable?" Roberto chuckled in Gunay's earpiece.

"*Veramente*," Gunay whispered, masking the wicked cockyness of his tone with a sip of the bubbly, and leaned toward the woman to make her think he was speaking to her. "Any man who fails to admit Your beauty to himself is but a fool unworthy of Your presence."

"Oh, stop it." The woman brushed a hand down his chest, obviously taken with his charm.

"Yeah. Stop it," Roberto cackled in a mocking sound.

"I am very fortunate to have accepted the prospect of a business venture with our host tonight," Gunay continued with his usual one-liners. "To think I would have lost out on the chance to meet You if my assistant would have declined the invitation."

"It would have been such a shame." She ran her fingers up the lapel of his tuxedo, unbothered by the idea of being so obvious in her intentions. After all, no one bothered to look their way. The crowd of self-absorbed millionaires was too busy with their own business. At least that's what she thought.

"Yeah, such a shame." Roberto clicked his tongue, clearing his throat afterwards.

"Maybe You and I can venture onto the beach after my business meeting concludes?" Gunay slowly skimmed over the woman's face, lingering his gaze on her lips. "My yacht is anchored not far from the shore."

"You certainly know how to make a woman wonder," she smiled.

"That makes two of us." Roberto raised his eyebrow, impressed by his best friend's effortless talent of captivating women. "Just remember to handle the business meeting You came there to handle. And that You flew and not swam there."

"Definitely, darling..." Gunay whispered, answering to both.

"Darling?" Roberto shook his head. "I've been called worse."

"Definitely." Gunay raised the champagne glass to his lips, running a finger down his momentary companion's neck. And froze.

There she was...

Damn the whole world, planets, and universes!

There... she... was...

The one...

The only one that got away...

Alarmed by Gunay's held breath and galloping pulse, Roberto sat up in his chair and double checked his best friend's vitals transmitted via Gunay's watch. A spike so sudden and so disconcerting was never a sign of anything good. In fact, it spelled out trouble. Ominous and formidable trouble.

"Gunay? Gunay?" Roberto rose to his feet. "What's wrong?"

"She's here..." was all Gunay was able to whisper, almost inaudibly.

"She...?" Roberto tipped his head back, confused, then opened his eyes wide. "No way!"

"Way..." Gunay swallowed hard, unable to move, unable to blink. He swore at himself on the inside. He was looking at the woman he once loved, if only for a heartbeat. A heartbreaking heartbeat too long. Iuliana Selenio...